KING INCUBUS
A NEW REIGN

THE CEDRIC SERIES

KING INCUBUS
A NEW REIGN

AWARD-WINNING AUTHOR
VALERIE WILLIS

4 Horsemen
Publications, Inc.

Published By: 4 Horsemen Publications, Inc.

4 Horsemen Publications, Inc.
PO Box 417
Sylva, NC 28779
4horsemenpublications.com
info@4horsemenpublications.com

Cover & Typesetting by Valerie Willis
Edited by Kris Cotter

Library of Congress Control Number: 2022931336

Paperback ISBN-13: 978-1-64450-059-0
Hardcover ISBN-13: 978-1-64450-505-2
Audiobook ISBN-13: 978-1-64450-048-4
Ebook ISBN-13: 978-1-64450-080-4

DEDICATION

This is for the alpha readers, the beta readers, the proofreaders, and the amazing people in my life who didn't let me give up and loved these characters as much as I do. Here's to book five and the ones that will follow!

TABLE OF CONTENTS

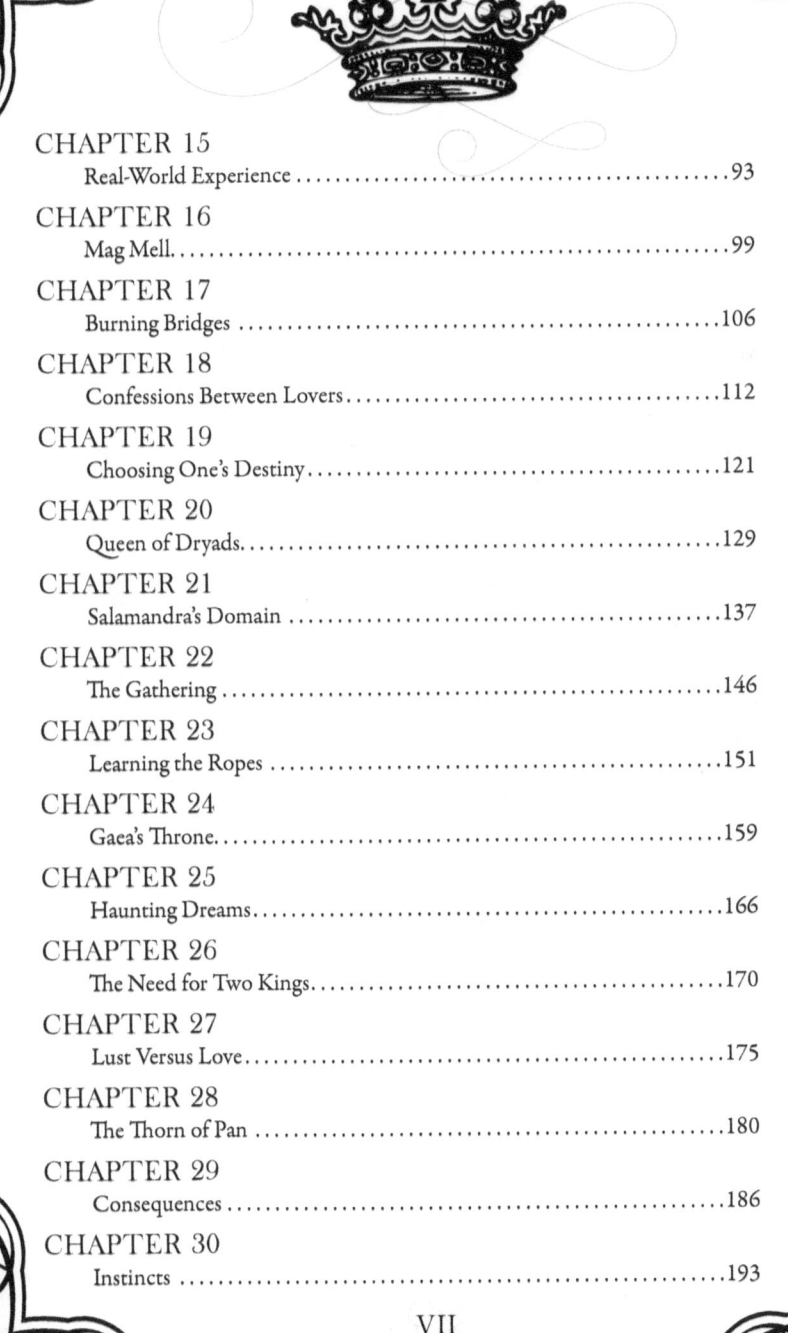

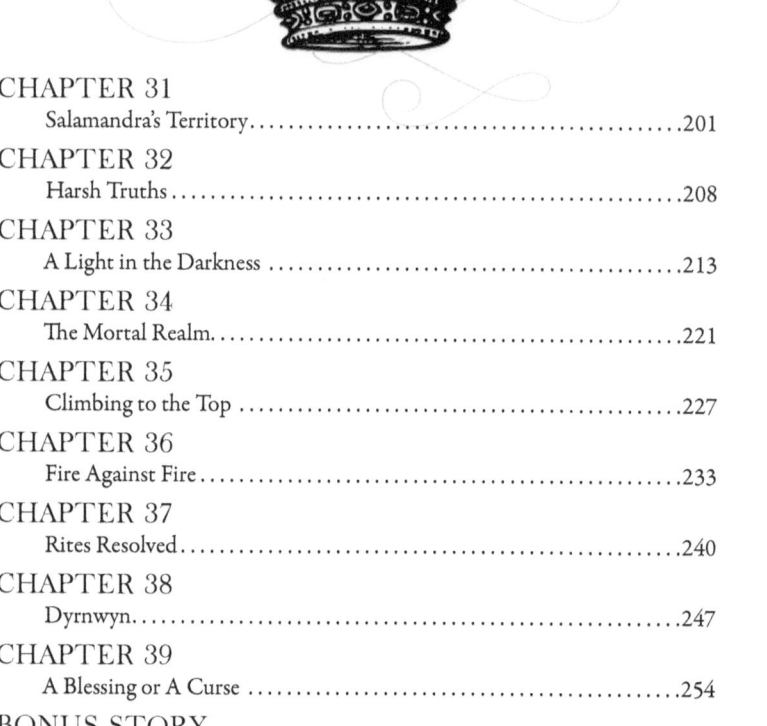

PREFACE

The mythology featured in this book takes us far from the Greek, Celtic, Slavic, and European-influenced names and ideas that have been heavily stitched into the series up until now. This story hints at Boto's namesake, and that the world within the *Cedric Series* reaches far and wide, across not only realms, but many cultures and beliefs.

As you travel on this journey with the characters, you will find more creatures and deities of the island and swamp variety: from the dog who takes the souls over to the other side from Maori beliefs to Caribbean folktales of questionable saucy ladies to the frightening deities who claim the swamp as theirs.

Much like my Russian, Polish, and Romanian-based readers who recognized many nuances, I want to place enough into this book that brings this same nostalgia to readers from the other side of the planet. There's so much to unpack in this world, and I am nowhere near unfolding the layers that have been hinted at since book one.

Regardless, everything comes with a layer of my own imagination attached and is not meant to slander or take away from the original versions that inspired their conception. I invite you to research or ask your family if they know about the douen and ciguapa. Have they ever heard the story of Papa Boi chasing rude folks out of his swamp?!

Happy reading and discovery!

Valerie Willis

CHAPTER 1

A NATURAL

The ringer on Tony's phone sent it vibrating across the nightstand. The phone danced and buzzed angrily to get his attention. He cracked an eye. *Just an alarm.* Over a month had passed, but Lillith hadn't been back since the night they... *I can still taste her, feel her orgasm lingering from where I felt it at my core.* Tony sat up, rubbing the sleep from his eyes with the palms of his hands. His body hadn't felt *normal* after that moment. Contractors had repaired the damage they'd done together to the bathroom: the vanity broken, and the mirror scattered into a million shards. In all his promiscuous years, he had never had sex so... *volatile? Explosive? Meeting my match in prowess? The chemistry between us was easily something on another plane, but was that her power being a succubus?*

Since Lillith hadn't returned a call or text, he had occasionally visited the Lion's Den to make sure it was still in working order. The bartenders he once thought were incompetent and bubbly were showing their real age and experience. At this rate, the place had been running without a manager to spearhead day-to-day operations for almost half the year.

Wonder if it's because they're afraid Cedric or Lillith will be pissed if they let the business go to shit while I deal with my curse? Granted, maybe they were bubbly around me for other reasons.

Regardless, both vampires seemed relieved to see he'd finally gained control over the incubine cravings. A pang of guilt struck a nerve at their reaction during his recent visits. That wild night in the bathroom had magically put the urges under lock and key, but he'd let every part of his humanity fade. *Is it the fact I'm no longer human, or the idea there's only one person I want?* Flashes of Lillith arching as her thighs shook made him groan in frustration. *These haunting hot flashes are killing me. Where the hell did she go?*

"Besides, my regulars weren't human to begin with, so what does it matter that I'm a..." Tony covered his mouth, every muscle in his body tensing. *King Incubus. What does that title even mean? Technically, it's Cedric's title, isn't it? Or is it a creature type? Who the hell do I even ask to know which it is?*

Shaking off the thought, he finished buttoning his shirt and rolled the sleeves up. "Did my clothes get tighter, or did I get more muscle?" he scoffed, having to unbutton a few on the top to make more room. "Shit, maybe I gained weight moping around here in sweats for weeks."

Tony tugged at his clothes as he rode the elevator down. As he crossed the lobby, the desk attendant flagged him down. He had barely noticed the staff working in the high-rise luxury apartments, let alone glanced their way. In tandem, they hadn't seemed to acknowledge him coming and going either. Slowing, he eyed the door, debating whether to pretend he hadn't heard her shout at him.

Did they finally notice it's just me living here now? Oof, this aura coming out of her. Coming in hot!

"Mister McCarthy!" The petite woman waved at him from behind the concierge desk, and thanks to his newfound abilities, he knew she found him *extremely attractive.* "I, uh, I have this for you." She tucked her hair behind her ear and batted her lashes at him. "How are you doing this evening, sir?"

"Better." *She's ready to rip my shirt off.* His face reddened, feeling guilty as his power slipped just then, like ripples in a tub, the arousal bouncing between them for a moment. "R-right. Thanks. Got to go." *This thing I can do and feel now is going to get me in so much trouble. How awkward life's going to be now that I know when and how sexually attracted people are to me and others in the room.*

"Well," she looked around the empty lobby before biting her lip. Her eyes dipped over him, and she finally whispered, "If you're not busy and alone tonight, I would love to..."

Nope. "Dating Lillith," Tony blurted, swallowing. "Have a nice day, lady."

He grabbed the envelope from her and fled outside, the frigid air blowing snow between the buildings. *What the fuck am I thinking?! Dating Lillith? Is that even a thing? She's going to choke me if that gets back to her!* Ripping open the envelope, he found a handwritten note and business card. Flipping the card around, his jaw muscles twitched. It read, "White Ram Law Associates, Nomius Panes Silvan, President," with an address reading, "Room One on Avalon." Tony was still furious over the nonconsensual kiss from the god of mischief. *To think, of all the careers he could have chosen, of course, he'd be a slimy lawyer.* Changing his focus to the letter, he read it, coming to a stop on the sidewalk where his feet slid on an icy patch for a second.

Dear Boy-Toy,

Lillith and I have discussed your current status after the deed was done. Needless to say, I've hired someone to prepare and teach you for what's coming next. Hope you're ready, big guy! You do realize as a king incubus, you're now in the top ranks of the demon caste system and will need to defend your throne. Congratulations on your worldly promotion! Sadly, you're too young to have enough experience and our initial plan won't work (casting a spell to fill your gaps). Indeed, a huge gap, dear me! It must be humiliating for you. Please call me when you're ready for me to start your training, my beloved and most admired bartender.

Always waiting for you,

Pan

Tony crumpled the paper into a ball, veins bulging at his temples. He tossed it to the ground, but it burst into a flurry of rose petals and scattered in the falling snow. *Typical Pan: an obnoxious, unwelcome romantic.* Snorting, Tony tucked the card into his back pocket and kept moving. Nearing his destination, he realized the stares and mutters of the passing pedestrians had been aimed at him.

Shit, didn't grab a coat and I didn't even notice, even with this wind and snow.

Pushing through the door at the Lion's Den, he found Lisa and Becca baring their fangs at a mohawked brute. The assaulter was shifting, tusks appearing with two halves of a broken pool stick in each hand as his clothes ripped under the pressure. A roar escaped him, and the vampires hissed in reply. In Tony's eyes, the scene looked like a bulldog cornering two cats. Tony's skin crawled with the excitement of an oncoming fight. Sucking on his cheek, he paused a moment to collect himself.

Is it normal for an incubus to feel aroused at the idea of a fight, or is this something else I haven't felt in a long time? Tony paled. *Regardless, I have to do something about this. I mean, I can actually do something for a change: monster versus monster now, assholes.*

"What's going on?" Tony demanded, letting the door slam shut behind him.

"This asshole-of-a-troll is a sore loser," Lisa hissed, retracting her fangs in embarrassment at letting Tony see her vampiric nature. "He lost his money in a game of pool and now he's breaking shit. This is the third time this month."

"I asked him to leave, but he threatened me," Becca added, also pulling back her own fangs and covering her mouth. "Sorry you had to walk into this and see us—"

"Shut up, bitch!" The troll lifted one arm, threatening to skewer her with the broken pool stick. "Not so tough without the damn wolf lurking in the back booth, now are you?"

"Romasanta. He has a name." Tony pulled at his shirt collar as he dared to get closer, aiming to force his way between the opposing forces. "You shouldn't talk so ill about a good friend and regular to my bar. Walk away now and I might still serve you drinks in the future."

"And who the fuck do you think you are, human?" A great roar of laughter erupted from the once human-looking brute. "I hear the owners are away in the Otherworld." The troll pointed the stick at Tony, saliva dangling from his chin. "So, who died and left your puny ass in charge?"

Man, the nerve of this guy. And how powerful is Romasanta to keep a monster like this under control by just being here? Holy hell.

The whole time, the man continued to shift into his troll form. Growing in bulk and height, he had lost the last of his human features. His skin looked as if made from cobblestones and bark, his face large and square, with tusks bigger than Tony's legs in width and length. The top of his head was scraping the drop-down ceiling tiles now, and his hair fell in a wild crest atop his head like a razorback boar. Tony looked up at the giant and cringed at the smell rolling from him, reminding him of the subway on sweltering summer days. Other patrons were grumbling to one another and holding their noses, eyes all watching to see what their bartender could even attempt to do without the powerful patrons present.

"I'm the owner." *Not a total lie; she did sign it over to me.* Tony began to roll up his sleeves farther off his elbows and unbuttoned a few more buttons on his shirt as it grew tighter. *Try to mimic how Cedric handles this and I might at least buy myself some time.* His green eyes were glowing with anticipation and excitement for a possible brawl. "And I'll ask you once more: get the fuck out of my bar and I might serve you again later."

The whole place seemed to be holding its breath. Becca launched herself over the bar top and ran for the manager's office. Lisa slid in behind Tony, gripping the back of his shirt, her knuckles digging into his back muscles. Tony's body was on fire with the desire to fight, and he was losing his ability to remain calm. *This isn't good. I feel like a kid again, ready to throw punches just to taste a bloody lip.* He'd never been the sort to *want* to fight immediately, without purpose. He'd always resorted to breaking up fights or defending himself under heated situations. Something inside him was boiling his blood in a way that reminded him of his past mistakes.

Old habits are hard to break … if you lose it here now, he warned himself.

Tony slowed his breathing, calming the eagerness stirring within him, refusing to cave to the desires clawing at his core. "I'm not looking for a fight," he offered the troll.

"Be careful," Lisa whispered from behind him. "You might be stronger in this new form, but you have no idea how to handle yourself. It can get dangerous for all of us. Trolls aren't an easy opponent in any scenario."

"Yes, I want a fight!" roared the troll, panting.

"If things get out of hand, you know how to call *her*, right?" Tony whispered to Lisa, his heart racing. *Lillith can put me in my place, and I prefer it that way. They might be worried about the troll, but I'm not sure how out of control I might become to satisfy this itch.*

"Y-yes, we're instructed to call her if matters get out of hand." Lisa gasped, taking a wide step back as a wave of arousal escaped him and hit her. "Please, Tony. I don't think this is going to go the way you think."

Crap, I didn't mean for that, but just thinking about Lillith makes me slip up. Dammit, focus Tony. Monster troll in front of you. "Look, this isn't the place to be fighting," reassured Tony.

"Oh, I don't care who I fight, even if it's against you, human." The troll grinned; a growling sound escaped him before turning into a snarl of bubbling spit.

The troll's solid black eyes reminded Tony of a great white shark, purely predatory and instinctual in nature. Chuckling at Tony, the troll dropped the pool stick pieces and cracked his stony knuckles together. There were shouts from other patrons, all jeering the troll to leave, that "this isn't worth the trouble" he would make for them all. Tony glared across the Lion's Den, and for the first time, he could sense how supernatural they were under their human facades. They were begging for the brute to stop, and Tony realized this was truly one of the few places they could feel like themselves or simply be human for a while. The bar had been doing them a great service, and even in this moment, they would all back Tony in this fight if it went horribly wrong.

"Look, if you want a fight, let's take it out back." Tony swallowed, conflicted between his own desires, of which he wanted more: *to fight or to be the dominant entity. Is that the king incubus in me? The need to defend my throne. What fucking throne am I defending?* "Let's not ruin everyone's night over this."

The troll grinned wide with sharp yellow and green teeth; his eyes widened, jeering, "You afraid of letting your pals watch you die?"

"No." Anger filled Tony, horns rising and his tone deepening as a button popped on his shirt. "But you already look like a fool for thinking I'm human." A sense of satisfaction filled Tony as he let this much of himself show; he would be spending the rest of his life decoding it. *Embarrassment. That always works as a good deflection. He'll back down if he looks like a moron on some level. Fortunately, I'm very aware I'm not human anymore.* "Are you sure you're the one who has the upper hand between us?"

"W-wait." Blinking, confused by the shift, the troll acknowledged, "What do we have here? Another incubus? This place is full of surprises.

Fine, I'll let you off this time, half-breed, but I'll be back. You'll owe me a proper fight." Turning away, the troll shrank back into his human form and shoved out the door.

As the door closed, the brute flipped Tony the bird and shoved a pedestrian, making them slip on the icy sidewalk before landing in a pile of snow. Everyone in the bar could breathe again. Tony was choking on the exhilaration building within him, his skin pimpling with the provocation of a fight. *To break skin and feel a fist knocking into a cheekbone.* Tony was thankful the bluff was enough to make the troll walk away. *What would have happened in the back alley?*

I used to square off with plenty of people in an alley, but with these kinds of instincts and power? I'm going to kill someone and enjoy it at this rate! I can't fight! I haven't been in a proper fight in years, let alone with a troll or with this body. What's wrong with me? Was I really lusting after a fight? Tony glared at his fists as he sat on a bar stool in awe, claws digging into his palm, healing as he continued to claw into his flesh. *What else did you not tell me about this form, Lillith? I think Cedric and Romasanta would have given me a better sense of what this meant. Shit, what all did Cedric tell me in his stories? Ugh, I should have taken notes!*

"You okay?" Lisa caught his attention, pouring him a shot of tequila. "Here, this'll cut the edge some."

"I've never had to throw a punch in this bar, and especially not because I wanted to be hurt by someone," he confessed to her, downing the shot. "I'm glad I wasn't starting with a troll to find out what that sensation was all about."

Lisa smiled, patting his arm. "Glad to see you got this whole thing under control, but your aura was a beast just now. Granted, the troll will be back after he decides how he wants to face a demon of your level. They've lived a long time, so I'm sure seeing a human aura reveal itself as something else is intimidating for even his kind."

"Wait." Tony grabbed her wrist, confused by her words. "What are you talking about? A human aura revealing to be something else? I'm pretty sure what human I had left is gone after—wait, do incubi have the ability to pass as human when they want to?"

"Oh, you don't know you're even doing that?" Lisa started laughing and he let her go. She sighed, starting again, "Tony, you're a natural at this.

Most demons have to work hard to mask themselves as human, and you do this like it's breathing. Maybe it has to do with the fact you started off human? I imagine it's easy to fall back into wanting to feel normal, but even I have a tough time passing myself off as a human. Normally, someone has to train and show you how to do this after your initial change. I mean, your aura was right there at the same level as Cedric and Romasanta when you slightly shifted just now. Keeping that under wraps means hardcore training. Did Lillith show you that?"

"No." Tony pondered the information, still feeling lost. "Let me get this straight: you can look like a human all you want, but there's some invisible sense, or aura, that says otherwise?"

Lisa digested his words and, at last, nodded. "In short, yes. Not unless you've got the skill to change your aura. But we're talking about a creature that has epic sorcery skills and can numb the senses of gods and titans. Normally, that's another god or titan fucking around with one another like a twisted game of hide and seek. Hence why Zeus went full animal mode because it's easier to mask his aura."

"Is that why, when Cedric sat here, I couldn't tell he wasn't human, but you could?" He furrowed his brow, trying to apply the new knowledge where he could. "And why Lillith felt so intimidating in an instant when she came through the door that first time?"

"Exactly." Lisa poured him another shot, and he drank it down, flicking his fingers for another. "See, some of us can smell it in the scent; others have the ability to see auras or sense them. At the end of the day, always follow your gut now that ... well, you're one of us, essentially." She cast a glare across the bar, but none dared to pry in their conversation.

The tequila burned, but he took the bottle from her and poured himself another. "Oh, that I can't do anymore. Following my gut is a terrible idea right now."

"Oh?" Lisa lifted an eyebrow. "Why is that?"

Frowning, he took the shot and shoved the bottle back to her. "Every part of me wanted that fight. It was a desire I didn't even know I had deep down anymore. All I could feel was this urge to rile him up, let him think he was winning before I let loose. I don't fight! I've broken up a fight or two since I've been here and even let my ass get kicked when I first got hired! I don't want to fight anyone or thing."

"You okay?" Becca came out of the office as Tony grew louder. "I called for backup, just in case."

"Backup?" Tony's eyes bounced between the two vampire bartenders. "Who is backup for a troll needing to be kicked out of the bar? Everyone is gone or in the Otherworld."

Becca bit her lip and answered, "Badbh."

"Badbh," repeated Tony, and his eyes grew wide. "Battle Goddess Badbh?"

"Yeah, she's the only one left willing to do the job of being the bar bouncer. Volunteered, in fact." Becca shrugged.

"She leveled this place already without a fight to be found." Tony pulled the bottle back and downed another shot. "My floor is still sticky from all the smashed bottles. Not even magic could undo that shit."

The bell on the front door chimed and Tony spun on the bar stool. Coming through the door was the scar-covered, broad-shouldered woman warrior. She looked like a pro-wrestler with her build. The ripped-up jeans and men's t-shirt with the sleeves cut-out didn't help make her any less intimidating. Arms as big as Tony's made it unclear who would win in an arm-wrestling match between them. Looking around, she turned back to the door and popped her head out, peering down the street both ways before coming up to the bar where Tony sat. Badbh flicked her fingers and Becca relinquished a bottle of Johnnie Walker to her.

"Where the hell is the troll?" Badbh peered over at the bar patrons, who all dodged eye contact with her in fear she would find a reason to fight them instead. "I thought you said he wasn't leaving without a fight?"

"Tony spooked him off." Dropping the information, Lisa then steered herself and Becca away, leaving Tony to Badbh's grinning.

Dammit, I didn't want her to know.

"You—of all people—scared off a troll without a fight?" Badbh glugged down the bottle and exhaled a drunken breath, laughing the words out, "Color me impressed."

"He said he'll be back." Tony eyed the tequila but decided to pass on another shot, putting the bottle back down. *I don't know what the hell I'm doing, and alcohol doesn't seem to be numbing me at all.* Inhaling deeply, Tony declared, "I've never been in a real fight like that."

"That's a lie," Badbh snorted, leaning closer and nudging his arm with her own. "There's more than one way of fighting, and there are different types of fights. It's true, you've never been in a real fight with a monster, but you've always fought with your tongue first anyhow. Now you've got more brute force as support, making your words slice deeper before you need to throw your punches, no matter who or what the opponent is. A fight is a fight."

"I never thought about that; different types, huh?" Tony mulled her concept around in his mind. *At what cost to me, though?* "This whole ordeal with my curse, accepting I wasn't ever going to be human ever again, was a hell of a fight, don't you think? I suppose it was wishful thinking that it would end there."

"Life is a war in which we face battle after battle. They all serve to remind us we can still bleed and feel, that we still breathe and thrive, even if it's just for one more day, hour, or minute." Badbh sipped her Johnnie Walker, another grin filling her face as she reminisced in silence before clunking the bottle down. "Hell, let's not sugarcoat it. The way you were keeping the incubine desires at bay shows you've got the willpower needed for greater things. Cedric couldn't wrangle it into his control immediately without getting desperate or giving into it. I think you'll surpass him in terms of control and talent as an incubus, though you're still green as fuck right now."

"I don't know about that in regard to being better at being a sex demon," Tony mused and took another shot of tequila. "Lillith had to come and bail me out on more than one occasion." Tony paused a moment, his eyes gazing through the cracked office door as emotions swelled in his chest, his desperation filling him. "At least she always showed in time to stop me back then."

"Or was it because you wanted her to come to you and you had a desire to submit to her the moment she appeared in the room with you?" Badbh threw a heavy arm over his shoulders, whispering, "I imagine you're one of those guys who enjoys groveling at her feet and licking her toes."

Tony choked on his drink.

Badbh's breath hot against his ear, she whispered her taunt, "I know a secret."

Tony glared down at the empty shot glass in his hands, his face flushed. "What kind of secret is that?" He poured another shot. *Is it a secret that Lillith and I, that we...?*

"When a lover of her liking even thinks about her sexually, wanting her to come to them," she giggled, feeling the tension build across his shoulders, "she can hear it, feel it even. At that moment, she can locate them and manifest as she wishes. Granted, it's meant to fulfill sexual desires. So, tell me, did she save you, or did you call her?"

Tony covered his face, recalling those moments of lustful struggles, seeing himself and the moment she manifested. *Thinking her name, uttering it during...* His pulse quickened. "Then I summoned her." *So why does it not work now? Is she refusing my call?*

Patting his back with hearty slaps, Badbh cackled as she sat up straight. "You didn't know? You're too much! So innocent—it's adorable!"

"I was a human. Why would I know that?" Tony quipped, the stinging from her slaps shifting to a wake of sensual warmth, stirring his incubine excitement. "And don't slap me like that."

Badbh's laughter died down, and she finished off her bottle of Johnnie Walker. "What if I hit you over the back of the head with this bottle? How would that feel?"

Tony paled, her glare and tone serious. "Let's not. I'm in no mood to experiment."

"Why not?" She flipped it playfully in one hand, twirling it with skill in her fingers, daring for an honest answer from him. "What do you think it would feel like now that you're not human?"

"I don't think it would be pain. Well, pain and something else," Tony corrected before pulling himself off the bar stool. "Look, I came to work today, not to talk about what happened to me. It's done and over with."

"Happening to you still," Badbh rectified, putting the bottle down. "This isn't the sort of work you can stay in without knowing how to properly defend yourself, Little Prince."

"Ah, that's right: the troll." Scratching the side of his face, Tony turned back to face her, pleading, "I can call you when he comes back, right? You'll take care of him when he comes here looking for that fight."

"Nope." Badbh stood and pushed a finger into his chest. "He'll come to fight you—and only you. You stood your ground and now the troll wants to challenge you. They're tacticians, and you should know that much from your silly nursery rhymes. Why do you think they attack and guard bridges? It's a weak point, forces the units thin, and can make it easy to pick people off."

Badbh's words sent a chill through him. *Nursery rhymes always creeped me out as a kid.* "We've been over this. I can't fight." Tony tried to brush past her to get behind the bar, but she grabbed his arm. "Let go of me."

"You need training to fight against monsters like the troll. That's why you're coming with me. Now." Badbh's fingers tightened, and he shuddered with the twisted sensation of pain and pleasure it sent tingling through him. "Didn't you get Pan's note?"

"They hired you." Tony could feel the weight of the realization. "Hired you to teach me to fight. How much danger am I going to be in for the rest of my life because of this?"

"Ah, he didn't tell you?" Badbh spun him around, shoving him toward the exit. "He's always speaking in riddles, that fairy prick. Lies or half-spoken truths. Drives me batty. In short, it's more like closing the gap in reflexes and experience. Then once you're fit for a battle, I'll cut you loose."

"I don't think this is a good idea. And you're dodging my question. Is this my life now? A series of fights to prove I'm stronger?" Tony spun, scrambling to stop her from shoving him out the front door. "Not with how I am—what I've become. I'm not a fighter. I don't want that life anymore, and I don't know what being *this* even means."

Stopping, she gave him an unamused glare. "What's my name?"

"Excuse me?" Tony blinked and replied, "Badbh?"

She snorted and rubbed her nose like a football coach does. "My full name," she demanded.

"Battle Goddess Badbh?" He felt like a child answering in a questioning tone.

"There's your answer. Come on. We have work to do." She yanked the door open and shoved him through it. "We've got to put a lot of battles in you before your life will no longer be in danger. There's your answer."

That's not what I want to hear!

CHAPTER 2

LILLITH'S REALM

L illith paced to-and-fro within her derelict castle. She hadn't been inside her own domain in ages, not since her time with Romasanta centuries ago. *1400s or so, was it?* In that timeframe, she had done nothing to maintain the castle she once called home. Claw marks across the stone walls brought back bittersweet memories of her and the secret lover she had let herself indulge in for a fleeting moment. *But Romasanta's heart belonged elsewhere, and we both knew that even then.*

A shudder brought her to a stop, and she groaned, holding her face as the weight of her emotions washed over her once more. She couldn't pull her horns, wings, or tail back in with the events with Tony still ravaging her. Weeks alone with her thoughts only added to the ache of want. *What's wrong with me? Why am I so drawn to Tony?* Plopping down on a dusty chair, she leaned on her knees, a leg shaking as she took it all in. *I can still feel his power throbbing through me. What was that? Something different than before... and the way he looks at me... I...* Her skin crawled and her heart fluttered.

She had found him attractive when he called her for the first time and decided to place her mark on him to serve as a means to keep tabs on him. *Not many can catch my attention like that anymore.* The curse he'd been served was indeed powerful. She could feel it loud and clear through her own spell after that. At first, she had mistaken her summoning for a reaction to the spike of lustful desires building in him as he undertook the change.

That last time in the office, though. He's been calling me the whole time, not the curse and not my magic. Him. And I ran to him without delay like a complete love-struck puppy! Covering her mouth, she glanced around the musty remains of her once elaborate bedroom. *Maybe I should have brought him here, but how would that have been any better? There's no one to distract us here.* Huffing, she played the night in the bathroom over and over in her mind. A wave of lust made her breath catch, and she struggled to swallow it down. *My body wants him. I want him...*

"It wasn't supposed to happen like this," Lillith muttered to herself, biting her thumbnail. "In fact, I didn't know someone could just take the title and not need me to bestow it. I was..."

An ache filled her chest, thoughts flying. *I was just going to fuck him to give him some relief, but I didn't think he was ready to be King Incubus yet. He was struggling ... and calling... fuck! What about the curse Gaea has me under? How does that come into play? Shouldn't I be on the verge of death by now? It's been a month now with no signs of reactions from the curse or having two kings in play. I've been isolated in this shithole trying to keep him—keep me from...*

Jerking back to her feet, she marched through the dark corridors, which seemed to be falling apart and overgrown with ivy and moss. Pressing against a door, she felt a shimmer of magic ripple, and the lock slid from the inside. It opened, and she walked in, the door slamming shut behind her as if intended to keep anyone from sneaking in or even peeking through the cracked door. Inside, it was cozy and dry, unlike the rest of the old castle. The library was scattered with scrolls and tomes from a time long forgotten. Magical flames kept the torches lit; a large desk awaited her, complete with a quill and ink bottle. Time had been frozen in this room for a long time. Pulling a scroll from the shelf by the door, she unraveled it and stretched it across the desk as she sat, knowing full well what she kept there and had last placed in it.

"Come on, Lillith. If this triggered the curse, then I would be feeling it by now," she reassured herself. "So why do I feel like I'm about to incur Mother's wrath at any moment? Did I find a loophole finally? Pan had a hard time coming up with one for it, but..."

Her eyes danced over the old language of the Oracles, who once had taken down Gaea's prophecies before abandoning the mother of titans to worship the new king of Arcadia, Apollo. The memory made her smirk, and flashes of her time with Romasanta prompted heat to flow over her. *Who wouldn't worship a man with a heart and passion as deep as his?* She sat slowly in her chair, reading the prophecy repeatedly.

For thee, Mother's warning, no companion will be found

Nor shall one come for thee. Lamentable tribal blood

Of Father's design, exhausted and much renowned,

Shall make thee impudent and desolate cursed flood.

Thou risk hot ashes to the wind, stretched,

As thou heart didst not foresee an end nor kneel to pray,

Thus, thou shalt not love the wretched.

Be you forever the mother and nurse of beasts of prey.

But when a sire of nameless birthright shall be born a man

Beautiful, boastful, brilliant; lost in a forsaken city

With a deep curse of thy forefather's blood right of titan,

By wondrous miracle, falling prone to lust and pity,

Shall thou weep in silence no more, alas arriveth thy fated mate.

Lillith paused in thought. *Mother Gaea cursed me to not be able to love any of the creations she and Father made. She was furious and jealous that he and the others had all stood up against her and Kronos in order to protect mankind. How did my birth go again? Ah! When she refused to give birth to mankind, creating those hecatoncheires instead, she eventually ripped me, her own heart and affection, from her chest to curse what little love she retained for mankind.*

A shudder rolled through Lillith just remembering the last time she saw the hecatoncheires. It had been the door greeter, Gyges, and his smashed mass of pained souls with numerous layers of arms, heads, and legs. All grasping or carrying weapons and the overall mass holding enough weight to smack like a mountain crashing down on someone. Inhaling deeply, she held it and walked through her own creation slowly in her mind, goosebumps rolling over her.

I was born from Mother ripping her love free from her very being. Unlike Aphrodite's creation when Father died, there was ill-intent in this act. She needed to make sure I would never love any creation they had made at that point, particularly mankind, or I would forfeit my own life. Wait, is that it?

"Is there really a prophecy and a chance that I would break free eventually?" She abandoned the current scroll and marched to another stack in a pot. "The Oracle did foresee a fated mate, but ... Tony? Really? He's clueless about this world... What kind of ... bullshit have they seen? I hate oracles... always meddling."

Opening a few scrolls, she finally found the one she was looking for and walked back, stretching it on top of the first. A grin grew on her face, a calm starting to take hold as she began to read over it again and again. *No, she only cursed me of her other creations and mankind. Does that mean Tony isn't...?* Her cell phone buzzed, and she blinked, shocked it could even work within her domain at all in its current state. Tony flashed on the screen, and she ignored it, along with the other dozen texts, missed calls, and voicemails with his name attached.

Not yet, not until I know it's safe. I imagine he's caving and going into work by now. I'll leave him to Pan and Badbh to get him trained and in shape. A war is coming, and he's just one more ally we could use, or he'll end up as another innocent who'll get wrapped into the battle against Kronos and Gaea.

Squinting at the scroll, she mumbled to herself, "It's always been about the wording when it comes to curses and prophecies, hasn't it?" She found the excerpt and sat down, mulling it over. "It says I can't love any of *her* creations, but..." Tapping her fingers on the desk a moment, she pondered, "Think about this, Lillith. You've been denying yourself love for so long, but it creeps up on you. She ripped me out because some part of her wanted to love all of Father's creations, hence why I'm drawn to... let's be honest. I can't say that some part of me didn't love Romasanta." Biting her lip, the confession stung at her core. "But he is a titan, which is considered one of her creations, so I knew I could slide under the curse because the love couldn't be fully reciprocated to me, but Tony... he's..."

She gripped her horns, furious she couldn't claw at her hair in frustration. *Dammit, I need Romasanta or Cedric here to get more infortmation. They got into Avalon because he has... Kronos. Shit. Tony's a descendant of a titan and a king incubus. Then, Cedric—he's an abomination created with ... Gaea's magic. So, what the hell does that make Tony now?*

CHAPTER 3

REGISTRATION PROCEDURES

Tony found himself some place different. This wasn't the bustling street full of people and snow, but instead a musky hallway inside a castle or... *a dungeon?* The stone walls were moist and moss-laden in a few places. Torches lit the hallway down each end, and he couldn't distinguish if the hallway even ended at all before it faded to darkness. Turning on his heel, he saw Badbh standing there in front of a wooden door with the number one carved into the center.

"What just happened? Where are we?" He twisted again, looking all around, feeling the cold stone walls to ensure he wasn't in a dream. "You just walked me out to the street, I thought?"

"Avalon." Badbh snapped her fingers and in a flurry of raven feathers was back to looking like a real ancient goddess, complete with weapons and her bronze and silver falcon mask. "We have to get you registered, though."

She opened the door they had come through, but it had changed. They walked into what felt like a law office and stood in a large waiting room with chairs. The secretary on the phone behind the counter was speaking in a strange language. Behind her were several doors, and at the end of that hallway seemed to be a conference room of some kind. *Everything feels normal except how we got here and who's in here.* Tony rubbed the back of his neck, confused by the place. There were people—or what he would have thought human if he hadn't changed and could smell and sense them. He furrowed his brow, trying not to meet their gazes.

I don't know anything about this other world I've been thrown into. What good will I be if I can't tell what is sitting in front of me? How does anyone sense a human is something else?

Tony couldn't help but take them in, picking apart details and wondering about Lisa's words about how hard it was to not only look human but to mask their true nature. Along the wall sat a man who seemed drenched head to toe as he crossed a leg and flipped through a magazine. If Tony had to guess, he had fallen into a river and immediately came here to file a claim. He was horribly pale in complexion, his feet bare, and his long black hair draped all around. His darkened gaze met Tony's, and when Tony's eyes darted away, he heard the man chuckle.

I feel so out of place.

Farther in the lobby sat a girl wearing a headdress fit for an empress. Her outfit was a pearlescent fabric, fitting for a wedding gown, draped over her like a sari seen in Hindu ceremonial garbs. Her skin was a vibrant red ochre, much like the warm color seen in a sard gemstone. On her forehead, to match the traditional attire and headdress, an ornamental Bindi made with a single pearl completed the ensemble. Her eyes were closed, but Tony couldn't look away. She was gorgeous and seemed out of place against the gray tones of the corporate office.

She's something out of an ancient tome or stonework on a palace wall or a special feature on a National Geographic *cover.*

Badbh smacked his arm, startling him as they approached the secretary's station. The petite woman behind the desk was chipper and stood up, though still shorter than the two of them by a long shot. A pair of fairy wings fluttered, translucent and iridescent in the fluorescent light. Her brown hair was wrapped tight and high in a classic beehive look from the 1950s with gaudy makeup to match. Tugging at her pink office suit, she waved them to come closer. On her lapel, she had a tiny nametag reading Karen.

"Hello, Miss Battle Goddess!" Karen seemed to be fangirling over Badbh, framing her face with her hands and wings fluttering. "What brings you back so soon?"

"We need to register this one." Badbh pointed a thumb at Tony and gave a perplexed expression. "Now that he's no longer human, that is."

"Not so loud," Tony hissed, feeling the stares of the other patrons burning through him at overhearing this news. "It can't be good to let people know I was human."

"Ah, good point." Badbh nodded, chuckling to herself. "Is Pan available?"

"Why, yes, I am." Pan had appeared in a flurry of rose petals beside Tony, winking before cooing, "For you, I'm always available, Mister Antonio."

"Let's leave." Tony tried to head for the door, but Badbh grabbed his arm and yanked him to a stop. "I'd rather not have his help."

"You don't have a choice in the matter," hissed Badbh, ending it with a growl.

"Why do I never get a choice in anything?" Tony spat in response.

"My! Touchy today, aren't we?" They both gave Pan a heated glare, and he threw up both hands. "Fine. Badbh and I will take a moment to sort out the details first. When we're ready for you to sign off on everything, we'll call you into my office. For now, take a seat. I'll be nice and keep the time you spend in my presence short, big guy. Such a pity, though." Pan slumped his shoulders and gave Tony puppy-dog eyes, his bottom lip poking out in a pout.

"Yeah, short works, and let's add distance, too." Tony sat in the seat next to the wet gentleman, who chuckled again as Tony gave Pan a heated glare. "Don't even think about pulling any more crap like last time, Pan."

"What did you do to him?" Badbh marveled, intrigued by the rising anger in Tony's docile demeanor.

"I'll share the story in the office." Pan winked at Tony again and made kissy lips. "Don't worry. Lillith made it clear I wasn't to touch you, or she'd have my head."

"Good." Tony crossed his arms and they left him behind in the lobby.

"Pardon my intrusion," the waterlogged man leaned over, whispering to Tony, "but to have Lillith tell Pan hands-off is an impressive feat. Here I thought she didn't have a jealous bone in her body." Clearing his throat, he nudged Tony's arm, adding, "I hear you're the new King Incubus."

Tony covered his face. The whole situation was spiraling out of control. "And who told you something so absurd?"

"Well, to be honest, no one. It's like an invisible crown. All non-humans can see, well feel, that you, sir, hold the title." Another wave of chuckling and the man mused over Tony's torment. "I was once king, you know."

"King Incubus or King?" Tony had learned his lesson: *leave nothing to vagueness with the non-human sorts or it'll burn you later.*

The stranger leaned in closer, icy water dripping across Tony's arm and shoulder as he continued to whisper so only Tony could hear, "King Incubus, of course. Shh, our secret."

Tony moved to stand up, but a wave of arousal hit him as the man gripped his shoulder and forced him back into his seat. The blood in Tony's veins was on fire. He could feel the desire and lust as heavy as it'd been when Lillith tried using her power on him. Once more, Tony tried to stand, but it brought him crashing back to his seat again and he looked at the former king. He wasn't even looking at Tony or touching him anymore. Just flipping through his magazine with an eerie smile.

Clenching his jaw, Tony replayed the wisdom of Badbh's words from the bar: *you have the willpower needed for greater things.* Inhaling, he gathered the sensation into his core and, out of pure spite, shoved it back at the man in lieu of an outward complaint. The man's eyes widened in surprise before his brow furrowed as laughter poured from him.

"Aren't you rather interesting?" He closed the magazine and tossed it on a table, meeting Tony's glare. "I don't know if you'd be so bold if you knew who I was, though."

"If I remember Cedric's story right," Tony glared at the man, accepting the challenge of guessing who sat next to him, "the only former king was Boto. Which means I'm sitting next to a dead man. I thought you died after that fight with Cedric."

The man caught his breath, whistling before offering a handshake. "Nice to meet you, Tony. Yes, I'm Boto, and no, I'm very much alive as you can see and feel."

Hesitantly, Tony shook the cold, clammy hand, grimacing as water dripped. Uncertain, Tony repeated his statement, "But I'm pretty sure you died."

"Oh, I did." They released their hands with no further attacks between them as Boto explained, "See, that's why I was the perfect test subject for Morrighan. I'm an undying god of the Amazon River and ocean, an incubine river deity who can never die so long as the water flows and the people believe in me. Hence, many of the creatures killed by Merlin, or Kronos, or whoever he was, are resurfacing since he's been exiled from Avalon. Many killed may never be seen again, including my own siblings. Sad business, that."

"Why are you here, then?" Tony grasped at his memory, those dark Thursday nights with Cedric seeming so long ago now. *Has that really been almost a year, or more, ago?* "Are you here to see Morrighan?"

"Oh, gods no." Boto grabbed the magazine again with its soggy pages and scoffed, "We're done. That relationship ended a long time ago. Consider us a peaceful divorce. I was asked here by Badbh, actually. I owe her, and well, I guess payback comes in the form of teaching you what powers and abilities an incubus possesses. It's not all about the sex, though..."

Tony shook his head. *Am I dreaming? Cedric's father, who died, is going to teach me how to be...* It made his head spin. "Shouldn't you have taught Cedric something?"

Boto frowned. "How the hell do I teach a thing like how to be an incubus? I left that to the moroi and magic that created him. He was something ... complicated with the powers of one of us."

"Right." Nodding, Tony couldn't stop the tension building in his body. "So, you're like my distant grandpa here to show me the ropes?"

"Don't fucking call me grandpa ... *ever*." Fangs grew in Boto's mouth, and Tony drew back as horns peeked out from under the wet black locks of hair. "We're cousins if anyone asks."

Tony slumped forward, burying his face into his palms with a despairing groan. "And my life has officially gone to complete shit."

The phone rang and Karen answered, her voice chipper and high-pitched enough to grind against the headache building in Tony's head. He regretted taking the tequila shots and allowing Badbh to drag him here. *I should have refused. In fact, I should have stayed in bed today. Granted, how anyone would be able to tell her no is beyond my imagination.* He overheard his name and jerked his head up, steeling himself.

"Yes, okay. I'll send Mr. McCarthy back." Tony had missed most of the call as she made eye contact with him. "They have the contract and registration paperwork ready to go."

"Contract?" Tony was glad to leave Boto behind. *What contract?*

The secretary motioned for him to follow her down the hallway. "I'm sorry. You'll have to ask Pan about that."

"Of course," Tony huffed.

21

Karen paused in front of a door and knocked. A gold plaque held Pan's full name and title, which earned another scoff from Tony. Badbh opened the door, motioning Tony to join her in the large office. Tony halted in his steps. The math wasn't adding up from the door spacing in the hall versus the sheer size of the office he stood in. It had large windows overlooking a forest filled with glimmering flying people and ginormous flora, including flowers the size of trees. At first, Tony thought it was some kind of television screen, but every nerve said otherwise when a frog the size of a car smacked and thudded on one corner of the glass and squeaked slightly as he settled into place.

It's big enough to eat a person. Shit!

Within the office was a minibar, a large square-shaped table, leathery couches placed to fill the gaps between, and three walls filled with shelves brimming with books and artifacts. Tony spun around until he circled back to where Pan sat at the center of the extravagant office, pushing glasses on his nose as he concentrated on the paperwork on his desk.

Pan's jade eyes shot up, gripping Tony's, and he flinched. "Come, sit. I need you to understand these documents before I can seal them."

Pan never sounded so official before, making Tony tense. Badbh motioned for him to go sit, and Tony sighed. Stiffly, he sat down and watched as Pan seemed to read the details in silence one more time. After a few minutes, he slid the left paper over and began to point at all the different sections as he began the process.

"This is the registration contract." Clearing his throat, Pan made sure Tony was looking at the paper, his tone sounding professional for a change. "All this is designed to do is acknowledge you exist. We aren't allowed to use this information against you in any shape or form. If someone were to acquire this document for the purposes of ill-intent, it would cast a nasty curse on them and dissolve your registration as a means to protect your identity. In the case of this happening, you aren't obligated to register again. It would purely be voluntary as it is now."

"What sort of information is on here?" Tony swallowed, seeing nothing but blanks and a foreign language that didn't look like any language he was familiar with. Pan waved his hand across, and it converted to English. "Okay, that's pretty handy. All my information is blank here, so I guess I need to fill this out myself?"

"Nope, I just need your signature here to allow us to keep record of it." Pan pointed to a spot lower down.

"Um… How can I sign this if there's nothing about me on here to confirm?" Tony arched a brow. *Still don't trust you, no matter how professional you sound right now, jackass.*

"Ah, in this circle, here, you need to give me your blood." Pan reached over to a flower vase and offered the thorn of a rose. "One prick and a drop or two will activate the magic. It'll fill in the blanks. It's my way of ensuring no one enters false information or pretends to be something they aren't."

Tony glared at the rose and refused the thorn. "I'll do it. A drop doesn't mean I sign yet, right?"

"Right, it just fills it in. Promise." Pan dropped the rose back in place and smirked at Tony. "A signature from us both and a witness will be needed to activate the magic in the registration."

"Ah, that's why Badbh's still here." Tony nodded, feeling more at ease.

Putting a finger in his mouth, Tony let a fang break the skin. He pulled it out and it dripped twice within the circle. The paper glowed and pulsed for a moment before information started to write itself in the blanks. Tony's blood faded into the paper, and soon there was no evidence he'd ever bled on the form. It was a little unsettling, watching his full name roll out: Antonio Devan McCarthy. He couldn't remember the last time he even thought about his middle name or had seen his birth name, having been called Tony all his life. His eyes read further, eye color: green, hair color: light blond, and classification: *still blank?*

"Um, do I need to drop more blood on the paper?" Tony looked up to see the serious glare Pan gave the blank spot. "What's wrong?"

"This usually takes a while, but this seems off." Pan's brow furrowed, his face tense. "You put two drops in, right?"

"Y-yeah." Tony's fingertip had healed.

"Exactly three more." Pan locked eyes with Tony. "No more, no less."

Swallowing, Tony pulled his finger from his lips once more. The blood flowed easily, and it was rather pleasurable breaking his own flesh. *I don't like how pain feels so arousing to me.* His shoulders shuddered, and he hovered over the circle on the paper. Two drops fell fast; the third swelled and at last gave way as he healed. Tony pulled away, sucking on his finger. The circle glowed and pulsed once again.

"You have no idea how sexy you look doing that." Pan smirked, glancing up at Tony from across the desk.

Yanking his finger from his mouth, Tony barked, "Stop staring at me like that!"

"Fine, fine." Rolling his eyes, Pan leaned forward to watch the writing unfold.

Tony leaned in as well, curious why it had such a hard time filling in this last blank. The writing started and stopped. Hum... was all it wrote, then it tried again with Hal... and again with Kin... and again went blank. Tony stole a glance at Pan, but his eyes were locked on the scribbles. Pan's eyes grew wide; the glowing scribbles on the form reflected in his eyes and brought Tony back to it. In the short few seconds, it had wiped itself blank again and started writing all the lines again, as if correcting its initial aim. It wrote quickly and with new clarity.

Classification: King Incubus, Titan

"You've got to be fucking kidding me," Pan muttered. "This can't be right."

"What's wrong?" Tony glanced at the paper and back to Pan, who had jolted to his feet in a panic. "It seems right to me. King Incubus."

"Lillith! When was the last time you saw her?" Pan leaned on the table, his voice in a panic. "Dammit, when?"

"After she turned me?" Tony's face flushed.

"Did she?" The pained expression turned to fear. "Or did you take the title?"

"D-do what?" Tony's heart was racing; he could feel the weight of Pan's interrogation. *I'm not telling him the details. Shit, we broke the vanity and fucked, but...* "I guess I sort of took it for my own. I mean, I started it ... in a way? I didn't think it mattered who made the first move? I mean, afterward, she rushed out and I haven't seen her since. In fact, she hasn't replied to any of my calls and texts, so I don't know where she is."

"You bitch," Pan muttered, pulling away from his desk and marching along his bookshelves, searching them for something. "She knew I would be the only one to be able to check this the proper way. Then again, she may not have said anything for fear of overthinking. I don't blame her. I can't believe I'm going to have to test this on you."

Covering his mouth, Pan's eyes leaped around the shelves. Pan had shed his aloof, mischievous aura and took on something foreboding. Badbh sat by the door, silent like a sentinel. Her only purpose was to bear witness, and she made that painfully obvious as Pan marched past her to the next batch of shelves. Pan turned down the wall, almost back to the desk, when he froze. Spinning on his heel, he marched three paces back and squatted. With a twirl of his fingers, something unlocked, and he flung the bottom shelf open to reveal a hidden compartment behind the books. Reaching in, Pan pulled out a tiny glowing bottle. He rushed back to the table, and Tony was startled to see Badbh standing at his side.

"Don't tell me that's a bottle of nektar?" Badbh seemed excited by the unraveling of the bottle. "It is. I can smell it!"

"You're not getting a drop." Pan made a quick glance at Tony. "I'll need a drop of blood from your finger for this. I need to know if it's true."

"If what's true?" Tony marveled at their obscure behavior. "I have no idea why either of you is freaking out."

"Nektar is the drink of gods," declared Badbh. "Well, the drink of titans."

"Titans?" The word bounced in Tony's head, and he realized what was written on his classification. "Titan. As in Greek Mythology titan?"

Pan froze. "Yes."

They all exchanged grave expressions. Pan popped the lid, and the room filled with an intoxicating scent; the very smell was more than enough to make them all feel buzzed and red-cheeked. *Almost a whole bottle of tequila did nothing, yet a whiff of this is enough to give me a buzz.* It was all things: sweet, savory, and delicious, just with the scent riding on his tongue. In a shot glass, Pan put no more than a few drops and capped the bottle. He wasted no time wrapping it back up. The ribbons covered in scrawls made it clear how valuable this item had become in the modern era. Finishing the last wrap, they heard the suctioning of air, and everyone felt their ears pop from the pressure of the magic cast. *No one will be opening that bottle, well, unless they aren't afraid of whatever curse Pan placed on it.*

"A drop of blood," demanded Pan. "In the shot glass. Let's see if my magical contract holds true on its word. If it does, then I outdid myself."

Tony didn't hesitate. A fang sliced his finger open a third time and a drop fell into the shot glass. Red shifted to a golden color like gold flakes seen in Goldschläger. Leaning forward, they peered into the shot glass as the golden droplet fell to the bottom of the tiny glass. After a long silence of staring, Tony sighed.

"Now what?" Tony leaned back in his chair, rubbing his fingertip until it healed. "It turned gold. So what does that mean?"

"Let me show you." Pan grabbed the rose, pricking his own finger. "You do know Lillith and I are siblings, yes?"

"I picked up on it after the argument in her apartment." Tony frowned; he didn't want to recall the chaos caused by the kiss Pan gave him.

"Watch." Pan let a drop of his own blood land into the glass, and it too turned gold.

"I knew it!" Badbh threw her arms up and marched back to her spot at the door. "You and Lillith were titans this whole time!"

"But how the hell did I become a titan?" Tony pulled the registration paper closer; nothing had changed. *King Incubus, Titan.*

"That comes from the curse that started this bullshit, I suspect. But a curse of that magnitude makes no sense." Pan flopped into his chair. "I'm dissolving your registration." He waved a finger, and the paper curled, then turned to ash. "We can't risk it. Badbh, we have a change in plans."

"I was wondering about that, too. You think I can train him in time to send him after it?" She locked the door, a spell glowing to signal they were sealed in, and no one would interrupt. "I have Boto on board to take care of the half I can't train."

"He's our best chance at this rate." Pan frowned. "I don't know if this is bad or good fortune. We'll make do."

Badbh flopped in the chair beside Tony and patted his shoulder. "We've got a lot to discuss."

Tony watched as the giant frog leaped away into the magical forest. *Oh, how I wish you'd take me with you. How the hell did I end up as a titan? This can't be right.*

CHAPTER 4

THE PLAN

Lillith jerked to her feet, pacing in the crowded space as a chill snaked up her spine at the thought.

Tony turning titan is the only thing I can fathom. I slid by with Romasanta and Boto, but how? It can't be. In this day and age? Aether has been dead since the beginning of Arcadia.

Her eyes were wide as she covered her mouth, her stomach knotting. Tony would soon be seeing Pan to be tested and registered after he sped up the curse and became a full-fledged king incubus. *But what else will it show? Pan will call me if...* She didn't know if it also sped up the other half of his bloodline.

Does Cedric's blood even matter at this point? Granted, that bastard seems to resist certain types of magic and thrives on feeding on it. Not like any of us are going to tell him that. If Tony has become a titan, then I cheated Mother Gaea's curse and found a way to essentially love someone who was formerly one of Father's creations? Then again... maybe Father has always considered all creations Mother's as well, and it's his will that decides how magic works, isn't it? Or is this nature finding a way on its own?

"Shit." Tail swishing and wings flaring, Lillith groaned. "I'm going to have to go to the Otherworld to find answers, but with the Underworld and Tir of Thuinn both blocked by Gaea, it's going to get ugly if I go near those locks." Marching out of the room, the door fluttered with magic as if to pause time in that single space. "And I can't necessarily cross paths with those fools, nor let Mother know I'm there... wait. With them there, I might be able to pull this off! I wonder how rough my gear in the armory is looking. Maybe Badbh could loan me some if it's bad."

She marched through the castle, rushing down the spiral steps to another hallway. Lillith put a shoulder into an old oak door. It creaked open a little before the metal hinges broke loose and it fell with a loud, heavy thud. A plume of dust billowed up, and she covered her mouth, coughing and choking. Waving it away, she flapped her wings a few beats and cleared the room. Looking around, she slumped her shoulders as she meandered around, kicking items that had fallen to the ground when their mounts and stands had rotted away.

"Shit. Everything here has gone to hell." Tapping a toe on a rusted blade, she watched it crumble with each contact. "I can't use any of my old gear. Some of this was enchanted and somehow still rotted away. Worthless trinkets." Squatting over another pile, she picked through it. "This is why everyone said to have a servant or two in your domain, but it's not fair to have someone under me. Who would want to be subjected to lusting waves, followed by me giving birth to a brood? Fuck my life."

She stood up as her words lingered in her mind and she held her arms. *I'm still cursed to mother monsters on occasion, which means...* Her hands slid to her belly, dread weighing down on her. *It was easy with Cedric and Boto. I didn't love them and felt no affection toward what we created. But what happens when I... with someone...* Swallowing, a wave of lust rolled over her as her phone buzzed with a text.

"How the hell are these getting through?" Pulling it from her jean pocket, she saw it was a text from Pan.

[FairyDork: He's a titan. And a King Incubus. Are you going to come out of your domain and help me with this mess you created?]

Lillith sucked on her cheek, another wave of arousal hitting her. *Tony is calling me... but I won't come. I can't until I figure this out.*

[Lillith: Deal with it. He needs to be taught survival skills. I'm busy.]
[FairyDork: Don't make me tell him how to do it.]

Another wave of arousal rocked through her, and she leaned on the wall, trying to shake it off. *He's already trying to figure out how to do that. He's done it a few times, but...* Steadying her stance, she used both thumbs to tap angrily on the phone. *It's so annoying you and he can use your magic to text me! Who knew we'd discover our auras and connections could cause cellular signals?!*

[Lillith: Don't you dare! I'm reviewing the terms of my curse and you should...]

The light all around shifted, and she looked up from her phone.
Did he just force me here?
In front of her was a large window that overlooked the Otherworld, a landscape view of the capital of *Mag Mell*, Hills of Honey, where all fae lived. Her hands dropped as a chill snaked up her spine, the heat of arousal unmistakable. *Tony, you asshole.* Turning, slow and reluctant, her eyes met Tony's green glare. Another blast of arousal rippled from him, and she couldn't stop the echo, watching as the muscles in his arm flinched.
Damn it all. He summoned me and he knows. He knows with that wave it wasn't because I didn't want him. Anger filled her as her tail swished back and forth.

"I'm sorry, but ... we need your advice." Tony's voice was soft, apologetic, and his eyes dropped away in guilt.
At least he's apologetic about it. Shoving her phone in her pocket, she crossed her arms and turned her rage at Pan. "And what advice would that be?"

"I'm going to send him for the *Dyrnwyn*, the White-Hilt sword," announced Pan flatly.

"The hell you are," scoffed Lillith. "He doesn't even know how to wield a sword, let alone survive entering someone's domain. Busting into Salamandra's turf might be easy, but the environment and creatures alone..." Losing her words, Lillith threw out her arm at Tony in frustration, proclaiming, "He's a fucking bartender!"

"That's what I said!" Tony rose to his feet, hand on his chest to join her proclamation.

"Look, I can teach him how to use a sword," interjected Badbh. "Though, I can't cast a spell to do it, so we're gonna use the training rooms here for it."

"Lillith, I'm sending him on this quest. I'm throwing him to the wolves so he can learn to fight and survive properly." Pan picked up the shot glass with the golden drop of blood. "We both know how this little fact has complicated everything. A titan not of Mother's making. That's what you crowned and fucked a month ago!"

I hate you so much right now. The smell of nektar filled the air, and Lillith's eyes lingered on the golden nuggets. "I admit I'm in over my head. We have a chance to get answers in the Otherworld, but I can't train him in..." Lillith choked and met Tony's gaze, her heart fluttering as they felt one another's arousal. "It's dangerous, isn't it?"

"There was no whiplash, then?" Pan smirked, his brow raising high with intrigue.

Of course, skirting any curse and finding a loophole excites you! "I don't know." Lillith's wings flared, and her tail swished like an angry cat. "It's too soon to know."

Badbh cleared her throat before cutting in once more. "I found someone more ... suitable to train him in Cedric's absence."

Lillith's hands were on her hips. "More suitable? Sure, there are plenty of incubine creatures not under Gaea's law like we titans and Greek descended, but... who the hell would be able to do it? I mean, a king incubus is an intense experience and a force of nature. I can't even handle one under the wrong conditions."

Badbh pulled open the door, whistling.

Lillith's eyes widened. *She couldn't mean... no. This has "bad idea" written all over it.*

"I don't think it's wise to—" Pan didn't make it to the door in time before Boto marched in; the door thudded closed behind him as the room fell into dead silence.

"My, not a face I thought I'd ever see again." Boto's tone was smooth and cool, his stare dark as it met Lillith's.

"No fucking way. Anyone but this Amazon-dickwad-of-a-deity." Lillith marched forward and leaned on the desk to meet Tony's grim expression. "This is dangerous. We all know he renounced his claim as a Greek titan to become something else, but you have no idea how much of a wild card he is because of it all. He's dangerous and... You can't be thinking of following their lead on this, Tony."

"I'm aware it's all dangerous." Tony sighed, searching the air before adding, "But I'm struggling and you're not here. You haven't been here.

I can't keep summoning you to compensate for what I don't understand. What I can't control."

I can. But I need more time to know that what's happening to me is not going to destroy me and you. Lillith couldn't hide the distress crashing down on her.

"Oh? This guy can force-summon Lillith?" Boto's smile faltered as he tilted his head. "No one's been able to do that in a long time. Not since the wolf, and before that..."

"Shut your mouth," spat Lillith. "Everyone out. I need to talk to Tony alone."

"C'mon, no hard feelings, Lill," cooed Boto.

I'd deal with a thousand Cedrics before you, Boto! Wings flaring, her aura stifled the air. Pan left in a flurry of red petals; Badbh did the same in a fluttering of raven feathers. Boto's toothy grin widened as he took a few long strides forward to show he was unfazed by the succubine blast. Tony, on the other hand, had horns and claws, adding to clenched fangs. His grip splintering and digging into the desk, Tony absorbed the blast of power coming out of Lillith. His veins filled with an adrenaline rush like nothing he'd ever experienced. Blood boiling and heart racing, Tony held his breath and digested it. Boto still stood, unchanged under the succubine aura she pressed down on all who remained in the office.

"Get out, Boto," growled Lillith. *Always wanting to be dominant in every fucking thing.*

"Make me." Boto took another step forward.

He's not looking at me; he's trying to get Tony to react. Lillith's lips pursed tight. *With a rookie king and a former king, I'm going to lose to the overwhelming pheromones starting to fill the room. Dammit, Pan, why him? You know what he did to me, and you dare let him near—*

CHAPTER 5

DOMINANCE OVER PATIENCE

I've got to do something. Tony glared down at the white-knuckled claws digging into the wooden desk. Flashes of Cedric back at the bar brought him to a calm. *This is what I am, and I need to use it to my advantage.* Waves of lust were slamming into him from both powerhouses. Lillith was angry and trying to overpower Boto. Still, Tony's body craved her power in so many ways, soaking it in like he'd been in a desert, thirsty. He had hindered her efforts, like a crack in the ocean floor swallowing up the waves before they could hit land.

As for Boto, he could feel how he pushed his power into them to assert dominance, forcing feral lustful rage. *He wants me to lose myself to it.* Swallowing, he thought back to all those times he would surge into a fever, the sensations now soul-crushing in heat and intensity. *There's no going back... she's here to stop me now. No need to hold back.*

"She said get out." Tony stood, his mass a wall blocking the windows and Lillith behind him as wings flared wide, horns rising like that of a minotaur's. *I can feel my power deflecting his now.*

"Look at you—thinking you can handle all this power and lust." Boto chuckled and hit him with a blast of arousal stronger than the ones before, but his smile faltered.

...and I will only submit to Lillith before any other power. I'm hers and only hers. Tony took in the blast, feeding on it, and pushed back with his own power, wings folding as he stood tall. "Get out," he snarled.

Boto threw up his hands, furrowing his brow as he backed up. "I see." He bowed, the power coming from him going cold. "We know how to establish dominance already, and we're not afraid of using lust for power." Continuing to slowly back out, Boto leaned so he could see some of Lillith's face. "He is a worthy match. I'll take care to train him and use those natural instincts to the fullest ... in the proper ways."

"Take heed, Boto. Tony is the true king and not his forefather, Cedric." Lillith walked around the desk, observing Tony's eerie calm before running a hand up his arm and leaning into him. "But this king is mine and no other shall ever befall this world again. A new reign has begun."

Boto was at the door now and turned to address Tony. "I look forward to teaching you how to fight with that power, though I might find myself on my knees sooner and not later." Boto turned and left, the door shutting and bringing relief to them.

Lillith took a step back. "Are you okay? That was a lot of lust to take in..."

Tony leaned forward, feeling like he couldn't breathe as the wings and horns faded. "Fuck. That was intense." *Well, I didn't lose myself, so that's a good start.*

"You know who that was, right?" Leaning down, Lillith gave him a pitiful expression.

"Yes. I'm very aware of who that is. Boto was in the lobby, but..." Sweat dripped down Tony's temple, prompting him to wipe his face with his shirt. *Crap, my body isn't calming down despite being able to pull that form back in. It's like hot flashes...*

"I should go, but I bought you some time alone." Lillith turned to walk away, and he gripped her wrist. "What's wrong?"

"Not yet," he ordered. *You owe me, Lillith. I know this scares you as much as me, but please. Just a little more time and help me get my shit together.* A wave of arousal escaped through their touch. *Shit, she's going to think...* She jerked her wrist free, and he sat back into his chair to show he didn't aim to try any further. "I just—just talk to me. Help me calm down."

"There's nothing to talk about." Lillith crossed her arms, wings and tail gone, but her horns remained. "They've told you as much as I know at this point."

She's still pissed off. Leaning on his knees, Tony steeled himself for the can of worms he knew he would be opening. "We need to talk about what happened that night. Not what I became, but about ... us."

Turning away to hide her expression, a sense of arousal slipped from her. "We fucked. Nothing special—"

"We both know there's more to it than that. I can feel it coming from you, and I know you definitely feel it from me. This isn't just a..." Tony sat up, unable to keep his own wave from hitting her. "Shit, sorry I just... it slips out." Lillith stood silent, arms still crossed, with her back to him. *At least I know she's listening, that she's not gonna run away just yet, so... here goes nothing.* "I didn't mean to summon you just now; I was panicking," he confessed. "And I didn't mean to summon you all the times in the bar before I broke my curse. Look, I don't want you to think I used you, and..."

Her head tilted and she shifted her stance.

"...and I want you to know that what we did. It was sincere." Inhaling deeply, he braved the next words, "I li—"

"Don't say it," she hissed, closing the gap to place her hands over his mouth with panic in her maroon eyes. "Don't you dare say those words to me. I can't. I don't need words of affection. You're right. I feel it. I know..." A wave bounced between them, and she pressed her hands on his mouth, not wanting to hear his words as he smiled under her palms. "This is new to me. I need time."

Tony pulled her hands down. "Fine. Just so you know, I will always prefer to submit to you. You know that, right?" Lillith's heart fluttered and he could feel that the thought of it brought on a provocative change in her aura. "I like submitting to you is what I was aiming to say," he dodged.

She laughed, hanging her head down as she leaned on his thighs. "You're killing me, Rookie."

"Don't call me that," his voice was stern as a finger raised her chin and brought her gaze to him. "I wanted to show you I could be dominant too and do it in a way that left," a shudder rolled over him as her arousal kept growing, "you begging for more."

"Fine, what do I call you?" Her hands were sliding up his thighs and over his waist, fingers hot on his skin and under his shirt.

Shit, I popped all the buttons out of my shirt. "We can't say I'm a rookie after how much pleasure I brought you, my queen." Tony slid his hand to cup her face, excited as her hands rode up his abdomen and the waves of their lust mingled between them.

"True." Her heart fluttered. "Then I shall coin you, my thrall."

"Yes, Queen," he murmured as she pulled away. "Tell me what you want of me, your majesty."

Lillith began to unbutton her shirt, the back already torn from her wings. "Get on your knees, my thrall. To the floor, now."

Tony slid from the chair, kneeling before her as if star struck by the goddess. The lustful power buzzing between them fed one another to the point of intoxication. Her shirt floated to the floor as she began to shimmy off her pants. The night of the vanity rushed back to Tony, his own excitement prompting him to grip his shirt, aiming to slide it off.

"No. Don't," her voice commanded as she stood naked before him. "I didn't give you permission to strip."

"Yes, Queen." Tony's heart pounded hard in his ears and left his chest aching. *Every fiber of me wants to leap up and take her, but the idea of giving myself over to her, relinquishing all control to her every command, brings an excitement like no other. She, too, feels my arousal, and it adds to her desires. How long have you denied yourself the kind of intimacy you craved from another?*

She marched slowly and purposefully closer, as if teasing and stalking him. Every muscle in his body drew tight, fighting the want to touch and taste everything her body offered to his eyes. Lillith circled him, her hand gliding over his shoulder and back. The heat of her fingers caressed the open rips in his shirt, and he shivered with delight. It made her pause, and she leaned forward, breast hot on his back, as her breath washed over his shoulder and neck.

"Tell me, my thrall," the sultry voice brought another wave of excitement, "what is it you desire from your queen? You deserve an award after shielding me."

"A taste," he whispered, closing his eyes tight before biting his lip. *I know how much she enjoyed this from that night and...*

"A taste?" Lillith's hand slid up his chest to his throat and tightened to draw another wave of arousal from him. "I will decide where you shall taste."

"Y-yes, my queen," he breathed, eyes rolling back as he completely submitted to her lust, drowning in the sea of her aura.

As Lillith pulled away, his bottle-green eyes watched her march back to where her shirt lay. Their power melted into one another until they could no longer tell who the lustful pressure belonged to. *Are we really going to do this here and now?* Lillith was slow and teasing in her naked state as she bent over provocatively to pluck her shirt up. Tony's breath caught. Marching back, she twisted it to make it rope-like before snapping it against him. The red welts were nothing compared to the pleasure they created. It had no pain behind it as it would if he'd been human. She circled him again and again, the shirt licking at him, unpredictable and teasing as he sat kneeling on the floor where she had left him.

Lillith paused before him, and he peered up at her as a shiver shook his body. He reached out to run his hands up her legs, hungry for her body to be against his own. Lillith punished the trespass with a tight grip on his hair and he retreated. She came nose-to-nose with him, hissing. The blood rushed through him with the wave of euphoria it brought him. He bit his lip again and couldn't keep himself from panting from the excitement rattling through his entire being. She shoved his face to the ground and let go. Tony stayed there, muscles tight with anticipation.

She walked behind him and demanded, "Arms behind your back, Thrall."

"Yes, Queen." As he did so, she pressed a knee into his back and began pulling off his shirt before using her own as a rope to bind his hands.

"You will not touch or taste me unless I allow it," she announced, and he shuddered under her weight. "As punishment, you no longer can use these greedy hands." Lillith leaned on top of him, her naked body hot against his skin. "You understand, Thrall?"

"Yes, my queen," he muttered under the intoxication of their arousal.

The cold she left behind as she pulled away made him whimper. Tony heard the squeak of a computer chair and his gut tightened. He didn't dare look to see what she aimed to do. Instead, he waited with patience until she rolled the chair into view and sat in it, legs crossed in such a way to hide what he wanted most to taste from her. Fingernails tapped the chair arm and his eyes snaked up her body. Her white hair shifted to black and cascaded down across her breasts, her head now crowned with horns. In this light, at this groveling level, she was both goddess and queen of his darkest and most lustful desires.

Lust built at his core steadily, as if drinking nonstop until the heat of alcohol made one belligerent. Still, despite the aching of passion and position, he didn't move as he soaked her in, waiting for her next command. Thoughts of why he had been there, whose office he found himself in, begging to lick and fuck his long-awaited mate, filled him with feral desires. Lillith uncrossed her legs slowly until she crossed them the other way, giving him a peek of what lay between her thighs.

"Tell me, Thrall," her voice hit him with a saddened weight, "how do you feel in this state?"

"Thirsty for you, my queen." His words held no hesitation, and he spoke in soft murmurings.

"Do you even feel human anymore?" The question made him look her in the eyes and see the grim expression there.

"My humanity was forfeit the moment I surrendered to my desire to be with you." He sat up, some part of him pulling out of the depths of the animal magnetism that had swallowed him. "I made that choice. Not the curse and not you."

Her tapping fingers halted. "You're impossible, my thrall."

A smirk crossed his face. "Lillith, there is something you have that I can't describe or have seen in any woman I've ever met or dated." She scoffed, and he spoke sterner. "I mean it. And no, it's not this power we push around into one another for the sheer pleasure of feeling it. You walk into the room, even on your shittiest day, with the odds stacked against you, and you dominate the situation and everyone within your reach. There's a prowess that I can only label as an ancient desire to make a change that can't be comprehended by anyone but you." Lillith searched his face and her lips tightened. "You've gotten this far alone, even helping others when you didn't have to, but..." Tony inhaled and he pushed his aura through her, using the new power to express what he wanted her to feel. "I'm here to serve you and your purpose. I've got nothing else to lose."

"You're a fool." Her voice cracked as she looked away, tears building in her eyes. "You don't even know what you're pledging yourself to be, and we both might die making my desires come true at this rate. The odds are stacked against me, and I still can't unravel what chains bind and constrict me."

Tony shuffled closer, arms still bound, before he ripped her shirt and freed himself. His lips were firm against hers in seconds, kissing her deeply as his arms wrapped their warmth around her. She opened herself to him, tongues twisting against one another as her knees opened to press against his hips. Tony broke away, kissing, suckling, and tasting her as he fell across her collarbone and between her breasts. As he sank back to his knees, she gripped his hair and pushed him to where she wanted him, where she knew he aimed to be.

"You make a terrible thrall." She inhaled swiftly as the heat of his tongue slid across her.

She let him look up, a goofy expression on his face making her scoff as he countered, "You make a horrible queen since you haven't commanded me to stop, no?"

For the first time, the tension she had held tight to for centuries loosened ever so slightly as she opened herself to Tony... and he could feel it. Tony kissed his way up her body once more. She arched into the heat of his body, legs wrapping around him as his arms reflected the motion. They connected, and they shivered to have one another, to grind and give way to the erotic wants that had haunted them since that first night.

She is giving herself to me, truly allowing herself instead of me taking it by force like last time. I think I could handle being immortal as long as I can be with her and drown in one another like this time and time again.

CHAPTER 6

PREPARATIONS AND TRIBULATIONS

L illith stepped out of Pan's office and marched into the lobby, where he and Badbh paused. Everyone shifted in their seats uncomfortably and shot quick glances her way. She could feel the provocative sensations and snuffed them out like flames on candles. *Shit, our little hookup in the office made it past the magical barrier and got the whole lobby hot and bothered.* She couldn't hold back the smirk. The very concept that together they could break powerful spells with their combined auras amused her. Another scan of the room and she was relieved to find Boto was nowhere to be seen.

"Well, didn't expect that little rendezvous to happen in my office of all places." Whistling, Pan aimed to march for his office, but Lillith grabbed his arm. "Ouch. Unhand me!"

"No, *we* are going to Badbh's armory. I need supplies and," looking over her shoulder, she shuddered at Pan's door, "and he's going to be riding out that parting gift for a while. I don't think you can contain yourself if you come into direct contact with his aura in his current state. Now, tell me more about why you think sending a rookie to Salamandra's domain is even a good idea in the first place. Lead the way, Badbh."

"Yes, ma'am!" Badbh chuckled, opening the door as she pointed with her chin. "Why are you wearing Tony's shirt all of a sudden?"

"We used my shirt to... well, it ripped." Clearing her throat, Lillith waited for them to lead her down the stone hallway.

"You're killing me," whined Pan. "My eye candy is shirtless, and you won't even let me take a peek."

"Oh, between my training and Boto's, you'll get your share of peeks," snorted Badbh, marching ahead.

"You're assuming he'll even allow me to be in the room," Pan mumbled, texting with someone on his phone. "Don't tell me you plan on going in his place, Lillith. I mean, it's not like you to request weapons and armor like this."

"I'm going to the Otherworld," Lillith announced.

"If Mother senses you, Hell will be the least of your concerns." Pan swallowed, giving her a side glance from his phone.

"Something tells me she is too preoccupied with Cedric and Romasanta entering the realm. Having her eye along means she's still half blind to our actions as well as..." She shot a glance at him as Badbh opened another door. "We both know she doesn't want it back. It was meant for Kronos—both for power and an excuse as to why she didn't see his sins against not only mankind but all other creatures and deities."

"True. What I don't get is why Alecto hasn't stepped in or started hunting him down at this point." Pan tapped his lips as they entered the massive armory filled with weapons and armor of all kinds, complete with a blacksmith workshop in the far corner.

"That's because Alecto only intervenes when a Greek god aims to do intentional harm to mankind. He's only done harm to non-human entities since he's been running amuck as Merlin. And there's that; he's trapped in a human body so it's man doing harm to man. Loopholes for days." Lillith halted to scan the warm room that pulsed with the heat of uncanny magic and power emanating from the forge. "Is that a ... dragon's breath forge?"

Badbh shrugged. "Maybe it is; maybe it isn't."

"You know you can make..." Pan paused and shook his head. "Never mind, you couldn't, not without the right anvil and materials. The forge is only the catalyst for a god-slaying weapon, much like the fires of Salamandra's volcano."

"Exactly." Badbh put her hands on her hips, looking over the assortment she had intentionally stopped in front of, and sighed. "And someone's gonna notice me hunting down certain critters and report it. I may not be under Gaea's law, but I've seen what happens to others who've skirted around the edge of what she watches. I don't do battle without knowing I'll come out winning."

"This makes me miss my collection." Lillith paced down one aisle, admiring all the weapons, fingers tapping across the various hilts and bejeweled pommels. "These would have sold for high coin back in the day. Why make so many in this day and age?"

"In a competition of sorts with one of Freya's Valkyries." Badbh snorted, adding, "You know me—it's all about proving oneself."

Lillith took her time weaving through the room. Tables, walls, and stands were filled and overstocked with enchanted weapons of a caliber she hadn't seen since the days when her father, Aether still lived. *Before Mother Gaea and Kronos threw all the realms into chaos...* Picking up a pair of raven-themed daggers, she could feel the magic that would keep the blades sharp and delay wounds from healing, no matter who or what she sliced open. *Not exactly aiming to do battle, but these might come in handy when war is inevitable later.* Not far from them was a chest halter for them; she snatched it up and sheathed them. Turning, she found thigh-high leather boots, breeches, some various packs that would strap to her waist, thigh, and back.

At least I have plenty of Otherworld cash and trinkets to use for getting around. Now chest armor... A leather tunic caught her attention, but Pan pulled it from her fingers and shoved a more scantily designed chest plate in its place.

"This is more your style," he teased.

"This is when I want them to know who I am and get them to give me some sexual energy to absorb." Lillith shoved it back at him, reaching for another light leather tunic that laced up and had images of the dryads embossed into it. "This, on the other hand, might be flattering considering who I'm aiming to see. The old tree has an ego as big as her forest."

Badbh arched a brow from where she'd started pumping the billows. "Going to see Hamadryades, are we?"

"Yeah. If anyone is well-rooted in information and the state of the Otherworld, she would know. She has as much skin in this game as I do." Holding the tunic up to her chest, she sighed. "Now I just need a cloak, something to obscure who I am, so I don't get spotted."

"Shouldn't you take something more long-range than the daggers?" Pan was meandering by the bows and arrows that lay piled high on a table. "That way, they can't see your face at all."

"I won't need it. Not there to hunt anyone or thing." Lillith took one last look at the armor selection before nodding. "This should get me to where I'm going."

"And I imagine you need a way in?" Pan resumed texting on his phone as he turned his back to her.

"If you don't mind." Lillith shimmied off her pants and pulled the tattered shirt over her head. *My gods, his scent even makes me...* her skin pebbled as she squashed the thought. "Can I make a request, or are you just dumping me wherever?"

"Well, I have a meeting with a client in the marketplace," Pan mumbled as his eyebrows rose high at an image sent in a text.

Stuffing the shirt in a satchel before anyone could notice, Lillith began to unlace the breeches. "That should work. I can gather what information I might find there from some of my contacts."

Sparks and loud pings filled the air as Badbh began to work on a piece of metal that she had heated. Lillith watched with interest as the fireworks of each hammer strike bounced off Badbh and the anvil before dancing across the cobblestone floor. It was mesmerizing as some part of her pained over the fact she would be walking away and leaving Tony to face his next tribulations alone. *But he'll wait for me, do this to be strong enough to stand with me. Besides, at least I know she won't go easy on him. If anyone can pound centuries of battle reflexes into someone, it's her.*

"By the old gods," Morrighan's voice echoed through the room as she marched down a parallel hallway. "What is it, Badbh, about your little friends always being naked? Hmm, dear sister?"

"We're born naked, sister," drawled Badbh, hammering the metal a few more strikes and pushing it into the water.

A pillar of steam hissed to life before she tossed it into a pile of plant materials off to the side. With her hands on her hips, Badbh gave her sister a goofy grin as she waited for her to climb the small steps to the work area. Morrighan's pitch-black hair was knotted high on her head and fell to her waist in thin braids with ornamental charms and runes. She wore a deep maroon gown and corset; her pale skin glowing in comparison. At a table, she snapped her fingers and several glass beakers appeared.

"I hear Boto is going to be here in Avalon for a while, training with you and the bartender." Morrighan smirked, tapping her nails across a bottle. "I desperately need something from Boto before he leaves again. Some materials for potions and experiments. Business, not pleasure, you understand."

Everyone shuffled uncomfortably as a silence followed her words. *Shit, I don't want to be here when those two cross paths. It'll make me nauseous.* Lillith began to dress in a hurry, though nothing coming from the powerful sorceress-turned-goddess signaled her interest in Boto was that of love, but lust. *I really don't want to know.* Trying to slide the loosened tunic over her, she failed to get very far, as her large breasts proved a bigger obstacle. Arms caught in such a way, she couldn't maneuver to grip it to pull nor push it off or on, she muttered profanities in an array of archaic languages, wiggling and trying to huff all the air from her lungs to make her torso thinner.

"Fuck, I'm stuck," she squeaked. "P-Pan. Help?"

"I got this." Pan gripped the bottom of the tunic and gave it a sharp tug down.

Lillith yelped, nipples on fire from the friction of the fabric. "You dick!"

Clearing her throat, Badbh ignored the shenanigans and pressed, "And what business do you have with the River King? What sort of materials?"

"Oh, just in need of resupply of materials. Boto is aware." Morrighan thrust a beaker into Badbh's hands. "Just some incubine saliva and blood is all. Anything else he's willing to provide is most appreciated."

"I thought you got some of that from..." Badbh set the glass down, twisting her lips, redirecting her words. "It wasn't easy to get anything from Cedric, you know."

"None of that half-breed bullshit works." Morrighan's voice came out flat and harsh. "It causes the spells to become too volatile, and then the spell spirals or fades out in a matter of seconds. I need higher-grade and nothing that is riddled with magic from unknown sources. He's eaten so much he's ... filled with auras like a melting pot of monster magic and souls. It's disgusting."

"Oh." Badbh crossed her arms, brows high at her sister's rant. "And what makes you think Boto's willing to do this for you?"

"That's a private discussion, sister. As I implied, he's already agreed." Another snap of her fingers, and Morrighan poofed away in a plume of smoke as ash fell to the floor.

"He has to be willing, or the contract will bite you both in the ass," drawled Pan, texting one last thing on his phone before shoving it into his pocket. "It's designed to prevent unlawful taking of one's ... 'materials.' Now, are you done dressing yet, Lilly?"

"Ugh, there are no words for the pain you brought me just now." Lillith shuffled on the cloak and began strapping on the bags and halter. "Just need to lace the boots."

"I suppose I should go get the man of the hour from your office." Badbh came down from her workstation and began looking through her collection of broadswords. "Are we letting him keep *Dyrnwyn* as his if he manages to obtain it?"

"Absolutely." Pan placed both hands into his pockets and rocked back on his heels. "If any being in the Mortal Realm could be said to match the stipulation of that blade's use, it's definitely him."

"If he dies by the sword," Lillith grunted, pulling the straps on the first boot tight and tying it before continuing, "I'll find a way to send you to see Hades and lick his boots personally."

"Ugh. Hades." A shudder rolled through Pan as he rolled his eyes. "That's one name and face I could live without ever hearing or seeing again. Though, we had our fun in the Mortal Realm a while back."

"What's the matter with Hades?" chortled Badbh, holding a blade in each hand to compare them against one another. "He's always been a good ally for me and an even better drinking buddy. Oh, Ares too. Wonder where that asshole is, though? Athena too."

"Of course, Hades would be there for you," drawled Pan, unamused. "He loves people who kill enough to send him souls in droves. But the fae tends to hold on to theirs for a very long time, and worse, to bless other beings with long life, luck, and immortality on rare occasions. We don't exactly help his quota, and we certainly only compete with our own need to collect just as many souls as necessary to bestow blessings like church dogs and the will-o-wisps to guide souls to the Otherworld, or change-lings to kidnap mortals."

"What happened between you two, anyhow? You were cussing him out every so often, not too long ago." Lillith stomped the boots, getting a good feel for them and making sure the heel of her foot was well-grounded.

"That's none of your business," Pan scoffed. "Ready?"

Reaching over the table, she grabbed a few small knives, tucking one in her boot, another in her tunic, and tossing a third in her satchel before slinging it over her shoulder. "Yes, I am."

"Fight well, my friend." Badbh dropped one of the blades with a loud clattering. "And don't worry. I've trained greener men than this in the past. He's got good instincts and reflexes, and he's going to be a fun opponent for some folks in the near future."

Before Lillith could say anything, she found herself in a dark alleyway of a bustling marketplace. *Dammit, Pan.* Rose petals were fluttering to the ground at her feet as a jorōgumo, spider-woman, wove with her six arms while drinking tea with the remaining two. *Shit, where did Pan go?* Tugging on the tunic, she took a moment to adjust to the dense magic in the air. *It's been too long since my last visit. I'm hoping to pass as alfin, but...*

CHAPTER 7

BEGINNER'S LUCK

Sitting in the office chair, Tony jerked to his feet and aimed for the minibar tucked between the bookshelves of Pan's office. Smelling a few of the containers, he settled for what he recognized as a rather old scotch and took a shot. *If only he had ice...* A shudder came across his shoulders, the moment that had unfolded between him and Lillith only adding to the desires burning in his heart. *We fed off one another, but the idea that I can feel when she peaks means...* His face flushed and he downed another shot of scotch.

The door opened and Badbh leaned on the frame. "You ready to get this party started, big guy?"

Tony glanced over his shoulder, muscles visibly tensing across his bare back. "Is that the sword?"

Badbh looked at what she had in hand and scoffed, "Nah. This one is built pretty close since it was inspired by it. But the real deal... well, you'll know when you hold it for the first time." She tossed it across the room at him.

"What are you—" Reflexes snatched it; Tony's heart raced as he paled. "What if I didn't catch it?"

"You're a monster with killer instincts now." Badbh crossed her arms, tapping her fingers in thought. "We're going to rely on those new reflexes, but I have to ask you something before we start."

"What is that?" Tony took a few steps before circling back for the bottle of scotch. *I'm going to need this.*

"Why did you lie about it?" she quizzed.

"About what?" Tony stiffened. *What did I lie about to her?*

46

"Making it sound as if you've never been in a fight," Badbh whispered and closed the door behind her. "We both know that's far from the truth."

Tony sat down in the office chair once more, his stare locking with Badbh. After a hearty swig from the bottle, he inhaled deeply and looked away. *Why did I think my past wasn't going to catch up to me at some point?* Drumming his fingers on the desk, he weighed his past against what Badbh could possibly know. *I never fought with broadswords, though these knuckles at one point...* He squeezed his fists closed, pumping them as if old memories could manifest old wounds. *How many times did I bust up my knuckles?*

"How much do you know?" Tony demanded.

"Do you really want me to expose how much I know of your fighting spirit?" Badbh slid off her mask and gave him a half-hearted smirk. "You realize I'm drawn to warriors, and especially those with a need to satisfy an itch."

"I was a thug," he mumbled, trying to read her face. *Oh, an itch indeed that I've drowned with no problem until now.*

"You were in the top ranks in that sorry-excuse-of-a-mafia." She laughed and sat on the desk. "It's hard to believe you never got any ink or branding. Loyalty is a big deal with those sorts, much like the mercenary guilds of old."

"About that," Tony puffed out his cheeks. "I used to shave my head in those days, quite the skinhead. Granted, you can't pull my hair in a fight, so..." Running a hand over his hair, he winced as he slowed and halted on the backside of his head. "I did get something, but someplace where I could cover it. They tried a few times to brand and mark me elsewhere, but ... I settled for a tattoo on the back of my head. Heh."

"How many teeth did you knock out of their mouths to keep your freedom?" Badbh smiled and excitement sparkled in her eyes.

"Not enough. Changed my name, changed towns, left a trail of blood only to end up in the..." He hesitated before snorting, "Well, the Lion's Den with you all."

"You do realize you should be scarred to hell." Badbh slid off the desk, leaning in to whisper into his ear, "But we both know that you've always known you weren't human from the start, little titan."

Shoving her off and back, he stood and slugged back another few gulps of scotch before grabbing the sword. "Let's train already. Where did that dickwad Boto go?"

"He's waiting in the training room, but we're going to start with what you don't know." She motioned for the blade and opened the door. "Let's go, Mafia King."

"Don't call me that." Tony brushed past, shooting her a dangerous glare. "I left that title in the fighting rings in the underground."

Badbh flicked her fingers, her mask flying off Pan's desk, and placed it back on. "As you wish, your majesty."

Tony groaned as he followed her through the twists and turns of Avalon's monotonous hallways. As they slowed in front of double doors, he could feel Boto's presence just on the other side. Tony gripped the hilt tighter as Badbh pushed through and they opened into an outside courtyard. He blinked a few times; the sky was clear and blue overhead, bright as if late morning. Boto was picking through weapons, giving each a test swing. Against the castle walls were vines, trees, and flowering bushes with the occasional stone bench. In the center of the grassy area was a cobblestone circle. A mosaic in the center had a bull's head, making it clear this was meant for training or fighting events.

How convenient...

Stepping into the ring, Tony's body tensed as memories of bloodied lips and swollen eyes flooded him. He looked to Badbh, who watched him from under her mask, her nod making it painfully obvious she was aware of what sensations rolled through him. Tony observed her as she marched up beside Boto and whispered something to him. Boto lowered his brow and shot a glance in his direction. Tony cracked his neck one way, then the other.

The faster I learn, the sooner I can be by her side. At least with this future, my past has no chance of ever catching up to me. Right?

Badbh smacked Boto, and he waved her off to continue messing with the weapons. She grabbed a broadsword and marched into the ring. As she circled a few times, Tony looked at the sword she had handed him. If he had been his former self, it would have been ridiculously heavy and needed two hands to handle. He swapped from one hand then the other, as if curious which he should use, before letting it sit in his right. *This feels best.*

"Good, you took your time to decide on which is your dominant hand. That's important." Badbh stopped in front of him and swapped hands so she could mirror him. "How fast do you retain and mimic moves taught to you?"

"It's been a while. It may take some time, but I learn best by fighting," he replied. "So, am I learning this with two hands or one?"

"Let's start with two, then move to one..." She took her first stance, and he could feel the aura of a knight flow from her.

"What is that? Is that a magic spell of some kind?" Tony mirrored the stance, despite being unable to shake the sensation flowing from Badbh.

"No, nothing like that." She smiled as she moved slowly into the second stance, and he mirrored her movements. "This is similar to what you've already been doing with your incubine aura, but there are different types you can develop with enough experience and willpower."

"So, this is what a sword master's aura feels like, then?" Tony followed her into a third, then a fourth move, and noted the importance of the motion of his hips needed for the swings.

"One type of sword master," Badbh corrected. "I'll be teaching everything I can on this front, since you'll need to know how to use a blade before picking up the *Dyrnwyn*."

"What's so special about this sword I'm going after?" A few more stances and swings brought them back to the first stance, and they began repeating the pattern, a little faster than the first time.

"It's a godslayer," answered Badbh. "There's a war on the horizon, and if things go as we think they will, all of us will be making a choice to join the fight."

"A war," scoffed Tony, following her pace as closely as he could. "And who are the big players in this game of war?"

Another round of the movements started, faster and more fluid as he mirrored her without hesitation. "We're waging war against Gaea and Kronos."

Tony flinched when the next round started, and their blades started to meet. *When did she step closer? I didn't even notice the gap closing!*

"We are gathering every godslaying weapon we know and can locate in the Mortal Realm." The power behind her strikes seemed soft in movement, but they jarred the hilt in his hand. "We'd rather arm who we can, whether they intend to stand with us or not."

"I don't..." He grunted; with the next round, she increased the weight of her strikes, her hips and torso quickening their movements ever slightly. "...I don't get why I have to get this sword. Send someone else."

"Each weapon has a stipulation." The strike almost made him drop the blade, and he gritted his teeth. "You meet that sword's requirements, but we also think a quest like this will give you some real-world training."

Tony began to mimic the weight of her strikes, the muscle in his arms aching and his grip numbing because of how tight he squeezed. "Was my past not tough enough for you, then?"

"You have no idea what power you hold, fledgling."

Without warning, she switched to one-handed sword swinging. The hits were harder with each stance as Tony tried to block the flurry of strikes in time. He sidled back, but she kept up with him. Sweat painted him as the adrenaline rushed in his veins. *If this keeps up, she's going to cut me in two!*

"Wa-wait! Fuck!" Again, he slid back, rushing to make distance in fear of losing his grip on his own blade. "I can't keep..."

"Keep up!" she roared, marching forward, the strikes jarring one hand loose. "Hold strong or be cut down!"

Tony's hand grasped air, his eyes wide in fear as the next strike jarred the sword from his hand. The blade sailed hard to the side, clanking loudly against one of the benches, and Tony threw up his arms. Badbh's sword cut, clean and true. Three fingers fell and the sword skidded across the bone in the other forearm. A roar escaped Tony, his body on fire with a mixture of pain and pleasure ripping him apart. Another slice slid through his shoulder, and he sank to his knees as his blood sprayed out, sparkling like garnets in the span between them. The last strike came thrusting forward and sank through his gut, ripping out of his backside. Shock rattled through him as she planted a foot into his thigh in order to rip the blade free of his body.

Another scream escaped him; his thoughts scattered as he kneeled there in the growing pool of blood. *Is this how it all ends?!*

Badbh's fingers gripped his jaw, bringing his eyes from the red and missing digits. "Do you hear me, fledgling?"

"You... you killed me!" Rage filled him before a sense of confusion met with excitement building at his core. *What is wrong with me?! I'm bleeding to death!*

"Heal fucking faster." Badbh's lips pressed against his, the provocative lust slamming into him, goading him on to kiss her back to reverse the damage she had caused.

Badbh moaned as he suckled on her tongue, his blood boiling. *What the hell am I doing?* Shoving her off, he jerked to his feet and rushed backward until his back slapped against the castle wall. Covering his mouth with a forearm, disgusted by the moment of lust he allowed to unfold between them, he felt sick to his stomach. Looking down, his fingers were back as if it had been some horrific nightmare. Searching the ground where he had been dying, he spied his fingers.

"What the fuck is happening?" Wiping his abdomen, he found the wound gone under the blood. "Did you heal me?"

Badbh huffed; he could still feel how she struggled with the lust that had been coaxed out of her. "No. You healed you. Look, I need you to understand this isn't that bullshit training the mafia put you through." She flung the sword and his blood splattered across the grass. "Now pick up your blade. We will do this until I can no longer put you down. Your former master was soft on you, but I'll not be so kind. Prepare to discover how well those powers can work to bring you back from the edge of death. You'll meet many deaths before you master all I need to teach you in the weeks to come."

"You're fucking crazy." Fear rattled through Tony. *This is suicide!*

"Don't tell me you've lost your nerve already, little king." Boto's dark gaze brought him rage like no other. "Just imagine how many times she's been cut down since the birth of mankind. This training won't even be worth a fraction of Lillith's suffering and the deaths she has faced."

He's right. If I want to be with her, I have to understand what it means to be one of them. Marching over to the sword, he picked it up and took the first stance. "I'm ready."

CHAPTER 8

BLACK MARKET WOES

Taking a few steps forward, Lillith stumbled again before she could leave the alleyway. Leaning on the wall, she held her head as it spun. *I feel drunk. Has the air always been this saturated with ether? I know the Mortal Realm is becoming unbalanced, but it seems it's happening here, too. I'm going to have to fight harder to keep my horns at bay. Shit.* Shaking it off, she straightened herself and pulled the hood back in place to cover her face better. Marching onto the busy market road, she turned and locked eyes with a familiar face. *Manannan?* Lillith's gaze floated behind the flamboyant wizard to see more familiar faces as Cedric rubbed his nose, glaring aimlessly in her direction. *How the hell did they get this far already? Shit!*

Manannan slowed his gait, tilting his head with a bemused expression. Lillith spun on her heels, marching to look at textiles at the jorōgumo's stall as an alfin joined her as if afraid she aimed to buy the same fabric. Peeking over her shoulder, Lillith watched them head for the alleyway she had teleported into, and she shuddered. *Too close.* She recognized all but two faces in their group, one short non-gendered shapeshifter of sorts and the other a tall Nordic warrior who was emanating lust wherever he lay his eyes. Almost meeting Cedric's gaze, she turned to the alfin next to her.

"I think this shade would bring your natural blush out and match your eyes wonderfully." She handed a fabric to the alfin.

"Oh! How kind of you!" Rolling the silken fabric between two fingers, the alfin woman smiled and tucked her hair behind a pointed ear. "You know, this might be what I was looking for. I've been invited to King Frey's grand banquet and hope to find myself a match. I've had a horrible time deciding on a color."

"Oh?" Lillith shuddered, Cedric's aura overwhelming in the Otherworld compared to the Mortal Realm. *Has he gotten stronger? What on earth did that monster eat to gain this much power?*

"Hey." Cedric's voice was loud and sharp in her ears, anger riding in the tone of it, making her stiffen.

Lillith swallowed, afraid to look over her shoulder. *I've been caught!*

"What the hell is all this?" demanded Cedric, but his voice had softened now. "In the Mortal Realm, none of them would dare let the other live on the same territory. Here they're shop buddies. What gives?"

At last, she dared look over to see them lingering by the alleyway entrance as Cedric visibly interrogated Manannan. *Cedric hasn't sensed me here.* Relief washed over her, and she grabbed her chest. They looked like a pack of fools following the wizard like a school field trip; she smiled, taking them all in as they looked about the market in awe.

Manny locked eyes with her and laughed. "You can't be serious? You do realize the Mortal Realm is where they send their criminals. It's like the Wild West of others by a longshot."

Lillith's heart leaped. *Where's Romasanta? He was there with them a moment ago and now...* A hand gripped her arm tight, and she swung away from the group. Swallowing, she glared into the familiar yellow eyes and square-jawed face of Romasanta. *I've definitely been caught.*

"What are you doing here?" whispered Romasanta, keeping an eye on the group behind her. "I thought you couldn't be here?"

"I shouldn't be here." She jerked her arm from him; he sighed as she explained, "But something's happened, and I need answers that I can't get from just anywhere."

"Do we need to return?" Romasanta tensed as Cedric aimed to turn to look their direction, but Manannan deflected.

"Oh? What sort of uncivilized life you must live? Speaking of which! Cedric!" The purple and yellow peacock-of-a-wizard threw an arm over Cedric's shoulder. "You like fighting? Right?"

"No, it's something I must resolve. Though it involves the boy." Lillith glanced over, looking at the rag-tag crew. "How are things progressing?"

"Cedric's angry, as always. Doesn't help that Artemis meddled and took Angeline to her *Tir.*" Scratching his chest, Romasanta thought a moment as they watched the bickering from afar. "So, what has happened to Tony?"

Brushing the arm off, Cedric grunted. "I like to kill and eat things, yes."

"He was cursed," Lillith confessed, a shudder rolling through her.

"Was?" Romasanta tensed and leaned closer. "Answer me. What has happened to him?"

"Eat?" Manny asked, then Cedric pointed to his fangs.

"Well, he's one of us ... now." Lillith's hand glided over Romasanta's chest, very aware that under it held the scar that made him into the werewolf he spent most of his life living. "He's a king incubus, so this may get complicated when Cedric returns."

"What do you mean—" Lillith covered his mouth and shot an aura of lust into him and the Nordic man.

"Go. Get your love back and get that eye to Gaea," she demanded as she shot a look at the blond warrior. "Do not speak of this. I'll find a moment to cross paths and tell Cedric as soon as I have all the information in line. Promise."

"Very well." A shudder shook him, and Romasanta caught sight of his lustful company sniffing the air as he approached a female centaur. "Shit, Fenrir."

Chuckling, Lillith watched as Romasanta gave her a knowing glare.

"Catch up to your wolf and try to keep the fools alive until then," she sniggered.

"Days like this make me remember how much I love and hate how clever and secretive you can be." Without warning, Romasanta kissed her and ran off.

Touching her lips, Lillith sighed. *As much as I appreciate the sentiment, my wolf, I'm no longer yours and you're no longer mine. It's time we move on; we have our rightful loves depending on us both to get them through their tribulations.*

"You don't have to lecture us on unpredictable." Romasanta grabbed Fenrir's arm and pulled him along, far from the centaur he aimed to approach from behind. "At the rate this quest has gone, I gave up predicting anything going down a straight and narrow path. Much like the life I've lived thus far."

Romasanta's words made her chuckle, and she started to weave past them as they entered the alleyway. *Good, he'll keep it to himself, as I thought.*

Fenrir frowned. "Romasanta, I wanted to sniff that..."

One last stolen glance exchanged between them before she pushed through the crowd and lost him. Lillith's heart raced, and she cursed under her breath. *Even when he's simply a man, the life he's lived as a wolf has made him beyond sensitive to my presence, no matter the place and time.* She looked around; it'd been a long time since her last visit to the black market of the Otherworld. What once was a main street fanfare of sorts had become its own bustling town, complete with towering walls and gates with guards. Searching the signs and listening into conversations, Lillith sought the soothsayer who once helped her in times like this. Recognizing a section, she rushed forward, but an alfin sentry lowered his spear in her way.

"You can go no farther," he drawled, his armor shiny and hair woven in many braids. "You don't have VIP status."

"VIP status?" she snorted, lowering her hood. "And where does one get such a status? Forgive me, for it's been a long time since my last visit."

The alfin picked her apart with his hazel eyes for a moment before answering, "It's bestowed on those whom the king favors."

Sucking on her cheek, she muttered under her breath, "Fucking Pan."

"Excuse me?" he furrowed his brow.

Clearing her throat, Lillith straightened herself to add a sense of importance to her presence. "I wish to see King Frey."

The sentry laughed. "You can't just ask to see him."

"The hell I can't," she growled, pushing a finger into his chest. "You tell him, or his advisors, that the king's blossom is here to have a few words with him about this so-called VIP status bullshit he didn't bestow on me."

He bit his bottom lip and let out an ear-shattering whistle. Another alfin warrior appeared. The sentry whispered into his ear, and the warrior went running off behind him. Lillith stepped back, crossing her arms in her impatience with the matter. She glared around, glad to see no further signs of Romasanta and company. Beyond where the sentry stood, she could see the wares and the customers interacting. The items were indeed of higher quality, both in craftsmanship and magic, in the so-called VIP section. Unlike the market filled with halflings, demons, and yōkai, this area seemed to be for celestials, fae, and alfin nobility.

"If you're lying," the sentry's tone darkened, "I'll be throwing you into the ring with the minotaur."

Lillith scoffed. "You're assuming a minotaur can overpower a queen."

His face flushed, and he spat, "What kind of queen dresses like a commoner?"

"One who has urgent matters that can't be trusted to subordinates," she drawled, mimicking his tone from earlier.

The other warrior ran up, passing the sentry, and bowed deeply to her. "Our apologies! The king will see you straight away, Your Majesty. Please, follow me this way."

That's more like it, though I didn't want to use my title and power in the open like this. Many frown upon me simply because of what I am and what I create, but they don't realize it's all part of the curse placed on me by Gaea herself. Maybe they think I am free from her torture and games because I'm made from part of her.

The alfin sentry seemed confused by the urgency of his companion as he ushered Lillith into the VIP area. Lillith followed him; the marketplace had mimicked the luxuries of the Mortal Realm more so than she had expected from what she could see outside. It reminded her of the markets and cafes of Paris, though the food of this realm was by far more enticing to one's sense of smell and taste. The alfin soldier spoke with several fellow soldiers, and they stepped aside and bowed slightly as she passed. None seemed to be aware of who or what she was, but King Frey was very aware, and he'd prove more difficult to deal with.

At least I got through this more discreetly this time. I damn near had to pull a move out of Cleopatra's book last time. Now, if Romasanta can keep his lips sealed, I can figure this all out. Then there's the matter of telling Cedric, as promised. Why did I even reassure him I would tell that buffoon? Let's wait until he has Angeline back. He's rather one-track-minded when she's not in his possession.

CHAPTER 9

A BLOOD BATH

Blood ran down into Tony's right eye, and he muttered curses as it painted the world in a red tint. The air was filled with a mangled scent of salty sweat and the metallic tinge of blood. Badbh stepped back to give him a moment to heal, but it was only thanks to the fact he had, at last, started to wear her down. She'd tossed her mask off hours before, disturbing Boto, who'd fallen asleep at a table in a far corner. They had advanced from two-handed sword training to one-handed sword teamed with a small dagger in the other.

"For what it's worth, you're doing better than I expected and are learning at a fast pace." Boto yawned.

Grunting, Tony reset his stance and tensed. *I don't even know how I'm still standing with so many revivals and healings having happened.*

"Damn, I haven't felt this strained in a very long time." Badbh stretched, her back to Tony as she did so.

Tony launched forward. *Never turn your back on an enemy.* She'd sliced across his backside twice for doing something similar; at this stage, he was angry and tired. *Payback's a bitch!* Spinning, she parried his strike, and he thrust the dagger forward and sliced her side. *It hit!* Badbh dodged just enough to keep it from being a deep wound. Tony pressed on, trying to overpower her, though she still managed to make the weapons in his hands feel as if she could jar them from his grip at any given moment.

"Dammit," spat Tony, retreating.

"Good, you're taking advantage of openings." She wiped blood from her side and grinned. "And we managed to draw blood finally."

"You've killed me over a dozen times." Tony glanced at the blood splatter and the sickening number of digits and limbs all around like abandoned trash and cigarette butts. "I can't believe I can grow shit back, but..." Another wave of nausea rolled through him, and he threw up. "Dammit," he choked. *Every time I dare to look at it, it fucks with my mind and stomach. I'm barely keeping my focus and mind from breaking...*

"Get used to it already," chortled Boto, heckling him once more from the sidelines.

"Then why don't you come in here and fight," growled Tony.

"As you wish." Boto stood and joined Badbh. "How about some two-against-one training?"

"Oh, let's!" Badbh's excitement sent a shudder through Tony.

Tony dropped the dagger and grabbed another broadsword from the weapon stand. He struggled to find a position or stance to start in. *Shit, at least she showed me how to do this. At this rate, what do I have to lose? I used to avoid taking a hit in a brawl, but now, fuck that.*

"Hold on. I can't be unfair about this." Badbh snatched Boto's sword from him and dropped into a starting stance. "You start in this position, rookie."

Once Tony mirrored it, she handed the sword back to Boto, who snorted, "You're softer these days."

"I want to see what he can do." She shrugged, spitting on the ground.

Swallowing, Tony slowed his breathing in an attempt to calm his racing heart. All at once, the two of them advanced, swinging in on him. Tony deflected and parried, arms aching. Boto's hits were every bit as skilled and jarring as Badbh's, and he couldn't dodge every thrust they threw his way. He began to willingly let them hit, now confident about how much and how fast he could heal. He'd managed to discover how to flip the sensation that had once stung and enveloped him in pain into pleasure to speed up the healing.

Badbh's sword sank into his abdomen, and he took a step forward. Tony parried Boto's next strike while striking down where Badbh's grip held and twisted the blade. Blood rolled into his mouth, and he spit it across her face; she let go, leaving the blade there. She retreated, cursing as she tried to clear her eyes. Tony tossed his sword and pulled hers from his stomach and wielded it; the pleasure his wounds brought him added to the power-high he rode as he came in striking.

A yelp escaped Badbh as she barely leaped out of the swing, and it sliced across the top of her thighs. Boto came in with a high swing; it made Tony stumble and drop to a knee when they locked blades. Tony turned his focus on Boto, roaring as he swung hard. Boto deflected and parried, pulling Tony farther and farther away from where Badbh muttered in another language and limped to heal herself with a spell. Tony managed a double upswing and sliced Boto's shirt open.

"Getting serious now." Boto backed up as they glared at one another, breathless.

"Well, it seems I'm better at two against one." Tony shifted into the starting stance again.

A shudder rolled through him as memories of being cornered in back alleyways and punching his way out flooded his mind. *I'm shit one-on-one unless I'm using my fists. As for being outnumbered, I prefer it every time.*

Pulling off his shirt, Boto seemed to have doubled in muscle mass; his arms and shoulders hidden under the black shirt had been deceiving. Boto came forward, his strikes hard enough to jar one blade from Tony's hand. Giving up on chasing the blade, Tony gripped the remaining sword two-handed as he defended against the flurry of one-handed strikes from Boto. Gritting his fangs, Tony pressed harder in an attempt to recover lost ground. Against Badbh, he couldn't shake the fear of cleaving her in two, but with Boto... *He can resurrect, so let's cut this asshole down to size.*

A hard under-swing sent Boto's blade sailing, and it stuck into the grass far behind him. Instead of retreating for Tony's next swing, Boto stepped into it. With a clawed hand, he caught the blade and jerked the sword from Tony as horns erupted from his head. Boto's other hand swiped out, the claws slicing across Tony's cheek and nose. *If he can rage out, then I can too! This is the fight I was itching for in Pan's office!* With a roar of frustration, Tony sprung forward with his own claws, slicing across Boto's abdomen. Boto crouched with a hiss and gripped Tony's shoulders. Claws dug deep into Tony's shoulder and brought on an orgasmic sensation.

Two can play at that game.

Tony's own claws dug into Boto's stomach. Smirking under his blood-soaked face, Tony pushed a wave of arousal and Boto puffed out his cheeks. They were gridlocked, neither willing to retreat as they clawed into one another ever deeper as blood dripped at their feet, tapping against the cobblestones of the fighting ring. Sweat dripped across them, glistening in the sunlight that seemed unmoving overhead, as if time stood still. The incubine auras shoved at one another.

This isn't like when Lillith's aura hits mine and they mingle with one another. Instead, they are shoving like invisible bulls fighting for dominance. This is what it would be like to face Cedric, but... if he could overpower Boto, so can I!

Another roar escaped Tony. He could feel himself growing in size. Horns accompanied by wings and a tail snaked into existence. Every bit of himself let the incubus within take hold, shoving back so as to not give Boto any more ground in the wrestling match. Boto's own incubine shape unfolded, the dual set of fangs gritting and the look in his eyes wild. Tony leaned back only to come smashing forward, foreheads and horns cracking against each other. Blood trickled down both their faces now; growling, they dug into one another, fingers twisting flesh.

Tony reached out with his other claw and gripped Boto's shoulder. In reply, Boto ripped a hand into Tony's abdomen to mirror his own state and tried to shove forward. Tony's wings flapped, and Boto's feet slid in the copious amounts of blood. A growl rumbled out of Boto like a thunderstorm. *He doesn't like that. Good.* Tony glared into his eyes, ignoring the red tint invading his vision. Pleasure erupted at Tony's stomach as Boto ripped it open and toward him. A sickening emptiness took hold and he felt light as guts began to slap against the floor between them. Tony didn't budge or flinch. *Not going to work on me, asshole.*

"Back down," growled Boto.

"You first," replied Tony, raking his claw from the shoulder down across Boto's chest, where he dug two hands into Boto's gut, fingers gripping what he could only assume were intestines. "Learn by doing, right?"

Tony pulled, gutting Boto as he coughed blood across his face. Before Tony could shake it from his eyes, a clawed hand was at his throat, lifting so his feet barely touched the ground. Another dip and rip of his own stomach and more blood boiled up his throat and gurgled. *I... can't... breathe.*

"Ungrateful twerp," sputtered and wheezed Boto.

Squinting with one eye, Tony struggled to gasp for air. Trying to pull Boto from his throat failed; with the last of his dying energy, he thrust both claws in and up under Boto's ribs, puncturing Boto's lungs. The howl from Boto made him drop Tony, shoving back to gain reprieve and gasp for air. Blood poured from Boto's gut and mouth as he stumbled back to lean on the wall. Tony scooped up his intestines, shoving them back into the tear as his desire to dominate over Boto grew. A familiar tingle rolled across his being, much like Lillith's mark had done to him in the beginning.

This isn't her magic; perhaps it's mine.

At last, Tony managed to inhale deeply, steam rolling off him as he healed incredibly fast. The moment Boto met his gaze, Tony charged forward on all fours like a wild animal. Boto tried to claw at him, but Tony blocked and uppercut him. The force of it sent him flying backward, smashing against the castle walls. Boto's eyes rolled back, and he fell in a crumpled heap. Panting, Tony stumbled back, only to slip in the blood and land on his ass.

"Excellent!" Badbh exclaimed, clapping and chuckling. "Nicely done!"

Tony spit the last of the blood from his mouth. Looking down, he wiped the blood away from his torso to find no wound or scar to show for the brutal battle. A tail lifted and moved in his sight, reassuring him that it indeed belonged to him. *Fangs, horns, wings, and a tail.*

"This is surreal. I should be dead." Tony stretched his wings into view and sighed. "But again, I find myself a monster."

"You're a king incubus." Walking over, she stood before Boto with her hands on her hips. "Oh, he's gonna be down for a while. I didn't think you'd take him down in the first match, but you do have more experience."

"Experience," guffawed Tony as wings flared open and his tail swished in reply.

"Brawling," Badbh confirmed.

"I don't feel like I should have won that fight. He's been around longer." Tony closed his eyes, trying to pull back the waves of arousal in hopes of making the monstrous form fade.

"No. You've been a brawler for some time with the mafia." Badbh spun to face him, and Tony's eyes fell to the new scars on her body, one at her side and one on each thigh.

"I'm sorry. I was trying to hold back." Tony stood, making a feeble attempt to wipe the blood from his face. "So much blood everywhere." *I'm feeling sick to my stomach again.*

"I was wondering there for a while." Badbh gripped him on each shoulder with a goofy grin on her face. "It is mostly your blood on the ground, my friend."

"I imagine so. You've been slicing parts off of me for hours." His eyes caught sight of a finger he had lost in the first round that had turned to a darkened color; he lurched his eyes up and away. "So many fingers everywhere."

"Hours?" Badbh snorted. "We're in Avalon, rookie. We've been at this for days." Slapping his shoulders, the blood was thick and sticky. "Let's get you washed up and well-rested before the next lesson."

"What do you mean 'days?'" He looked at the sky. "The sun hasn't moved."

"Oh, does this mean you really don't remember the few times I accidentally beheaded you?" She was shoving him toward a door and whispered, "Don't look in the bushes; it's a little unnerving to stare at one's face like that. Boto thought it best to roll them in there until we can clean it up."

Tony began to feel faint; entering the dark corridor, the cold air was a nice reprieve. "Exactly how unkillable am I?" he demanded.

"You're definitely built like Cedric. It would take a lot, and they'd have to find a means of turning off those incubine powers to get any advantage over your healing." They didn't get far before she shoved him through another door. "Here's your room and the bath should already be drawn with a table set with food and drink. Rest up and I'll be back."

The door thudded behind him, and Tony stood baffled by the extravagant medieval bedroom fit for a king. Looking around, the only lighting was flames from a massive fireplace. Next to that, he spotted the steam rolling from a tub of water. Unbuckling his pants, he let what was left of the blood-soaked rags drop to the floor. Sinking into the scalding water, he settled in and let his muscles relax.

I wonder how Lillith is holding up. Does she feel what is happening with me? Coming up for air, he rubbed the back of his neck and a warm tingle pulsed for a moment. *If she can bestow this upon me to connect to me, I wonder if I can do the same for her?*

CHAPTER 10

KING FREY'S COURT

Relief washed over Lillith when she saw she wasn't going to the formal waiting hall with the others. It wasn't her first visit to King Frey's mansion here in the Otherworld, where he came for entertainment before returning home to his castle on his own *Tir* and domain. Instead, they weaved down hallways and into the area for esteemed guests and bedrooms. The guard spoke elvish to the other alfin stationed in front of the guarded room, and they stepped off to the side.

"King Frey and his guest await you." The soldier bowed deeply as the sentries opened the door.

And guest? Lillith's boots clacked on the marble floor as she passed between guards. The room was bright with embellishments and golden flairs, complete with faux columns. She could hear snickering. The *thud* of closing doors and *ting* of teacups echoed throughout the grandiose sitting room as the tea drinkers hid behind a high-backed Victorian couch. Lillith stopped in the center of the open space and bowed, holding the stance over the rug that led to where King Frey and his esteemed guest whispered excitedly to one another.

"I'm sorry to disturb you, King Frey." Her voice seemed loud and crisp in the acoustics of the vaulted ceiling painted with satyrs and faeries. "It seems I need your permission to even walk through the VIP area of the market."

Another round of giggling made her bite her tongue, still holding the pose. After more hushed whispering, she glanced up to see two men standing before her, holding teacups in hand. The taller one, King Frey, was lithe and athletic even under the white silken paisley vest and suit, while the other had his back to her, his suit strangely familiar. King Frey's silver hair was long and pulled back into a series of golden clasps;

golden chains and earrings decorated his pointy ears, and silvery irises held a playful air about them as he leered down at her. His thin lips drew tight with his grin as he took a sip of tea before deciding to reply.

"You're right, dear Pan," cooed King Frey. "The blossom still blooms, even wrapped in leather and cloaks."

Standing straight, Lillith met Pan's over-the-shoulder glance. "Fairy Dick." She reached into a pouch and started pulling up the contacts in her cell phone.

"Wh-what are you doing?" Pan placed his teacup down in a hurry, brow furrowing.

"Changing your name in my phone as a stark reminder of what you are," she answered flatly.

"Oh, c'mon. I thought you were here to shop, not to see Frey," Pan scoffed as Frey raised his brows high.

"Sibling rivalry! This I can get behind." Another sip of tea and he walked over to sit in an armchair to get a front-row seat to their bickering. "Come, sit and talk with me for a spell, my little blossom."

Shoving her phone back in the pouch, she took a seat and leaned in to grab a pastry before pouring her own cup of floral tea. "So, what's all this business with VIP status and being thrown to the minotaur?"

"Ah, well, I've decided to have my own game of sibling rivalry," King Frey mused. "You see, someone has to challenge those silly Amazonians that my sister cherishes so much."

"And how do Alecto and Artemis feel about this little challenge?" Lillith took a sip of her tea and smirked.

"Well, that's why we have the minotaur," reassured Frey.

Pan walked around the table and stole a tiny chocolate off a top-tier dish before adding, "And the birdcage."

"I see. So, you first need a champion who can survive the agreed-upon trials?" Lillith giggled. "It seems like a pissing contest, since your beloved sentries aren't strong enough."

"Lillith," hissed Pan, sitting on the arm of Frey's chair, "why must you be so rude all the—"

Frey lifted his fingers to silence Pan. "No, I rather enjoy it. Reminds me of my own sister's forked tongue. You're insightful as ever, I see."

"They don't call me Queen for nothing, deary." Lillith took another bite of the pastry.

"I thought you had business in the market." Pan changed topics, turning his gaze to the painting of a majestic unicorn and its virgin maiden.

"I do, but I don't have the King's blessing to enter the high-class side of town, it seems." She finished the last bite and tilted her head.

"Nothing I can't solve, my blossom." Rolling his fingers, a coin pendant appeared on a silvery chain. "Your ticket."

Lillith took one last sip of her tea and set it down. "And the cost?"

"You two are deplorable." Pan stood up and walked to the painting. "I'll have no part in this agreement." He vanished in a burst of red petals.

"He's so adorable when flustered," Frey hummed, standing to circle the petals.

Lillith stood, watching as he rolled the pendant to and fro across his knuckles. "The price?"

"Ah, yes." He flipped the coin to her, and she caught it. "Let's say this is a pact not to meddle in any of my affairs while you're here. Someone is bringing me something of interest, and rumor has it you might intervene if I decide to accept it into my games."

Lillith snorted. "Manannán's your dealer, huh?"

"Lillith, you're impeccably quick-witted. Does your brother know he may lose his title?" He scooped a handful of rose petals in his hand and inhaled their scent.

"He lives for the sleight of hand," answered Lillith, placing the necklace on and peering at the seal of King Frey upon the pendant, the metal holding an opalescent shimmer to it. "I'd rather just call you out on your shit."

Dropping the petals, Frey smirked as he thumbed an earring in thought. "No interference then?"

"If this involves that crew of misfits, good luck to you, King Frey." She bowed deeply once more and shot him a dangerous glare. "You better not get between that one and his fated mate, or he may burn your kingdom to the ground. Does Pan know of the mischief you plan?"

Frey laughed, leaning on the back of the chair, and looked away. "You know how I am, my blossom. I rather enjoy surprising him with my own mischief—the expression I hope to draw out on Pan's face when he sees my new champion enter the ring! So, what manner of creature is he? No one seems to know, not even the wizard, presumably."

Lillith stood and spun away, chortling. "Oh, you'll see. He's the only one of his kind for sure, except his counterpart, who is said to be heir to Artemis's legacy."

"And that is worth the price of a favor from me later." The magic in the room became heavy with Frey's excitement.

"I had hoped it would be. I'll save that one for when the time is needed." Shoving out the door, she held her chin high as she let the waiting soldier lead her back out.

Stepping into the dust of the bustle of the marketplace, she peered around. Frustration filled her as nothing from before seemed the same. *So much bigger and busier than before. Is she even still here, I wonder?* The soldier bowed deeply to her and mumbled his goodbye, but she grabbed him by the arm. He shot her a disdainful glare and she let go.

Sighing, he brushed his arm off. "What do you need of me, Your Majesty?"

"I'm looking for the Gander & Goose," she whispered.

His eyes widened, and a smirk crawled across his face. "You know one needs a reservation to get into that joint?"

"Just point me in the right direction. Back in my youth, they were just a little tent in the market," she scoffed.

"You haven't been here in centuries," he snorted and seemed impressed. "Well, keep traveling deeper in that direction. You should be able to see the willow trees from here."

Lillith shuddered. *Dammit, it's in the direction of where that uncanny wave of lust is emanating from, which means...* "Really? You made a red-light district in the black market?"

"What's a red-light district?" The soldier furrowed his brow, but Lillith marched past him.

This is going to be difficult. Willow trees lined a dark alleyway, with strands of flowers and leaves falling in a colorful burst of yellows, whites, pinks, and green. Lillith halted as another wave of lust slammed through her and she winced. *This isn't like lust from humans. Between the magic-laden air and lust from magical beings, this is potent, and I don't want to show my horns here.* Tugging the hood up and over her head, she swallowed down her nerves. *I wonder if Romasanta could see how uneasy I felt being here.* Up ahead, she saw signage written in old Sumerian reading Gander & Goose. *Bingo!*

Slowing her approach, the peak of the lustful and arousing aura wafted out of the establishment she aimed to enter. *I keep forgetting she's also a fertility goddess. Nice to see she's doing well for herself these days.* Inhaling deeply, she digested the power emanating from the building, her entire being craving to devour it. Another shudder rolled through her, tiny nubs of her horns peeking through. *This will do. It's not so blatant and doesn't immediately scream succubus.*

Throwing open the door, she walked into a scene that reminded her of the old west saloons but more sophisticated and harem-like. A few steps in and she was stopped by a hostess of some kind. Her dark hair was long and filled with flowers; a headband of yellow and red feathers and petals circled her head. A large tropical flower burst into a colorful array of pink, purple, and green that matched the dress and shawl she wore. All the jewelry, bracelets, and earrings were fruit-themed and done in the old ways of the Manipuri ancients. Lillith couldn't quite place where the goddess was from, but the power flowing from her was more than enough to manage the door and take down any who might try to force entry.

"Welcome, esteemed guest of King Frey." Her voice was soft and sweet, pleasing to the ears. "What has brought you to the Gander & Goose today?"

"I'm here to see the headmistress." Lillith bowed her respects. "It's a rather urgent matter."

The woman blinked and asked, "You wish to see Miss Yuki-onba?"

Lillith choked, making a befuddled expression. "No," she blurted in confusion. "I'm here to see perhaps the owner. I'm an old friend of Nanshe and Nindara."

"Hmm." The woman narrowed her eyes a moment before raising two fingers to summon one of the courtesans. "Let me see if they're ... available." She whispered a few words into the young faerie's ear, who fluttered off in a hurry. "Now we wait."

"My apologies," Lillith added. "It's been several centuries since I've last seen them. Last time, they simply had a tent, and I didn't have to wear one of King Frey's trinkets to even get close to the shop."

"I see." She leaned on a podium where she took a bite of a strange faeland fruit.

Great, I've only been in the Otherworld barely an hour and it's been a complete shit show. I wonder how many days, or weeks, have passed since I've been here? If Tony is even able to stand his ground against those two at all? Memories of Tony kneeling before her in Pan's office sent an enthralling shiver up her spine. Shaking it off, she turned back to her hostess, who crunched on her snack with a judging glare. *Ah, she thinks I'm bullshitting her about knowing them. Fair point seeing how much they've grown and now need... who is this?*

Clearing her throat, Lillith started some small talk to ease the tension growing between her and the hostess. "Manipuri goddess?"

Swallowing, she gave an amused expression. "Not many people can guess that much."

"I apologize; I'm not well acquainted with your hierarchy since I spent those years with the Greeklings."

"Ah, what a rowdy bunch they can be." Offering some fruit, she announced, "I am Heinu Leima, the queen of fruitful abundance."

"From one queen to another, I'm honored to meet you." Lillith bowed her respects.

"And may I ask what kind of queen you might be?" Heinu Leima crunched another bite from the fruit, curious now.

"A queen of another kind of fruitful abundance that goes alongside fertility in the most monstrous ways." Lillith chortled as a dark-skinned hunk with an aggressive aura approached. "And here's the Gander himself, Nindara!" Lillith pulled back her hood and revealed herself to him; a wild smile and laughter rolled from him. "It's been a while since I've seen the bull in the rushes in person!"

"Lilly! It's been so long!" Nindara embraced her, hugging her tight and swinging her around. "Come! Come! Nanshe said you would be coming soon to see her and here you are, as prophesied!"

"I figured she'd know before I did that I would be coming." Lillith turned and bowed again to Heinu Leima. "Thank you for your hospitality."

"You're most welcome. Lilly?" She arched a brow. "I didn't expect you to be received by the Gander so brightly. Not very often someone's claim ends with truth."

"Understandable." Lillith hooked an arm with Nindara, his build making her blush as it reminded her of Tony's. "How is my favorite consort these days?"

"Busy." Nindara waved his hand across the room as they started up the grand staircase. "We've come a long way in the last few centuries, though so many are seeking Nanshe for guidance and, well, she can only do so much, as you know."

Sighing, Lillith remembered how she first met Nanshe and demanded where she had found that scroll, where she had found and written down her deepest, darkest secret. "I hate to admit this, but I, too, seek her for that purpose today."

"Ah, but unlike the others, your destiny is the one that speaks to her the loudest these days." Nindara brought her down the maze-like hallways, the corridors twisting and turning unnaturally. "In fact, listening to her whispers during trances leads me to suspect you may have found a bull more skilled in running through the rushes than myself."

"I, uh..." Lillith choked. "How could you say that to me?"

Chuckling, Nindara patted her arm as they came to a stop in front of a white and gold set of doors. "Don't worry. Your secret is safe with the Gander and the Goose."

The doors were painted with two geese, one on each door to represent both Nanshe's beloved pets and also a self-reflection of the goddess and her consort. The room tilted, her body weakening as a wave of magic slammed into her. Inhaling deeply, she pulled Nindara back before he could open the door. She was falling and used him to keep herself upright a moment longer. Panic filled her. *Shit, what's wrong with me?* He gave her a baffled look, his blue-green irises flashing down on her. Her breath drew short, tight, stinging. She couldn't catch her breath. Nerves drawn too tight; she began to shake under the state she found herself in.

"Are you..." Lillith sank to her knees, gasping for air. "Breathe, Lilly, breathe!"

Shit, is this a panic attack, or is the curse taking me at last before I can get any answers as to why me... and why him... Tony! Is this how I end? Without confessing...

CHAPTER 11

SNEAKING AROUND AVALON

Taking another chunk out of a bread roll, Tony looked around at the medieval furnishings of the room. *I feel like I'm living inside some renaissance fair themed hotel.* Grabbing the goblet, he snorted to himself before chugging the water. Returning his gaze to the fire, he let his thoughts wander back to Lillith. He couldn't shake her; the sensations and power of the connection they had just being in the same room were surreal and frightening. *My thrall...* a shiver shook him, and he set his cup down and jerked to his feet.

Pacing the floor, he felt trapped with every glance at the door. *Even if I walk out of here, how the hell would I find my way back? It's not like I'm aiming to leave Avalon, but shit, I just need to go for a walk.* Every muscle in his body seemed taut. Restlessly, his arms and back twitched as if his body was begging to be put through the paces of sword practice again, the reflexes itching to be used now that they had been established.

Something about this all seems to be bringing me closer to ... myself? I was always a brawler, but holding a sword felt ... right.

Scooping up one more bread roll, Tony pushed into the dark hallway. Looking right and left, he found no sign as to where the paths led or what he might discover farther down. Cobblestones protruding out of the wall around the doorframes were some indication of doors lingering in the far distance in the darkness. Turning, he dared to pull his door closed.

"Besides Pan's office, none of the doors seem to have signs," Tony muttered to himself before braving to walk down the hall to look for other doors. "There has to be a method to the madness."

Tony strode a few steps down to the left and saw no other door, although moments before he had clearly seen stone sticking out as if one had been a few paces down. Circling back, he walked past his door and looked down the other way. *Nothing.* Cursing under his breath, he decided to retreat back to his...

"Where the fuck did my door go?" Tony stared at the cobblestone wall where his door had once stood, a sense of betrayal and dread filling him. "Well, guess I'm going for that walk no matter how I feel about it." Taking a deep breath, he tried to calm down. "They'll be looking for me soon enough, I'm sure."

Taking a bite of his roll, he began walking down the now doorless corridor. Sometimes a torch or lantern would appear to keep just enough light in the hall that he wouldn't trip or bash into the occasional table or rogue cobblestone tilted out of place. It was damp and musky, everything a castle dungeon's ambiance was expected to be. Roughly half an hour had passed, and he was still walking down a constant curve with no doors.

Slowing down while chewing on the last bite of his roll, he decided to turn around and start to go back the way he came. *Maybe my door will show back up?* Again, the hallway seemed to curve as he marched down it, but it made him stumble to a stop. *This isn't right. It's curving to the right still.* A chill snaked up his spine and his shoulders shook. *Magical castles are a pain in the ass.* Swallowing, he pressed forward again, trying to keep the same pace in hopes of ending where he had started. Another half hour passed and still no doors appeared.

"C'mon!" Tony's voice echoed through the corridor. "Can I just go back to bed?"

As the echoes faded to haunting whispers, they distorted until they stacked on top of one another, giving him a harsh reply, "NonoNonononoNonononoNononoNono..."

Fear shook Tony, and with one step, he triggered the torches in the hall to all snuff out without any indication as to how. The darkness crushed down from all around, cold and silent until a howling started to build in the distance. A harsh wind hissed as it rushed over him, shoving him back a few steps as it kept going. Clenching his jaw tight, Tony blinked in desperation at what nightmare might unfold, begging his eyes to catch some hint of light or what might be causing the chaos. The pressure in the room shifted and his ears popped. *Is that some kind of magical barrier being cast? Isn't that what Pan's office did that day?*

Looking all around him, Tony's eyes seemed to fail peering through the abyss. Reaching out to touch the walls, he found nothing. *Shit! Where the hell am I? Did the room change?* A wave of arousal hit him, and he spun to face the source. Far in the distance, where the wall had once stood, was a new corridor with many embellishments of faeries and other creatures that he wasn't so familiar with. At the end, a white set of doors waited under the glowing sconces lit by blue flames of magic. Another shudder shook him, and he willed himself to walk toward them.

"Where are you taking me?" he muttered, glancing over his shoulder to see a solid wall where he had once stood. "You're not giving me much choice in the matter, I see. This better not be some kind of trap."

The lights by the doors glowed brighter in response and the doors came closer in a rush. Tony's heart leaped to his throat as his back slapped against the wall behind him. Taking in the fine craftsmanship, he saw it didn't match any of the other doors in Avalon. The glow of the lights pulsed as if promising to take him some place completely new and different. No other door had looked as if it came out of a mansion from a far-off land. Before Tony were double doors adorned with gold featuring a pair of birds, one featured on each door facing the other. Reaching out, he saw his hand trembling.

"I feel like this is all a bad dream and I'm going to wake up in that cheesy renaissance fair room." Sucking on a cheek, he added, "Those are some fat and ugly swans painted on these doors."

Another wave of arousal flowed from the doors, but this time there was something alarmingly familiar. *Lillith?* Tony swung open the doors in alarm, squinting his eyes at the bright lights that filtered in from... As if someone had turned up the volume, Tony was met with the bustling sounds of a crowded building as he tried to gain his bearings. *Where am I? This place feels ... different.* Laughter and moaning filled the air. His skin crawled at the amount of lustful power that he took in with ease. *I would normally have been screwed encountering this much power. Thankfully, I'm still exhausted from training.* Another few blinks and his eyes adjusted to the bright lights. Something grabbed his leg, and he dropped his gaze.

"Lillith!" Rattled, seeing her sprawled on the floor where a mostly naked man held her head, his heart fluttered. "What's going on? What did you do to her?"

"How did..." The man let Tony scoop her up as the doors shut behind him. "Where did you come from? How did you get into Nanshe's room?"

"Look, I got teleported here, but what the fuck happened to Lillith?" Tony growled, horns and fangs creeping forward. "I want answers now."

"Ah, so you're her bull." With a sigh, the man gave him a softened expression before bowing to introduce himself. "I'm Nindara, consort to the goddess Nanshe. Lillith and I are close friends, but she fell ill before we could," Nindara opened the doors to reveal a bedroom filled with cushions and fabric swaths hanging from the ceiling, "see Nanshe. Here, lay her inside. We'll discuss how and where you came from after we tend to her."

So, Avalon knew she was in trouble and sent me to her. Or did Lillith summon me like I've summoned her in the past? Picking her up with ease, Tony hesitated before passing through the doors again. "She's been gone for over a month. She must be exhausted."

Nindara closed the door behind him. "That's quite the impressive spell you cast to come to her side like this. And your name?"

"I didn't... It's—" Tony wasn't sure which question to answer first.

"Antonio," whispered a female's voice, some place deeper in the room.

Every nerve twisted inside Tony as he held Lillith's limp body tighter. "Who are you?"

"Nanshe," she replied from somewhere behind the waterfalls of fabric.

Nindara waved for him to follow him. "Come, let's have a closer look at her. Perhaps Nanshe knows what's the matter."

Weaving through the room, they passed a fountain where two geese played in the water. One flapped its wings at them as they walked past, dodging in and out of the fabric. Eventually, the room opened to a space with fruit piled on tables and a half-naked woman smoking a hookah. Nanshe's hair, dark and wavy, fell all around her, harshly contrasting the soft tones of the pillows and fabrics that decorated the room. A large golden crown sat on her head; a glow of power emanated from her that only added to her body's voluptuous curves, from her bare breasts to her hourglass waistline. A skirt wrapped low on her hips teased the eyes as if it could fall off or open if she were to stand. Smoke billowed from her thick, dark red lips as she watched Tony with dark eyes.

"Lay her down." Another whisper, though her lips seemed to barely move, as if she spoke directly to his mind.

Tony did so as she gestured next to her. Nanshe abandoned her hookah and flowed her hands over Lillith as if reading the unseen aura. Another wave of arousal rolled out of Lillith and hit Tony. He winced, trying his best not to echo it back to her, or worse, hit the strangers with it. Nanshe's necklace jangled as she muttered in a strange language. *I feel so useless.* Lillith seemed to shift and at last, inhaled deeply, as if she had been stuck underwater and was catching her breath at last.

"What's wrong with her?" Tony furrowed his brow.

"She's drowning." Nanshe frowned as her eyes shot up to meet Tony's gaze. "He's brought you here to see what purpose you intend to take with her. It's your turn to show your intent without her interfering."

"Who brought me here?" A wind filled with magic blew across him again, as if sneaking out from Avalon and into this strange place. "I don't even know where here is, to be honest."

"You're in the Otherworld," answered Nindara, tilting his head. "And I assumed you brought *you* here."

"No, Avalon forced me through a door." Tony slid strands of hair off Lillith's face and lips. "I've never seen her so ... vulnerable." His chest ached with a sharp pang. *Has she always been this vulnerable and was hiding it away from even me?*

"It seems he's made a decision to join the fight, has he?" Again, a whisper and plume of exotic smoke filled the air. "You, there, choose how you wish to serve your queen. The gods and fates of old demand an answer."

"E-excuse me?" Tony arched an eyebrow, confused by her murmuring that seemed to fill the massive room. "What does that even mean?"

Nindara crouched and gave him an expression of understanding before explaining, "Do you intend to stand behind her in servitude as her consort or stand in front of her as a king?"

Tony's face flushed red as a chill of arousal rolled through him. *My queen... but I'm her thrall.*

"He forced you here because you are the only one this child has accepted, entrusted with all her being and fragility. The thorns on a rose bite hard, but their petals bruise if touched too harshly." Nanshe stood in a flurry of jingling, her steps silent, her aura darkening the room until she stood behind him and whispered into his ear, "But you have touched petals that no one has seen blossom, little titan, and did not aim to bruise them, but cherish them. Have you not?"

Swallowing, goosebumps rolled over Tony. "Look, I don't know why I was practically thrown through a door or what it is that makes me so damn special to you all." Fangs and horns pulled forward as his anger and frustration bested him, his voice grumbling, "But what's so fucking wrong with being in love with someone who's been thrown the shittiest of paths in life?"

Nanshe blew smoke across his face and hissed, "Then which path do you choose in order to stay with your flower?"

Tony searched Nanshe's face; her wide pupils overpowered the black-brown irises. "Neither. I don't need titles that will put me before her or in a position where I can't protect her at all."

Another wave of charms and jewelry chimed as she moved to his other ear and murmured, "Then what title would you take for yourself?"

Tony's head was spinning in the weight of the intoxicating fumes, the weight of arousal from the Willow District, and lust pouring out of Lillith as if a cup overflowed. "If I choose..." He searched his swimming thoughts. One caught him from an old fantasy novel he once read at the bar; the girls had told him it wasn't meant for men to read at all. "King Consort."

Nanshe pulled away, laughing as she settled back in the pillows where she had started. "Very well, King Incubus Consort of Queen Succubus Lillith. What will you do to help your partner, and equal, at this moment where the lust and magic have overwhelmed her for the first time in all her existence?"

"I will take back what she has taken from me," muttered Tony, pumping his fist, staring at his palm as the idea crept forward.

Is it possible to do to her what she has done for me? His eyes took her in, the memories of how she had placed the mark on the back of his neck and how it would tingle as his lust grew too much in those moments before he took on the change for himself. *Shit, she's going to know it's me, and she's going to feel this the next time and for a while, but just maybe...* Again, he scanned her entire body. He started tugging at the threads of the leather tunic until he could weasel a hand over her navel. A chill made his shoulders shake. *I can do this. Think of it as a means to always know where she is, to find her, to save her...*

He let his hand land softly against her warm, soft skin. She winced and a wave of want and arousal hit him, and he let himself soak it in. *Okay, just like what happened in the office. The only difference is she's not going to be able to talk me out of this...*

"You may want to stand back; this is my first time..." Inhaling deeply, he could feel the familiar tingling building in his hand and buzzing against her.

At first, it seemed as if it wouldn't work, but the grimace on her unconscious face meant she was resisting. Remembering their tiff in Pan's office, he pressed his hand more firmly onto her. With renewed confidence, he pulled the overflowing arousal from her, and she arched. Her shallow breathing erupted in a deep inhale, as if she could breathe again. The tingling mark he imposed upon her peaked, and he yanked his hand out and slid back. His heart raced, adrenaline rushing through him as his pupils dilated and he felt the connection close tight between them. The sensation, eerie and surreal, reminded him of the shared pleasure that had happened between them in those secret moments.

"Dammit, I don't know if I did this right..." His eyes widened as a wave of lust slammed him. Unlike the wave from before, this blossomed from his core like a spiritual eruption. "Is this what it was like for her?"

Gripping his chest, he balled his shirt into a fist. Sweat poured over him as his entire being boiled with the heat of the excitement filling him from her. Looking at Lillith, he could see the relief and tension melting away. *Good, it's working.* Her hand moved and slid to touch his mark and pleasure snaked up his spine as if she had rubbed her naked body against him, against his soul. *I am so fucked.* Panting, he stumbled back and lost balance, splashing into the pool where an angry pair of geese honked.

"He must go before she wakes," Nanshe's whispers rolled through the room like a quick breeze.

"Come on, big guy." Nindara jerked him to his feet and began to pull him away.

"Are you okay touching me?" Tony became hyper-aware of the wave of arousal that flowed from Nindara now.

"I will have a means to release later, unlike you." He chuckled, letting go.

Tony stood in front of the doors once more. A sinking feeling and fear filled him. He reached out, but the doors opened before he could touch them. The dark castle hallway filled the other side that once housed an exotic faerie whorehouse. He turned to steal one last look at Lillith, only to find himself lost in the hallway, save one wooden door. An aching filled him, but the arousal burning through him like a spring at his core reminded him he would be the tether that would help Lillith control her powers in the Otherworld.

"Fucking go in already. Wash the blood off, champ." Badbh smacked his back, and he gave a frightened expression. "What the hell were you thinking about?"

"Is it possible for time to get scrambled here in Avalon?" His arms and body were covered in blood as if the bath had never happened, but his connection with Lillith was indeed still there. "To go back in time?"

"I don't know. Time here normally matches the Mortal Realm last I checked." Badbh furrowed her brow and frowned, adding, "There's a lot we don't know about what Avalon can and can't do."

"Time just went backward on me." Lillith's mark on his neck tingled, and in turn, he made hers do the same. "I was forced..." Glowing green eyes in the dark corridor glared wildly at him and what little of the figure he could see lifted a finger to its lips. A man of some kind was shushing Tony; a harrowing wind blew through the corridor. "Never mind. I'm tired." And he shoved into the bedroom, bewildered and rattled.

What was that in the hallway? Is that the person who sent me to Lillith? Why didn't Badbh notice him or the wind?

CHAPTER 12

GOOSE AND GANDER

Lillith sat up in alarm, her hand over her stomach. The tunic loose with threads unraveled told her volumes of how much of her fitful dreams weren't her imagination; the scent of Tony filling her senses confirmed her worst fears. Scrambling to her feet, she searched the room, shoving Nindara out of the way and rushing out the door. Clinging to the railing, she lost his essence and swiveled back, slamming the doors shut tight in an attempt to trap him in. Tony's mark on her belly sent chills through her; the way it pulled the edge off her overwhelming lust made it easier for her to bring herself to a more human or alfin state.

I'm still being overwhelmed by the lust flowing in this part of the marketplace, but can he really handle taking this much? It's far more potent than what I pulled from him back when he struggled with lusting.

Marching back to where Nanshe puffed on her hookah, she felt anger rising in her. "Where is he?" she growled.

"Back where he belongs," she whispered as smoke escaped her lips with each syllable.

Holding her stomach, she sank back onto the pillows. "Why'd you let him do it?"

"It was his choice as your King Consort." She blew smoke from her nostrils with a wide grin. "I suppose this answers the question you came to ask me, no?"

Looking at the ceiling, Lillith held back the tears begging to be released as she clenched her jaw tight. *You love-struck fool... I'm supposed to rescue you, not the other way around.*

"Child, this will be your last time to cry without revealing your open wounds of the heart." Pulling in more smoke from her pipe, Nanshe looked away. "I advise you to let the rivers flow free."

78

"I know." Lillith's voice trembled with the weight of her despair. "You know, I didn't want this for him."

"I know, child." Smoke filled the span between them. "But he's capable of choosing his own path. This was not for you to decide."

Gripping at the tunic, Lillith closed her eyes and reached out to her mark, and his echoed, warming her belly once more as if he were physically touching her. "You fool, how could you do this as if it's as easy as breathing? It took me so long to know I had this ability."

"He's meant for this life." Nindara brought a platter of tea and food of all kinds. "More so than you, I dare say." His face blushed before adding, "And I will do well not to touch such a strong incubus ever again."

Pulling the tunic threads tight, Lillith stared at the platter with a scowl. "Why did you call him King Consort, Nanshe?"

She chortled, smoke running away with her breath. "That was the title he gave himself. Does he not get to decide his place and how he intends to serve his wife and queen?"

"We're not an official union." Lillith flopped back and covered her face with her forearm. "This will be a dangerous union if it happens, and it complicates my bidding and curse. Gaea will be outraged when she figures this out. I wasn't supposed to be joined with a king of any kind that I love with all my being. It defeats the whole concept of one ripping their heart out and cursing it for what it was designed to do: love."

"You should see what Hamadryades thinks of this," Nanshe mused, reaching to pluck a piece of meat from the platter.

"I'm regretting coming here already," Lillith confessed as the tears started to fall.

"Aw, Lilly, don't say such hurtful things," Nindara whined as he sat a bowl of food for the geese by the pond. "We have missed your visits these last few centuries."

Lillith was watching them eat when she realized the vase and statue near the edge were lying on their side. Sitting up, she could now see water splattered across the ground that stopped shy of the door. Chasing it back, she could see where someone heavy-footed stomped on the pillow and fabric, and she touched her belly once more.

"Did... did he get into a fight with you?" Lillith's heart leaped to her throat.

Nanshe giggled, coughing on her food before answering. "He fell into the pond and startled my beloved pets."

Lillith couldn't contain the laugh, wiping tears from her face. "Of course he did."

"Now eat, rest, and prepare for your journey." Nanshe waved her hand to the platter. "Where do you intend to go next?"

"Well, I need to see my brother next and see if I can get a more direct route to the forest or an update on what's happening in the Mortal Realm." Sighing, she finally grabbed a chunk of meat and munched on it, her stomach growling in reply to getting proper food. "What do you want to ask me now that you've met him?"

"He's very protective." Nanshe abandoned her pipe and sat up with a promiscuous smirk. "And quite striking with those emerald eyes, no?"

Lillith's face flushed. "Yes, that's no doubt, Tony." She nibbled on a cracker and chewed slowly in thought. "Wait, how did he get here?"

"He said Avalon forced him here." Nindara was coming back to sit behind Nanshe, who lounged into him.

"Avalon?" Lillith choked, sputtering, "What the hell does that mean?"

Nanshe shrugged. "It seems Avalon has chosen a side. This is good news for you, is it not?"

"You make it sound like Avalon has its own free will." Lillith lowered her brow and grabbed a goblet of mead, taking large gulps.

"Dear child, it does," announced Nanshe, sounding taken aback that Lillith didn't know this much for herself. "It's just the first time since its creation that he's taken action."

Finishing the goblet, Lillith cast a dangerous glare. "He, you say?"

"Yes, he." Nindara started to kiss his queen's neck and groped her breasts.

A shudder rocked Lillith, the arousal slamming her, only to be whisked away by the heat of Tony's mark. "And why would my condition invoke him to choose a side after all this time?"

"Now we're asking the right questions." Nanshe moaned as Nindara's hand slid down her stomach, snaking under her skirt. "But I don't have those answers."

Another rattle of her shoulders and Lillith stood, holding her stomach. "I've taken up enough time." Shoving the hood up and tugging the tunic into place, she turned for the door. "My time is limited, and I have far to travel."

"Sorry, Lilly," Nindara murmured from Nanshe's neck, where he nuzzled her. "Your bull's touch has me in quite the state, and I can't shake it."

Lillith sniggered, casting one last look their way as Nanshe moaned under his touch. "Yes, I've had a troublesome time with it myself. Enjoy."

Marching out, Lillith made haste to exit the Willow District and gain distance between the swells of lust and herself. Pausing in the open marketplace, she pondered a moment. She pulled out her cell phone; the signal was non-existent, so calling Pan to get her wasn't an option. *That would have made matters easier.* She tried pushing out to use her magic to connect to the Mortal Realm. A surge of lust hit her, and she winced as Tony's mark seemed to pull it away too eagerly. *I can't use this method, or I might drown Tony. I'm all over the place with my magic in this ether-rich air. Should I see King Frey?* A mental image of Frey's wild grin and cashing in on the favor for the meager matter seemed a complete waste. *No, but I need to talk to Pan. Shit. He puffed away. So that means I'll have to go to Mag Mell and see if Glorianda will even entertain the thought of helping me.*

Walking through the market, she searched the vendors' wares until she came across a scarf bejeweled with pearls and opals and with gold and silver stitching. Tossing a few coins down, she overpaid, unwilling to haggle for a fair price. She opened her pouch and froze. *Tony's shirt.* Closing it, she thought better of it and placed the scarf in a different pouch. *No way in hell am I going to let that sex harpy get her nostrils on his pheromones. She's been staying here, but she's overdue to prowl the Mortal Realm for her next sire.* The sentries let her out of the VIP section of the market, and she aimed for the gates out of the bustling township that the black market had become.

The crowd had grown thick and before she could weasel herself out of the wave of patrons, the gates slammed closed. *What?* Lillith's heart leaped to her throat, and she stood like a boulder in a rushing stream as the crowd parted around her, all headed in the opposite direction. *What the hell? Why are they closing the gates?* More thuds echoed into the air before the sound of trumpets and a distant gong called for silence. *What is happening?*

"The games are beginning!" someone shouted in excitement.

"What games?" Lillith twisted and realized where everyone was heading.

Crap, I bet those buffoons entered Frey's little gladiator games. I wonder which of them was dumb enough to do it. My bet is Cedric, ha! Glaring back at the closed gate that was heavily armed with alfin warriors and mages, she changed course and followed the flow. *No, not getting out until this fight ends. I guess I'm seeing a show before I leave.*

CHAPTER 13

INNER PEACE

Again, Tony stood at the door. He had slept off his exhaustion, but... *What the fuck is happening here? Who was that and why are they messing with me?* With another deep breath, he stepped out into the hallway once more. A shiver ran up his spine, making him stand more erect. Letting the air out slowly, he turned and started walking. Within a few steps, another door presented itself and relief washed over him to see the White Ram Law Associates plaque. Pushing into the lobby, he found it empty, and the receptionist was gone. In fact, it seemed entirely closed. Marching down the hallway, he pounded on Pan's office door.

"Who let you—" Pan's words stopped as he met Tony's glare. "My, look who came knocking on my door first."

Tony shoved the door open and pushed past Pan. "I don't know what the hell is happening in this place," he announced.

Pan puffed out his cheeks, closing the door and the magical barrier shifting the pressure again. "What has you all worked up more than I am?" Fanning himself, Pan looked winded as he blurted, "And when the hell does a mere touch from you hit this hard?" Pan swallowed and shook his head, starting again, "You're dripping in sexual aura, and I don't think that's normal."

Flopping into a chair, Tony drummed his fingers on the desk and stared at the view of *Mag Mell*. "I placed my mark on Lillith and it's been a non-stop onslaught."

"You're dreaming," guffawed Pan, marching to the minibar. "Though you should be humping everything in sight with how much you're packing." Pan snorted.

Tony shot him a dangerous look. "I can't explain how or why, but I ended up in the Otherworld."

Pan paused before setting the bottle in his hand down. "Again, you're dreaming. It's a cute thought, but you have no means of getting there on your own."

"Exactly, but..." Tony thought for a moment before deciding his next words, speaking sternly, "Nanshe didn't seem surprised to see me pop in through her door."

Pan choked on his drink, sputtering, "Nanshe?"

"And Lillith wasn't doing too good, so I decided to return the favor she did for me before... well, before I became King Incubus," reassured Tony.

"Wh-wha..." Clearing his throat and setting down his cup, Pan held on to his chest a moment. "Wait. Are you saying you cast a bonding mark on Lillith?"

"I guess?" Tony shrugged. "Whatever she gave me on my neck— that mark."

"First, I'm impressed." Pan slugged back the rest of his drink and started to pour another. "Second, do you even know what that means for you?"

Furrowing his brow, Tony could feel the hairs on his arms rise. "No," he confessed.

Walking back to his chair, Pan sat down and glowered at Tony. "If she were ever to come near death, you will replace her. Literally, instantly healing her while taking on her grievous wounds at best. Granted, for titans it's normally not a big deal." Pan set the drink down to rub his temples. "But I have no idea how badly this magic gets twisted with marks cast onto one another. I mean, I thought only she had that ability, but ... you seem to be breaking the norm. Wait." Pan's eyes grew wide, and he whispered, "Who the fuck took you there?"

"I don't know." Tony grabbed Pan's drink and chugged it. "And strangely, when I came back, time was ... distorted."

"Distorted how?" For the first time, Pan's expression and tone were filled with deep concern.

"When it pulled me into the Otherworld, hours had passed since Badbh had taken me to my room. I'd eaten, bathed, catnapped even." Leaning in, Tony couldn't help but feel he would need to whisper this in secret. "When I got back, I was standing in front of my door covered in blood again, as if all that had never happened. There was someone there, in the hallway, watching me in the darkness, someone who didn't want me sharing this information. Badbh didn't seem to notice them or the shift in time, so... Who the hell is strong enough to do that?"

"I only know of one, and he's been dead a long, long time." Pan leaned back in his chair. "Let me do some digging. Until then, let's get you back to training, in hopes of burning off that sexual aura before everyone caves to the desire to make love to you." Frowning at his empty glass, he added, "Including me."

Snorting, Tony stood and took a few steps back. "I can't help it. Whatever is going on with Lillith over there, it's just pouring all of her excess power into me and..."

"And you don't feel the least bit lustful? Like an incubine urge of wanting to be ... well, frankly put, sexually feral?" Pan walked around to the desk, arching a brow.

"No. I just know that I can't seem to keep it inside?" Tony struggled to find the words to describe how the power at his core, flowing through every fiber of his being, felt.

With a snap of Pan's fingers, Pan sent them back to the courtyard where Tony had been training. No sign of body parts or blood, nor the destruction he'd left behind, seemed evident. Looking around, there were no signs of Badbh or Boto. Pan walked over to a bench and began pressing buttons on his phone. He tsked and shook his head before punching more keys.

"What's wrong?" Tony walked to the sword rack and browsed the options.

"I can't reach Lillith. So yeah, she's unstable." Pan frowned, putting the phone in his pocket. "You do know time flows faster there, right?"

"Faster where?" Tony grabbed two broadswords and strode to the center of the fighting circle. *Might as well practice until we figure this out. Burn off this energy at best.*

Pan nodded, scoffing. "Here in Avalon, no one seems to know where it falls in the timeline, not even I know. It seems to follow Mortal Realm time for some odd reason. As for the Otherworld, time travels so much faster. Meanwhile, in another domain, it has the possibility to flow slower."

Tony began going through the paces of the maneuvers Badbh had taught him. "Why is that?"

"Well, being in a domain gives us the advantage to literally gain time to heal or protect ourselves. Meanwhile, the Otherworld is dense with ether, or magic, that speeds up nature in a lot of ways." Pan's words paused as he watched the training unfold and added, "There are so many stories about mortals going to the Otherworld and coming back decades later. What was a fleeting moment visiting the Amazonians or Fae can measure to be twenty years in your time."

Tony paused and soaked it in as Lillith's mark tingled at the back of his neck. "In short, the magic pouring out of me from her, from there, is like a week's worth of overflow in just a matter of an hour or so?"

"Precisely." Crossing his legs, he folded his hands on his legs. "So, my question now, lover boy, is how the hell are you handling this so well for a rookie? What are you not telling me?"

The door opened and Badbh walked in, catching the heated exchange of glares between them. "Whoa, what did I miss?"

"Nothing." Tony tossed a sword at Badbh, who caught it with ease.

"How does someone who was merely a bartender hold up among the inhuman for so long without being bothered by the auras, I wonder?" Narrowing his eyes, Pan wasn't leaving without an answer. "It means that you grew up among our kind, had faced us, even if they never exposed their true faces to you. Granted, that leaves me to wonder about your past and those responsible for the life you led before becoming a bartender in a big city."

Badbh came in swinging, and Tony deflected. The exchange of strikes clanged loudly in the courtyard as Pan watched without saying a word. Much to Tony's relief, Badbh's strikes didn't seem to jar the hilt as badly as before. Even the muscles in his body seemed less tense, though they provided plenty of power behind his swings. Her speed increased, and he misjudged it. The blade slid grotesquely between two of his ribs. As the metal blade pulled free, the silver now red, his wound closed nearly instantaneously. Her eyes fell on it, and he swung, nicking her chin with an upswing.

Crap, she can sense there's something drastically different about me. Let's see how much it's impacted my ability to stand my ground with her. She's only going to turn the difficulty up, seeing how fast I healed.

Badbh whistled and another sword from the stand flew across and into her free hand. Jaw clenched, she came at Tony with a new resolve. The swings were stronger, faster, and he struggled to block them at all with the single blade. Anger rolled forward; his body took the power and found a place for it. Wounds barely existed as he rapidly healed. His horns and claws seem more monstrous, as he did all he could to keep the tail and wings from forming. Now he braved deflecting and parrying with a claw while swinging a sword in the other. Badbh laughed, retreating. She quickly flanked him, blades biting at him.

Why didn't I think to combine the two sooner? She seems to be excited—

She muttered an incantation and the swords in her hands began to glow and buzz. *Shit!* The very scent in the air shifted and every nerve in Tony tightened. *She's not holding back now!* A new barrage of strikes came and there was a significant difference in power this time. His claws ached and stung while the sword in his hand showed signs of chipping. He took an opening with his sword, but the double parry with both blades snapped it in half. Dropping the hilt, it clattered at his feet, and he lurched forward. *Now or never!* With it, a wave of sexual power made her drop her weapons. Before he reached her, she was gone in a flutter of feathers.

Clapping, Pan stood. "Quite the warrior we have here."

"Yes." Badbh had reappeared by the forge, fanning herself as she sat. "He broke Boto last time; I don't even know where he ran off to, but I think Tony's a natural. Good instincts, teamed with good reflexes, can go a long way in a survival situation."

Pan crossed his arms. "Yes, it's rather strange, don't you think?"

Catching her breath, Badbh snorted. "Not when you grow up as part of a mafia."

"I said I didn't want anyone to know about that," hissed Tony, walking back to the weapon rack for a two-handed sword.

"Mafia?" A big grin crossed Pan's face, and he tapped his chin. "You being Mafiosi makes sense. Oh, let me guess, somewhere in New Orleans? Maybe Dallas? Had to be one of those two, right? I'm right, aren't I?"

Tony swung the sword, casting a death glare at Pan. "Why'd you open your mouth, Badbh?"

"Nothing to be ashamed of. There were some great battles fought between the mafia groups and good times to be had during the roaring '20s there." Standing, Badbh began to heal her chin and the other slices Tony had made. "I don't understand why it's so secretive for you. Get over it. No one fucking cares."

"Oh, I care." Pan seemed giddy with a sparkle in his eyes. "Dallas it was then. Boss died and everyone split to New Orleans or to the Triads."

Stabbing the sword into the ground, Tony licked a fang. "You seem to know a lot about this yourself, Pan. Guessing you spent some time in the mafia, too?"

Flicking his eyebrows up, Pan threw up his arms. "I'd be lying if I said I wasn't involved. Though there was quite the tiff and... did you get out before the Dallas boss went, or after?"

"Before whom went," Tony said flatly, unamused at Pan's confession.

"Edgardo DeCarlo."

Tony bit his tongue, drawing blood as he met Pan's stare. *He was involved. Maybe his speculation wasn't too far-fetched that I might have been around other beings this whole time. It just bugs me that I've gotten this far without noticing.*

"Before, I take it?" Chortling, Pan started for the door. "I don't think we knew Edgardo in the same essence, since I know his true face, but ... one day, I can say, you'll see him again."

"That's one face I never want to see again," scoffed Tony, yanking the sword out of the ground.

Pan laughed louder. Tony poured the anger and frustration into training the swings he had learned. Badbh was perusing her collection as if wondering which weapon to choose next. The sun beat down on Tony, sweat trickling down his spine, only adding to the unnerving thought of it all. *Have I been tiptoeing around the paranormal all my life and was just completely blind to it? Or was there some level of denial that I've always known? The day Cedric revealed himself and became part of my life, I couldn't turn a blind eye to it anymore.*

CHAPTER 14

KING FREY'S CHAMPION GAMES

As the crowds funneled into the stadium in the underbelly of the black market, the path lowered ever deeper underground. Shoulders and hips bumped into one another. Lillith tightened and locked the buckles on her satchels and murmured an incantation to keep pickpockets from getting anything but blistered fingers. The aroma of sweating magical beings made Lillith's stomach turn. *Do we always smell so sticky sweet? I really do prefer the more masculine musk of men, titans, and...* Her hand touched the pouch holding Tony's shirt. *Ugh, I've really fallen hard.*

Following the crowd, she soon found herself able to sidle onto the benches. Looking down, she was impressed by the size of the arena battlegrounds. *Frey is really pouring in a lot of mana and fame for this. Dammit, his ego was already obnoxious, but this...* Sitting down, she sat stiff-backed, arms crossed. Lillith was annoyed to be delayed in her quest to reach *Mag Mell.* Trumpets blared and criers took turns rolling through a menagerie of ancient dialects to inform spectators to take seats quickly, look forward to vendors, and that soon their host, King Frey, would mark the start of tonight's battles.

The movement all around came to a crawl, and as promised, vendors were selling food and drink. Lillith bought herself an Otherworld alcoholic drink. Settling in, she sipped on her drink, enjoying how it warmed her and numbed her senses. Horns blew once more, and as if in a magical edition of a major ballgame's opening ceremonies, King Frey came out waving like the Queen of England. *So ridiculous.* Lillith rolled her eyes, taking another gulp, unamused as the audience squealed over their beloved King of Elves. *He's lucky that his head can fit through a door anymore.*

The muscles in her body were starting to relax as Tony's mark helped ease the imbalance that had rattled through her. *Maybe with this, I can get by, but I wonder how badly he must be struggling. I suppose it's Badbh's and Boto's problem.* Another sip and she smiled. Closing her eyes, she remembered the moment Tony stood up and won dominance. *Boto's expression... he knows there's something more about him, about our connection. Is it because I...* Dread knotted her stomach, her entire being terrified to even think the words or label the emotions haunting her.

Another round of ear-screeching trumpets made her wince. The stadium fell silent, and doors were opening on the far side. Clearing her throat, she let her focus fall to the battlegrounds as she finished her drink. *Maybe getting another drink or two would help me just stop...* She choked on her drink, sputtering onto the alfin man in front of her. Walking out of the door was an all too familiar flash of red hair and gleaming green eyes. *I KNEW IT!*

"What the fuck were they thinking using him for this?" Lillith stood, heart racing. "And what is he wearing? This isn't Rome!"

"Sit down!" roared a dwarf behind her.

Lillith shot him a sneer and sat down. *Are they out of their minds? If he rages out...* Crushing the paper cup in her fist, she could sense that he had his power in check. Another gate opened at the opposite end and a massive minotaur stepped out. Lillith rubbed her temples. *Of course, Asterion, of all the minotaurs. They're going to kill one another.*

Flagging down another vendor, she muttered, "I'm not drunk enough for this bullshit."

"Ha, good pun." The fox spirit took her money and was off to the next waving hand.

Lillith scowled, gulping the drink down. Asterion and Cedric were flinging one another from one end to the other in the arena. *They are two bullheaded morons who like to feel their muscles burn and the sting of a punch to the face. I'd like to see how they'd take a punch to the throat. I mean, what is Romasanta thinking? Worse, Nyctimus should have said something. Are they really playing along with that fruit-ball-of-a-wizard's shenanigans?*

A wave of arousal struck her, and she paused and lowered her drink, scanning the battlefield. She sensed it again and tilted her head. *Is that coming from ... that horrid-looking armor? What in the hell did they do?* The fight grew in violence, blood splattering the ground, making the crowd roar louder as they thrashed at one another. *If they get caught entering an Underworld class creature or even wearing enchanted armor...* She finished her drink and started another. *It's one thing to compete, but this farce is just asking for it.*

Both Cedric and Asterion were exhausted, standing there, clearly talking to one another as they caught a moment to recover. They had made a good show of it. Blood spilled, and arena walls smashed, making patrons back away. It was thrilling to think the fight might leak into the audience. King Frey sat on the edge of his throne, watching with a straight face, as he ate and drank. Lillith glared down at Cedric, every nerve tight as she took in a new fact: *he's missing a horn. Yet I don't sense a loss in power. How could he be... I mean, am I the only one struggling? Is my magic broken, or is this just the start of my own curse breaking me down?*

They were back at it until Cedric managed to deflect the charge and send Asterion to the ground. A great plume of dirt obscured her view. *That crazy asshole is trying to get his hands on a minotaur horn from the highest ranked. I mean, if he plans on making some godslaying weapons, that has to add some oomph, but can he really do it?*

Lillith's breath caught as a wave of power came from Cedric. *But that's not his power. I know this power. It can't be.* She shoved the half-empty cup to a dwarf and scrambled down closer. *It can't be his power. Is that strange armor Cedric's wearing broadcasting this aura? Where the hell did he find it?* She climbed down, shoving her way closer, until she hung over the edge where Cedric ran. Lillith could hear the words huffing from him with each stride as he left a trail of blood in his wake.

"Fuck Manny, fuck that dwarf bastard." A wheeze escaped him as he winced. "And fuck you, Romasanta, for making me do this."

Asterion was up on his hocks and closing in fast, speeding past where Lillith watched, trying to gauge what it was she sensed. Something about the magical armor made every fiber of her being scream. Impaled on Asterion's horn, Cedric stumbled back. His energy dwindled, his stamina sucked from him as he failed to show any signs of healing now.

Am I going to have to send a blast of sexual energy into him to help him recover? He can't keep fighting in this state! Lillith's heart raced. *If I do that, he's going to know I'm here and who the hell knows how big of a tantrum he's going to throw over that. Come on, Cedric. Pull your shit together!*

Asterion and Cedric squared off, both showing signs of how spent they felt. The audience surged forward, chanting for their favorite warrior. A mix of Asterion and... *Theseus? Really?* The noise of it all made it unclear who had gained more favor from the spectators.

"Look at him! I told him to keep it a secret, Fen!" Manannan's voice startled her, and she pulled the hood up to cover her face and twisted away. "Your horns are showing!"

"Ha!" Fen chortled. "He doesn't seem happy with you meddling with him right now."

Lillith shot a glance over. *Fenrir. That lust was Fenrir; what was that crazy wizard thinking giving him shapeshifting abilities?!*

"Shit! He's threatening to use his magic." Manannan was holding his head. "Nonononono!"

Lillith spun around, panic filling her as she watched Cedric fade into the shadows. *Holy shit, he's going to use his vampire abilities for the first time ever. At least he has enough sense to play the part of a bloodsucker here.* The audience grew quiet as they watched Asterion get clawed and bitten by the shadow bursting in and out of existence. Gasps rang out, and they began to speculate what this ability spoke loudly of: *vampire.*

Relief washed over Lillith. *Phew, I don't have to intervene. I better get out of here before I'm tempted to help again.* Lillith began shoving her way out of the stadium. *Cedric should be finishing him off and healed any moment.* She reached the top section and slipped out the archway as a collective gasp and wild roar celebrated Cedric's win.

I'm going to have to look into what that armor is later. Just need to get a little closer. Regardless, I need to connect with Pan and see what in the hell is happening in the Mortal Realm to have sent Tony here and back again without Pan, or some other powerful deity, involved. Some strange magic is afoot both here and there. Who in the hell is meddling with us?

CHAPTER 15

REAL-WORLD EXPERIENCE

"So why did you bring me to the armory?" Tony stood just inside the large armory, taking an interest in all the different weapons and armor. "Did you make all of these, Badbh?"

"For the most part." She rummaged through a table filled with daggers and pulled one from the pile that was bejeweled. "Sometimes I collect pieces like this, though. They inspire future designs." Dropping the blade again, she walked over to a lineup of greaves, some having ornate engravings. She pointed to a pair before adding, "On occasion, I get gifted things from others who share my love for blacksmithing."

"When you choose your armor and weapons, which do you prefer?" With his hands on his hips, he took in the wall of broadswords. "Would you rather use what you made, or what you find, or what gets gifted to you?"

She scoffed. "That depends."

Tony arched a brow and looked her way. "On what, exactly?"

"Who my opponent is and what sort of battle I'm going into." Badbh began pumping the billows on the forge, the entire room heating with each pump. "You see, that's why I like war and battle so much. There's a lot of preparation and thought put into it. It's not like a street brawl or two mafia gangs crossing paths."

Why does everyone keep bringing up my past? Grimacing, Tony joined her on the raised area of the blacksmith's workshop. "I can see that. More time to pump yourself up for the fight and develop a tactical plan."

"Exactly." Removing her mask, Badbh chucked it on a far table and began to pull her wild locks back into a haphazard ponytail. "Since you're starting to break so many weapons in training, I figured now is a good time to make you more reliable ones."

93

Tony gazed down at the overstocked armory with a baffled expression. "Can't I just use something here?"

"You can, but there's something special about working the metal and being part of the process." She continued to remove all the armbands and other metal elements of her armor until all that remained was the skirt and wrapping suppressing her breasts. "This is hard, sweaty work. You may want to toss the shirt. Chances are it's going to be riddled with holes and drenched before we even get halfway through." Badbh walked over to a table that had various metal ingots laid across it, far more organized and well-kept than the rest of the armory. "Do you have a preference for your blade?"

"Not really." Tony reluctantly pulled his shirt off and tossed it beside her own discarded items. "I'll leave this up to you, the expert weapons smith."

"Good, consider this a gift from your mentor, then." Picking up two ingots, she looked torn between the two. "Hmm, considering your powers and strength, I'm going to have to use something that can channel that energy better."

Tony leaned against a barrel of water and furrowed his brow. "But is it necessary for me to have a sword at all in this day and age?"

Badbh began to chuckle, tossing both ingots into the forge to heat them up. "You do realize that you're going to need some real-world experience, right? Now that you're part of our society, being challenged to a duel or sent someplace where guns don't do shit is common."

"Define real-world," drawled Tony, crossing his arms. "I thought I was in the real world before you all walked into the bar. So, what is this experience you'll be sending me to get?"

"We're sending you after *Dyrnwyn*, which means you'll need a weapon to get there." Badbh picked up two big hammers and shoved one into his chest. "Much like Delphyne's stance, Salamandra's domain will eliminate anything of modern tech or design when you step into it. No guns, no phone, nothing of the sort. Magic and brute force are all that will be accessible to you."

"You guys are really sending me on a mission to do something I have no fucking clue about?" He followed, hot on her heels, back to the raging heat of the forge, where she pumped the billows a few more times. "I have no idea what I'm doing."

Badbh smirked, cooing, "It didn't stop you in the mafia, so why would it stop you now?"

"Not this again!" Badbh shoved him to the side as she grabbed tongs and pulled the first glowing metal ingot out and held it on top of the giant anvil.

"Hammer it and I'll hold it," commanded Badbh.

Tony grunted, pulling the hammer up and over, much like one would to chop wood. Sparks flew with each strike, biting at his skin as they bounced off his arms and chest. The ingot was slow to change its shape and once the glow faded, she pulled it away, only to bring the next one. His muscles and shoulders ached as sweat poured off of him, the combination of heat and labor building upon one another. He hammered relentlessly as she pulled and pushed the ingots into view until he was hammering and twisting the pieces together, melding them into one combined rod. Badbh would toss dust or herbs onto it as each round unfolded. Now she dunked it; the hiss and sputtering of white-hot metal meeting water made him realize how parched he had become.

"Goblets of water on the far table there," she muttered, focused on watching the metal cool and rushing to add it again to the forge and pump the billows.

Scooping one up, he gulped it all down before confessing, "I can't imagine you doing this alone."

She laughed, pulling the blade out, and began using a smaller hammer with the other hand. "It's strangely hypnotic and satisfying work. I enjoy it just as much as battling, to be honest."

"I see." Tony rubbed a shoulder; the muscles were being worked in a new direction compared to all the sword practice that had unfolded for months now. "Why do you cool it so rapidly only to heat it again?"

"To harden the metal." For the first time, the blended ingot began to take on a familiar shape.

"And all those things you were sprinkling on it?" The goblet he was holding refilled itself; he didn't let his mind think about it long before guzzling down more water.

"Well, normally, that's to add flexibility to the sword and metal, add some fiber, or even influence the blade to take on a pretty look later when the blade is sharpened." Another steaming dunk and shove into the forge gave her a moment to rest. "But we're also imbuing it with magical abilities, so it's a little more complex. You ready to lend your hammer again?"

"Y-yeah." Tony grabbed it and returned to his position.

Again, he struck in the same spot, leaving it to Badbh to move the metal to best beat it. Sweat dripped across the metal, sputtering and steaming as soon as it hit the blade. After a while, it became a sword before his very eyes, and she signaled for him to stand back. He watched her tweak and nitpick at the blade as if adjusting its balance or removing any leftover imperfections. At last, she gave it one final dunk before dropping it in a strange red sand. From there, she covered it until the blade was hidden, save for the steam coming from the sand. It billowed up in blues and purples, the smell strange, and brought on an image of flowers at a funeral.

"What is that stuff?" he marveled over it, inhaling the fumes to place the scent.

"Sand from the Underworld." Badbh coughed and pulled a handkerchief over her nose and mouth. "And the steam is miasma."

"I thought miasma stinks. Isn't that the stuff demons make?" Tony's skin goosebumped. *Encountering the real thing is a little unnerving. All I know is from fiction, but this is… the real deal.*

"It stinks to everyone but those for whom it's meant, like demons." Badbh shot him a glance and his face mottled. "In case you didn't know, incubi count as demon, so it makes sense to imbue your blade with it."

"Is this the last step?" Tony looked away and went for the goblet of never-ending water.

"Oh no. We still have to mark it as yours, create a hilt, and sharpen it." Picking up a blade from the table, she walked over and sliced his palm open.

"Ouch. What was that for?" She had a firm grip on his wrist as she tugged him closer to the sandbox and forced his blood to spill across it.

"Marking the blade as yours," she sliced the palm back open, flustered. "Your healing is making this part a little hard. Where are you getting the sexual energy from to do that and rattle even me?" Badbh let go. "I can't hold on anymore, or you might see a more feral side of me." Shoving the knife in his chest, she demanded, "Keep spilling blood onto it until the sand dissolves. The blade will show and be black."

Grunting, Tony ripped the blade over his hand again and again. Watching the sand melt and become absorbed into the metal under it.

"You didn't answer me." Badbh was gulping water from her own goblet before clanking it on the table. "Where is all this sexual energy coming from?"

Shit, do I tell her, or should I keep it quiet? No, this is between Lillith and me. Swallowing, he sliced his palm open. "I can't say. But the moment it happened is the day I asked if time could shift."

Badbh slid onto the table and pondered for a few minutes. "I see. I'll trust your decision on this, then."

Relief washed over him. *I thought she'd pry it from me.*

"How's it coming?" She changed the subject as if uncomfortable at the thought of it all.

"One more." Another slice and the last bit of the black blade rose from the red sand.

"Excellent. You can relax now. I'll take care of the rest from here." Another gulp of water. He turned to see the uneasy stare she gave him.

"What is it?" Tony couldn't hide how he flinched when he met her fierce gaze.

"I think you're in over your head." Her voice was stern and sharp. "Then again, Cedric would have buckled under the weight of what you're dealing with. One of these days, you'll have to tell me more about your past. I think there's more than what you remember."

"It was one group of thugs going after another until they finally killed each other off. I was just lucky to get out before that point." Turning away, he aimed for the door. "I'll make it to my room alone."

He shoved out the armory door and found himself in complete darkness. Spinning around, the doorway was already gone.

"Fuck." Looking all around, he almost missed the glowing eyes in the distance. "What do you want from me now? Who are you?"

The eyes faded and the sound of glass smashing brought him around to where another door had appeared. He could hear roaring and women screaming. Another wave of glass breaking made him flinch.

"Where does this go?" He shouted into the abyss around him.

A heavy clawed hand hit his shoulder, and he froze, the power from it snuffing out his aura with ease. "To real-world experience..." it hissed in his ear.

Turning, it was gone. Another shout rang out and brought his focus back to the door, the voices sounding more familiar. *Was that Becca? Is this the Lion's Den?* Swallowing, he gripped the doorknob. Closing his eyes, he turned the knob and stepped through the threshold. *This better not get me killed. I'm starting to wish I had a weapon in hand. Carrying a sword has never made much sense until now...*

CHAPTER 16

MAG MELL

Lillith had waited until nighttime, far enough outside the territory of the black market, before using her wings to fly to *Mag Mell*. It had taken some time, resting by day and flying during the night, to hide her presence. Every time she shifted, her magic would feel unstable; she could feel Tony's mark buzz with heat. *That's so much magic flowing into him; he can't be handling this well.* Reaching out on occasion, she would allow her own connection to reach him as if to say thank you. *This is all I can do for now.*

Landing on a platform within the fae village, guards greeted her. Unlike the militaristic armor regale of alfin warriors, the fae looked like a tropical variant of the mafia. Three of them surrounded her where she stood on the edge of the platform. Their village was built in the trees among the kaiju-worthy plants and flowers that kept the realm both beautiful and dangerous. They weren't as tall as her, except for the one in the middle. They were dressed in a random mixture of timelines, one a throwback to the 1920s, with a bowler hat and suspenders with wings like a butterfly. The other short one was something out of an 80s punk rock band, complete with wings like a moth that were translucent except for the black outer edge.

Covering her mouth, she stifled the relief washing over her when she recognized the wingless one as a changeling she had crossed paths with in the Mortal Realm. *How long has it been since I last saw Gregor? Those were wild times.* Towering in the middle, he was dressed in a suit and had his hands in his pockets. Throwing back her hood, his expression softened, and a grin crossed his face.

"Didn't expect to see your face around here, sweetheart." He embraced her with a hug. "It's been a few decades."

"Gregor, those were the days!" Lillith's heart fluttered with lustful memories of when they had used one another for survival and companionship. "Glad to see you alive and well!"

"Who's your friend, 'ere?" asked the 1920s fae thug.

Gregor chortled. "Pan's sister. I got her from here, Mikey, Zephyr." He waved Lillith down the path, and she stepped between them. "Are you here to see Pan?"

"Is he here?" Part of her wished for the answer she knew wouldn't come. *I doubt it.*

"Afraid not, though he's been spotted in the Black Market with King Frey a few times." He rubbed the back of his neck as they entered the large estate that seemed fused into the trunk of a massive tree.

"I thought so." Lillith rubbed her stomach. "In that case, let me see Glorianda."

Gregor grabbed her shoulder and spun her around. "Are you sure?"

"Yeah, I don't have much choice." She brushed his hand off, and they ascended the winding stairs that snaked in and out of the tree as they climbed higher.

Reaching the grand wooden doors and other guards, Gregor waved his hand, and the doors opened. No one gave them a second look as they disappeared between them. A long hall spread before Gregor and Lillith and at the end was a grandiose platform with two thrones. Behind the thrones was an ornamental tapestry as well as a mosaic of butterfly or insect wings of some kind that shifted in an iridescent manner as the light came through the elongated windows on either side. The long carpet cut down the middle, bordered with braziers lit with blue and green flames.

Sitting on one of the thrones was a curvy, plump woman in a pink and orange gown. Her laughter filled the hall as she spoke with a servant serving her drinks and food on a platter. She didn't seem alarmed by their presence as they approached. *She's in a good mood today, so I might get pretty far.* Reaching the bottom of the platform steps, they both fell to one knee to show their respect. Another howl of laughter erupted from her before she waved the servant off to acknowledge her guests.

"Pardon me, Gregor." Glorianda had striking blue eyes and a wild mane of hair that fell in golden waves and braids all around her. "What may I do for you and your ... friend here?" Flowers and vines could be seen dipping in and out of her hair as she shifted in her chair; glass slippers peeked out from under the frills and chiffon of her dress. "Hold on." She stood and hopped down the stairs like one would expect a child to. "Is that Lillith beside you?"

"Indeed, it is I." Lillith stood and Glorianda hugged her. "It's been a while."

"By my wings, I haven't seen you since..." Humming to herself, she pulled away to tap a foot, the clinking echoing in the room. "...we fooled around with the Romans, and I hooked up with Julius Caesar!"

A nervous laugh escaped Lillith as Gregor made a face that said plenty about him not being aware of that side of his queen. "Those were the days. If I recall, you spent more than a night with him."

Glorianda's laughter filled the great hall as she slapped Lillith's arm, leaving it stinging. "Says the one who got me in the tent by fucking his general... What's his name? Manny, Manmun?"

"Marcus Antonius." Lillith rolled her eyes, crossing her arms.

"Surely you know who we speak of from the Mortal Realm, Gregor." Glorianda's wings fluttered with excitement, similar to that of a dragonfly's, but with the look of a magical stained glass window.

"I believe all the realms are familiar with the stories of Julius Caesar and Mark Anthony." He coughed, shooting a bewildered look at the servant, whose face flushed. "I knew my queen was ... picky about her consorts, but..."

"Which reminds me!" Glorianda threw up her hands and shook Lillith by her shoulders. "I wish to have you guide me through the Mortal Realm for another wild night, Lillith. I crave adventure and something new!" She grinned wide. "Find new men to conquer with our—"

Lillith shoved her fingers against her lips to silence the next vulgar thing about to fly into the air. "Yes, we can take you to the bar and pick up a man there. At the moment, I need to get into contact with Pan."

"Deal." Glorianda snapped her fingers and in a flurry of pink petals, Pan appeared wearing a toga of some kind with alfin ornaments. "My, off on adventures with Frey again, are we?"

"Lillith!" Pan ignored Glorianda. "We need to talk!"

"That's why I'm here," she sneered, hands on her hip.

"Forgive me, my queen," cooed Pan, bowing deeply before Glorianda. "What price must I owe you for my time?"

"You don't owe me a thing this time, my beloved consort." Glorianda's tone shifted from playful to dark and haunting. "Lillith will owe me the moment you're done talking in private. You are to return her to me immediately."

"U-understood." Pan gave Lillith a confused expression and she lipped, *it's fine.* "As you command."

A snap of Pan's fingers, and Lillith was standing in his private quarters in *Mag Mell.* "I haven't seen this place in ages," she guffawed, picking up fae trinkets off a dresser. "But I need to know what's been happening with Tony since I've been gone."

"Training, but he's lasting longer than we anticipated. Badbh says he's tapped into a power source we aren't familiar with and plans on cornering him about it when she's exhausted him. Boto is even struggling to stand against him, and well, abandoned training with him at all at this point. He's a quick learner." Pan crossed his arms, waiting for her to face him. "So, is that constant overflow of sexual energy what you did before you left Avalon, or is that coming from the mark he gave you?"

"He actually told you." Lillith sat the item down and leaned on the dresser, unable to face her brother. "That's his mark's doing."

"And why would you teach him something like that?" Pan paused a second before pressing, "How could you allow him to do that spell on you?"

"You got it all wrong." Lillith's voice shook, and she held her stomach, feeling the tingling warmth pull her power back into alignment again. *Fuck, even anger is throwing me into imbalance.* "I can't control my powers since I've been here. The ether and imbalance... I..."

Pan stood in silence, a look of deep concern growing on his face.

"I was passed out the whole time." Balling her hands into fists, the tears began to fall against her will, hot and stinging as they escaped her. "Ask Nanshe or even Nindara. I collapsed, and the door opened, and he was there, fresh from Avalon. He cast the spell, intuition, or instinct, but if it weren't for his mark..." Spinning around, she choked out the next confession, "I wouldn't be able to stand before you. Some part of me hoped to find out you sent him, but if you didn't..."

"Then who the hell is in control of Avalon and what agenda do they have with him? Or even you at this point?" Pan began to pace the floor, deep in thought.

"I don't know." Wiping the tears from her face, Lillith grew frustrated over everything. "How many times has he suffered from lusting? I'm sure Boto has had to struggle to—"

"That's the problem." Pan paused, and his glare sent shivers through her. "He's perfectly fine, though exuding the aura."

Lillith paled. "What's happening with him?"

Pan shrugged, stumbling on his words, "I wish... we can't seem to unravel..." Taking a deep breath, he tried again. "Look, he's dripping more sexual energy day by day, but he's improving his ability to pull it inside himself. Heaven forbid someone touches him; he'll dominate anything with his incubine aura; they'll desire to have him bend them over and fuck them silly."

She searched Pan's face; the information seemed so wildly different from her own encounters with Tony before that night. "It doesn't make sense; he was always struggling when I went to see him at the Lion's Den."

Pan scoffed and started laughing. "Dear sister, of course, he would be. That stubborn fool is yours and only yours for eternity. Whether that was your intent or not, it's certainly his aim. All his sexual energy is for you, and you alone." A snort escaped him to see her distraught face. "Don't make that face. You know you love the idea of it, the fact that for the first time, you are truly the focus of someone's lust, unconditionally at that. Cedric loses it around Angeline, but we all know he's madly in love with her, even though I don't think the hot-headed buffoon would ever confess that to even himself."

Lillith bit her lip. Her world spun and she felt sick with the truth of the concept. *Of course, he's lusting and struggling near me. We're in... we're in... how am I any different from Cedric at this point?* She cringed.

"Speaking of Cedric." Pan cleared his throat and broke her panicked thoughts. "You're running out of time. He's managed to impress Frey, and he's preparing to be sent to compete with the Amazonians. Once he gets Angeline back from Artemis, they'll be heading for Gaea."

"We need to figure out what or who is in control of Avalon. For now, let me follow through with seeing Hamadryades." Blinking, she recalled the burst of power from Cedric's armor. "Have you come in contact with Cedric recently?"

Pan rolled his eyes and crossed his arms. "Unfortunately."

"Did you sense anything familiar with his enchanted armor?" she pressed.

"I didn't notice his armor was magical until that last fight. It was dormant when I was close, but yes, it does have its own aura." Pan drummed his fingers on his arm in thought. "We'll have to try and get closer. A lot is unfolding. Up until now, it's always been something that our side or Gaea's side has put into play, but lately, things are coming from an unknown source or sources."

"You think they are helping or hurting us at this point?" She swallowed.

"It's too soon to tell." He motioned to her. "As far as what has happened with you and Tony, it seems symbiotic at best."

"But since when does Avalon take action without some sort of master involved?" Lillith couldn't let it go. *This is dangerous. Our plans were to use Avalon as a safe realm to build an army to rise against Gaea and Kronos, but if it can harm us....*

"Let me do some digging. Until then, I hope you can make it home after Hamadryades." He gave her a pitiful look.

"I'll be okay. There's always a way, and I'm resourceful, even if I have to crawl out of the Oracle's spring and face Delphyne. I hate how fast she can be reborn." Scoffing, Lillith used her cloak to wipe her face and steeled herself. "Okay, send me back to Glorianda."

"Are you sure?" Pan seemed hesitant for once.

"Just do it." A snap of his fingers and she stood before Glorianda and bowed. "I'm here to fulfill the favor, my queen."

"OH! Excellent!" She hooked her arm in Lillith's and they started to walk down the great hall. "So, tell me more about this bar or club stuff."

"Oh, um, in the Mortal Realm, women dress scantily and take part in drinking, and well..." Lillith sighed and leaned in to whisper into Glorianda's ear about all the promiscuous activities and things that could possibly unfold.

Glorianda giggled, wings fluttering with each juicy bit of information. "Oh, you don't say. That does sound like fun." Stopping, she gripped

Lillith's shoulders. "I want to experience this firsthand! I hear you own such a place in the Mortal Realm."

"I do." Lillith gave her a perplexed expression. "But it's not the best place to find these sorts of ... hookups. I mean, the Lion's Den is nothing more than a dive bar with pool tables for—"

"Then it might provide more context for me!" Glorianda snapped her fingers.

Lillith blinked as the pink petals fell away. Becca was sweeping up glass off the floor and looking up at her, baffled. "What in the hell is happening around here? This is twice now that someone has appeared out of thin air!"

A wave of arousal slammed everyone.

"Tony." Lillith abandoned Glorianda and rushed out the door, heading for the back alley.

Shit! Why is he here? What is happening for that much power to be released here, of all places? And if Glorianda sees him, I'm in for a fight against the Faerie Queen to keep him for myself.

CHAPTER 17

BURNING BRIDGES

A brisk breeze blew from behind Tony as the door disappeared and he found himself standing inside the Lion's Den. Every patron in the bar who hadn't risen to their feet now stood in alarm at his sudden materialization. Clearing his throat, Tony turned his gaze to where Becca and Lisa cowered behind the bar top. The liquor bottles behind them were partially missing or shattered, the mirror backing was in a billion shards and missing chunks. Between them stood the culprit: *the troll.*

"Didn't I make it clear the last time I didn't want you here?" A shiver rolled through Tony strong enough for him to crack his neck one way, then the other. *Real-world experience. Really? A bar fight? I don't think this counts.*

"Well, here he shows at last." The troll wasn't in his true form other than the tusk starting to rise from between his lips. "Where have you been, incubus bitch? It's been months."

"None of your business." Tony looked at the girls, who flinched. "Are you okay?"

"Y-yeah," squeaked Becca.

"Tony," Lisa hesitated for a moment, as if she barely recognized him, before speaking again, "are you sure you can handle this?"

Huffing, Tony took in the eyes of all the bar patrons. *They're curious to see how this plays out, but I'm not going to wreck this place. Besides, I have an itch to satisfy for myself too.* Tony turned back to the troll, and the punk snorted and cracked his knuckles. Again, unbridled excitement rolled through Tony to an arousing level, and he could feel power seep into his core from Lillith. Her mark buzzed and his echoed back to reaffirm he was very aware that he was helping her through whatever was unraveling in the Otherworld.

"You, me, back alley now." Tony pointed at the door and the troll's excitement waved out of him. *Lust comes in flavors, I suppose.*

"Fine, but don't blame me when I slam dunk you in the dumpster." Laughter rolled from the troll as he shoved out the door, nearly breaking it off the hinges.

Tony took a few steps toward the door and heard chairs squeak. "Hey." Tony turned, and they all sat down as if caught doing something wrong. "No one follows us. It's dangerous. Girls, give everyone a round on the bar while I take the trash out."

"Tony, I don't think you should—" Becca snapped her jaw tight as he flashed her a look and pushed out the door.

It was dark out, a cold wind was blowing, and the ground was covered in ice. Tony couldn't tell if this was the start of winter or the beginning of spring, seeing no obvious signs of holiday decorations, or if it had even been an entire year since last winter. *Time is all messed up. I know I've been training, but I've missed entire seasons while training and dealing with this curse.* The alley turned twice before the last stretch, with a dead-end filled with a large dumpster.

Snow flurries were falling, melting as they touched Tony's skin, and his breath rolled out in puffs of steam. His blood was boiling with the rise of his frustration and anger. *I just want to throat-punch this dick.* The troll was pacing and growing large with each step as he left ice shards where he stepped. *Shit, he has magic. We didn't train for that.* His tusks were a little larger than those of a wild boar, and his overall size was a little bigger than Boto in full demon mode. It wasn't his size that bothered Tony. It was the fact the alley was painfully cooler, and the ground and walls were icing up all around the creature. *Real-world experience, huh?* Tony shoved his hands in his pockets and took in the huffing and puffing.

"Keep that up and you might blow someone's house down." Tony smirked, raising his eyebrows high.

"Yet you come out of nowhere shirtless like you're some hot-shot, incu-bitch," snarked the troll. Taking in the overall look, Tony thought the brute was uglier than he remembered from last time. His face and exposed skin were covered in warts; it all looked as tough as bark on a tree. "You can't talk me out of this fight."

"Who said I wanted to talk you out of this fight?" Tony shrugged, licking a fang in thought. *He's in trouble because my curiosity is piqued now that I've seen what I can do.* "If I win, you won't cause a ruckus in my bar or my neighborhood again. Be thankful I'll even consider letting you on my turf again after this ass-beating."

Spitting, the troll lowered its brow. "You sound like a street thug. Who are you fooling? Ha!"

Tony winced. *I suppose at some point, I can't deny I was one.*

"What's your name?" The troll rolled his shoulder and shifted in the rags of what was left of his punk rocker clothes.

Tony thought a moment before answering, "My mother named me Antonio Devan, but my friends call me Tony."

"Well, Antonio." The troll stood taller in an attempt to overpower and dominate Tony; the temperature dropped again as ice began to nip at his bare skin. "Be sure to tell folks you got your brains scrambled by the warrior, Kesil Ymir. Descendant of Ymir, the first frost giant and troll who escaped the constellation of Orion of my own willpower." Roaring, spit flew from the gaping jaws and splattered at Tony's feet, only to turn into icicles in seconds.

"I didn't realize I was supposed to give my title and heritage." Tony blew his breath out and let the steam of it roll between them. "In that case, I'm the chosen King Incubus of Lillith herself, descendant of Cedric."

Snorting, Kesil snarled, "Fucking bullshit!"

Kesil came fast and hard, ice casing his fist and arm to harden it. Tony raised both arms and took the hit, sliding back from the power of it. His arms bled for a moment before they healed, and Kesil smirked. Tony shook his arms out and regained the distance, slow and watching. With another roar, Kesil punched the ground, sending a sharp row of ice at him. Leaping back out of the way, Tony lost his footing and dropped to one knee. *Dammit! This ice makes it hard to keep my footing!* The troll didn't wait this time, rushing forward again.

Tony managed to duck under the first right swing, jabbing into the opening and popping Kesil between the eyes. Retreating, Kesil held his nose as blood dribbled down to his chin. Seeing how easily the troll's demeanor shifted with one hard jab, Tony went on the assault. An ice shield met his first two swings and crumbled. The troll made a sound that let Tony know he was alarmed by the power behind his punches. Gritting his fangs, Tony ducked low, parrying an uppercut, and gripped the brute by his tusks for several high knee hits to the gut.

The air forced out of the creature. Ice began crawling up Tony's legs and he retreated immediately. The distance was barely enough to get him out of being frozen entirely. Ice shards spiked outward; one sliced Tony's side wide open. He grunted, eyes still locked on Kesil and blood slowing as he healed.

"That's annoying," grumbled Kesil. "I've heard your kind could heal like that, but it's my first time seeing it."

"You should have seen the first day of my training." Tony raised his fists, ready for the next onslaught.

Another snort escaped Kesil, and he broke an icicle and held it like a spear. "I also know your kind has no magic."

Dodging the ice spear lugged at him, Tony took the next one in his shoulder. He launched forward, breaking through Kesil's spiked ice wall. Another tossed spear thudded into Tony, and he took it. The coldness of the ice slipping through his abdomen did nothing to deter him from the flurry of strikes. Tony jumped up, punching down. Again, Kesil had made a shield of ice only for it to give way under the power Tony let loose. Horns and claws showed themselves as he slashed up, slicing the troll's chest.

Another roar and Kesil managed to land a few punches, a crunch filling Tony's ears as his cheekbone broke under the weight. Leaning back, Tony fell forward and head-butted Kesil, who stumbled back until he thudded against the dumpster. Tony clenched his jaw, yanking out the ice lodged in his stomach. The act of it was pleasurable and his skin crawled, wanting to experience more. Kesil ran forward like a charging boar; he slammed into Tony and sent them both sprawling to the ground, ice shards scattering all around. The troll's hand was large enough to grip Tony's entire face as he began to smash it over and over into the concrete.

Shit, this is... Tony's eyes were rolling back as each *klonk* and *crack* of his skull brought erogenous joy. Fighting the urge to let Kesil bash him to pieces, Tony did the only thing he could do: *How about I share the pleasure?* A wave of sexual arousal blew out of him, reflecting the desire that the pain brought him. *Yeah, that's right, dickhead. This feels good!*

Kesil gasped, and Tony could feel the sexual desire shift inside the creature. "What the fuck was that?"

"My... magic..." Tony sat up, the blood in his eyes painting the world red as he felt himself heal. "Just thought I'd share the sensations you brought on." Wiping the blood from his face, Tony shuddered. *Oh, this is bad. Didn't think it would send the neighborhood into the gutter.* "But apparently, I turned the whole neighborhood on. Didn't think it reached that far."

"What kind of sorcery did you cast!" Kesil roared, still trying to make distance between them.

"Oh, no sorcery." Tony rose to his feet, healed fully. "Incubi feed off of pleasure. Just nature taking its course."

"Don't you dare come any closer," mumbled Kesil, eyes wide as he shrank to a more human size.

Tony shrugged. "What's wrong? I thought we were fighting?" A smirk crossed Tony's face as he felt another rise and fall of sexual desire escape Kesil. "Oh, excited about touching with our fists again, are we?" Tony got back into an offensive stance and another wave made him chortle. "I mean, I'm not done if you aren't."

"Fuck you." Kesil shook his head, trying to fight the influence Tony's aura had over him. "I can't even focus to use my magic. You bitch, take it away."

Tony rushed forward and landed a hard uppercut, knocking Kesil into the dumpster. He slid limply to the ground, incapacitated. Leaning on his knees, Tony relaxed, his horns and claws gone, as he tried to sort through the sensations invading him from all around. *Holy crap, I need to be careful releasing that energy. This poor neighborhood is going to see a baby boom like no other. Fuck.*

"T-tony." Lillith's voice made him turn. "Did you just down a frost giant barehanded?"

"Uh." His face flushed as he peered back at Kesil. "I guess so. Didn't seem too hard to do."

"Without a weapon?" Her brow furrowed.

"Well, define weapon." Tony rubbed the back of his head and found it caked in blood. "When someone is smashing your skull in, there's no time to be fickle about defense. You use what you've got in the heat of the moment."

Lillith touched her stomach, and he paused, feeling it before daring to turn and see the motion. "I'm sorry about that. I didn't think I pushed or pulled through our connection if you want me to try and undo it—"

"No, don't," she whispered, her steps growing closer.

"It seemed like the right way to deal with it," he offered, afraid to see the expression on her face, closing his eyes tightly as she approached. The hood began to fail at hiding her expression. *I can't look her in the face. She had to feel that blast. How upset is she?*

She gripped his arm and shoved him into the brick wall. "Open your eyes and look at me," she demanded.

Opening one, his heart raced as she gave him a haphazard smirk. "Why did you come back here?"

She's not mad at all. To see her smile like this feels ... good. Tony snorted, running a finger along the side of her face. "I didn't, but I'm rather glad it sent me here. It was worth it for a chance to see you."

Shoving his hand down, she scowled. "But you're a mess."

"And I thought you were in the Otherworld," he countered.

"Lillith? Lillith." A sing-song voice called from afar.

"Who's that?" Tony went to look over her shoulder, but Lillith's lips met his as she kissed him deeply. He shoved her back, fighting the feral desires creeping to the surface. "I don't think that's a good idea, I'm on a little high and—"

"If I don't claim you now, Glorianda's going to take you from me." Her lips were firm on his again, lips parting as they deepened the kiss, and she pushed her intent into him, adding to the high and making his control slip.

He pulled away; he needed to catch his breath. *She's scared.* For the first time, Tony saw fear written in Lillith's eyes. Reaching back, the wall behind him produced a doorknob nesting into his palm. His heart fluttered. *I shouldn't put trust in the unknown like this, but my gut says this is our safest bet. Let's hope we end up in my bedroom so we can ... release the pressure building between us.*

CHAPTER 18

CONFESSIONS BETWEEN LOVERS

Tony's arms wrapped tightly around Lillith, his lips tickling against her ear. "Hold on."

"Wait, what do you mean—" Lillith's eyes locked on the wooden door behind him just before it opened, and they fell into the darkness.

Where is he taking us?

Tony held on as he landed hard on the ground with a thud. Neither of them moved as the door slammed shut just as Glorianda cast a spell in their direction.

I'm going to hear an earful from Glorianda. Even worse, she's unsupervised in the Mortal Realm. Pan's going to kill me. But when did Tony learn to cast spells? I can't even do many of those.

Lillith swallowed; she could hear Tony's heart racing as she pressed into him. Tony's shoulder blades ached where he held onto her tight as the hard ground bit into him. Even with her strong night vision, she couldn't make out anything in the pure black that surrounded them. A strong aura suppressed everything around them.

"Did you just summon a door?" she mumbled into his chest.

"No," he whispered. "*It* does this all the time to me. I just, well, I at least have a witness now."

The only thing Lillith's eyes could see was Tony and his glowing green eyes. "Well, I saw the door appear behind you. I assume you opened it. We fell through the door. So, who summons the door?"

Tony sat up and began squinting through the darkness until he did a double-take and held her closer, pointing into the distance. "*It* does."

Looking in the same direction, she could see eyes similar to Tony's, or possibly Cedric's, far off. It didn't move or make a sound as they sat there exchanging glances with it. Lillith's heart leaped to her throat; the aura coming from *it* was drowning the world out. *I've felt this before, a long time ago; it's similar to what Cedric's armor seemed to emanate. What kind of cosmic or celestial magic is this?* Underneath her, she could feel cobblestones. A harsh wind blew past them and they both scrambled to their feet in alarm. The eyes had disappeared, and they were left alone in the darkened silence.

"Where are we?" Lillith held onto Tony's arm, afraid of being separated. *How is he not afraid? This has me on edge and I've seen some shit over the centuries?*

"Avalon? Someplace in between maybe?" Tony looked around and swung his arm out and found nothing. "Don't know. Sometimes there are walls; sometimes there's none. Eventually, a door shows up, but where it leads beats me."

"You said this keeps happening to you," she hissed into his ear. "So, how do you get out of here?"

Tony huffed. "It usually leads me to a door, and I have no choice but to wait it out."

"Wait," she blurted. *He can't be serious!* "For how long?"

"Minutes? Hours? I hope you like going for long walks..." He pulled her closer. "I mean, literally, it shoves me in a direction if I even try going the wrong way."

A whispering mingled with the wind and a breeze, pulled past their feet. The magic tugged at them to follow, to go into the darkness. No light, no sound other than the surreal harsh, "*...thiswaythiswaythisway...*" echoing in the space; a chill fell over them.

"And here we go." Tony slid his hand down to hers and clasped it tightly. "I have to say, it's nice not to be alone this time."

"How often has this happened to you?" Tony went to walk in the direction of the wind, but she pulled him back. "Is this how you found me at Nanshe's?" The sensation on her stomach warmed with his power at the thought of it. *And is this door summoner after Tony or me?*

"It has happened almost every time I enter a door by myself since the day I started training, to be more specific. The whole time I've been on Avalon." Tony reached to where he knew his mark lay but retracted his hand. "And yes. That's how I appeared in the Otherworld." Tony pulled her along, reassuring her, "Now let's see if it will let us out of here."

"Wait, maybe we should..." Lillith turned to find a dead-end wall hot on their heels. "A wall?" Spinning back, a hallway materialized out of the darkness. "Is this ... Avalon?" She ran a hand over the wall and scoffed, peering down the doorless hallway. "But where are..."

Another exasperated sigh escaped Tony. "Doors. Part of me wonders if it thinks this part is funny, taking the doors away. I walked over an hour once before it even gave me one."

"Have you told anyone about it?" Lillith walked in pace with him, squeezing his hand tighter as she glanced over her shoulder to see an endless hallway stretching beyond. *The dead-end is gone.* "This is... I've never heard of this being a thing."

"I tried to tell Badbh, but it intervened." Tony pulled her closer, whispering into her ear, "But I managed to tell Pan. I suspected his barrier would be enough for me to get the word out." A light brightened from behind them, and Tony stiffened. "I feel like I'm stuck in a real-life horror movie at this rate. How's that song go, 'Hotel California' ... something about never leaving?"

"I see. Should we turn around?" Lillith squeezed his hand again. *I can't get my heart to stop racing and I'm afraid to let go of his hand. What kind of creature has been hiding in Avalon or even controlling it? This is dangerous. We shouldn't—*

"What choice do we have?" Tony tilted his head and changed direction, spinning them both around to head toward the only door, next to a lit torch. "Uh, this is my bedroom door."

"What? Are you sure?" she pressed. *How can he be so confident in this situation?*

Tony pulled her along until they stood in front of it. "I left a mark at the bottom last time." Tony pointed to claw marks gouged into the wood. "All the damn doors look the same on a normal day." Grabbing the doorknob, Tony hesitated. "But why bring us here? You think this is a trap? Though, I was hoping for this..."

"It seems to have helped me in the Otherworld and both of us in the alley just now." Lillith reached out, placing her hand over his. "Let's just get some place safe and figure the rest out later."

The door opened, and a wind shoved hard from behind. Hands shoved them over the door's threshold, slamming the door tight as they tumbled to the floor. *Who the hell pushed us?!* Tony landed flat on his back again with Lillith straddled on top of him. The room was prepped in the normal fashion, as it seemed to reset itself every time he left. Fresh food was laid out on the table, a warm fire was crackling in the fireplace, steaming bathwater, and the bed made. On a chair were fresh clothes for them. Medieval tapestries and mounted beasts hung on the walls. Relief filled them and Lillith kissed him quickly, laughing as she cupped his cheeks. *We're okay! I was so worried something bad was about to happen to us!*

Smirking, Tony cooed, "You should really stop falling for me like this."

Rolling off him, Lillith laid on her back. "I'm sorry you've been dragged into this mess."

"Trouble has always found me." Standing, Tony began to shed his pants. "I smell like a troll, so make yourself at home. I got to get this guy's funk off me."

Has he always been so quick to adapt? I wonder what he was like before we stepped into his life. Could it be he's a lot stronger than he lets on? Lillith smirked from where she lay and watched his naked form sink into the claw-foot tub. "You got room for two in that thing?"

Tony looked into the tub and back at her with an arched brow. "Maybe. How about we test it out and see if we both fit, huh?"

"How can you crack jokes and talk a good game after some creepy thing whisked us away, kidnapped us, then dumped us into your bedroom?" She scoffed, unlacing her tunic and boots. *A bath sounds divine... I still smell like dirt and sweat.*

Dunking under the water and coming back up, Tony leaned back, staring at the ceiling as steam whirled all around. "Ever since that day you walked into my bar, I accepted my life would never be the same." She stood and Tony watched her as she slowly undressed, casting the occasional glance to make sure he was indeed paying attention. "And when you made me watch Romasanta change, I realized there was no turning back or fighting against it all. Especially if..." Tony furrowed his brow as Lillith pulled the tunic up and off, freeing her breasts, her body pale and curvy even in the warm glow of the fire.

"Especially if?" She dropped the leather to the ground, hips swinging as she walked up to the tub and slid in between his legs to lean into him. "Hmm?"

Tony couldn't keep the arousal from escaping him as she nestled into him, too afraid to move a muscle as he mumbled, "Especially if it would be impossible to be with you."

I think this is it. If my curse doesn't kill me tonight, then this is the thing Gaea has feared the most. Unconditional love... but can I really let this happen between us? She pulled his hands off the edge of the tub and pulled them around her. *I'm scared, but this all feels...* "Yet here you are. With me. What do we do next?"

Both of his hands covered the spot where his mark warmed her as he felt her mark buzzing on the back of his neck. "Yes, here we are ... being sent to my room," he murmured, kissing her shoulder once before resting his chin on it. "What a horrible turn of events this has been for us both, no? Completely traumatizing," he added flatly.

"Horrendous," she replied, mimicking his tone, enjoying their bare skin pressed against one another in the heat of the water. *I want more moments like this. These stolen tender interactions with someone who loves me unconditionally. Someone who knows what I am, what my power is like, and is not afraid of me. He's not with me for power. In fact, he took that for himself. Instead, he's taking a step into the unknown just to save me and has grown in power in my absence. He doesn't need me to gain power, but I wonder, how much would he grow if I...*

They sat in silence, watching the fire until he whispered, "Are you okay with this?"

"With what?" Lillith could feel exhaustion settling in as she little by little let her tension cut loose.

Tony nuzzled her, inhaling her scent and holding it before pressing further. "Settling for me. The clueless monster and love-struck crush."

Her hands rubbed up and down his thighs in the water where they hugged her hips. "Clueless and love-struck, huh?" *Which of us does that really address at this point?* Tony's arousal slipped out and he shuddered behind her, prompting her to answer, "I'm not settling."

"Well, that's good," he scoffed and suckled at her neck.

"And you're not clueless," she offered, shoving one of his hands downward as she raised her knees, the water sloshing as her own arousal echoed into him at the touch. "You seem to know me better than I know myself."

Moaning, Tony shifted behind her and whispered into her ear, "I'd like to reaffirm I wasn't talking about being clueless about this part." Tony's other hand rode up and groped her breast, the rise of their auras mingling, adding to the excitement rattling through them. "I meant about this world you live in, my love." He bit her ear, and she moaned.

"Then who was the love-struck crush?" Lillith's hands cupped his own, encouraging the erotic play to continue.

"You tell me," he gruffed with a smirk, daring to go farther and pushing his arousal into her.

She echoed it back and the dam broke loose between them, unwilling to keep a slower pace. Rolling forward, she gripped the far edge of the tub, water splashing the floor all around from the swift movements. Tony pressed his hips hard against her, entering her, grinding in response to the lust that waved from her. Gripping her hips, Tony paid no heed to the water rocking out of the tub as she panted and moaned. Her wet hair slapped against the metal tub, and he arched, his motions hard and hungry to have her once again. Tilting his head back, he groaned with pleasure.

"Stop there, my thrall." The demand released a breathtaking amount of incubine desire. *Can he obey in this moment so close to peaking?*

Tony's heart fluttered at the words, and he froze. "Yes, my queen."

Her skin pimpled... *impossible with this aura flooding out of him.* She pulled away, twisting to sit eye-level with his groin. "I didn't say you could have your release yet." Chin tilting up, she let her eyes soak him in until their eyes met. "Hands behind your back, Thrall."

"Yes, my queen." A smirk crossed his face, the provocative aura building between them.

How well can he keep himself tame under this dreadful weight of bottomless lust? Her lips were hot around him, tongue a wet silk before her lips popped to look at him once more. "Are you going to obey this time?"

Licking a fang, Tony countered, "I didn't disobey last time."

Again, she took him in between her hungry lips, suckling as her hands rode up his thighs and abdomen and back down. A grunt escaped Tony, muscles in his arms twitching to grab her, to hold her there where she brought him pure bliss. The aching to fight the release that begged to be let loose only added to the agony of staying in line with the orders she had given him. Another pop of lips, and he was brought relief and a deep yearning all at once.

This is it. I'm willing to do this even though he hasn't asked it of me. He doesn't lose himself, not like the others. Perhaps he's even more in control than I was ever capable of being.

She stood, her long legs stepping out of the tub, and left him there, standing at attention. Lillith cast a devious expression back at him. He wanted to give chase, but he knew he wouldn't get the level of satisfaction he'd gotten from her in Pan's office. *He wants to see where this will go if he's a good boy.* Agonizing patience lingered between them as he waited and watched as she approached the table of food. Picking up a strawberry, she suckled on it, eyes on his, before eating it. *Tonight, I will give him the only gift I have left to give in hopes of keeping him alive through all that he has still left to face. He will get the one thing I have never truly bestowed on any since the very inception of this horrific power.*

"Don't move, my thrall." Lillith plucked another strawberry up before sitting on the table facing him. "Face me." Tony turned on his heel, the tub water sloshing. "Have I told you how gorgeous you are naked?"

Shaking his head, he licked his lips. "I can say the same about you, my queen."

"Oh?" Eating the strawberry, she leaned back and opened her legs. "You know what drives me crazy some nights?"

The lusting building at his core made him shudder, claws digging into the other arm to hold his position and horns crowning his head now. "N-no."

"You," she confessed. "Those eyes looking up between my knees as you took your place as the next king. I still see and feel it every night." Her hand slid between her thighs, and he bit his lip. "I've never felt lust so unconditional as what you released then and even now." Lillith played with herself, watching how his eyes locked on her, grunting. "So hungry to have me again, huh?" She could smell the blood that dripped into the water where his claws dug into his palms. "Are you okay if we do this with no restrictions?"

The question jolted his glare back to her face, the tone of her voice dangerous. "No restrictions," he echoed, and visibly shuddered. "Is that incubus succubus code to just give in to..." Unfolding his fists, he leaned forward to brace himself on the side of the tub as he let some of the sexual desire go. "...this?"

Lillith's breath caught as it slammed into her. Her legs closed as she fought the orgasm it shook from her and she whimpered, "Y-yes. Are you willing to see how this unfolds? It can be dangerous for us both." *I'm willing to take that chance only because of how well he's holding up.*

A shudder rolled through him again, desires itching to be let loose. "If at any point I... I stray... you command me, my queen." Shaking his head, he looked back at her with a fierce green gaze that made her heart race. "You put me back on my knees. It's intimidating, the idea that there's no end of how high this is stacking. It's like having aggressive sex, but all it takes is being in the same room without even the need to touch one another."

"I've only tried this one other time, and it went horribly wrong." She touched her broken horn and jerked her hand back. "But I've never met someone so enamored with me for who I am, not what I am or the power I can give." Her heart fluttered as they kept the distance in place, unsure of what they hoped this would bring out in either of them.

"I want more moments of just being with you. It's not the sensations, but just..." Another wave pulsed between them, and he closed his eyes and took it in.

"Then, I release you, my thrall."

"As you command."

The tub tilted and spilled across the floor as he closed the gap. Both had let their horns, wings, and tails take form and let their auras release, feral and animalistic. Tony's wings cleared the food from the table, dishes and food splattered and clattered across the cobblestones. A hand at her throat, firm and gentle as he pushed between her legs. He released her, gripping her hips to tilt her to a better angle, connecting deeper with her. The sexual hunger he felt from her startled them both, yet the sense of control somehow clung on in the wake of lust drowning them. Lillith pulled him down to her, kissing him deeply as she suckled his tongue. She climaxed, and it sent him over the edge. Her scream of pleasure was only matched by his own roar. At that moment,omething slammed into his core, a stirring of his soul, as if it broke apart and snapped back together in an instant. Looking down at Lillith, she too had felt it and he paused, heart racing.

"What the hell was that?" Tony asked in alarm.

It happened so fast, so naturally... She cupped his face, grinding into him to encourage him to keep going, to give her more. "We are bonded. I've taken you as mine and I am yours."

Tony kissed her, continuing to let himself spiral deeper to satisfy both their desires.

This is like nothing I have ever known.

CHAPTER 19

CHOOSING ONE'S DESTINY

A knocking at the door stirred Tony from his sleep. Under his arm, Lillith simply rolled, mumbling to herself, "...coffee and maybe some eggs." Slipping out of the covers, he paused. *Did I always have furs for covers?* Standing, he stretched his naked body, muscles aching as he scanned the room. *We trashed the place.* The tub still lay on its side; most of the water had evaporated or soaked into the cobblestones. Food and dishes lay scattered everywhere he looked, with the table broken in half. His face flushed. *Is that going to happen every time we—*

KNOCK-KNOCK-KNOCK!

The knock at the door made him grab his pants off the chair. *At least these and the bed survived us last night.* Pulling them on, he looked back to where Lillith lay snuggled in the furs, still asleep. *She's a big girl; if I need to leave, I have no intention of making her stay by my side.* Opening the door, he glared at Pan, who furrowed his brow.

Pan's eyes wandered over Tony, who cleared his throat. "My eyes are up here and I prefer yours to be there, too."

"You moron," growled Pan. "Who did you bond with?"

"Uh, what?" Tony didn't quite grasp the question. *First, they can see king status, and now they know we... shit, I hate this.*

"Look, don't get me wrong, you'd put Adonis to shame with that body, boy toy." Pan pointed where his heart was located. "But as a fae who specializes in curses, pacts, and bindings ... I see that shit." He shoved Tony back and slammed the door closed, his voice filled with rage, "Who did you do this with? How could you betray her like this?!"

"Wait, betray...?" Tony marveled at the reaction, perplexed.

"That power and those markings." Tony watched as wings unfurled behind Pan and his eyes went black, fangs and antlers growing from him.

Crap, he has a form... wait, what markings? Throwing his hands up, backing up, he reassured, "Look, I'm not going to fight you, but I think you're assuming—"

"I want to know who you bonded with now!" The wings fluttered as he hissed, wagging his finger at all of Tony. "Because I'm about to perform my first attempt at untangling someone's bond!"

I don't know if I was meant to stay quiet about this, so... Wincing, Tony declared, "It's not my place to say." Keeping Pan's attention on him, Tony sidled to the fireplace and tub.

"Oh, you're going to tell me," Pan threatened, wings black as night with dots of brilliant blue and purple along the ragged edges. "I don't care if I have to strangle it out of you. Don't you know she loves you? Do you realize how hard it is for her to even admit that or even come to terms with it?"

"W-wait, Pan." Tony could feel an ominous aura flowing from the angered King of Fae, and he could sense the aura his curse had given him building between them. "I think there's been a misunderstanding. Calm down—"

"Don't tell me to calm down!" Pan roared, the force pushing Tony back and sending the tub sliding. "I thought you were different! You were different! Lillith deserves someone—"

"Nomius!" Lillith's voice made them both flinch.

Pan turned slowly, the fae form retracting as he saw her lounging in the bed. "Lillith?" he questioned.

"Glad to see some part of you would defend your sister's honor." Lillith arched an eyebrow, smirking. "I don't think I've ever seen you in full fae rage before."

"Ugh." Pan covered his face, scoffing. "You aren't supposed to be here!"

"Agreed." Sitting up, she wrapped the furs closer. "So, what's the status on everything in the Otherworld?"

"Oh, no you don't," fussed Pan. "You aren't changing subjects! Do you know how dangerous it was to bond yourself? Are you trying to activate the curse?"

"What curse?" Tony started to pick her armor up off the floor. *What else is she hiding from me? Is she even going to talk about it to him with me here?*

"Oh, the curse is there." She flopped back onto the pillow with a forearm over her forehead. "But what do I have to lose? If my feelings haven't triggered the starting process, then ... perhaps there's a loophole after all."

It could have ... killed her? Tony dropped the armor on the bed beside her, locking eyes. "In short, were you going to tell me before you died the moment that happened last night?"

Grabbing her items, she turned away. "If I had said something before, you wouldn't have let me take the risk."

"You're right." Tony crossed his arms, a mixture of rage and fear filled him. "And were you ever going to tell me?"

The muscles in Lillith's back tensed.

"No. The word you're looking for is no, you weren't." A sense of betrayal rolled through him; Tony turned back to Pan, who wore the same expression. "And apparently not you either?"

"No, and she's right. We both would have stopped her." Pan rubbed his forehead. "So, how the hell did you get here?"

Tony puffed out his cheeks and rubbed the back of his neck. "We took an impromptu door here ... but ... she was at the Lion's Den."

"Wait a minute." Pan closed his eyes and shook his head. "What were *you* doing at the Lion's Den, Tony?"

Oops, he caught me. Tony took in a deep breath before blowing out his confession. "Fighting a troll?" he offered.

Pan's eyes got big, and he turned to Lillith to avoid any further details. "And you? Why were you at the Lion's Den?"

"Shit!" Lillith rushed to put on her clothes, panic riding in her voice. "Glorianda!"

"What do you mean, Glorianda?!" Pan grabbed the sides of his head. "What the hell was Glorianda doing in the Mortal Realm? I can't decide what part of my fucking day is the worst! King Frey trying to contract Cedric, you fighting a troll and leaving him unconscious in a back alleyway—"

"Oh, good you took care of—" Tony tried to cut in and failed.

"Or the fact you that two morons fucking BONDED!" The wings popped back out as he waved his hands about. "This was not part of the plan!"

"Look, port me back to Lion's Den, and I'll catch Glorianda." Lillith hopped up, tugging on her leather breeches.

"NO!" Pan shouted. "I need you in the Otherworld meeting with Hamadryades! Cedric is on his way to pick up his wife as we speak."

Tony piped up, "Do I need to go get this... Glorianda—"

"NO!" Tony flinched at the immediate reply from them both to his question.

"We can't let her see Tony. Ever." Pan began pacing. "My mistress will hold you captive as a sex slave. I stole a kiss, but she'll steal you."

"I don't know if she got a good look at him in the alleyway." Lillith pulled the boots on, rushing to lace them. "Let me deal with her." Pulling on the cloak, Lillith marched up to Tony with a stern look. "Please be careful when you go to Salamandra's domain." She kissed him deeply; the overwhelming desire had calmed and brought itself to their control for a change. "Now, let's go, Pan." She opened the door, then halted. "Shit. This again."

A breeze blew through the room with a floral scent, bringing all eyes to the scene that lay beyond the threshold. *It's happening for her, too. Doors leading elsewhere.* Trees, tall and enormous, filled as far as the eye could see in the shadowed forest. Magic-infused wind hit Tony and his mind fell back to Otherworld. They all three shuddered on inhale. Lillith looked to Pan, then to Tony, before back to Pan.

"Is this ... where I think it is?" Looking back, Lillith didn't dare step into the forest just yet. "Because it seems Avalon has other plans for me, or at least intends to help us."

Pan nodded, confirming, "That's Hamadryades's forest."

"Okay, so now the two of you have seen this shit in person." Tony sighed, relief washing over him as he shot looks at them both. "It's crazy, right?"

"I question it," Pan started, lingering on his words before at last saying, "But between her being here and now, this, Avalon, or someone controlling portals, is pulling the strings. The real question is, what do they want from you two?" Pan tapped his lips, eyes bouncing between them. "Are you really going to trust this blindly?"

Tony shot a look at Lillith, and she turned, confessing, "I don't think we have a choice. Whatever it is, it can use high-power magic and swallow both our auras."

Rustling brought their eyes back to the forest. A woman's silhouette formed on a tree before stepping out. Her wooden body was painted with flowers, moss, and mushrooms to imitate some form of clothing. She kneeled before the door. As if sensing this, a few more beings came out from their own trees, some carrying shields and spears as if guards of some type. *There are creatures I couldn't even fathom that these two have seen. I'm so useless to Lillith like this.* Tony huffed, amazed by the creatures appearing in the forest.

"Queen Lillith." The kneeling dryad's voice was like the rustling of leaves and pitches of songbirds. "We have anticipated your arrival for some time now."

Chills rolled over Tony; his heart raced as Lillith bowed. "Very well. Let us not keep her waiting any longer."

Lillith shot one last look at Tony, his chest aching only to be calmed by her mark on his neck. She stepped through and a harsh wind slammed the door shut. Turning, Tony searched the room for his clothes, unsettled by how much they were being shoved in a direction. Pan watched, lost in thought, as he tried to piece together who or what was interfering. *I'll leave it to Pan to investigate, since that's what Lillith is doing. She has her own mission; it's about time I set off on mine.* Approaching the door, Tony hesitated to open it.

"Do you need me to teleport you to where you need to go?" Pan gripped his arm, furrowing his brow with a pitiful expression.

"I don't need your pity or protection," Tony huffed and shook his hand off.

"Fine. I need to locate my mistress anyhow." Pan's eyes dropped to the side before meeting his gaze once more. "Look, it's dangerous to be bonded to someone. She's never done this before, and well..."

"I know. Don't forget I've heard from Cedric what happens." Some of Pan's tension eased. "I'll be mindful of that when I get hurt. At least I'll know if she's okay. I think I understand Cedric a little more now." Tony laughed. *A crazy bar story is actually helping me here and there.*

"So be it." Pan evaporated in a flurry of rose petals.

Tony opened the door to see the armory and marched in, feeling a little better having a chance to prepare. Badbh was sitting at the table polishing a black-bladed sword, completely ignoring him, as she chanted and murmured things to it. *Time to go shopping for gear.* He began digging through armor, pained over what kind to choose. Looking to the side, he saw padded leather breeches and greaves and began undressing to put them on. *I don't care. I need to get my hands on that sword, and I need more real-world experience.* Turning back to the chest armor, he grabbed a metal piece up and began to make an attempt at buckling it on.

"Not that one," Badbh drawled, holding the blade up to inspect their handiwork. "You're going someplace hot. Leather will be better."

"R-right." Pulling it back off, he dropped it on the table and dug through the leather options. "Aren't you going to stop me?"

"No," she snorted. "Nice work on the troll."

"Does everyone know about that already?" Tony flustered, pulling on a leather tunic similar in style to the one Lillith had on. *There must be a reason she chose this style out of everything here, I imagine.*

"Well, what you don't realize is you've been back for a few days." Badbh stood, coming down the few steps. "I don't know what all happened, but your door couldn't be found until today, so I sent Pan to check on things. It seems some powerful magic is meddling with you, after all."

Shit, how long were we having sex for then? I mean, I know my drive and stamina are off the charts with this and when it comes to her, but... Tony's face flushed as he tried to focus on lacing the armor. "What else do I need to do for this quest you're sending me on?"

Badbh arched an eyebrow and smirked, "Well, here's your sword. It should pair with the other one when you get it, but for now, let's get you a shield." She pulled one from the wall, bypassing the pile on the floor, and reached under a table for a cloak. "You will need these. Both are fire resistant and should shield you as needed."

"Thank you." He took them from her, pulling on the cloak and weighing the shield before daring to reach for the sword. "Is this it? The completed blade I hammered with you?"

Grinning, Badbh nodded. "Yes, it is, and I must say, you did very well. We need to make more weapons together when you get back."

Tony gripped the ornamental hilt and power rolled through it and into him before pulling his own power back into itself. "What was that?"

"Ah. I forgot to mention this is a new recipe." She gave a toothy smirk, patting his shoulder with heavy slaps. "It's a little experiment of mine."

"Experiment?!" Tony gaped.

"You see, these kids nowadays are always writing stories and playing video games with demon blades." Licking her lips, she had a wild look in her eyes. "So, I thought, *I can fucking make a real one. Watch me.*" She leaned in closer, poking his chest as she spoke. "And I thought, maybe some demon sweat and blood, or even some aura treatment, might do the trick." Nodding proudly, she patted his chest and confessed, "That's when I remembered I had a King Incubus at my disposal. Let me know how it goes."

Walking away, he fussed at her, "Are you serious? What kind of shit does this sword do? Does that mean it's magical?"

Badbh shrugged, marching away. "Who the hell knows?! But I suppose you'll find out and let me know when you make it back."

"You can't be serious! Aren't we training with it first to make sure it works?" He was hot on her heels.

"Here." She tossed him a sheath and halter from the table. "And no, we aren't testing it here. What if something bad happens when you try to use it?" She scoffed, taking a gulp of mead.

"That's my point!" Tony sheathed it and started to buckle it in place.

"Look, it shouldn't kill you," Badbh reassured.

Tony stared at her in disbelief. He opened his mouth to say something, but she was downing more mead. Looking at the gear, all he had left was to strap on boots. He would have to take the risk. *I mean, I'll just be careful when I use it. Not like I don't have claws to rely on. She's made thousands of weapons, so what are the chances of this one being a bad apple? Right?* He swallowed; his thoughts weren't the most convincing. Grabbing some leather boots, he strapped them on and marched for the door.

A blast of heat slammed into him as he opened it. Beyond the threshold was a sweltering tropical island scene, and he sucked on his cheek. *This is going to be the shittiest vacation ever.* In the distance, a volcano smoked and rumbled; the floor shook underfoot.

"You better come back and get me when I'm done here, Avalon," he warned.

As he stepped through the threshold, a creepy hand stopped him, lips hissing in his ear, "Prove you are worthy."

The door slammed shut, shoving him forward. Tony spun and flicked a finger at where the door had been. "Fuck you, too!"

CHAPTER 20

QUEEN OF DRYADS

Inhaling deeply, Lillith gave herself a moment to react. She could feel the magic soaking into her once more and the tingling of Tony's mark warming her. *Compared to the first time, Tony's able to bring instant relief.* Unlike before, she was in control, steady. Being bonded to Tony had changed more than she had anticipated and some part of her no longer felt connected to Gaea herself. *Could this be the reason for the curse not triggering? To make sure I didn't break my chains to her, she's been linked to me directly on some level that I'd been too scared to admit to. An unchained heart is a dangerous force, is it not?* She smiled to herself at the thought.

The dryad servant led her through the forest, the trees shifting as the light filtering through leaves and branches made a disorientating kaleidoscope across the ground. A clearing came into view and at the center sat Hamadryades. She sat upon a large toadstool, drinking tea from a flower teacup. Today her hair seemed to be pinned up in a cluster of green and white ivy with a large pink hibiscus bloom for decoration. A smaller mushroom sat next to her with a cup of tea steaming, waiting for Lillith's arrival. The servant bowed deeply and sank into the ground, leaving Lillith alone. *She's always so classy about these meetings, but even a calm meeting with her is unnerving, knowing how powerful an entity she is. I mean, she was friends with Father, not a creation of his. She's older than Gaea, though not as powerful.*

Lillith approached and bowed, speaking softly. "Thank you for seeing me, Queen Hamadryades."

"Sit, child of Aether." Hamadryades's hair rustled in the breeze as she sipped her tea once more. "We have much to discuss, don't we?"

"Y-yes." Lillith picked up her cup of tea. *I feel like a child being scolded by my great-aunt.* Sipping the tea brought on an uncanny calm as Lillith sat on the giant mushroom. "I want to start by saying sorry for any trouble my comrades have caused you, my queen."

Hamadryades spit her tea out and began to laugh.

Lillith stared at her, bewildered. *I don't think I've ever seen her laugh like that before. She's always so serious or scary.*

"I'm sorry." Hamadryades caught her breath and wiped a tear of sap from an eye. "No, dear, you have nothing to apologize for. Much of my trouble is what your father set in motion or what I've inherited responsibility for during his hiatus."

"What do you mean?" Lillith furrowed her brow. "Aether's been dead for millennia."

"Ah, I suppose to some of you it feels that way." Hamadryades grinned, another sip of tea. "The one called Angeline is quite the talented one, no?"

How dare she change the topic on me! "I wouldn't know." Lillith silenced herself by gulping more tea down. *But I'm not in the position to challenge her on the matter. Perhaps I should let Pan know the old tree doesn't think Aether's dead at all.*

"She summoned me the other day."

Lillith snorted her tea out, sputtering and coughing. *Someone can summon Hamadryades?!*

"Impressive, yes?" Hamadryades let her flower teacup go and the petals fell apart and drifted on the wind. "And Cedric, he reminds me of... well, let's circle back to why you are here."

Lillith inhaled deeply, trying to recover from choking on her drink, rasping, "Artemis didn't summon you?"

"Oh no, Artemis has to bargain with me. Though I ignore her." She spun to face Lillith more directly, looking her over before adding, "And how are you feeling now that you've found a mate to bond with?"

"Is it so easy to read?" Lillith stared at her reflection in the cup. *It's embarrassing. Like it's written in marker on my face.* "Gaea is going to chase me to the ends of the world over it."

"The heart will always find a way," cooed Hamadryades. "And you were the last bit of good Gaea had left. It hurt Aether deeply when she tore you from her chest and dared to curse you. He cried many oceans-worth of tears over the matter."

"I find that hard to believe," scoffed Lillith, drinking the last sip of tea.

"Believe what you want." Shrugging, Hamadryades took the cup from her and let it fall to the wind as well. "But he swore to find someone worthy of you."

"If we rise against Gaea," Lillith ignored the words, changing topics, "will you stand with us?"

"That depends on her final act involving Daphne." Hamadryades let a butterfly land on her hand.

"You don't think she would go back on her word after everything?" Lillith's heart broke with the idea of Romasanta losing the only thing that had kept him going all this time. *Granted, a love like theirs is enough for her to kill one or both of them out of the sheer jealousy of it.*

"Don't fear. We dryads have grown to adore little Daphne and blessed her with our power." Hamadryades sighed and watched the butterfly flutter off. "But I fear Gaea's hatred of mortals, love, and Aether's children, save one vile child, has grown to a festering depth of sorts."

"I see." Lillith stood and stretched. "But I agree. It's gone on too long and too far. She's locked the Underworld now, and the key to the celestial realm is behind her throne, right?"

"Indeed. You've been gathering information without my help, I see." Hamadryades pulled her legs to her and hugged her knees. "You will know what my decision is when the time comes."

"Fair enough." Lillith nodded, enjoying the serenity the forest brought. "I still need to meet with Cedric."

"I can manage that since I will give him passage to reach Gaea." Hamadryades gave Lillith a sad expression.

"What is that look for?" A chill snaked up her spine and the hairs on the nape of her neck stood on end.

"It saddens me it took so long for you to find love, only to have it dragged into this war."

Lillith winced, confessing, "I agree, but what choice do I have?"

Hamadryades slid down, and the toadstools shriveled away. "Come, let's cross paths with Cedric. You stand here; I'll bring him to you."

"Wait, I do have one last question." Lillith hesitated as the old dryad paused and looked back at her. "Avalon. Do you know who controls it?"

A wicked smile crossed her face. "So, he's taking action at last?"

"Who is ... he?" A sense of danger rolled through Lillith. *That expression unnerves me to think she knows who it is and has said nothing.*

"That's not for me to reveal." She turned and disappeared into the forest.

What does she mean by "he" and "taking action?" Why the secrecy? And how does it all tie to Tony and me?

A fog settled in all around the tiny meadow she stood in as it fell dark. A wave of sexual aura slammed into her, and she let herself shift to help tackle it. *How much stronger has he gotten since the minotaur?* Horns, tail, and wings helped ease the friction of their power brushing against one another before seeing one another. Tony's mark buzzed and kept her from being overwhelmed, as if his power could shield her against the aggressive aura of another incubus. Crossing her arms, she bit her lip in annoyance. *This is going to get exasperating when we're under one roof, but perhaps the ether here is still causing me to be unstable?* She turned, sensing his approach from behind her. Cedric appeared through the fog; the muscles in his cheek twitched as his eyes fell upon her. He had stopped a few steps from her. *He feels the friction, too.*

"I was hoping to catch you in time." Lillith unfolded her arms, gauging his expression. "Pan said he let it slip."

"All I want to know is who you two really are." Cedric crossed his arms, lowering his brow. "I've already figured out you're trying to take down Gaea and Kronos, but I'm missing the direct link. Something tells me you aren't being honest about who you really are."

How much should I say? I don't think holding anything secret will get me far with Cedric at this rate. Cedric's not the child he was when I first met him.

"Well, about that..." Taking a deep breath, Lillith at last locked eyes with Cedric—what she would say next was as truthful as she could manage. "My name is Lillith, especially in the Mortal Realm, but my birth is muddled in their history. It is true that I was the first woman to walk the earth. You see, Gaea wanted to love her husband's creation so much that she took a piece of herself and gave it to the first man of humanity. Sadly, that's where the last of her goodwill toward Aether would end."

"I knew you were ancient, but made from Gaea? Why turn on your own maker?"

"You're one to talk." Lillith smirked. *Of all people, you know the hatred that comes with being born for the sole purpose of creating chaos.*

Snorting, Cedric turned his back to her. "So, what happened next? I imagine something happened and Gaea is to blame?"

"Well, Aether frowned at how much of herself she didn't place into me." Her voice broke a little and Lillith forced herself to continue. "The thing he pressed was the ability to procreate. She didn't want to do it. In fact, at that time, Lamashtu and Kronos were a thing."

Cedric shot a glance over his shoulder. "Lamashtu?"

"Yeah, Lamashtu. Granted, Kronos's original body isn't too flattering, so it makes more sense. Trust me. Regardless, Aether denied Kronos the Mortal Realm and when he gifted it to Adam and me, all hell broke loose. It was then that Gaea decided to give me the ability to procreate, but it wasn't..."

"That, I see." Rubbing his forehead, Cedric inhaled slowly before starting again. "And let me guess, Aether got pissed because she wouldn't undo the malice she bestowed upon you, her jealousy incarnate, so he took a piece of Adam and created Eve, an equal creature to him."

"From there, tables were flipping in the other realms. The worst of it was watching how Aether distanced himself from Gaea more and more with each vile act and move she made. Constantly a sleight of hand to destroy humanity. I was abandoned here, left to breed like a monster, with monsters, and make more monsters if none were to be found. Delphyne found herself in the same predicament. She was made from the earth, gifted to Kronos to ravage humankind, but it failed, and he gifted her to his eldest son, Zeus, who gave her a place, a task to protect the Oracles and Phoebe."

"Now things are clicking into place. So, what was so special about Phoebe?" he asked.

"Your direct connection is the fact that she's the mother of Apollo and Artemis and sister-in-law to Kronos, me, and Pan." Cedric spun back as she spoke. *He needs to understand how long this shit has been going on before his involvement. There are more lives and higher stakes.* "And, at one point, she served as Gaea's personal oracle, until she went into hiding. Hence, why Gaea snatched up little Artemis the moment Kronos let it out that she had powers that rivaled her mother's."

"Then what's Artemis's aim? She's been pulling my strings more than anyone else in my life." Narrowing his eyes, Cedric closed the gap between them. "Can she be trusted at all?"

Good, he's listening and wanting to learn more. We might have a chance of pulling together an army against her. "She wants out," Lillith hissed. "But Gaea watches everything she sees and hears. Meanwhile, she practically handed her eye over to Kronos so he could destroy Aether and wreak havoc on the Mortal Realm. If the eye is returned, she has to let Artemis go."

"Why?" Cedric knitted his brow. "What reason does she need? And didn't she task Apollo to bring the cursed thing back?"

"She's been trying to kill Apollo, knowing full well he would come for his sister and his wife. What she didn't count on was Kronos using her eye to bind him to Fenrir, and in doing so, making him almost unkillable." Huffing, Lillith tapped her fingers on her arm. "Look, Gaea lost most of her alliances when Aether was killed, and she let it happen. After that, the Celestial Realm was cut off from the Otherworld, and the Underworld is heavily gated after Kronos pissed off Hades. The returning of the eye quest was her trying to maintain what little control she had left at the time, but as time passed, many still walked away. She's growing bolder by the day."

"And why should I give a shit about all of this?" Cedric spat, turning away.

Shit, here we go again. "Because her interest has turned to you and yours." Lillith grabbed his arm, and they locked eyes. *Please take this seriously, Cedric. I know you only care about yourself but...* "Look, fucking hate me for all I care. Gaea and Kronos are trying to create proper mortal vessels, and they are looking at you and Angeline. Shit, do you even know you have a daughter?"

With a rotation of his arm, he broke her grasp and gripped her arm. "And when were you planning to tell me? Isn't that the reason you dragged me from my bedroom? How long have you known?"

Lillith broke her stare, confessing, "It wasn't my place to tell you." *It was hers, and worse, you've known and didn't want to accept that was the case. Who could blame you?*

"I figured it out."

A wave of magical energy hit Lillith, and her eyes fell on his armor. *This sensation of malice. I've felt this before. Is it the same as Avalon?* "Where'd you get that?" Jerking her arm back, she gave a bewildered expression. "That bracer, no..." Her eyes darted to the other bracer, the boots, and the leather tunic. "That armor. Where did you get it?"

"It found me," he declared, muscles taut. "You know something about it?"

Another wave of magic and nostalgia slammed her. *Aether. This magic is Aether's magic.* "N-no. In fact, I didn't know anything still remained of Aether and..." She bit her lip, despair weighing down on her. "Look, just know that I'm every bit of a victim as you are. We have a common enemy, always have. Right now, everyone is scrambling to locate weapons we can use against her and Kronos."

"So, I've heard." Cedric licked a fang. "Rumor has it something happened to Tony."

"Yeah, and your daughter started that mess. Tony finished it." Lillith's face flushed and lust escaped her as thoughts of their bonding crossed her mind. *Fuck! He's going to know. And since when do I get defensive and prideful? Pull it together!*

"You must be kidding me." Shaking his head, Cedric scoffed, "So he took the throne from me, after all?"

"Technically, there will be two King Incubi in play when you return." Lillith spun away, wings flaring. "He saved me." *No, I can't reveal he was here in the Otherworld so...* "After I came for Romasanta, Tony ... saved me."

"But that's not the reason you're falling for him, is it?" Cedric's words stung her.

"No, it's not." Another flare of her wings, her tail started to swat side to side. "Cedric, he's part titan and part incubus. I don't know how this will work out."

"Something tells me Aether consulted Phoebe and placed a lot more into motion."

Why didn't I think about...? "I never took into consideration that my father would seed solutions to take down Mother..." She spun back to him. "My time here is up. I must return, or Gaea will know. Don't take any longer; we may need you for a rescue mission if Tony hasn't returned, and we fear the Salamandra may have been compromised." *I assume he's left, but the few hours here have been days there.*

"Why send an amateur?" Cedric scoffed.

"We'll talk later."

If you only knew that he's making this look like a cakewalk in comparison to your rise to power. Granted, there's got to be something about Tony's past that makes this all easier for him to just persevere, but what could it be?

CHAPTER 21

SALAMANDRA'S DOMAIN

Scoffing, Tony spun to get a good gauge on his surroundings. *I feel like I was kicked off the boat on a secluded island.* Behind him, a tropical beach worthy of a travel magazine cover was a stark contrast to the complete opposite direction where he saw his personal version of Mt. Doom. *Tolkien would be proud.* There was a lot of jungle between the beach and the base of the volcano. Coconut trees and signs of crab holes littered where he stood just at the edge of the tree line. A sinking feeling hit his gut and a single thought hit him.

"Where the hell am I supposed to go?" He paced back and forth in the sand, nerves wrapped tightly in his joints. "I got all cocky and didn't even ask. No one thought to give me a map or briefing?" Flashes of watching Cedric and Romasanta go through a portal came to mind. "But they took next to nothing. No one in fact in that lot talks about maps, so how do they do it?"

The ground shook once more, and he turned to face the volcano. Birdlike creatures took to the air, cawing at the angry mountain. They looked like weird owls, stocky-bodied but too far off to make out much else. A bigger plume of smoke, darker than the first, snaked to the sky. Red lines indicated the rivers of lava spilling forth, and a shudder shook Tony. *I can survive being killed by the blade, but can I bounce back from being burned or melted down to nothing?* Readjusting his gear, Tony made his decision. *Well, I can only assume he's in the mountain. Let's hope I can figure this out the closer I get.*

Stepping into the forest made him pause. A chill rolled across his entire being. He looked back at the beach. The heat of it was gone, and it seemed eerily darker. *It's dense here, much like Avalon's aura when he's fucking with me.* Swallowing, he scanned the shadows between the trees and saw no signs of anything. Other than the distant caws of birds and ocean waves, the forest was silent. Licking a fang, he started down the path. Occasionally he'd slow and look back or even check for paw prints, any prints. The trees grew larger, and no longer did he see the constant cluster of palms. Now a more robust canopy of trees nearly took all the sky from him.

Shit, this is going to make it hard to know what time it is and if I'm going in the right direction.

Stopping, he started to mark trees with claw marks. *Sorry trees, I don't have any breadcrumbs.* Cold and wet, he no longer seemed to be in a sweltering junglescape. Swarms of bugs hadn't attacked him, and he stalked deeper, eyes darting. *This place feels so wrong in so many ways. At first, I thought the forest was getting denser...* Tony slashed another marker, taking a moment to look all around him. *...but it's just getting darker.* Staring up, he could no longer see the sky; there was just *nothing.*

Another tremor, and he took it in. *It feels like it's coming from ... that way.* He turned to the right and clawed another tree to correct his path. It seemed like hours had passed when he decided to take a break, sitting on a fallen log. *Why do I feel so damn lost already?* Staring into the shadows, he squinted, hoping to find signs of *anything. There are no signs of animals or even insects, but clearly, something is eating the bananas and coconuts. Even a crab carcass here and there, but...* Standing, he stretched his muscles. Another slash and...

"I wouldn't do that anymore."

A voice came from behind him, and he spun. Leaning on the tree was a dark-skinned man, wearing a blue and pink loincloth with a leather cowrie shell belt. Looping around his neck and across his chest were several necklaces made of turquoise and more shells. Large golden bands wrapped around his upper arms in the shape of snakes with turquoise eyes. A white tignon adorned his head and a tribal harpoon hugged between his arm and body. He was the same height as Tony, but thin and toned, making him seem half the mass or less. If he'd been dressed more feminine, he could easily pass as female, though. Seven thin braids laid split across one shoulder and the other. Golden yellow paint stretched brilliantly in a band across his eyes and colored his lips, giving him a look worthy of a fashion model with high cheekbones. His eyes, a steel gray, didn't seem threatening, but unmoved by Tony's presence.

"Do what anymore?" Tony questioned, inhaling deeply through his nostrils, but not smelling anything other than the earthy tones of the dirt and salt in the ocean breeze. *Isn't that how Romasanta and Cedric do this? Constantly sniffing out danger before it sneaks up? Why can't I smell shit? Is it because I'm neither a vampire nor a werewolf? How the hell am I to compensate for that little tidbit?!*

"Clawing Papa Boi's trees." His glare fell to the claw marks Tony had been leaving. "He doesn't like rude people, and that's as rude as they come."

Tony tensed, asking, "And who might you be?"

He smirked, his eyes dipping over Tony before answering, "Inle." Tilting his head, he seemed intrigued, adding, "But the real question is who are you?"

"Um, Tony?" he offered. "I was sent here to see Salamandra?"

Inle snorted. "You have a long way to go, brother, and a dangerous path to cross. Salamandra's domain is home to many creatures, good, evil, and otherwise."

Well, this guy seems helpful. Clearing his throat, Tony rubbed the back of his neck, confessing, "Yeah, I've been told a few times that I'd have to literally fight my way to where I'm going. Honestly, um, what are you doing here? It's not exactly the kind of place to go meet new people to shoot the shit with, now, is it?"

It earned him a chuckle. "Hunting, but I'm in need of assistance." Inle smiled, pushing himself off the tree. "You seem capable enough for the task, I think. Perhaps we can help one another out, so we may go home sooner and not later."

"Hunting what exactly?" Tony could now see a dagger and short staff made of coral hanging from his belt, a spear decorated wonderfully, now that Inle's body didn't hide them away.

"Baccoo are blocking me from going after my bounty." Stopping, Inle put a hand on his hip, looking over the gear Tony wore. "You were indeed coming here ready to fight with that gear, but can you use it?"

"And what exactly is a baccoo, and who or what is your bounty?" scoffed Tony. *Why does everyone always want something from me? Regardless, this might be my chance to not go through this solo.* "And if I offer to help, can you take me to Salamandra?"

"For a healthy boy like yourself," hummed Inle, looking Tony over once more, "yeah, I'll take you there afterward. You should be able to handle it."

"You didn't answer all of my questions." Tony crossed his arms, scowling. *Always half-truths and riddles with these people.*

"Well, for starters," Inle leaned to the side and pointed, replying, "that is a baccoo."

Tony turned, pulling his sword, and dropped into a ready stance. Between the trees, he could see movement for the first time since he entered the jungle. The creatures were half his height as the first one came fully into view. A large head and eyes were off-putting, its body thin, and the skin looked as if made of driftwood washed ashore. As it came closer, Tony could see the occasional stretched skin covering parts and hints of red flesh peeking through the cracks. They were ape-shaped, tiny legs lacked the kneecaps of a normal humanoid, as if they were nothing more than crude, living, wooden totems. A smell wafted from them, a mixture of decaying flesh and rotten bananas. Branches and underbrush snapped and crackled behind as two more shambled forth. Nothing but black pupils bounced between him and Inle in the bloodshot white eyes. A chill snaked up Tony's spine.

The deeper I dive into this side, the more I feel like I'm in a living nightmare. Well, I'm kind of glad not to have such a sensitive nose for this part, but damn, these guys reek. "Are they here for me or you?"

"What does it matter?" replied Inle, walking up beside Tony and looking back. "It seems they have us surrounded."

Glancing over his shoulder, Tony could see more stepping out of the shadows from all sides. "Shit. I suppose I'm about to find out how strong I am."

"Wait, this is your first battle?" sputtered Inle, taking a more readied stance. "Who is crazy enough to set foot on this island as a rookie?"

"Outside of street brawls and that fight with a troll, yeah, it's my first battle," confessed Tony. "And I was sent here by... well, that's a complicated answer. There are a couple of names I could drop, but the one who opened the door is another matter."

"Your aura and overall build say you can take on anything," fussed Inle, who leaned his back against Tony's. "So please tell me you've trained for a fight? This isn't a street brawl!"

"Yes, I've been trained," scowled Tony. *Crap, keep in the sexual aura. Keep it in. I can't have everyone under the sun getting the hots for me by brushing up against me or touching me.*

A baccoo screeched, bringing Tony's attention forward as the initial three rushed him. He made a slash across them, none of them making any attempt to dodge or defend. The sword seemed to hug his hand firmly, rather than him grip it, making Tony hesitate on his second slash. The blade lodged into one creature, just out of reach to claw at him; it seemed to have no sense of pain... *and no sense of pleasure escaping them either, luckily.* He kicked it off and slashed again, pushing them back. One came into his periphery and before he could react, Inle's spear stabbed it in the forehead, and it hit the ground limp.

"The head, aim for the head, or they'll keep standing back up." Inle swung the harpoon, using it more like a javelin the way he battled with it.

"Head, right." Tony slashed across two more, this time scalping them, and they dropped instantly, as if cutting the strings on a puppet. "Is something controlling these?"

"Yes, they are summoned mercenaries made from the dead, flesh and fauna alike." Inle roared, jabbing several back-to-back. "La Diablesse is using them to keep me from following her."

"Uh, did you mean El Diablo?" Tony corrected, cutting down three more. *I got this.* The task seemed easy as he lopped off heads and jabbed through eye sockets.

Inle laughed. A grunt escaped him as two baccoo pushed him to the side. "Muddascunt!" He lost his balance, falling to the ground with a yelp.

Tony swung his sword, taking the head off the last of his own adversaries, and reached back. Grabbing the head of one in a clawed hand, Tony crushed its skull and tossed it into the other. Inle blinked his eyes, baffled by the change in his appearance; horns and claws appeared as Tony clenched his fangs. Marching past the shocked warrior, Tony ravaged the remaining baccoo until howls rang out and they retreated. Panting, the rush of his blood both familiar and exhilarating, Tony looked back to Inle, who stood back up, brushing dirt off himself.

"You know how to fight, indeed, brother. Not only like a beast, but as a beast." Inle tapped a foot on a headless baccoo. "I suppose you might be more helpful than I thought."

"Well, it seems they only retreated." Snorting, Tony sheathed his sword and crossed his arms at Inle. "Now tell me more about La Diablesse. I've never heard of it before."

"Her," corrected Inle, who checked the bodies and pulled trinkets from a few.

"Her," echoed Tony.

"How good are you without your armor and weapons?" Inle arched a brow, curious to know more.

Tony licked a fang and gruffed, "Bruh, you don't want to see that side of me."

Inle threw up his hands. "I got you, brother. Let's just work our way into her territory, then I'll take you to Salamandra."

Turning, Inle started to walk deeper into the forest and Tony followed at a distance. Silence fell heavy between them again, with no scurrying of anything nor signs of life coming from the trees. Thoughts rolled through Tony as he followed aimlessly behind Inle, his mind and instincts conflicting with one another. *Ugh, this is not the situation I was ready to face. My gut says I can trust him, but I can't help but think I'm being set up.* Looking up, Tony still couldn't see the sky, or perhaps night had fallen at some point, and he had failed to notice. *I wonder how long I've really been here. Has it only been hours, or is this like the Otherworld, and days or weeks have passed?*

"You come here often to hunt?" Tony pressed for conversation. *At least I can pass the time and learn more about who I'm naively trusting.*

"When I seek out certain individuals," answered Inle, casting a glance back at Tony with a smirk. "From what you were saying, this is your first time in battle?"

"Yeah, it is. Of this kind, anyhow. Swords and monsters weren't my first career choice." Tony glanced to the left and right, checking for any signs of suspicious activity as the icy jungle slowly morphed into a warmer swamp environment.

"What was your first career choice?" Inle had slowed his pace to walk side-by-side, indulging the conversation and curious.

Tony smirked, casting a glance at Inle. "Bartender."

Inle scoffed, "Bartender turned warrior! Ha! Brother, that's a hell of a career change."

"Who said I stopped being a bartender?" Tony arched a brow.

"Where at? Perhaps I'll make my way there for a drink." Inle slapped his shoulder, smiling wide. "I promise to leave a good tip."

"Lion's Den, in the Mortal Realm." Tony stopped, searching the environment and feeling the nature continue to shift and change rapidly. "What is up with this place?"

Inle paused a few steps away and followed his gaze. "It's not abnormal for the environment to shift depending on who is influencing that territory. Salamandra, Delphyne, and many other powerhouses can make their own domain, private realms, but those less powerful beings, they simply influence a limited range of territory." Inle started walking again as if he could see a road Tony failed to notice. "It's normal for someone like Salamandra to open their domain to creatures such as these, both to provide sanctuary to them but also to provide a level of protection or an alarm system for their domain."

Tony trailed behind him, taking in the information. "Does everyone do this? The whole bringing in outside monsters?"

"Depends on who we're talking about." Inle shrugged. "As a deity of estuaries, it doesn't catch my attention a lot."

"Okay, interesting alignment," remarked Tony.

"Delphyne is the most famous. She only nurtures her children, or types of dragons, and they protect her as much as she protects them. That's more of the mother-child caste system for a domain." Inle paused, looking around, and took a right turn in the direction of a fallen log. "But here, this is more of a symbiotic relationship as long as they stay out of Salamandra's way. They can stay here and thrive."

"Okay, so won't he be pissed you're here to take away one of his lackeys?" Tony challenged him.

"Not when he's the one who hired me to take her out," cooed Inle. "As a deity who protects estuaries and promotes health, it's not uncommon for me to be asked to hunt and take down the parasites that dare to disrespect the balance of these sacred places."

"What about Lillith's domain?" Inle came to a hard stop, and Tony spun to meet the scowl on his face. "What's wrong?"

"That place is barren," announced Inle, his brow furrowing. "Why ask about her of all choices, brother?"

Shit, I didn't realize how risky it is to drop her name. Tony's heart fluttered, his thoughts flying before pulling his answer together. "I've met her before."

"Badwud," muttered Inle, shaking his head and walking again. "If you want to know, I think it's because that domain is an incomplete creation."

"In-incomplete how?" Tony chased after him, Inle's pace increasing. *This wasn't the sort of information I thought I'd be getting, but I want to know more about what it means to be her.*

Inle stopped, turning and bringing Tony to a halt once more. "Well," pausing, Inle gauged Tony's expression and sighed, "she's never brought a king to the shared domain. Rumors say she's never really bonded with a king to make her sanctuary stable, but it could have something to do with Gaea. It's quite sad."

Tony blinked, a knot formed in his gut, and he paled. *Until now, I can't press further without revealing too much. Does this mean I'm partially responsible for a place like this?* Tony's throat tightened as he glanced all around; the ground vibrated underfoot from the volcano. *Is it barren of animals and creatures? Or is it a wasteland or desert? Did she abandon it knowing—*

"What's wrong?" Inle tilted his head, picking apart the emotions written on Tony's face.

"Since this seems to be your expertise," Tony's heart raced with the idea that crept up in him, "is it because she hasn't brought a king there, or is it just uninhabitable because she's abandoned it?"

"Oh!" Inle chuckled, waving it off as he started to walk again. "Now, that is a very good question. There are very few domains with shared entities, so who knows which is the case with that one? Come, come. We are getting closer, and we've been able to keep out of Papa Boi's way. I'm starting to think you're lucky, brother."

"R-right." Tony inhaled deeply and held it. *But how does it work when you have a domain? Do you just go there anytime, like Romasanta, or how everyone goes to Avalon? What are the stipulations to cross into it? Do I need a door, or because it's part mine, can I just snap in and out of there?* Looking down at his hand, Tony pumped his fist. *Is it like leaving a mark? Is it the same magic or something entirely different?*

CHAPTER 22

THE GATHERING

Leaning on her knees, Lillith felt drained from merely being in the presence of Cedric. *When did he grow so monstrous? I think he might be able to take Gyges down with that much power.* The forest shifted all around her and Hamadryades marched out of the trees. The expression from the Queen of Dryads was very sobering as she stood up straight to greet her.

"Impressive, that one," commented Hamadryades. "Why choose another king over that him?"

Lillith tensed, casting a dangerous glare at Hamadryades. "I've chosen my king. Cedric was never mine to have and took that title only to retrieve the queen of his own making."

"Ah, the heir of Artemis's power." Hamadryades cracked a smile, her fingers fluttering to bring back the toadstools from before. "Tell me, Lillith, why do you still pursue this war even now with newfound love?"

Lillith flinched, reluctant to sit. "Is it wrong that I feel we're the only ones capable of stopping her?"

Hamadryades cupped her cheek and nodded. "To be honest, many would have never even entertained the thought if it had it not been for a few factors: first being that you set much of it into motion and second being the world deities refusing to follow Gaea's lead. Her magic is old and deeply rooted. However, her hatred for mankind and blind love for Kronos has brought too much poison, not only to the Mortal Realm, but here in the Otherworld as well. They threw it all out of balance."

Relaxing some, Lillith scoffed, "No one paid attention to my warnings until it was too late, and she had locked the celestial realm to anyone strong enough to easily overpower her."

"Indeed." Hamadryades sighed. "I think everyone took alarm when she went as far as locking the Underworld and when Hades threatened to raise his army against Kronos for meddling in his affairs in the Mortal Realm."

"Don't remind me... the great Satanic Panic and the other cult-based attempts only lasted long enough for Pan to meddle and piss Hades off further." Lillith rubbed her forehead.

"Granted, when she figured out that Hades found a way to hide away in the Mortal Realm and catch Kronos in the act..." hummed Hamadryades, casting a knowing expression.

"Well, that didn't help me much because that was Hades wanting to play war games with Pan when she wouldn't let him near Kronos and he refused to leave Avalon," groaned Lillith.

Hamadryades giggled.

"But I figured we were done talking." Lillith arched a brow, pressing further, "So why am I still sitting here?"

"Waiting, my dear." Hamadryades turned, the rustling of the leaves making up her hair soothing as Lillith looked in that same direction.

Alecto and Freya were walking out of the trees, chattering with one another. More toadstools were appearing, and just behind them a large number of Amazonian warriors. Lillith tensed, squirming on the toadstool as her heart fluttered. *This whole time I thought Hamadryades was going to stay out of the fight, but it seems she's been the catalyst bringing it all together.*

"Today, we get to free the third queen of the Amazonians," boasted Freya.

Alecto shoved her, rolling her eyes. "I'm more excited to fulfill my role as justicar. She must honor the terms with a mortal, though Romasanta is a titan, he forfeited that life long ago and is powerless besides the gifts bestowed to him by Fenrir."

"Regardless, I have children and it appalls me to see how she takes from her own family and never truly fulfills her promises. She had better do right by him. Apollo is in good favor here for his tribulations in giving back her dreaded eye." Freya fussed, taking a toadstool next to Lillith. "Gods not fulfilling promises to other gods is a dangerous quandary."

"And let's not forget the treaty we enacted with her over the matter." Hamadryades bowed her head at the two powerhouses. "Today, ladies, I believe we get to open up the celestial gates once more in hopes of relieving the imbalance in magic."

"Oh, yes, indeed," Freya chortled. "Granted, to completely fix this farce, someone will have to pop that lock on Hades's cage."

"Ah, Lillith!" Lillith turned to see Manannan coming from a different direction; he bowed deeply. "Sorry for not saying hello in the market the other day."

"That's okay. Romasanta was quicker than the rest," drawled Lillith.

"He saw you?" Manannan stood with his hand on his hip and looked obnoxious in purple, gold, and green attire in the forest setting.

"He spoke to me." She cut him a glare. "But thank you for redirecting Cedric. Out of the two, it was the better choice at that moment."

"Ugh, Cedric. What a beastly creature that one is," Manannan scoffed.

Freya and Alecto chuckled at the comment.

"Is your brother joining, Freya?" Hamadryades had produced a teacup and sipped from it as she crossed her legs on the tallest toadstool.

"You know Frey; he'll wait for a dramatic moment to enter." Crossing her arms, Freya snorted. "He said he'll appear, if needed."

"Better than a no, I suppose," cooed Hamadryades as she turned to Lillith. "In your absence, we worked diligently for this moment."

"How so?" Lillith furrowed her brow. *Yet, centuries ago, all of them told me I was crazy for wanting to find a way to take down Gaea.*

"Well, we placed a large treaty and contracts into place to keep Gaea from being able to break her promises to anyone." Alecto gave a wild smirk.

Lillith blinked. *Did they not trust me at first until I had pushed too far?* She had been unaware they had been pushing matters after Gaea had chased her out of the Otherworld. "In short, you gave her a taste of her own medicine. Ha!" Laughter rolled from Lillith. *Gaea's law had turned on Gaea herself, or at least, the powers that be had used the principle against her. Genius.*

"Look, it's no secret that I was close to Aether." Hamadryades's smile faded, and she stared into her flower teacup. "At one point, she truly loved him. I can never forgive her and Kronos for trying to kill him."

"Yes, but he did provide sanctuary for all beings when he fell. His body, soul, and power divided out to create the realms as we know it," added

Alecto in a sobering tone. "Not many with his power would have been so selfless."

If anyone might know the answer to this, they might. Lillith looked across the faces around her and cleared her throat, mustering the courage to ask, "Do you think Father had a plan, or if some part of him is still out there in hiding?"

All eyes fell on Lillith, the gaunt expressions sharing her thoughts on the matter. They tossed eyes to one another, nodding and thinking. The silence spoke volumes toward the indecisiveness on the matter even now. *They know something but won't say a damn word of it in front of me beyond the hints that he might not be dead. What good does that do me when I've seen no sign of his aura... Well, until now.*

"Well," the wizard Manny started first, "he left living armor behind instead of wearing it himself. For some strange reason, it took a liking to your buddy, Cedric."

"I noticed." Lillith nodded. *Finally, some affirmation.*

"Knowing Aether," Hamadryades smirked and winked at Lillith, "he definitely knew the betrayal was coming and he's the sort to at least protect his children."

"Did anyone ever figure out where Kronos hid his head?" Alecto's voice earned everyone's stare. "What? It's true! The only body part that was missing, and the main thing Kronos wanted, was Aether's head. Gaea shrieked like a banshee from her castle for decades over the matter. Sent armies of her creations to look for it to no avail."

"I didn't realize it was missing," sputtered Lillith. *His head? Then he didn't die, but where the hell is it, or is he? What form remained? Surely, like me, being Gaea's heart, his head has its own entity, no?*

"Yes, though I speculate Gaea has it in that shitty thing she calls a castle," drawled Freya.

"I do know she has some of my siblings imprisoned there." Lillith scowled. "But I don't think we're able to rescue them. We're just going to be lucky if that gang of misfits makes it to the throne room alive."

"Oh, they'll make it," reassured Freya.

"I know our girl is strong enough by herself," chuckled Alecto. "That's one stubborn queen Cedric's chosen for himself. Which brings me to my next question," Alecto wagged a finger at Lillith, "when did that happen? Doesn't Gaea have a curse preventing that?"

"This is why I hate being near all you old hags," flustered Lillith, covering her face. "I don't want to talk about it."

"Well, it seems we've finally found a loophole, huh?" Freya patted Lillith's shoulder. "I hope he's a warrior strong enough to protect his mistress. Ottar has been a wonderful companion in Odin's absence while he's been stuck in the Celestial Realm."

"Poor humans think the Mortal Realm is godless, but it's because they've been all locked away." Hamadryades snorted, "How much of a warrior is this one?"

"About that." Lillith's cheeks flushed; she rubbed the back of her neck. "We sent him on his first quest."

Hamadryades spit her tea out.

Lillith puffed out her cheeks and avoided the judgmental stares. *That's right; I'm robbing the crib at this rate.* She bit her tongue to stifle a laugh over the thought. *Here we go. I'll have to explain everything to them. Perhaps they might take pity on him and help me out on this note. I hope he's handling Salamandra's domain well. It's a haven for curses, but he should be fine... right? Shit, did any of us give him a map? FUCK. Pan, this is your fault!*

CHAPTER 23

LEARNING THE ROPES

The occasional bullshit banter did nothing to pass the time. They'd been walking for hours, *or has it been days now?* Tony shifted in his armor, sweating in the hot humidity of the swamp they trudged through. They had dipped in and out of knee-deep water, sulfur springs making the whole place smell of rotten eggs and mildew. Worse, the mud threatened to rip their boots off and left the skin burning with the bacteria it produced. *Never going through a swamp willingly in the future.* Once more they found a dry spot, and Tony stopped, sitting on a stump.

"Don't tell me you're tired already?" Inle scoffed.

"No, but I just want to get some water out of my boots and dry up for a moment." Tony unlaced a boot and let the water dump out. "This is rough."

"Well, that's why I'm not wearing boots." Inle gestured to his bare feet.

"Rub it in, why don't you?" Tony pulled off the other boot; more water splashed out. "Maybe I should try to go without boots, too."

Inle looked all around as if gathering his bearings. "Let me see if I can gauge where we are or at least find a smoother path. Wait here."

Tony watched as Inle faded into the darkness of cypress trees. *Shit, I should have followed.* His elbows on his knees, he rested his forehead on his clasped hands. *I'm so in over my head here. My only way to Salamandra just left me, and I have no way of knowing if he's coming back.* Peering around, he no longer could evidence of a tropical island, but instead seemed to be wandering into a place worthy of a Louisiana bayou at best.

Reminds me of the places I passed driving in and out of there for mafia business. A shudder rolled through him. *Is it possible I was working for one of these deities or creatures this whole time?* He sat up straight, covering his face in frustration. *Maybe there was something I knew wasn't right. All that night-shine in their eyes didn't bug me in the bar because I had seen it before...* Tony's gut twisted. *Did they really die, or do their sudden "deaths" just mean they went back home to the Otherworld or even the Underworld? There is an Underworld, right? Yeah, Badbh said something about that, and Pan mentioned Hades another time, too.*

Tony unbuckled his halters and pulled his tunic off to free himself of his shirt. *It's soaked.* Wringing it out, he dropped it to the ground and held up the leather tunic. *Dry as a bone. Maybe it has an enchantment to solve chafing. Amazing.* Weaseling it back on, he looked down at his breeches and sighed.

"At least they don't seem to be heavy or uncomfortable when wet." He looked at the boots in betrayal. "But the boots are hell on my feet. Let's take a note from Inle..."

Crouching down, Tony began to roll up the leather breeches to his knees. Turning back to his sheaths, he strapped them on before sitting back down to shake the mud from the boots. *I guess I can lace them together and lug them over my shoulders like I used to do with my tennis shoes at the beach.*

SPLASH!

Glancing up, he saw no signs of Inle. Squinting, he peered out through the darkness, which seemed to be lifting ever so lightly. *Did someone's territory waver or come closer? Or does the darkness imply two entities trying to dominate one another, like Inle is leading us to a meeting point where two collide? I suppose that would make it easier to slip through without either noticing us, but...* Something shifted, and Tony tilted his head, alarm building in his core.

"I-Inle?" he stuttered.

A voice called out, "Come this way."

Tony jerked to his feet. "Who's there?"

"Come," it whispered again. "This way."

Pulling his blade, Tony looked at his boots. "Shit." Leaning down, he knotted the laces together and slung them over his shoulders. *I'm too afraid to go without; even if Inle can do it, that doesn't mean I should. What could this be? It sounds like a woman now, but I swore it mimicked Inle's voice at first.*

"Hurry." Now it sounded fully through the darkness in a female's voice. "Help. Please come."

Swallowing, Tony shuddered. "I hate this. Why is everything so damn creepy?"

Looking around, he saw no signs of Inle, but the mysterious voice kept whispering and calling from the same direction he'd disappeared in. *What if he's in trouble? This thing could be helping or...* Every nerve tightened in his joints, the tension in his muscles burning. The instincts screamed, *beware.* Much to his surprise, a path started to form, and slowly the swamp retreated and tall grass with jungle trees started to come forth as the light started to dabble through the trees in clusters. The whispers were coming to his ears from all around now, and he halted.

"Don't stop," they hissed and whined. "Come, this way. Please. I need you. I want you."

Inhaling deeply, Tony tried to smell and scoffed at himself. *Yup, still just a Cedric and Romasanta thing.* The tall grass next to the footpath started to rustle, and he gripped his sword's hilt tight. Tiny straw hats fidgeted between blades of grass, hiding the faces of the tiny creatures that wore them. *What in the hell are these tiny things?* More scuttling came from behind and all around him, and dread weighed down on him. *I'm surrounded, and there's a lot.* A massive hoard of chicken-sized creatures was stepping out onto the pathway where he stood. Their legs were humanlike, bent in a peculiar manner like that of a bird, with backward knees and tiny arms that reminded him of porcelain dolls. Tony pulled his sword free, ready to fight, and they hissed all around him.

This is going to suck ass. I've never fought something smaller than me. Tony swung out, the tiny pack of creatures scattering back. A hat fell off one and it shrieked, turning to retrieve the hat with its tiny three-clawed hands. *Well, that's an odd reaction.* Looking up at Tony, it was a clean slate of skin where a face should have been, minus the tiny, sharp-toothed mouth. *Fucking creepy!* Jabbing forward, Tony managed to kill it with ease. The rest hissed and shrilled in anger and tightened their circle around him.

"I don't know what the fuck these are, but nothing good can come of them." Glancing beyond them for a quick moment, Tony still saw no signs of Inle.

AWOOOOO!

Howls rang out from the jungle, catching Tony and the small creatures off guard. Several things were loudly shoving through and getting closer. Branches popped and excited yelps filled the air. *Wild dogs?* The tiny straw-hatted goblin-like creatures scattered. Tony twisted and turned, ready for an attack as they thudded closer, coming in fast. Something big broke out of the trees. Through the parting grass, Tony caught the panicked eyes of a floppy-eared dog. *What the*—it tried to stop, but the momentum was too much as it tumbled into his shins.

The excited yelps had fallen silent, drawing Tony's eyes back to where the dog had come from. *Why is there a dog here, and what was chasing it?* Golden eyes glowed from between the gray wash of tree trunks. *Wolves?* Snarling and growling rolled like thunder as another tremble shook the ground from the volcano. The dog at his feet stood again baring, its teeth, barking, and snarling. *What the hell is happening here?* At last, the first of the dog's pursuers stepped into the little light that filtered in overhead. A wolf, massive and slightly humanoid, crept out. Saliva dangled from its jowls as it growled.

Is that a werewolf? Images of Romasanta flew across his mind and he tensed. *No, these are similar, but something is wrong, off. Maybe it's more … feral?*

The werewolf-like creature pounced. Tony swung wide to meet it in the air. Unlike with other foes, he barely slashed open a wound; the pelt was tough to slice, and the wolf yelped and retreated. Another one launched out of the grass. He swung the other way but failed to be quick enough. Teeth gnawed at his forearm. Another clawed at his back. Eyes wide, Tony's pulse raced. Pain quickly shifted to overwhelming pleasure. The stinging and burning he should have experienced at that moment were nowhere to be found. All that remained was his growing excitement for the fight.

Roaring, Tony dove his sword into the head of the one latched onto his arm. It released and thudded at his feet. *One down.* He spun around; two were crouched down before him. Seeing his blood on the left one's claws, he charged forward with a downward strike. It dodged and the other one snapped at him. Sidling, Tony missed the gnashing fangs and swung wide. Lopping off an ear, one yelped and retreated into the grass, hiding itself while the other circled.

Again, Tony spun around and found the other one. Stepping forward, he aimed with a flurry of jabs, half of them hitting their mark. *My footwork is shit barefooted on unlevel ground like this!* The lopped-off-ear one launched out of the grass. Tony raised an arm in defense. The floppy-eared dog knocked it off course, and the two ripped and bit at one another. Another wolf-creature charged out of the grass.

"Dammit!" cried Tony; he watched as the dog's blood splattered the dirt.

Inle burst from the forest and tossed his spear with a roar. The creature buckled and skidded across the ground from the force of the throw. *Two down now.* Another werewolf came barreling out of the grass at Inle, and he pulled his dagger and fended off the snapping fangs. Anger and pleasure rolled through Tony. *I don't like how this is getting me so thrilled. I should be scared shitless. It's too hard to focus on what's happening.* His sword buzzed in his hand in reaction to the onslaught as horns grew forth. A familiar thrill for the fight and blood to spill boiled up within his core.

"Careful!" Inle warned. "There's a whole pack of loogaroo, and we're still outnumbered ten to one."

Another roar rolled out of Tony. His fangs clenched tight and his tail swished in anticipation of his claws meeting their mark. Every fiber of his being wanted to take them all down, alone. His instincts screamed that they wanted to smell the iron of his blood and theirs paint the ground.

I want to show them who is king here.

Tony shoved his blade into the ground. Abandoning his weapon was enough to draw four into his striking range in an instance surrounding him.

"Brother, what—" Inle found himself pinched in by two creatures now; he cast a bewildered look at Tony as he abandoned his weapon in the heat of battle.

Claws aching and his back already healed, Tony was ready. His eyes fell to the dog, still breathing and unmoving in a heap on the road, as the loogaroo with the missing ear met Tony's rage-filled gaze.

"Come at me," growled Tony.

It leaped forward and Tony clawed upward, slashing open its throat. *Three dead.* As he twisted, two more jumped him. One slashed out, ripping through the tunic and opening his abdomen. The other snapped its jaws at his head; a raised arm caught the heavy fangs. Tony paid no heed to the ripping of his flesh. Another yelp signaled Inle taking down the fourth, and Tony snarled. His claws popped and crushed the snout and pulled it off. His bleeding arm healed as the canine teeth left it and he gripped the bottom jaw, ripping it apart. *Five now.* Dropping it, Tony launched forward. Pouncing the last loogaroo in sight, he slashed at it with both claws until it stopped breathing.

Whimpers and yelps filled the air as the rest of the pack splashed through the swamp and smashed their way through the jungle. *Retreating, even though they had us outnumbered. Ha!* Panting, Tony glanced around, looking for any signs of more loogaroo remaining. Tony's gaze met Inle's as he yanked his spear out and frowned.

"How often do you rage out like that when fighting?" Inle arched an eyebrow before adding, "And do I need to worry about my own throat when you do?"

Tony stood, the tunic in pieces, as he ripped the last of it off and dropped it. "It's a new sword, and it made me nervous..." He met Inle's wary gaze. "I did say most of my experience is street brawls, didn't I?"

"It shows, brother, it shows." Inle came closer and scanned past him, squatting at tracks in the footpath. "Wow, did you run into the La Diablesse's douen?"

"The what?" Tony looked around until his eyes spotted the dog.

"Hat-wearing chicken goblins." Inle followed Tony as he dropped beside the dog. "What is this? Is that a dog?"

"I was dealing with those douen things, but this dog was being chased by the loogaroo." Tony petted its head, and it whined, breathing fast and shallow. "It attacked one that was going to get me. You didn't have to do that, little guy. I can heal really fast, and clearly, you can't."

Inle squatted beside him and pressed a hand into the blood-soaked beige pelt. "Fortunately for you, I do have the ability to heal." A glow pulsed out from Inle's hand like golden waves rolling over the dog's body. "Bumba, you have strange luck, brother." The blood vanished, and soon after, the bite marks as well. "Do you know who this is?"

"N-no." Tony watched as the breathing deepened and slowed, the dog's eyes still shut. "I just thought it was a dog caught in a bad spot."

Inle chuckled, his hand pulling away. "He's going to be out for a while, so we'll have to camp in the road. Don't move him."

They both stood, and Tony rubbed the back of his neck. "Are you going to tell me who he is or just keep that to yourself?"

"Irawaru," answered Inle, picking up loogaroo corpses and tossing them into the trees.

"And that is?" Tony began to mirror the action.

"He's a long way from home." Inle looked at the dog with a pitiful expression. "That there is a Maori god. The husband turned into a dog to serve as a guard to spirits traveling to the afterlife. I wonder how he ended up in the predominantly Caribbean domain here?"

"Yeah, which means he's on the wrong side of the earth." Tony chucked the last loogaroo corpse and picked up the chicken-legged goblin. "This, these are...?"

Inle scoffed. "Douen. So, you did run into those. La Diablesse isn't far, so we'll have to be mindful. She may start hunting us instead."

Tony tossed it to the trees. "Are there creatures out there that will eat those?"

"Oh yeah, Papa Boi will send the scavengers of his forest to take care of it. He might see it as an offering, which will be helpful to win favor for safe passage from him in a tight spot." Inle circled Tony, glaring at the blood smudged across him. "Not a scratch, muddascunt. You are an interesting one, Tony."

"Uh, thanks, I think." He pointed toward the Irawaru. "So, does he speak?"

"Oh no. He's been cursed to that body since his sister did that to him." Inle started searching the grass for branches. "Come, let's get a fire going and we can talk more."

Tony started his own search, the tingling of Lillith's mark reminding him he had to make it through this. *I'll get through this, promise. At least I've quickly made some interesting friends. Perhaps I've got some uncanny luck.* He shot a glance at the sleeping dog, Irawaru. *At least my curse led me to be able to fight; this guy, he can't even communicate. Shit, I got lucky.* Tony froze, his heart fluttered, and his throat tightened. *That could have been me...*

CHAPTER 24

GAEA'S THRONE

Sitting with her lips drawn tight, Lillith waited for Freya and Alecto to catch their breaths. They had tears in their eyes and the red in Lillith's face wouldn't let go. *Why did I even share my dilemma with Tony with these old hags?* Hamadryades couldn't even meet her gaze, though she had managed to keep to a giggle, unlike the boastful cackles of the other two.

Alecto wiped another tear away, catching her breath, "So, let me get this straight. He's only been a god for, what, a century by mortal terms?"

Lillith bit her tongue. *Should I even tell them?*

"No, it's shorter than that." Freya waved, snorting. "By a few decades, I thought she said."

Again, Lillith glared angrily, still biting her tongue to keep silent. *Surely someone can change the topic now.*

Hamadryades sipped her endless cup of tea some more, gauging the expression Lillith held before the epiphany hit her and she sat her cup down abruptly. "It's barely been a year."

They gasped and waited for her answer.

Lillith opened her mouth, reluctant to confess the truth before at last, revealing, "Barely six months."

Silence fell over them as if the answer had been spoken in a foreign language.

"Uh, how long?" Freya leaned in, eyes wide as her blonde locks slipped off her elven ears. "I don't think I heard you just now."

"You heard me," spat Lillith, narrowing her eyes at them.

Hamadryades covered her mouth. "Will he live?"

"Yes," hissed Lillith. "You act like I'd send a fledgling into battle."

"Well," Alecto made a cringing face, her makeup and warrior ensemble softening under the empathetic expressions. "I mean, compared to other demons at the same level, he's a fledgling. It's not like he knows how to use a sword."

"He does," reassured Lillith. "I had Badbh train him."

Hamadryades spat her tea out again.

"He's as good as dead." Freya stood, stretching.

Lillith sighed, crossing her arms. "You'll change your mind if you ever meet him."

"Why bother?" Alecto waved it off. "Unless they have an army or domain, I don't bother to acknowledge them."

Biting her lip, Lillith turned to Hamadryades. "How do you intend on getting into the castle as needed without the brothers stopping us?"

A smirk crossed Hamadryades's wooden lips. "You forget that there will be two sorceresses with a pact with me in that throne room." Arching a brow, she added, "Though Angeline can force me there if need be."

Nodding, Lillith reached out through her mark. *Good, Tony is intact and doesn't seem to be in trouble.* The familiar warming at her belly made her smile. Looking up, the three old goddesses stared at her in alarm. Blinking, she shot a glance behind her and forward again, baffled. *Why that reaction? I didn't say or do anything that—*

"What power was that just now?" Lillith realized Hamadryades had dropped her teacup.

Heart racing, she whispered, "That was his. Tony's power."

They cast glances at one another; a sobering expression shared between them as Alecto spoke first. "You didn't say anything about him being a titan."

Lillith scowled. *How could they possibly detect that through his mark?*

"Which one have you made a pact with?" Hamadryades's voice crackled as anger rose from her, thorns bursting over her.

"If you think it's an old titan, you're mistaken." Lillith raised her chin, standing her ground. *They think I went to one of Gaea's children!*

Alecto rushed her, gripping her by the throat. "Who did you bond with? Oceanus?"

"If you don't believe me..." Lillith rasped, grunting from the claws gripping her. "I'll take you to him. A moment ago..." Alecto tightened to cut her words short.

"Are you telling us he's a new titan?" Freya shot a glance to Hamadryades, who shook her head, unsure. "That's impossible."

"It..." Lillith could barely breathe now.

"Alecto." Hamadryades's voice boomed with the force of storm winds and Alecto dropped Lillith.

Coughing and sputtering, Lillith kneeled before the ancient deities; she didn't dare stand to her feet. "It was a shock to me as well. He was human before being cursed to have his bloodlines consume him."

"Who sired him?" demanded Freya, the air getting cold.

"I suspect Kronos, but he's also a blood relative to Cedric." Lillith's heart raced, panic filling her. *Are they thinking about going on a headhunt?* Glancing up, they had gathered with their backs to her. "Please..." They froze at the sound of her trembling voice. "I've had everything taken from me, or her wretched curse stood in the way of me from all I ever wanted..."

Alecto turned, rage still in her uncanny eyes, pupils small and piercing. "After we finish facing Gaea, we'll use Freya's astral projection to see this king for ourselves."

"Be warned, heart of Gaea." Freya seemed stern. "If this proves to be other than what you have implied, we will snuff him out."

Clenching her fangs, Lillith couldn't keep the horns and wings from bursting to life. "And if you aim to harm him, I will protect him with my life, even from all of you."

Hamadryades sighed, cutting into the middle. "I wouldn't expect any less from you on the matter. Now stand, we have a bitch to put in her place, and afterward, we shall return here to proceed with our investigation from the safety of my forest."

"Agreed." Alecto sucked on her cheek, seeing worrisome the reaction in Lillith.

"It's time." Hamadryades cast one more pitiful glance at Lillith, whispering, "All will be known soon enough, child of Aether's affection."

Lillith went to speak, but within a blink, they were inside Gaea's castle, standing before the grandiose doors that led to the throne. Inhaling deeply,

Lillith bit her lip, still exchanging heated glares at Alecto and Freya. *How dare you threaten what is mine!*

Within the doors, Artemis spoke loudly, alarm rising in her voice. "Mother Gaea, are you implying when you return the girl's humanity that you intend to keep her age the same? That would mean she would be nothing more than ash."

"Precisely," Gaea's voice answered sharply.

"May I propose something?" Artemis cut in; a long silence hung in the air.

"Fine. What do you propose, annoying little sorceress?"

"She remains a dryad, but one who can walk freely like her sisters." Everyone looked at Hamadryades, who smiled warmly at this suggestion.

"Oh, but little one, don't you know that Hamadryades..." Anger rose on the Dryad Queen's face, and she pushed on the doors, "...and I are no longer on talking ter–" Gaea's words stopped as the doors flew open, knocking Gyges to the ground.

"She has become one of mine, Gaea." Hamadryades's voice boomed loud and clear for all to hear.

Gaea gripped her throne, leaning forward to hiss, "How dare you trespass into my home!"

"We have come to cash in on your sworn word and honor, the contract *you* made centuries ago." Freya stepped out from behind Hamadryades. "Alecto, dear, what were those terms again?"

Alecto appeared from the shadows beside Hamadryades, Furies and Valkyries pouring into the room. "Ah, there were many things discussed at that last round table. For starters, after Apollo so diligently returned her eye from Kronos, who you still swear you have no allegiance to—"

"I don't," Gaea snarled.

"Right. Seeing Apollo has fulfilled the quest, you are to break your curse on Daphne. Changing her back to human after Hamadryades has gifted her the right of being a dryad would be breaking your truce. Ah, but there's more... now if Pan wasn't the contract holder, who was?" Hamadryades lifted her brow high, seeing the contempt in Gaea's face.

"I drafted said contract since I was the only neutral entity available." Manny stepped out from between a cluster of Valkyries and unraveled the contract. "My, there were so many stipulations to be undone when, and if, Apollo could get you your eye back. How's your sight this fine evening?"

"Get on with it," Gaea hissed.

"Yes. So Daphne's curse is lifted?" They all eyed Gaea as Manannan cleared his throat, "I would love it if you took care of these matters as I list them so we can settle and dissolve this nasty document for good."

Gaea's returned eye glowed for a moment. "Done."

A dryad appeared, whispering to Hamadryades, who announced, "And confirmed."

"Ah, next was the freeing of his sister, Artemis. We've outlawed such servitude in this realm, especially after gaining so many rights for seers and oracles alike." Manannan motioned between Gaea and Artemis. "Please, do so..."

Artemis stood, stretching her arms out before Gaea. Gaea hissed at the watching eyes as a claw came closer, shackles appearing on Artemis's wrists. She tapped it and the manacles dissolved. Gaea kept her jaw taut with her building rage.

"Rise and stand with them." Artemis motioned as she cut down the middle of Cedric and the crew.

"That's your cue, Fen. Whatever unfolds next is fair game." Cedric released him, making his way forward to meet Angeline halfway. "You have definitely made some powerful friends, haven't you? I think they just saved our asses."

"I'm starting to think Gaea didn't mean for Romasanta to make it this far... ever." Angeline and Cedric rushed to the group, Alecto winking at Angeline. "Thank you."

"Has the bond of servitude been broken as promised?" Manny looked to Freya, and she waved her hand over Artemis, who kneeled before her.

"Yes, our trinity of queens has been restored." As Artemis rose to her feet, Freya hugged her. "Welcome back to the free world, my sister mage!"

"Ah, very well. Let's see; next was the dissolution of Gaea's law." Again, Manny cleared his throat. "This was ordained by the Nordic Alliance, Dryad Alliance, the Otherworld Trading Company, the Blacksmithing Faction, the Sibylline Sisters Sorority of Seers, the Trinity Daughters of Calatin, the..."

"Enough. I am very aware of who signed that ridiculous document." Gaea stood, and everyone tensed. "How dare you corner me like some beaten dog!" she howled, the cry blowing wind over them.

"Gaea." King Frey stepped through the doorway, and she shut her mouth. "I advise you to calm down and let the wizard do what he was tasked to do."

"And if not?" A wild look crossed Gaea's face.

"I'll devour you!" Fenrir erupted from the crowd, fur rising and his size twice fold. "You have wronged this man even knowing he is of your pack!" Anger rolled out of Fenrir, growling and barking. "An alpha who turns on the pack will die by the fangs of her pack."

The room fell silent, but Romasanta closed the gap with Fenrir. Giving him a few hearty pats on his leg, Fenrir backed his aggression down a few notches. The ether was thick in the air now.

"Tell me, have you been honest with me?" Gaea hissed. "Keeping your pact to not create new beings? Leaving that task to me?"

"Madame," Manny smirked, "I assure you my contract has that spell intact. After all, I am a wizard of my word."

"Fine." Gaea settled back into her throne, regaining her composure. "I will dissolve the curse laid on my children."

"Please do. The moment that comes into effect, this contract shall dissolve itself entirely." Manny walked into the fray where everyone in the room could bear witness, holding the parchment high. "Please, Gaea, this is the last remaining task, seeing fit that you had only dissolved this for Kronos previously and left your other children defenseless against his attacks."

"Are you accusing Kronos of single-handedly wiping out my other children?" Her tone was dark and sinister. "How could a mother sit back and allow such travesties to unfold?"

"Please, dissolve Gaea's law and free the rest of your children from servitude per Otherworld laws as promised," Manny demanded, his tone and stare stern.

"Very well." Gaea took a single claw, cutting open her palm. "Here. Take it."

She tossed a key covered in black, acrid blood across the floor. Miasma wafted from the metallic item, sending everyone scattering. There was a wave of whispers and murmurs. She stood, a wicked grin filling her face and her eyes wild, glowing. Again, the room darkened, and the ether thickened in the air. *There are only three demons strong enough to grab it.* Lillith went to take a step forward, but Alecto caught her arm and pointed a chin.

Cedric marched up to the key. "Where should I take this?"

"Ah, Vampire King!" Manny gleamed. "If you could do the honors, there's a padlock of sorts there behind her throne. Unlock that, and the law shall be nevermore."

"There's no Underworlder here—" Gaea inhaled sharply.

Cedric plucked it from the ground, marching past her. Gasps rang out as Cedric retreated, the contract in Manannan's hand burning up. As if sensing their freedom, Lillith and Pan appeared in a flash of roses. *He didn't realize I was here! Did he think I would be afraid to show myself or was this for show?*

"W-wait!" Lillith shot a look at Freya; she nodded. *She's allowing this.*

"No time to explain, but we need to leave. Now." Pan snapped his fingers.

Are they going to chase him down without me? Can they even do that?

CHAPTER 25

HAUNTING DREAMS

The swamp crept closer by the minute as Tony sat there, glaring aimlessly at the crackling fire. Inle would stand and disappear, only to return with more firewood or report no signs of anything. Tony offered to do so once, startled to see no traces of the huge corpses anywhere, let alone evidence of what took them. Irawaru slept deeply and Tony would glance at him in fleeting moments. Nothing about the dog gave him the impression this was a god of any kind. It reminded him of the dog his grandmother had, beige and shaggy, nothing but a floppy-eared mutt with a black nose and average size.

"How can you tell what he is?" Inle had finished throwing another log onto the fire. "He just looks like a dog to me."

Glancing over, he huffed in thought before replying, "Being a deity of health, wellness, and transition ... you can say it's in my nature to know. On that same note, aura readers or creatures who deal with binding spells or curses can also see through the veil."

"Will he ever be ... normal?" Tony gauged the painful look on Inle's face.

"Brother, normal has never existed alongside the fables of perfection and peace." He frowned and leaned back to stare up at the sky. "Granted, it never stopped anyone from aiming for those trivial things and many other matters. Perhaps one day he will find a way to change back, but..." Inle narrowed his eyes, pausing a moment before daring to speak further, "...perhaps he's happy being a dog."

Tony blinked. "Well, maybe?" Rubbing his chest, Tony laid down on his back and stared up at the swaying Spanish moss and branches. "Is it night or day?"

Inle squinted. "I suppose it's whichever one you need it to be."

Tony laughed. "How does anyone function like this?"

Smirking, Inle shrugged. "Why do we sacrifice ourselves for others in the name of love without knowing if they feel the same?"

Tony snorted, glancing over at Inle as he rose to his feet again. "Who doesn't want to know what it feels like to have someone love you unconditionally?"

Inle pointed at him, wagging his finger. "You, brother, are a smart one. Can't learn to love until you know what true love looks like."

Tony rolled his eyes before closing them. "I'm going to take a nap."

"Rest for the mind and heart is good for the soul." Looking all around, he sighed before adding, "I'm going to scout the area and see if there are any signs of trouble."

"Sounds good..." mumbled Tony as he drifted off to sleep.

Darkness and quiet rolled over him, melting away the tension. A breeze rolled through the grass, the blades rustling in hushed whispers all around. The fire popped and crackled as a log crumbled and he found himself dreaming. The abyss was void of light as the sounds of his environment muted, making him feel like he was back standing in the unknown presence of whatever *Avalon* was.

"Prove you are worthy." The whisper made him turn a few times until he caught the glowing green jewels far off in the distance of the bleak nothingness.

"Who are you?" Tony inhaled deeply, holding it in as he waited for what was next. *Am I dreaming, or is this a strange spell?*

A deep chuckle rolled through the air, vibrating in his chest. "I am the forgotten. I am the dead. And I am your ancestor."

Sighing out the breath, Tony echoed, "Ancestor. Then you're Kronos?" *Shit, this is dangerous.*

"...noNonononoNononoNoNoNoNoNonono..." The strange, harsh echoing of the word was unnerving as a cold wind blew all around him.

"But an ancestor?" Tony circled back, losing the eyes in the darkness, heart thudding hard in his chest.

Fingers tapped his shoulder, and he spun to find nothing, just words lingering, "Yes, to you, the new one... the unplanned one..." The words were spoken as if by someone just out of view, walking circles around him.

"My titan, my human, my child made from her essence and mine in hopes of bringing about change."

Tony swallowed, his throat aching with the rise of anxiety. "I thought that was Cedric." *If this thing is involved, it should know something, right? Isn't the plan to build Cedric up to face Gaea and her army? I mean, that's where I thought this was all leading, but...*

"He is the second coming..." hissed the voice from all directions. "You are both my mirth and the affliction of my own making."

"Of your making?" Tony's gut knotted as something alarming stirred at his core. *Wait, is this thing implying I'm related to it and not Kronos? But that can't be right. I mean... can it?*

"Yes," the voice whispered into his ear, the breath tickling across his skin, making him freeze. "I wandered the Mortal Realm, watching and waiting."

Tony's pulse raced, thoughts trying to decode the riddles. "What about my connection with Cedric?"

"He held *her* magic." Clawed hands crossed over his eyes and mouth, the whispering in his ears continuing. "Listen well, last child of Aether. You will be tested; this is just one path, but the eyes will be here soon, and I will not be able to interfere nor protect." A burning sensation began to build inside him, and Tony tried to shift uncomfortably. "You will need to prove your worth to those who guard the realms. Know I have given you the last seed, the one that harbors my will and the power to break what stands before you and..." The blood in his veins was on fire as his breath quickened, but still, he couldn't speak or see in the monster's embrace. "... any who shall do her any more harm. I give my blessing, but now you must show me you will take her as yours, take this power and make it your own, and teach them the value of your humanity despite it all."

Tony's body jolted, and he took a step forward. Sweat glided across his skin, soaking him as he stood on a footpath. Looking all around, there were no signs of Inle, Irawaru, or even the fire. The swamp bordered both sides as he panted. Every fiber of him was on fire. Power mingled and snaked through him like a foreign spirit trying to push his own out. A wave of pain rolled through him, and he gripped at the fire searing inside his chest. The monster of Avalon had given him something, something that could burn away his existence, and fear shook Tony.

"Shit!" He stumbled through the grass to lean on a cypress tree.

Jaw clenched; *something is wrong with me. What the fuck did it do to me?* A roar escaped him, the burning sensation peaking as if all that made him human inside was burning away. He couldn't bear to inhale; his eyes widened as he descended to a knee. *Am I going to die?* He gasped for air, the pain throbbing a few times, burning through his veins, and rose again. Closing his eyes tight, he tried to calm himself through the waves of the rising fever rolling through him.

"What did you do..." Cringing, he swallowed and looked at the water's edge. *I need to cool down...*

Crawling over to it, he reached his hand into the water, and it boiled in his cupped hands. *Fuck this. Tuck and roll.* He let himself fall into the water with a splash; steam rose above him and blocked the sky overhead. Another wave of agony made him curl, drowning in the water that boiled all around him. *What spell was cast on me? I feel like a nuclear reactor over-heating and threatening to melt down!* As the core of the heat exploded through him, he roared and stood in the swamp with rage and torment fueling him. Something snapped; a chord in his soul popped free as if something trapped had been set loose within his core. Relief washed over him, and he could breathe again. Panting, he climbed to the shore and laid down exhausted. The excruciating pain still sharp in his mind, he searched inside himself with a bewildered expression.

What has it done to me? Lillith's mark throbbed, and his pulse quickened with a sense of arousal. *Or did it do something to her, too? Was he really after her?*

CHAPTER 26

THE NEED FOR TWO KINGS

L illith's chest tightened with the rise of her panic. *Hamadryades, you wouldn't dare let those two go without me. What if they decide... if Alecto decides...* Inhaling deeply, she found reprieve free of the thicker magic in the air. All around, she heard the cheers and bickering of Cedric and the team. *What will happen to Tony now that Cedric is back? Will having two King Incubi in this realm cause issues?*

"What is this magic that I sense coming from you?" Artemis's voice jolted Lillith. "This isn't something we intended, but ... it's dangerous."

"I..." Lillith searched the shaman's eyes. "It's not of his doing, not intentionally."

"I see." Artemis glanced back at her brother Romasanta rejoicing. "Do they know?"

"Not the extent, but Hamadryades does." Artemis whipped back to Lillith with her eyes wide. "And what does she—"

"They want to pass judgment." Lillith raised her chin, heart fluttering.

"Alecto and Freya have caught on?" A scowl deepened on Artemis's face.

"Yes. Well, he left a mark, and when he activated it, they felt the power behind it." Lillith huffed and added, "And I imagine you are more sensitive to magic."

"I thought the plan was to use two kings to overpower her, but instead, we have whatever he's becoming." Artemis's eyes shot a glance at Cedric, who seemed to be gauging who all returned with them. "And now whatever you fools have done in my absence."

Cedric's voice caught their attention, "... that voice from before."

"Ah, yes, did you figure it out?" Romasanta scratched his jaw. "You were back rather fast; it surprised me."

"Well, she said she would meet us here in Avalon, but..." Cedric paused as a chill rolled through Lillith. *Could he mean...* "Gaea had Phoebe in a locked room."

"My... my mother?" Romasanta's eyes widened. "I thought she ran off?"

Shit, this whole time, we thought the titans and Greek gods had abandoned us, but they've been imprisoned this entire time? Lillith gave Artemis a heated glare. *How much has she kept from the rest of us? How could she not say or find a means to let us know that...*

"I'm starting to think Gaea needed your sister under lock and key, too." Cedric caught Artemis's attention, and she turned, marching up to him as he drawled, "Speaking of the devil..."

"Cedric," Artemis hissed. "What have you done?"

Everything we've planned over the centuries is starting to crumble in a matter of days, if that. Lillith swallowed. Her stomach knotted and her body tensed. *Will we fail before even moving forward from here?*

"Done?" Cedric blinked.

Wait, is she pissed about...?

"We had a plan, and you go and waltz over to grab the key, you imbecile." Artemis scoffed, "You painted a target on your back!"

Cedric roared back, "Like I wasn't already a target! Who else could have picked the damn thing up, huh? It was clear to me she thought she was using a power play."

"And so, you thought to take it upon yourself to deflate her ego to inflate your own?" Artemis marveled, swinging her arms about. "It is beyond me how you've survived in this world at all."

"A lot of blood, sweat, and tears ... and part of that is your doing, old hag." Cedric pointed at her with disgust written across his face.

Silence took hold. *Well, I suppose a lot of this is falling apart. He's figured it out and is up to speed, so what are we going to do now? If we can't keep Cedric on our side for the fight, we aren't strong enough to overtake Kronos, let alone Gaea.*

"Is everyone here, Pan?" The sing-song voice sent chills through Lillith.

"Yes, Phoebe. I think I grabbed everyone you requested." Pan turned to the door and bowed. "It's good to see you, Sister. I didn't think we'd get a chance to rescue you."

Pan knew about this. A sinking feeling rolled through Lillith. *What else have they all kept me in the dark about? Have I been out of the loop because I'm technically part of Gaea? Did they think I would... I would betray them?* An aching sensation tightened in her chest as she frowned at Pan, and he flinched. *You fucking owe me for this one. And you know it!*

"Ah, that reminds me." Phoebe turned, meeting Cedric's gaze, and bowed. "I am in your debt. Thank you."

Everyone in the room faced Cedric. The looks seemed baffled and confused. He frowned, unsure how to read the mood shift in the room. *Idiot doesn't realize how important it was to at least have Phoebe free and on our side. Reckless and unknowing of the weight of his actions, as always.* Cedric sighed and what little urge for fight and anger he had left was gone. *He seems drained, even exhausted. I can't say I don't agree; if the ether in the Otherworld impacted him much like myself, then he must be...*

"Many of you need to rest," Phoebe addressed the room. "But I do have one important offer for you all. Gaea must be taken down. She may have followed her contractual duties, but I assure you, she will continue to aid Kronos until he summons her into this realm. We cannot allow this to happen."

"Shit." Cedric's mumbled words jolted Lillith as he paled.

Something's wrong. All of a sudden, I can't feel Tony's connection and something about Cedric's power is shifting. I need to get back to Hamadryades!

"C-Cedric?" Angeline's words stumbled. "You look pale and..."

"I just... I need rest," Cedric reassured.

"I implore you all, please join me and my brothers and sisters in our fight against Gaea," Phoebe continued. "She has already placed targets on many of you, as has Kronos."

"Then let the War of Roses begin," Manny chimed in, bowing before Phoebe. "I will gladly assist where I can, Goddess Phoebe."

Fucking read a room, Phoebe. Oracles are so socially awkward, but clearly, the unstable aura is making most of us uncomfortable. Something's not right, so... "Everyone out," Lillith cut in, the mood changing to dire. "Cedric, Angeline, Pan, Phoebe—you four, stay."

The room cleared immediately, and after some stolen glances, they knew why. Cedric wobbled where he stood, holding his face with one hand. His breathing rattled; Angeline pulled him to a chair, forcing him to sit. His speech slurred and muffled, and he didn't seem to hear any of the questions asked of him.

I can feel it; there's something happening involving the power tied to Tony, him, and me. There was a chance, but the tie with Tony went dark. Someone's interfering, and if it's hitting Cedric like this, what is happening to Tony?

"Cedric, listen." Lillith stood, arms crossed. "This is my fault; I didn't think about the complications of two King Incubi."

"Just re-establish your link with him as the queen," offered Pan.

"Fuck that," Cedric breathed.

"No, if I do that, then my connection to Tony might put him in a similar state. We still don't know where he is." Desperation weighed down on Lillith. "We need those weapons, and we need both of them to maintain their power. I don't know what to do."

"He needs a queen, yes?" Phoebe tapped her lips and looked at Angeline. "And it seems he has one."

That's why. Because I bonded with Tony, I threw the balance into a spiral, but...

They all turned to Angeline as she winced. "But I'm no succubus."

"But you are, my dear." Pan smirked at Lillith. "Looks like you have an apprentice, after all."

You've got to be fucking kidding me—I don't have time for this shit! "Are you two implying I pass this shit curse to someone?" Lillith's blood boiled with rage.

"More like, share it... it might even break it." Pan gave her a mischievous grin. "Oh, why didn't I think of this sooner? It's a rather barbaric way... No, no. This should work wonderfully!" Pan rushed to his desk, opening and closing drawers. "Oh, you'll hate me for this, but yes. Sometimes a curse can be split and shifted into a yin-yang effect. Daoists were so clever."

"I am not giving this to her!" Lillith chased him, hot on his heels. "I'm used to it, but she... I can't do this to someone else."

"That curse—was it Father, or Mother's, doing?" Phoebe held her chin in thought.

"Mother's." Lillith calmed. "Mother made me, but when Father insisted on making me fertile like her, she..."

"Right, right." Pan turned and opened another drawer. "Isn't that also how we ended up with Three's Company: Gyges, Cottus, and Briareus?

Ha, Dad wanted her to give birth to mankind; she agreed to it and had a botched abortion, expelling it from her body into those three. So gross..."

What does this have to do with me and my curse? Are they mad?! I can't willingly split my curse with her. Who wants to be like this? Like me? I don't even want it!

"Pan," Phoebe warned. "It seems that these two were made with Father's magic."

Lillith and Pan froze, paling. *What did she just say? It couldn't be...* "Are you sure?" Lillith whispered.

Phoebe nodded. "Positive."

Then that means... Tony... but it couldn't be. Wait, even with Cedric. Then that means he's still here, alive, but why? Swallowing, Lillith couldn't get her heart to slow down.

"I don't care," Angeline interjected. "If it means saving him, I am willing to do anything."

Cedric's eyes rolled back, and he fainted. A burning sensation rolled forward in Lillith's gut, and she dropped to her knees. Tony's mark was on fire. She inhaled swiftly, but the pain made it nearly impossible. *What the hell is happening to us...? This isn't my magic...* Glancing up at Phoebe, she saw the goddess smirk. *What does she know? Fucking oracles.* The pain spiked and Lillith passed out.

CHAPTER 27

LUST VERSUS LOVE

C almer now, Tony lay on the ground with a forearm thrown over his eyes. His heart had reached a calm, but nothing felt the same. *This is the second time I've felt as if my body is foreign and new to me. I fucking hate this... When will the changes stop?* Every muscle felt taut, much like the moment he started to change with the curse after he and... *Lillith. What happened to her?* He reached out through his mark, but there was no reply from hers. *Nothing.* Sitting up, he glanced through the gray and black landscape of the bayou before him. Inhaling deeply, he held it there, thinking before something crossed his mind. *What about ... our bond? Did this break it? Did I change into something ... else?*

Closing his eyes, he searched deep within himself. The sense of connection, though quiet after the night in Avalon before he came here, was still there. *It took a hit, but there's something still there, though not our marks. Is it the bond?* An electrical exhilaration made him shiver and lust boiled up through his core. He inhaled swiftly; a soulful desire gripped the thread tugging at his core, and there, he could feel Lillith. A wave of arousal chimed from him to her, only to be met with a pleasure that made him moan. *Holy shit, what was that? This makes the mark look like child's play.*

Sitting up, he blinked as his skin pimpled. *It's as if I can feel her touching me, kissing me, and even feel...* Swallowing down the nerves, he closed his eyes to try once more. This time, the wave he sent reflected the sensation of submissive desire he held. In a flash, his body tensed under the provocation reflected at him as if she stood before him, hand on his neck. He folded forward under the weight of it. His body buzzed on the verge of peaking, and he panted with want.

"Fuck me..." Shaking it off, Tony stood and shuddered once more. "That's on a completely different level than the mark." *No, that lets us transfer power. This is a connection of desire, of being one...* His eyes jerked up, feeling the lustful desire of something else coming from the swamp before him. *Shit, I think I might have sent a wave out. This could get dangerous, but something is strange about how the power is working. I'm a little more aware of its function. What the hell did Avalon do to me? Or do I call that thing Aether, now that he's let his name slip?*

Another pull, and he swiveled his head to see a woman behind a large cypress. Her hat hid everything but smiling red lips, large golden disc earrings, and the golden chokers stacked on her thin neck, which made her tall and slender in appearance. Her red dress was form-fitting and made the curves of her chest and hips dip in and out of view from behind the trunk. A white boa fluttered in the breeze and danced loud in his eyes against her mulatto skin and the dark tones of the swamp framing her. Dark hair fell behind her in large, frizzy, wavy locks swaying just behind her lower back. His eyes fell to the leg peeking out from the hip-high slit; until his view was met with a group of douen.

Frowning, Tony reached for his hilt and was met with nothing. *Shit, I left it at camp... wherever that is. Did I sleepwalk, or did Aether just snatch me up and dump me here on purpose? Asshole.* She shifted again and he could see flowers, ribbons, and moss decorating the hat almost enough to hide the set of small horns. *Ha, who is she fooling?* A wave of lust hit him from her again and Tony snorted. *Sorry, that's not enough to do shit to me. This must be the one Inle was looking for. What was her name again?*

A giggle escaped her as she stepped out from behind the tree. The douen stayed crowded at her feet. Tony arched a brow and crossed his arms. *Those chicken goblins freak me out. Nothing sexy about this, lady.* She sauntered closer; her giggle haunting and unnatural as the pendulum of her gait and hips added to her attempts to seduce him. Another wave of provocation slammed into him, and he grunted with annoyance. *I think she thinks she's seduced me. She's got nothing on Lillith.*

Tony narrowed his eyes. A cow tail slid into view behind her and retreated suddenly. With each step, her breasts bounced within the open top of the bodice and corset, which he hadn't noticed initially. She bit her lip, pulling the skirt over her other leg and the douen retreated as she came within arm's length. Tony tensed as another wave of lust rolled from her and he snuffed it out within himself instantly.

"Sorry to tell you, but I'm taken, lady," Tony gruffed.

Her head tilted; her face remained obscured by the floppy wide-brimmed hat as her red lips frowned. *"Eres un hombre guapo. Ahora, entrégate a mí."* Another hard blast of wanton desire rolled from her.

"Sorry, I don't speak Spanish either, but," Tony sent a blast of incubine lust into her, and she stumbled back, "I don't think you're paying attention; I'm not one to fall for that." Another push of lust, and he saw the cloven hoof as she stumbled back again and the douen circled him, hissing. "Guess it doesn't work on creepy chicken goblins, but you definitely can feel the threat this has."

"How dare you..." she hissed, the brim of the hat lifting to expose cracked flesh surrounding blood-red eyes with black pupils. She looked like a broken porcelain doll with sharp teeth.

"Well, I suppose we wait for—" Tony jerked back as she lunged forward with a clawed hand. "Look, you don't want to do this."

"¡Cobarde!" Another swipe and her hat fell off.

Devilish horns rose sharply from the top of her head as her claws grew longer. The douen bit at his legs, taking chunks out of his shins and feet. *I really miss my boots right about now.* A shiver rolled through him. His own horns grew, and he blasted a more dominating aura over her. *Douen don't seem phased, too dumb of a creature, but with her, I can gain the advantage.* A gasp escaped the serrated row of teeth now visible between the painted candy-apple red lips. She fell to her knees, panting as sweat began to form across her skin.

"You're in a losing battle with me." Swinging around, Tony slashed out with his own clawed hand, shredding three of the goblins. "Annoying."

They scattered, abandoning the succumbed devil woman. *"¿Cómo es posible que no te enamores de mí?"* She tried to stand, and Tony pushed the aura over her once more, making her scream and shriek in frustration, face and bosom flushed from her arousal rising against her will. "How can you not love me?" she managed to snarl up at him in her fury.

Squatting, Tony smirked. "There's a difference between lusting after something or someone and truly being in love with someone."

"I have taken many men already in love," La Diablesse spat, hissing.

Tony nodded, and after a moment, added, "But being a creature of lust has taught me there is a difference. As a man, before I met *her*, I would have had a tough time telling the difference." Standing, Tony marched a few feet away, looking for signs of the douen. "I guess your little chicken demons aren't much for a fight, huh?"

"*Vete a la mierda, perro enamorado.*" Charging forward, she was faster than he expected.

A spear thudded into her midair and she flew off into the waters of the swamp. Turning, Inle panted from running and Irawaru was growling at his feet. A screech rose from her so sharp it made Tony cover his ears. Inle pulled the dagger from his belt and tossed Tony his sword. Before Tony could follow him to give chase to the wounded devil woman, Tony caught the loogaroo breaking through the brush and jungle behind his companions. Pulling the blade free, he threw the sheath to the ground. Irawaru ran past, following Inle into the water with a splash while Tony traded spots and gave them La Diablesse.

"I got the loogaroo. You kill whatever the fuck that thing is," called Tony as five loogaroo came sliding to a stop in front of him. "I really don't like this place. Everything bites."

Snapping and snarling, one came charging forward. As Tony swung the sword, black flames lit the blade and shot out in a crescent shard of magic. The drain of power that pulled from him made him drop to one knee in surprise as he finished the swing. All the loogaroo were sliced in half in a flash, blood spraying out from where the black flames had cut. The trees behind them buckled and fell with a great drumroll of thuds. Wobbling to his feet, Tony turned and caught Inle knocking La Diablesse out. At his back, Irawaru barked and snapped at the douen until they sensed his approach and scattered. Taking another look at the splattered loogaroo and trees, Tony sighed.

"So how pissed off does Papa Boi get when you cut a tree down?"

Inle dropped the woman and rushed to bind her wrists and ankles. "La Diablesse is caught, but I don't think he'll let us off lightly if we decide to chop a tree down."

Rubbing his forehead, Tony glanced back at him with an apologetic expression. "How about, roughly," a quick look back and he returned to Inle's worried face, "Ten or so?"

"Brother, please be joking." Inle clambered up the hill and froze. "Muddascunt."

"New sword. Not sure how to use it, and, well..." Tony cringed, a thought crossing his mind. "I don't suppose you can heal trees?"

Inle gave him a nasty look as Irawaru whimpered, covering his face with a paw. "You're a funny guy, brother. But we're in big trouble with Papa Boi over this."

"Make a run for it? To Salamandra?" offered Tony.

"We have to now. It'll slow us down carrying La Diablesse—"

Tony scooped her up and lugged her over his shoulder. "Lead the way. I can do the heavy lifting."

Inle and Irawaru snorted and began their walk deeper into the swamp. Tony glanced back at the mangled mess of loogaroo and trees. He sensed something there watching them, but saw nothing. Adjusting La Diablesse on his shoulder, Tony groaned. *I'm making a mess out of this, but how was I supposed to know that my blade can cast magical flames?*

"Hey, why were you being chased by loogaroo?" Tony picked up his pace to walk beside Inle.

"Not me," Inle pointed down to Irawaru. "They're chasing him. I think it's the idea that another canine is treading on their territory. They'll keep coming until we get onto the black sands."

"Black sands?"

"Salamandra's territory is covered in black volcanic sands," explained Inle.

Looks like I'm getting closer. Now, if we can avoid whatever Papa Boi is. If this bitch on my shoulder and the loogaroo didn't faze Inle, I'm a little hesitant to face the guy he'd rather run away from. Granted, I wonder what Inle would think of Boto or Cedric? Would they be on par with Papa Boi? Am I on par with Papa Boi?

CHAPTER 28

THE THORN OF PAN

Darkness surrounded her. *Did I pass out? Am I dreaming?* Turning, she looked all around and found nothing. *Maybe a spell?* Her mind flashed to Cedric passing out and the moment she had been engulfed in pain. *Pain... real intense and unrelenting pain.* A shiver rolled over her and she hugged herself in the black nothingness. *I've been feeling that again after so long; it scares me.*

With no signs of anything, she began walking as the aching in her chest grew tighter with each step. *If we passed out, then Tony definitely got knocked out.* Using her power, she tried to reach out through her mark and halted. The magical rope no longer found its anchor where she had left it in Tony. Her pulse began to race even faster.

"Come on. Wake the fuck up, Lillith." Gritting her fangs, she pinched her arms, yielding no results. "Am I in a coma?" She spun again, her eyes seeing nothing through the dark.

Biting her lip, she started marching again. Her fists swung as her fear turned into anger. *This isn't a dream. Something broke between the three of us. This magic stems from me. I've got to figure it out, or Tony's going to be in danger.* Again, she stumbled to a stop. Looking at her palm, she tried to muster the power of her mark once more, holding it out and away. At first, nothing stirred.

A crackling sound hissed to life in the abyss. She turned toward it, and her palm warmed when she pointed it in that direction. *Well, better than nothing, I suppose.* Swallowing back her worry, she marched in the direction of the sound, the warming sensation slowly growing hotter. On occasion, she would have to turn left or right, like a boat lost at sea trying to navigate a changing tide. *What is this? Where the hell am I?*

She furrowed her brow; something glowed in a heap up ahead. Part of her wanted to rush forward, while another part of her brought her pace to a slower, more cautious gait. As she closed the gap, the glowing form looked more like a heap of flesh and it became hot like a fire. Her heart leaped, and she blinked, still far off, but close enough to recognize it. The muscles in his back, the way his arms tensed as he balled into the fetal position, and even the horns curling from his head.

Tony.

She stopped, her heart racing like the beating of a panicked canary in a cage. Glancing all around, she seemed wary of all that was unfolding. Still, nothing but darkness greeted her. The rise of her anxiety made her breathing shallow and fast as her mind circled endlessly: *Dream? Spell? Passed out? Dreaming... trapped... spell... coma...where am I? Which is this?*

The heat rose higher, and she flinched as it stung at her skin like a bonfire gaining momentum. Tony hissed, steam spewing from between his clenched teeth. She could see the silhouette of his face, sweat dripping from his nose and chin. Eyes tight as he rode out the uncanny heat boiling forth at his core.

Lips whispered in her ear, "If you intend to keep him as your mate, now's your chance to break free of Gaea's wrath."

She spun, but no one stood in the nothingness that filled this place. Tony's roar brought her back to him, and she watched in desperation. *What do I do?* Another howl escaped him, and it was enough to break her free. Rushing forward, she didn't care if the heat erupting from him burned her flesh. Cupping his cheeks, the panic in his face broke her heart.

She pressed her lips against his. They burned as they parted, and the steam stung in her mouth. A wave of desire escaped her, and the heat faltered for a fleeting moment. Tony kissed her back, his arms burning across her back. Arousal flowed from him like cool waves, calming the flames that had burned at them both as they embraced one another. He pulled away, blinking.

"Is this a dream?" he muttered.

"I don't know," she answered. "But what the hell was that?"

"Avalon did something to me," he answered. "But I think it's Ae—"

Jolting upright, Lillith found herself in Tony's room. *Did that Avalon asshole just tug or corrupt our bond?* Flopping back down, she inhaled deeply. His scent floating up from the pillows only made her chest ache, and she bit her lip. *I actually miss him, don't I? It feels so strange.* The fire crackled, and she rolled to her side to see Pan sitting in the chair, elbow on thighs as he leaned forward, staring aimlessly at the bed. Stiffening, it took a moment for Pan to realize her eyes were open and glaring in his direction. He had a deep frown and opened his mouth to say something, but decided to close his mouth instead.

"Did you find Glorianda?" Lillith dodged the question lingering in the air between them.

"N-no." Pan huffed air from his nostrils and added, "But according to the bartenders, she had a good time and found someone to go home with." Sitting up, he cleared his throat. "If she wants to club hop and enjoy a spree of one-night stands, so be it. As long as she doesn't bring about a calamity like last time, no harm, no foul."

"I see." Lillith hugged the covers and furs into herself, Tony's scent thick on them. "So why bring me here and not my apartment or castle?"

He half-laughed. "Yeah. About that." Motioning at the door, he seemed annoyed. "Every door took me here. I can't teleport; something or someone is blocking my abilities."

Lillith sat up, heart fluttering from her time with Tony. "Who do you think it is?"

"Someone strong enough to detain a titan?" Pan rubbed his jaw, thinking it through. "Considering they were fucking with Tony before the celestial lock was destroyed, the only person I can think of is long dead."

"Aether," Lillith shuddered, saying the name out loud. "But why now, of all times?"

"I ... don't know." Pan stood and stretched, stifling a yawn. "So, what happened to you? Was that connected to Cedric?"

"We suspected two kings in the Mortal Realm would conflict, but that wasn't it. Something else happened." She hugged her knees and thought back to the sensations. "I think, I think Aether has done something to Tony. Maybe, there's something else he's doing to those two?"

"But what would he want with Cedric to the point of making that monster pass out cold?" Pan walked to the table of food and plucked a grape, popping it into his mouth.

"It's as if..." A chill rolled over her. "It's as if Aether forced the King Incubus curse out of Tony and into Cedric? I don't think he was able to get rid of it, but he may have found a way to pass the buck to someone more accepting of it or immune to it? I don't know... it's a guess."

Pan choked on the second grape, coughing for a second before rasping, "What makes you say that?"

Lillith shot him a disconcerting expression. "Check. Our bond shifted, and the marks were burned away. Someone cast some powerful magic."

Walking over to the bed, Pan sat and motioned for a hand. Reluctantly, she handed it to him. Memories of Tony's reading made her nerves tighten. With a flick of his fingers, Pan began invoking the underwriting to reveal any bindings and curses she possessed. She watched as his brow furrowed. Abandoning that hand, he grabbed her other wrist and tried again. Her heart raced as he shot her a bewildered expression.

"M-may I?" Pan whispered, unsure of what he was seeing in the old magic traces. "I know this is the more painful method, but I need to see..."

Inhaling deeply to steady her nerves, Lillith began to unlace the tunic. Despite passing out, no one had dared to touch her in her vulnerable state. *Granted, if Tony had been here...* Shaking her head, she pulled the tunic off and sat naked before Pan. Eyes tight, she waited for the pain that would unfold. *He's only done this once before on me, and I still can't wipe it from my memory.* The smell of blood and flowers made her tense. A finger drew a rune over where her heart raced in anticipation of what would unfold next. Pan's palm pressed firmly over it, and they both stiffened.

"I'm sorry," he murmured apologetically. "I never thought there would be a need to do this twice."

"We need to know," she reassured.

A thorn ripped deep into her heart and soul. A blood-curdling cry escaped her despite her attempt to stifle it. Her eyes were wide with the pain that engulfed her. There were no physical aspects, but the magic was designed to uncover any deep-rooted curses that lay deep within one's heart and soul that one might not be able to see. *This is how we found out about the initial curse...* Tears streaked down her face as Pan cringed, working fast as his black, soulless eyes teared up. He pulled away, and with it, she could breathe again.

Hugging the covers to herself, swallowing, she insisted through her pants, "So, so tell me, what, what has happened?"

A tear rolled down a cheek on Pan's face, and a smile crested his lips. "It's all gone."

"What's gone?" Lillith blinked, the words strange.

"Gaea's curse is gone. Your connection with her... gone." Pan searched the air and his thoughts for a minute. "All that remains is the bond with Tony. It's as if his bond swallowed it and expelled it, but that's dangerous magic. Both of you could have died... I wonder what made that lovesick fool think of that as a solution to free you, but does he know anything of that caliber?"

"I think he had help," she laughed, a great weight lifted as the tears started to fall faster now in celebration of her shackles officially being dissolved. "Can you believe it...? I'm free, brother."

Pan smirked. "Yeah, you're free, but what about Angeline and Cedric?"

Covering her face, she began to sob at the relief. *Thousands of years with no solution, no help, no way out from under that cunt's curse... and to think...*

"Will there be a way to fix Cedric? Granted, I'm afraid to even ask to check his bonds and curses." Looking at his phone, Pan pulled away and began pacing. "They say he hasn't snapped out of it, and no one can get near him thanks to that vicious living armor."

Swallowing, Lillith turned to Pan. "I might know a way after seeing what happened to me, but I'll need you to take me to Hamadryades. We'll have to find a way to get the answer from Tony, and seeing that the two sisters of the Amazon trinity want to test him..."

"Fuck. Testing Tony? Don't you mean passing judgment on whether he's allowed to live? Why can't we catch a break?" Opening the door, Pan sighed to see the hallway. "Can you give me some time to prep first?"

"Y-yeah. I want to wash this shitty rune off anyhow." Wiping the tears from her face, Lillith scoffed, "And I need some time to let my emotions settle. I will not be able to do Cedric and them any favors until I know Tony's safe."

"Agreed." Pan nodded, the door thudding shut.

Silence fell, and she looked around the room as lustful memories rolled through her. As always, the steaming tub of water waited on the far side, ready for whoever sought to cleanse themselves. Shedding the last of her leather gear, she slid into the tub and cried. Tears of joy, of pain, of frustration, of ... every emotion she had denied herself in an attempt to harden her heart. For the first time since her creation, she could allow herself to feel, and more importantly, *love. By the fates and old gods, I absolutely love this foolish man that I was willing to forfeit my life for, and he's willing to do the same for me. What a blessing and strange new curse I face.*

CHAPTER 29

CONSEQUENCES

The heat and humidity had increased drastically as they continued marching through the wetlands. At times the mud and swamp would have them waist-deep in the water, legs aching to push through the soft, muddy floor. Inle would signal for everyone to pause on occasion. There was no mistaking the fact that something or someone was tracking them down with a flutter of birds or the snapping of a branch. It had gotten dangerous enough that Irawaru needed to be carried in Tony's other arm, where he whimpered, clinging onto his shoulder.

I don't understand how this dog is some powerful deity. Still seems like a Plain-Jane dog to me. He's shivering so bad.

Somewhere beyond the trees, he could hear the rumbling and gurgling sounds of the volcano getting closer. *Finally, feel like I've made some ground. I was starting to think I'd be lost in this swamp forever.* The tremors would send limbs, leaves, and moss falling all around the swamp from time to time, obscuring any hopes of grasping where the entity following them could be coming from or moving closer. All around, mysterious growling, chirping, and even the occasional splash unfolding only an arm's length away had them all on edge.

Whispering, Tony drudged closer to Inle, "Who or what is Papa Boi? Whatever it is, it's got you on edge more than that pack of loogaroo or La Diablesse."

"He's the protector of the land and animals here." Inle tilted his head, listening closely. "And I can't decide if he's closing in on us or if we've got Mama D'Leau on our side."

Tony huffed and Irawaru licked his face in reply as he shifted La Diablesse on his now aching shoulder. "Look, treat me like a fresh-off-the-boat mortal. None of these names mean anything to me."

"Brother, you make me worry for your well-being." Inle turned, spotting a dry patch up ahead and a footpath. "You come all this way to see Salamandra, and yet you don't know one name of the creatures who protect his domain. Then, there's that thing you call a sword; you don't know how it works, and it slew a pack of loogaroo in one swing." Pulling up out of the swampy water, Inle flopped onto the ground to give his soggy feet a rest. "And let's not count how much power you have on a physical level to not hesitate to face La Diablesse head-on."

Tony let Irawaru down first, then flopped La Diablesse beside Inle before joining him. "I've faced worse, I think." Tony shrugged.

"Like whom, or what?" Inle chuckled, giving him a skeptical look. "You're a strange man."

Smirking, Tony confessed, "Badbh and Boto. They trained me with the sword by beating it all into me over and over again."

"Muddascunt..." Inle covered his mouth as he sat back up, staring off into the swamp.

The tense expression and body language from Inle made Tony uncomfortable, and he changed the topic. "Enough about that. Let's keep going. I can smell sulfur, so the volcano has to be getting closer." Back to his feet, Tony reached for La Diablesse, but Inle's hand gripped his wrist.

Meeting his gaze, Inle signaled to be quiet and nodded up ahead on the footpath. There stood a bulky, grotesque creature. Its cloven-hooved legs and hairy humanoid top half sent chills through Tony. *Like a satanic Bigfoot, shit.* Tusks like a troll, horns like a goat, and beady red eyes set in yellow stared back at him. In one hand, it gripped a gnarled club while the other scratched its hairy chest. The fingers were short and stubby, a beard like a billy goat hung from its chin, and a loincloth with a satchel was all it wore. Moss hung from its horns while the hair across its body was filled with beggar's lice and other sticky seed pods. *Like a mangy dog, wonder if he's got ticks or mange.*

A low growl rolled from it, and the murderous intent slammed them, making Tony bite his tongue. *This is Papa Boi.*

"Look, I didn't mean to down the trees. I was defending myself and overshot." Tony threw up his hands, and he saw Inle's panicked look. *I did the damage, and he knows it with the way he's staring me down and not Inle. No sense in dragging them into being punished with me.*

A low grumble rolled out of Papa Boi, before baring razor-sharp teeth as it hissed at him in reply. The hand gripped the club tighter, and it took a few steps closer. Shadows were growing deeper and pulling in all around Papa Boi as he snorted and roared. *Boto is civilized. This, this is a monster.* They stumbled back, heels at the edge of the dry land, before it dropped back into the swamp. Tony looked over his shoulder, the water looking more like tar as bubbles rolled to the surface. *Something is there in the water, something he's had following us.*

Papa Boi turned to Inle, his voice harsh and rasping, painful to listen to as it attempted to speak. "Inle, is this one with you?"

"Look, Papa—" Inle started.

"No, I'm not." Tony cut in, stepping in front of Inle in a shielding manner. "Look, he was after this thing, and I helped with that as a favor to have him guide me to the volcano. I'm here to see Salamandra." Tony motioned to Irawaru. "While I was doing that, I came across this guy being chased by a pack of loogaroo, and they just wouldn't stop coming. I got desperate," he confessed.

Papa Boi raised his chin, unfolding his hunched posture to reveal that he was monstrously tall, taller than Boto, and had hunched to keep the horns on his head from tangling with the limbs of the cypress trees. Again, a toothy snarl and hiss escaped the black lips and gums of Papa Boi. The look he gave Tony was frightening enough to send his pulse racing. A shiver rolled over Tony as the last of the shadows connected; the land visibly shaded from all goodwill that had remained. *I totally fucked myself over with this one.* Tentacles wrapped around Tony's ankles and yanked hard. His chest slammed hard against the ground, knocking the wind from him.

"Tony!" Inle jerked around, shocked.

By the time Tony released the whine of a gasp to inhale, he was being dragged into the murky depths. Irawaru's barking muted as his head sank under the water's surface. The suckers on the tentacles dug hard into his flesh. Something bit hard across his shoulder, chomping and large enough to dig its teeth into the base of his neck, across his shoulder blade, and halfway down his upper arm. Tony's body ached with the want to breathe as he flailed his free arm, hoping it managed to break the surface of the water.

I don't know if I can come back after drowning. Or is it that I keep drowning every time I come back... Fuck this! I'm not in the mood to figure this out the hard way.

The tentacles wrapped tight around his leg and torso, tugging, and tearing. Tony thrashed his arm in the direction he could only hope was up. His one free leg seemed to not find the bottom of the swamp they had literally been walking through minutes before. A hand gripped his forearm and tugged hard. *Inle!* The creature didn't relent its constant gnawing where it attempted to eat him. Tony's head broke the surface of the water and he inhaled, desperate for air as his lungs stung.

As the creature broke the surface, Inle yelped and released Tony. Back to the depths, he fell with the offending creature. Reaching over to it, he dug his claws into it. It shrieked, letting go of his shoulder. The side of his torso lit on fire with pain as it found a new place to chomp and bite. *At least I have both arms again!* His hands found the shore and roots. Roaring under the water, a burst of bubbles led him to the surface, where he burst free from the swamp waters. He clawed his way to shore, the monster still gnawing at his side and tentacles shredding at his leg.

Able to breathe and see, Tony glared down to take in his assaulter. A shark's head tore into his torso, eyes black and lifeless, only hidden in white eyelids with each bite as serrated, triangular teeth cut into his body. Just past the gills, the creature had a body on par with that of a large octopus or squid. The suction cups were lined with their own tiny shark's teeth; blood poured from him. Horror filled Inle's face as he stumbled back and fell onto his ass. Irawaru lunged forward, biting and tugging at the tentacles wrapped around Tony's leg.

Tony shot a look down the footpath where Papa Boi still stood. Gritting his fangs, Tony turned back to the smaller monster. *I'm going to kill them all.* Claws ripped into the shark's head, shredding and slicing through even the bone and cartilage until it stopped moving. Irawaru tugged it off him as Tony stood, horns large and wounds healing fast. Papa Boi raised his chin, looking down at Tony.

"Quite da monster, no?" rasped Papa Boi.

"Papa Boi, he means no harm to your swamp," Inle pleaded.

Tony cracked his knuckles, snarling. "What else you got? Or are we going to go nose-to-nose?"

A smirk crept on Papa Boi's face before he began laughing, exclaiming, "*Kèt! Bon bagay!*" He rubbed his forehead and spoke more softly, "Have to give it to ya, Fanchon; not many would confess and live." Biting his lip, Papa Boi whistled an ear-shattering pitch. "Mama D'Leau will see to you boys. Take care." His expression shifted to a serious scowl, voice growling as he warned, "But this swamp isn't for you; leave my trees be."

Tony blinked. *What the hell just happened?* "Fanchon? You mean me?"

"Ya' you." Papa Boi hunched once more and pointed with his club. "You some kind o' demon from da Underworld, no?"

Blinking, Tony folded his brow. "No. Though, I suppose incubi are demons."

"Fanchon, for sure. *Sa pa regade m!*" he muttered, waving them off. "No more trees. Mama D'Leau, they are yours, cher."

"Very well," spoke a female voice as she reached down and caressed the torn-apart sharktopus creature. "Poor sweet lusca."

Spinning on his heels, Tony saw a woman standing on the water's surface, skin dark, hair wild and long. Her eyes were golden and slit, like that of a snake. A golden comb pulled some of her long hair to the side. The white gown she wore was a stark contrast against the black locks, and the skirt shifted unnaturally where her legs should have been. Instead, snakelike appendages kept her upright. Tony wondered if her walking on water was really her ability to rise to this height on the split snake body hidden poorly by her white skirt. A shudder shook his shoulders, thoughts filling him.

What other fate could I have met? I could have been a monster like these two. There was so much that could have happened, yet why was I lucky enough to be able to hold a form no different from who and what I was before? I may not be human, but I still look human, unlike these poor... monsters? Deities? What are they anymore in modern times where they're no longer worshiped? Where they are believed to be fiction, yet here they stand before me as solid, irrefutable fact. Is that why they have all retreated to the Otherworld or their domains? Here they can remind one another of their existence and possibly find... A sensation of lust flowed between Papa Boi and Mama D'Leau, and Tony's gut dropped.

"Forever Papa's loyal pet." The wounds on the lusca healed, and it came back to life, scurrying back into the swamp waters. "Go join your brothers and sisters, sweet child."

Another wave and Papa Boi glanced at Mama D'Leau with a look of longing before fading into the swamp. The darkness and shadowy aura faded and the sound of birds cooing and frogs croaking returned for the first time in a long while. The natural order restored, Mama D'Leau smiled with a tired look in her eyes. She flowed closer, her white dress recognizable now as a toga, and a golden rope at her waist served as a belt. Golden bracelets adorned her tiny wrists, and her thin, pink lips smiled sweetly.

Tony's mind wandered back to classic Greek mythology, and the thought fell from his lips. "Scylla."

Her eyes widened and her breath caught.

Inle's eyes bounced between them. "You know one another?" he marveled.

"No." Tony shook his head, rubbing his side where he swore he should have been still torn open or be missing something. "But I was a big fan of Greek mythology."

"I haven't heard me birth name in a very long time." Mama D'Leau's hand clasped over her heart, and she sighed. "But you are of Greek blood too, are you not?" She moved closer, excited now. "Whose offspring are you? Which of the gods and goddesses are you born from, godling?"

Tony's heart raced. *Shit, how do I even answer this? What did he call me? That's right...* "I've been told I'm a child of Ae—" A wave of arousal took his breath away. *Lil-Lillith?* Every part of his being tensed. *The mark's gone, but the bond...* Searching deeper in the swamp, he could feel the tug there, somewhere. "Lillith."

"A child of Lillith?" asked Scylla.

"No, no..." Tony blurted, still searching the swamp where he swore he sensed Lillith's presence. "Um, I recently became King Incubus."

"Oh my!" Scylla covered her mouth and flushed. "Then, a moment ago, you felt..."

Tony's face flushed, and he rushed reassuring words, "It's none of my business. Everyone needs someone, right?"

Inle snorted. "Brother, you just keep impressing and confusing me at every turn." He stood, patting Tony's shoulder with hearty slaps. "The fact you're healed without even needing my help truly amazes me."

Clearing her throat, Scylla motioned behind them. "We've set a table of food and a shelter. Please take rest." La Diablesse's corpse started to move and a snake from under Mama D'Leau's skirt lunged out and sank its fangs into her neck. "She's not dead; I imagine Salamandra wanted her alive. This one is hard to kill, strangely enough. Her deal with Beelzebub must have been strong."

Tony flinched. *And to think I was carrying it this whole time, and it was waiting to strike. And Beelzebub? Isn't that who caused trouble for Morrighan and Boto in Cedric's story? Something seems strange about it all... perhaps Kronos isn't working alone, and I don't mean Gaea. Does Lillith know, I wonder?*

CHAPTER 30

INSTINCTS

Checking the straps and belts of her armor, Lillith opened the door to head to Pan's office to only find Hamadryades's forest in view. Sighing, she bit her lip and looked at the door frame. *This is unnerving. It's as if Avalon knows my next move before I have even considered it. But how reliable is it? At what point, will this entity decide I'm a threat and turn on me?* Lillith balled her hands into fists, staring out aimlessly. Her heart beat hard against her chest, gut knotting. She took a step back, then another. *No, I can use Pan to get here. I won't follow its lead.* Another step back and she smacked into a wall of solid muscle. Stiff, goosebumps rolled over her entire being as her breath caught. Before she could find the courage to turn, two hands shoved her forward.

"I demand you to go," Avalon growled; by the time she stumbled to catch her balance, the door was gone.

"Fucking aggressive asshole," she spat.

"Well, that was an interesting bit of magic." Freya's brow raised high. "It's been a long time since I've seen something of that caliber. How about you girls?"

"Quite some time, indeed," Hamadryades murmured, sipping her tea and dodging the glances thrown in her direction.

Alecto furrowed her brow, staring where the door had once been. "Far too long, and now I wonder how much of this is *his* involvement."

"That's why we decided on this little venture, is it not?" Hamadryades let the petals of her teacup fall away as the ancient goddesses gathered all around Lillith. "What took you so long, child?"

Lillith's body stiffened, heart racing away against her will. "Forgive me." Lillith softened her voice and bowed her head in respect. "I ... fainted. It's been a long journey, and before facing this, I wanted to be well-rested to prevent any ... shortcomings on my part." Her confession stung, but none seemed surprised or dismissive of her words and honesty. *At least they took this as sincere. Though I regret not taking a moment to consult Phoebe.*

"Freya, this is your forte." Alecto motioned, clearing her throat to change topics. "Let's see what this new titan is up to, shall we?"

A flurry of ice and snowflakes left Freya's fingertips, swirling until a portal showing a swamp opened before them. Alecto gripped Lillith's arm while Hamadryades hooked an arm in the other. *Nothing about this feels friendly. This is their way to make sure I don't go anywhere as they observe and pass judgment. Please don't be doing anything fucking dumb, Tony.* A cold wind made Lillith shudder as the portal closed behind them. Catching Freya's expression as she sniggered, Lillith twisted to look to where her eyes fell.

There stood Tony, sidling himself between another deity and a dog and... *shit, Papa Boi?* They were too far off to hear the conversation; Freya watched the confrontation unfolding from a safe distance. Lillith couldn't keep her pulse from racing, and she shifted uncomfortably under her captors' grips. Alecto let go, crossing her arms with a bemused expression on her face. *Oh, this is just great. They know how green he is...* Hamadryades was unreadable as always, stoic and expressionless, while the dryad's thoughts could very well be betraying Lillith's hopes.

Why can't I do that? I've lost my touch because of him. Lillith took in Tony. His muscles taut in his back, shoulders wide, and arms thick muscled. *He's growing stronger, both physically and magically. This could make it hard to hide him any longer, or perhaps I need to accept we've long passed that moment already. I just wanted him to enjoy his human life a bit longer. Or is it I wished to join him in that simpler way of life?*

Tony stood tall, chin high, waving his hand at the others as if to own up to something while the other beat on his chest to point the blame at himself. *Hopeless hero.* Tentacles were bubbling and snaking out from the swamp waters. Lillith opened her mouth, but abruptly shut it. *He won't hear me, and I'll only cause more trouble if I do react.* Helpless, she watched as it gripped Tony's ankle and jerked him. A great thud and wheeze rang out. *Heard that from here,* she scoffed, rolling her eyes. Her gut twisted into knots as Tony was dragged under the black surface of the swamp waters.

Hamadryades tightened her hold and shook her head in warning before adding, "You are not to interfere."

"I know," Lillith spat, frustration in her tone.

"My, we get to see him fight, it seems." Freya grinned wildly, her Nordic love for battle shining through as her eyes glowed. "He's quite handsome even from this far off."

"That's Papa Boi," Alecto announced. "He's short-tempered, but he doesn't attack without reason." She scowled. "I wonder what trouble he caused."

"Not much." A new voice made all but Hamadryades jolt. "You wished to speak to me a moment, Queen of Dryads." Mama D'Leau bowed deeply before them. "It's a pleasure to see you after so long a time."

"Yes, I was wondering what your thoughts were on this creature invading your territory." The snakelike eyes glanced to where bubbles rolled up, tentacles and a hint of a thrashing hand on occasion breaking the water's surface. "Reckless, but full of good intentions."

"Oh?" Alecto gave Mama D'Leau a hug, her interest piqued. "I was wondering who had upset your beloved husband, my dear cousin."

Mama D'Leau giggled. "You know, Papa. He's just messing with the new godling. He's a little miffed about the trees, but more good than harm came from that one's actions at the end of it all. But what about this being has brought all of you out here to watch over him? Is this a Rite of Preeminence?" Lillith flinched, confirming her suspicions and her grin widened. "My, what a brave one to find himself under such judgment."

Shit, Scylla isn't dumb. This will bring more attention to Tony than...

"We may need to slay this one if he shows signs of going against the Trinity," Freya's voice cut like ice across them all. "If he proves a threat, we intend to resolve it here and now."

"I see." The words knocked the smiles from everyone, and after sighing, Mama D'Leau reassured, "He has worked hard to keep Inle and Irawaru safe. He even rid my swamp of La Diablesse and a pack of loogaroo that were causing issues for Papa Boi."

"Then why the fight?" Alecto watched as Tony broke the surface, gripping the shore and gasping for air with a lusca still attached to his torso. "He's not one to give up easily."

"It's just boys asserting dominance; what else?" scoffed Mama D'Leau, waving her hand to dismiss the blood-soaked events unfolding before them. "No need to worry. I'll give them rest before I cut them loose to Salamandra's territory. They'll need it. What else would you like to know?"

"What weapons is he using?" Freya glared intensely at the claws and horns that had shown on Tony. "It seems he's more than just a titan."

"He did the most damage with an enchanted sword, reeked of Badbh's magic," answered Mama D'Leau, brushing her skirt out in hopes of covering the snakelike appendages. "Why?"

"We fear there was meddling in his creation, or someone thought dead was involved." Hamadryades's expression made everyone pale with the aura that came with it. "But speak nothing of this."

Her power is startling. Lillith watched as blood painted the ground, the lusca's shark head chomping and ripping at Tony's torso as tentacles shredded his flesh. *You've got claws; use them! Ugh, this is painful to watch. Cedric and Romasanta would have flung that tiny beast at Papa Boi and spat in his face by now. How could I have fallen for someone so... so... soft?!*

"I see..." Mama D'Leau looked to where Tony rolled on the ground with the lusca, roaring in frustration and panic. "But I must say, there's not much about him that *screams* short-tempered or dangerous—"

Tony's aura exploded, the weight of it invoking a jolt and tightness in all of them. All eyes shot to Tony, his horns and claws larger now. His eyes glowed in the shadowed swamp, shining eerily like Avalon's and Cedric's. Lillith held her breath and bit her lip, waiting to see what the old goddesses would do or say, feeling the weight he unleashed. *This is on par with Cedric, but horrible timing...*

"My, that murderous intent—did you feel that?" Alecto shot a look at Freya, who nodded in agreement. "That's not from someone who is wet behind the ears. That's god-level and taught to him." Alecto glared at Lillith. "Did you teach him that?"

"No," blurted Lillith. "I didn't know you could read that deeply into it?" Lillith had goosebumps as doubts began to take root. *Do I really know this man... or... no, I can't waiver now? He's given me no reason to. He hasn't pried in my past and I've simply avoided asking him about his own. I can trust him. I have to trust in him now. We've... he doesn't realize...* Panic tightened in her chest as she kept the thoughts and truth from boiling up from her core.

The goddesses all watched unmoved as Tony ripped and shredded the creature from his body and stood. Blood painted him, crimson washing down him like a wet cloth. More words were exchanged between him and Papa Boi. Within a blink of an eye, Tony was healed in full, without lust and without Inle's assistance. Lillith swallowed and watched the goddesses.

That's not a good sign. They can't see that as an okay thing. That's as fast as Alecto or me.

"My, that didn't take long," Freya snorted.

"Haven't seen healing like that since Hades and I got into a scrape," confessed Alecto with a smirk. "Interesting fellow you've bonded with, Lillith."

"His name is Tony," snarked Lillith, tightening her arm around Hamadryades's own.

Hamadryades patted her arm. "He's proven to mean no harm, and using murderous intent during survival is smart."

Freya tilted her head. "True."

"Excuse me, Papa Boi has asked me to be there as well, and it seems he wishes to see these boys off with rest and food in their bellies." Mama D'Leau's stare stopped to meet Lillith's own. "What's so special about him to get you, of all titans, caught up in a rite?"

"None of your business," spat Alecto, eyes wild.

So glad she spoke before me.

"I'm sorry." Mama D'Leau swallowed. "I misspoke. Take care, cousin."

Scylla, or Mama D'Leau, rushed off and Lillith snorted. *Good riddance.*

Alecto grunted. "Nosy, that one."

"Always snaking her way into matters that don't concern her is in her nature, Alecto," offered Hamadryades. "Now, let's come listen to this conversation some."

Lillith was half-dragged closer, the smell and presence of Tony exciting her entire being. *What the hell happened to him, to us, the other night? That wasn't a dream. Something is different and—*

"Scylla." Tony's recognition of Mama D'Leau brought the goddesses to a halt, glancing at one another before glaring down at Lillith.

"I don't know how he knows her!" Lillith exclaimed in alarm.

"You know one another?" Inle marveled.

"No." Tony shook his head. "But I was a big fan of Greek mythology."

Lillith sighed in relief. *Mortals and their obsessions with those dolled-up tales about us.*

"That makes sense," nodded Freya. "Most mortals are into studying such things."

"I haven't heard me birth name in a very long time." Scylla's hand clasped over her heart, shooting a glance over her shoulder at the goddesses with a sigh. "But you are of Greek blood too, are you not?" A wicked smile and glimpse at Lillith before Scylla pried, "Whose offspring are you? Which of the gods and goddesses are you born from godling?"

That bitch. She's going to expose him! If they find out what he figured out, what I suspect at the rate this is going...

"I've been told I'm a child of Ae—"

Desperate, Lillith shot a wave of arousal through their bond. *Fuck, too much!* His eyes met hers and her heart leaped to her throat. *Can he see me? Us?* Alecto, Freya, and Hamadryades all stiffened and glared at her. *Oh no...*

"Why'd you do that?" hissed Freya.

"It slipped out?" offered Lillith, staring at Tony helplessly. *Please don't see us. Don't say my name...*

"Lillith," Tony muttered before his eyes shifted to look behind them and all around.

Lillith's legs felt numb with panic.

"That was close," Alecto chuckled. "But he felt you there; that's some bond."

"A child of Lillith?" asked Scylla.

"No, no!" Tony blurted, meeting Lillith's gaze again.

Can he see me? Lillith's stomach turned again. *If he doesn't, the longer we're here, the higher the chance he'll break Freya's spell and they'll know more than I've speculated about his ... bloodline.*

"Um, I recently became King Incubus." Tony looked away, and Lillith could breathe again.

My heart can't take much more of this. I swear he's staring me in the face.

"Oh, my!" Scylla covered her mouth. "Then, a moment ago, you felt..."

You're trying to get him to confess he felt me! You bitch!

Tony rushed a reply. "It's none of my business. Everyone needs someone, right?"

"And you've picked quite a someone," nudged Hamadryades. "Come, ladies, let's head back for a moment and watch from my viewing blossom, no?"

"Yeah, let's wait for something more exciting to happen." Alecto motioned to Freya, who opened the portal back up.

Freya and Alecto chatted with one another in hushed tones as they stepped through the portal. Lillith stood, staring at Tony. Another stolen glimpse of him with that lost puppy dog expression pulled at her. *Why does some part of me wish he saw me?*

"I don't think I've ever seen two people search for one another so hard amongst turmoil," Hamadryades whispered into her ear. "It seems he has a good heart, but what of his connections and past? Hmm?"

Lillith let her gaze break, and she gave Hamadryades a stern expression. "He never asked about mine and I didn't want to know his either." Inhaling deeply, she made her decision and spoke to stand her ground on the topic. "We both just want to capture the present and move forward for a better future. Like he said to her, it's none of my business, and everyone needs someone."

"My, intriguing." Hamadryades pulled her through the portal as toadstools bloomed in a circle around a bromeliad with water in its center. "Let's see what unfolds next. Sit, eat, drink."

At last, Hamadryades had let go of Lillith and she sank onto her designated toadstool. Dryads came and went as tables made of wood bloomed in time to be filled with food and wine. The knots in Lillith's stomach only added to her growing fears about what would become of Tony. Food was the last thing she wanted. Instead, she wanted to crawl into a hole and be free of watching this unfold, wondering at what point would his magic break through and see her. *There's no way he wouldn't be quick-witted enough to not react. He felt me. So how long will it take him to see me?*

"She looks like we've sentenced him to death already," snorted Alecto, plucking meat off a platter.

Freya chuckled, gulping mead and chortling. "Lighten up, Lillith. We're just having some fun, is all!"

"Leave her be." Hamadryades cut through them, and they looked away in shame.

I don't know what good will come of this, if any. Should I be questioning him about his past? Perhaps Pan has already done so, but wouldn't he tell me if there's something to be worried about? At least I know he can fight, and despite seeing monsters for the first time, he's following his gut. Just don't let them know you're a child of Aether. You have no idea how dangerous this information can be and how much bigger that target on your back will grow.

CHAPTER 31

SALAMANDRA'S TERRITORY

The food warmed Tony's belly, though he'd been reluctant to eat it. Creatures of all types had appeared from the shadows and swamp: setting up a tent, starting a fire, and laying a table of food. The smell of the roasting meat turning on the spit made his stomach growl and he realized, *I haven't eaten in days or maybe weeks.* He bit into the large drumstick of what he could only conclude might have been a douen. *Definitely smaller than the huge birds I keep seeing flying overhead. Taste isn't bad...* Raising his brow high, he devoured piece after piece.

"You were hungry, brother," chuckled Inle, who set a plate on the ground for Irawaru. "But I suppose you've done far more running around and fighting than we have."

"I just, ever since..." Tony took another bite, chewing and swallowing the large heaps of meat. "Honestly, it's been a while since I felt hungry."

Inle gave a befuddled look. "You talk as if being a deity is new to you."

Tony froze. A chill rolled over him and he shuddered, his gaze rising to meet Inle. "What did you call me?"

"Deity?" He arched a brow, curiosity rising in his tone and posture. "Do you not know what you are?"

Tony's stomach twisted, and he abandoned his food, pushing back the plate. "I didn't think a King Incubus was considered a deity," he confessed, grabbing for a goblet of what he could only assume was moonshine from smell and taste.

"Why wouldn't you be?" Inle motioned as if the items that were on the table between them were enough evidence. "Just like well-being, health, and body, plenty, worship, love, and lust, go together and separately. More so, an incubus, unlike its counterpart, is the very being of pleasure and pain involving one's dreams and physical desires."

Staring down at his reflection in the goblet, Tony frowned. "I hadn't given it much thought."

"Much thought?" scoffed Inle, leaning closer now. "Brother, are you telling me you were just born into this life despite being naturally suited for it?"

Tony shot him a pained look and began gulping the moonshine. It burned in tandem with the thoughts and emotions running through him. *I feel like a fucking idiot. We're talking about gods and goddesses that I've found myself being involved with. I mean, Lillith herself slept with me...* Tony paled and choked on his drink.

"Muddascunt," muttered Inle.

"I don't think it's official, nor am I finished with my ... change," announced Tony, reaching for the pitcher to refill the goblet. "Is that a possibility, to be new and still ... changing?"

Weighing Tony's grim expression, Inle sighed.

"Look, it's not your responsibility," snorted Tony, furrowing his brow.

"But I owe you." Inle gave a half-hearted smile. "What do you think is happening to you?"

"I don't think..." Tony paused, searching the air for the racing thoughts that never left him. "I don't think I'm done evolving. Every time I get close to feeling comfortable in my body, it shifts again, and I have to relearn what this is that I have to be in charge of." Tony frowned, glaring at a fist as he pumped it as if assessing his body to see if it still functioned as expected.

"You make it sound like someone cursed you or cast some magic to change you, brother." Inle started to laugh, but it stumbled to a halt as Tony puffed out his cheeks and drummed his fingers. "You—You're kidding?"

Shaking his head, Tony confessed, "Started as a curse, then a baptism for King Incubus, but something cornered me and did something. I was on fire and what spells and curses I could feel attached to me were burned away and something ... changed."

Irawaru whimpered and yelped.

Even the dog feels sorry for me. Tony rubbed his forehead. "Never mind, I've said too much."

"Irawaru is right; you shouldn't tell anyone about this." Tony arched a brow at the dog. "It's dangerous information. All of it." Inle took a sip of his mead. "The idea that you're new, changing, spellbound, and curse bound ... that's a lot of magic pumped into one body and soul." Inle finished his drink. "That's a lot for a titan to take in."

Tony tilted his head and corrected, "Human, you mean."

Inle gave him a skeptical look, countering, "No way, brother. You've been a titan from birth. Don't forget my specialty is well-being; you can't trick me on this matter."

"How?" Tony tensed, suspicious of his own past more than ever. *How is that even possible? I have a birth certificate and pictures.*

"I am a deity of physical being, what one is on the inside and out, no matter the gender or lack thereof, I know what a being is made of." An eerie white light shone in Inle's eyes, making Tony stiffen further. "You were a titan from the start. Never sick and quick to heal."

Tony's mind flickered back to the golden droplets of blood in the nectar. "Okay, let's say some part of me believes that. I didn't think titans needed to sleep or eat."

Irawaru groaned and gave out a muffled bark. It seemed to hold the expression of *everything must eat and sleep and...*

"Well, I can't say I'm an expert on supernatural anything." Tony huffed and pressed for more information. "So let's circle back to your initial observation." Tony swallowed, joints aching as every nerve tightened in his body. "Are you saying someone is packing magic into me on purpose?"

Inle looked at Irawaru, who raised his ears before they turned back to him. "We think so, from what we've seen." He pointed at the sword now leaning on the table. "That's made with your blood, forged with your essence?"

"Y-yeah." Tony shuddered; the idea they could tell made him feel exposed more and more.

"That pressure you released is only the tip of the iceberg. Whoever helped you forge that weapon knew you needed a means to vent the magic swelling inside." Irawaru barked and gruffed at Inle, who nodded, adding, "And that's where it's strangest." The pause made Tony's stomach sour, the food churning in his gut. "Normally, it stays steady, or you use it, and it refills back to the initial cap. Inside you, it seems limitless, as if you are capable of creating ether itself. I've never met someone capable of getting stronger with every breath."

Is that why I'm struggling and burning up inside? This is why Boto stepped out of training without warning and why Badbh forged the weapon, but... not one fucking word of explanation. I don't think Lillith knows, but that means I only added to it when I linked with her and later when she ... What was the word for it? Bonded with me. Granted, without that bond, the marks were burned away and ... perhaps they couldn't withstand the amount of magic I took in from Aether or Avalon or whatever damn name it goes by? If that's rare, then what about Cedric? Doesn't he get more powerful at every passing moment? Did I inherit this through his bloodline via the curse?

Frowning, Tony glared at his reflection in his drink once more, his green eyes aglow. "I only know one other person who does the same thing; granted, it's because he can eat and absorb the magic of others, but that may have changed for him, too."

"Is it your father?" Inle took a bit of mango.

"Uh, more like my ancestor?" Tony scrunched his face. "Like, hundreds of years removed?"

Inle choked on his mango, blurting, "Then how were you born this way?"

"Not by choice," offered Tony, finishing another goblet of moonshine.

With that, Tony grabbed the sword and began walking down the path. Before them, the path, mottled with ash and trees, withered and charred, led to the open rocky, barren landscape. The bubbling and hiss of lava flowing or coming to the surface was only matched by the sulfur that stung his nose. Inle rushed to his feet, lopping La Diablesse over his shoulder before catching up. Irawaru stole one last slab of meat from the table, swallowing it down as he came trotting hot on their heels.

"You don't have to follow me or guide me." Tony's temper had grown with the rise of bitter thoughts. *I'll find my own way to deal with it. Who needs to rely on old gods who are in over their heads?*

"Look, you've saved and helped us without even being asked to do so. We're going to the same place and there are a lot of dangerous creatures between here and the entrance at the top of the volcano." Inle shifted the passed-out being on his shoulders. "Someone needs to be your guide."

Rolling his eyes, Tony flustered, "At least someone gives a shit."

Irawaru growled and Inle laughed. "He says not to let it get to your head. I have a bounty to trade, and he says who he's here to find was brought here to serve Salamandra against their will. It seems we all have our reasons for going, but at least we've been in good company."

"Well, I don't want you two caught up in any trouble I make, so I'll cut a path." Marching forward, Tony couldn't shake the bitter emotions twisting at his core.

Irawaru sneezed and paced ahead, sniffing around before whimpering back at them.

"Look, brother." Inle jogged ahead and halted Tony with a palm against his chest. "You've got a good heart, no matter what happens with this body." Tony inhaled deeply and held it in thought. "Don't let whatever happens to this," Inle patted his bare chest and smirked, "change who you are in there," and he flicked Tony's forehead.

Irawaru barked and wagged his tail.

Tony brushed his hand away and bumped past him. "I don't plan on any of this changing who I am. It just pisses me off, is all."

Inle looked to Irawaru, whose wagging tail slowed to a stop. "Yeah, brother. He's pissed, alright."

The heat rose in waves from random spots across the black and gray terrain. Towers of steam or geysers splashed up on occasion as Tony trudged down the footpath. His gaze peered up at the smoke rolling from the top of the volcano as lava sputtered from it. *No idea how much hotter this is about to get.* Tony stopped; sweat trickled down the divot of his back as he watched a flock of birds scatter in reply to the tremor that shook underfoot. *This sucks. I've lost my boots, my shirt, my cape, and my tunic. At least I somehow still have my sword and shield.* Over the swamp, the flock of owl-like chickcharney rushed up and settled back down into their trees. Around the glowing peak of the volcano, birds made of flames circled in vibrant reds, oranges, and yellows. One showed bright blue and purple, larger than the rest, like a male peacock, even from this distance.

"Hey, Inle." Tony waited for him to catch up. "Are those ... phoenix?"

Inle grinned, nudging his arm as he started to walk ahead. "Yeah, gorgeous, aren't they?"

"But I thought they were ... rare?" Tony caught up to him; his frustration melted away by his curiosity.

"Everywhere but here," answered Inle, grunting under the weight of La Diablesse.

"Huh." Tony gave the flock far overhead one last look, marveling over it a moment.

Looking all around, this landscape did very little to hide the tiny creatures who scuttled around, unlike the swamp. The path didn't lead straight up, but instead zig-zagged on the softer inclines that lay on the edge of the mountain as they began to climb. As Tony glanced one way then the other, he caught glimpses of lizards that looked as if they were on fire and of what looked like dog-sized chicks chasing after them. Suddenly, by an open pool of lava, he spotted a little figure, like a flaming Barbie doll. Tony stumbled to a stop and kneeled, watching as it peered up at him from the edge.

"What is this?" Tony caught Inle's attention; he flinched when he saw the little humanoid made of fire.

"Oh no, brother." Inle marched over and grabbed Tony's biceps, tugging him down the path and far away from the creature. "You don't mess with the tiny ifrits or any of the little ones here."

"I just wanted to know what it was," defended Tony.

"A newborn ifrit, or fire spirit," answered Inle, dropping his grip.

Pointing at two chick things chasing fire lizards, Tony demanded, "And those things?"

Waving them off, Inle announced, "Newborn cockatrice and firedrakes. Easy for them to grow close to the food the swamp makes and the abundance of water. They are learning to handle their fire for the first time and hunt."

"So, these are the babies," confirmed Tony as he watched two cockatrice chicks rip a firedrake in half. "Do we need to worry about the parents?" Tony glanced around, wondering how anything could sneak up and attack them in the barren land of lava pools and boiling water. "I don't see anything big."

"We haven't entered their hunting grounds yet." Slapping Tony's arm, Inle pointed farther up the mountain.

Squinting his eyes, Tony swallowed. Lines of lava drooled down in rivers. The boulders only became larger, sharper, as if trying to replace the trees that once stood in their place. Dark smoke loomed over the midsection of the mountain as if stuck in a perpetual state of low-hanging thunderclouds with streaks of lightning flashing in reds and purples.

Tony froze and stared up at it, eyes wide. "Is that a thundercloud on the ground up there?"

"No, brother. That's a never-ending cloud of ash, heat, and lightning made from the friction of it all." Motioning to a dead cockatrice being eaten by baby firedrakes and two more ifrits, he added, "These are going to seem adorable in comparison to what waits for us there."

"And why did you take this job again?" Tony noticed the tiny ifrit spirit from before peeking at him from behind a rock.

"Because I needed a favor that requires Vulcan's fire," Inle mumbled.

"Vulcan... as in the one who forges Zeus's thunderbolts?" Tony's skin pimpled as the weight of the situation began to hit a legendary peak. *First Scylla, now I get to meet Vulcan? This is wild!*

"Yes, Vulcan, or Salamandra." Inle paused, a profound thought hitting him as he spun back and declared, "You didn't know Salamandra *was* Vulcan."

"No, I didn't, and now I'm a little intimidated by this." Tony pumped his fist as a tiny firedrake crawled out onto the footpath and licked an eyeball. "Guess this is my personal version of out of the frying pan and into the fire."

Looking at the stormy midsection, Tony steeled himself. *Real-world experience, ha! Prove I'm worthy... bullshit. When I get back, Avalon, I'm going to pry answers from you.* Tony gripped the hilt of his sword. *Since I have a means to vent my magic, it seems like your halls might be a good place to start when I get back from this fiery hell.*

CHAPTER 32

HARSH TRUTHS

L illith scowled down at her teacup. "Is it too much to demand I get some wine?" *This is pure torture. There's nothing I can do. If it were just one of them, I might be able to escape, but all three... forget it.*

"Come now, I'm trying to calm your nerves," defended Hamadryades.

"Alcohol numbs the nerves." Lillith abandoned her cup on the table and picked at the fruit. "I much prefer that method." She smiled to herself for a moment. *Besides, my bartender is on a tropical island at this given moment.*

"Perhaps you should reconsider your drinking habits, Gaea's heart. Is that why you landed in the bartender's bed in the first place?" Freya's snide remark earned her a heated glare from Lillith.

"Let's make something clear here and now." Lillith tossed a grape at Freya, which halted midair, turning to ice before shattering. "We didn't end up in either of our beds to start with." *By the stars, they better not be planning to pry into my personal business.* "I sensed something, had Pan evaluate the curse, and we devised a plan to essentially beat the curse to the punchline," explained Lillith as a dryad appeared with a wooden goblet and pitcher of what looked like wine. "Something that's been in practice for eons."

"And by the punchline, you imply..." Alecto motioned for Lillith to elaborate.

Drinking a glass and pouring a second, Lillith offered, "To make him a King Incubus."

"But there's already one in existence." Freya looked confused.

"Ah, so that's why there was a sense of urgency over the matter." Hamadryades had pieced it together in an instant. "Cedric was here, and though not due to shedding his mortal body, it created a loophole to Gaea's curse so you could create a new king in the Mortal Realm. Clever."

"But what of Boto?" Freya waved a hand. "Wouldn't he have been the better choice? I mean, the man can't die with his ties to the Amazon River."

Lillith's face flushed. "We were never truly a thing, and I don't think either of us wants to rekindle whatever that was that we had between us."

"Oh," Freya's voice pitched higher as she flapped a hand at the others. "What about Himeros?"

Hamadryades slammed her cup down. "Absolutely not. Baron La Croix would be a far better choice. He dresses nicely, quite debonair."

Alecto groaned. "That man thinks people dying is a joke. I don't think any of us could handle an asshole of that caliber."

"Min!" Freya flapped her hand once again. "He's rumored to be well-endowed! If she's going to make a new King Incubus, he needs to be a big guy!"

Lillith mottled. *I hate when they talk about my curse as if it's some trivial matter. You don't have to live with it, to fulfill its obligations and endure lust without love until... until...*

"If you ladies are going with size matters." Hamadryades arched a brow and cooed, "Then Priapus would be the taker of that crown."

A round of laughter erupted between them, though Lillith remained dead silent. The weight of her emotions nestled in her chest, aching as she began to drink the so-called wine. *This isn't hitting the mark; who is she fooling?* Glaring into the cup, she realized, *This is just fruit juice. Damn her.*

"Oh, and trust me, they aren't rumors at all." Alecto raised her cup with a sheepish grin. "I can't believe I never shared with you ladies that night Priapus and I..."

Lillith's thoughts spiraled her mind inward, the cackling of the goddesses seeming to fade. Closing her eyes, she clung to the way Tony gazed at her. The way he pulled her into him and gave her that crooked grin that made butterflies flutter in her stomach. *No one ever seems to sincerely be glad to see me, other than you. For a moment, when we're alone, I almost feel as if I'm nothing more than...*

"...Lillith? Did you hear me?" Freya seemed offended that she had checked out.

"No." Lillith sipped her drink. *Definitely not alcohol.*

With a huff, Hamadryades repeated, "What do you intend to do with two kings? You've already crowned Cedric and..."

"Tony, the only one appointed by me and accepted fully into the role in the full capacity as a true King Incubus is Tony." Lillith took a swig and added, "Cedric and I only did what was needed to be done per my curses, just as I did with Boto before. The creation of a brood supersedes any actual bond."

"First time truly bonding with one in all this time, is it?" marveled Freya. "And they call me the ice queen."

"But I thought you already had a bond with someone?" Alecto stuffed a chunk of meat between her lips, talking with her mouth full. "So, was that your mark or a bond we felt earlier?"

"There was both at one point, but..." Lillith sucked on her cheek before relenting, "...something happened last night and only the bond remains. Something has taken away both our spells and possibly ... both of our curses with it."

Alecto choked on her food and Freya sputtered out her drink.

As I thought, they find this idea unsettling as well.

"I was wondering if you were going to say something." Hamadryades narrowed her eyes. "As for the other matter, we will discuss it in private. In the meantime, who or what do we know that has enough power to unravel a curse written by Gaea herself?"

Annoying, old hag can see too much, but I suppose the fact that she's nature incarnate... who could hide anything from her? Defeated, Lillith began to eat the fruit on the platter before her. "I only know of one, but we all know Aether's been dead for millennia."

They all fell silent, solemn faces speaking volumes. They shared the heartache or perhaps something more unsettling ... *or is it the expression of knowing that's not true? He's very much alive, and no one has been brave enough to say it bluntly.* Each of them sipped their drinks and nibbled, the once playful and teasing tone squashed in a single moment. Flashes of Avalon and being in the darkness and shoved through doorways came back to the forefront of Lillith's mind. Alarmed, she shot up. *I'll make them say it. Confess it all.*

"Who can summon doors at will?" Lillith demanded.

They looked at one another, Hamadryades speaking up, "Like the one you just came through, if I'm not mistaken? I thought you knew someone."

"I went to leave the bedroom, and it opened to here." Lillith's heart raced; some part of her curious whether the old goddesses would have more knowledge about Avalon. *I mean, if they know who has the biggest prick, surely they have more useful information.* "I didn't prompt it. It knew and when I didn't step through, I was physically shoved."

"A liminal deity who can bypass and untangle magic, hmm..." Alecto leaned her elbows on her knees.

"Precisely." Lillith crossed her legs, relaxing at last. "And has a strange fascination around Tony and me, apparently. He's been helpful, but unpleasant and dark at best."

"Janus comes to mind, even Hades," offered Freya.

"No, Janus is more of a keeper of doors in the Mortal Realm," Alecto contemplated the matter. "Hades is locked in the Underworld for the time being. Hamadryades, did you sense the doorway here in your forest at all?"

"No, not at all, but the magic did remind me of someone." Hamadryades smiled, a nostalgic look crossing her wooden face.

"It can't be." Freya stood in alarm. "All this time, while Kronos and Gaea destroyed and mettled with every realm the way they did?"

There it is. Recognition. "I thought the same." Lillith shuddered. "But I don't know. This seems to be more disjointed, angry." Lillith held herself a moment, reflecting on the presence. "And I would think he would have acted sooner? Perhaps revealed himself?"

"But his body is gone." Alecto clasped her hands, grimacing.

"True, and his ill will, good will, and neutrality fill the very air of all the realms and adds to the magic we feel." Hamadryades bloomed a flower in her fingers until the dandelion shifted into a ball of seeds and she blew them away. "But no one ever found his head, where his mind's eye survived and lived. Where the emotions, thoughts, and memories... all that made him who we miss and wish to have returned to us."

"If it's true that he's out there, why hasn't he shown himself?" Freya seemed miffed at the thought.

"Without a god's body, he's a weak mortal, I imagine." Alecto's darkened tone changed the mood further. "Gaea and Kronos would snuff him out if that were the case."

"Very true. If he were still able to act indirectly, what might he do, I wonder?" Freya hummed to herself.

"I know." Hamadryades smiled, cooing, "Make a new titan, find a new heir, and save the very heart that stole his." They all turned and faced Lillith. "Isn't that what is happening now, Lillith?"

"Tony is no heir," she guffawed.

"No, he isn't meant to be the heir." Alecto rose to her feet, holding the sides of her head. "That crazy old fool, he wouldn't! Freya, the girl! Artemis's heir and Cedric!"

Freya knocked her table over as she stood in alarm. "He wouldn't!"

Hamadryades sipped her tea and replied, "He would. His time of ruling has passed, and they will take their place. As for Lillith, he's trying to find someone worthy. He's the only one who can manipulate all magic without any consequence, since all magic originates from him. To open doors without effort, to unravel curses of any being—there's always been one entity capable of such feats."

"I don't know; I find this rather hard to believe," dismissed Freya. "We will need more proof."

"True." Alecto sat back down and grabbed her mug. "Perhaps we are hoping for it to be him. Despite that, now we have two entities to watch and judge."

Lillith inhaled deeply and looked off to the forest. The darkness between the trees brought her back to the swamp, where she swore Tony met her gaze in that moment. Her skin pimpled, and deep down, some part of her hoped he had. The way her heart had fluttered, the fear and excitement that rattled through her in that fleeting moment. Her hand rose to her chest, hoping to protect her still-racing heart from being ensnared by so many unknowns.

Part of me wishes I could be there on this quest with him, but how much more careless would he be?

CHAPTER 33

A Light in the Darkness

Before them lay a black curtain with heat radiating from it that made the sweltering beach and humid swamp feel like a cool shower. What had appeared to be a thundercloud was actually something far more harrowing. Tony coughed and took a few steps back in disbelief. Geysers of ash and hot rocks vented endlessly here. Looking at Inle and Irawaru, he gave them an exasperated expression.

"It's the vents for Salamandra's forge that make this," explained Inle. "All that heat has to go someplace, and it stirs up the ash and rocks."

"And we have to go through this?" Tony hacked some more, lungs stinging from the hot, ashen air. "I'm questioning you more and more about taking on this job, Inle."

"Here, brother." Inle handed him a wet cloth and motioned for him to tie it over his nose and mouth. "This should help you breathe while we travel through there."

"Breathing is one issue, but how are we supposed to see through this shit." A spark of lightning spiderwebbed through the ashen wall, the footpath lighting for a quick moment. "I hate everything about this." Tony coughed.

Once everyone had their cloths, they nodded to one another and stepped through the threshold. The air stung at his skin and eyes. Hot was an understatement. Lightning from the heat and friction lit the pathway, and Tony sped up. Another flash and they were turning between two huge boulders. Here the ash lightened up and the falling rocks clattered softly against the boulders and rolled down into piles all around the base. It began to bottleneck, making Tony sidestep to fit his shoulders as they started to brush against the walls. *This is a tight fit.*

Inle and Irawaru let Tony take the lead, hot on his heels. The crackling of lightning snaked overhead once more, and they could barely see the end of the crevice. After one last tight squeeze, the rock scraping Tony's chest until it bled, he was free from being pinched between the boulders; he had thought he was going to get wedged there for a fleeting moment. He leaned on his thighs and wiped his chest. Blood smeared his hand, though the scrape had healed quickly without the need for lust and prompting. *Still not used to this. To bleed and find no wound by the time I get a moment to assess.*

Upon taking a few steps farther into the darkness, rocks rained down like sharp hail. One knocked the top of his forehead, slicing open his brow long enough for blood to sting in his eyes. Tony wiped it free; lightning lit the area. Something was towering in the pathway up ahead. Every muscle went tight. *That's not a rock.*

"Something's there," Tony barked back at Inle and Irawaru, still sliding through the crack.

"Y-you're bleeding," Inle remarked. "Is it a shadow or glowing?"

"Sh-shadow." Tony swallowed, trying to peer past the falling ash, skin on fire.

"Cockatrice," announced Inle. "Watch for the glow when they shoot fire from their beaks; they hunt in small packs."

"Packs," guffawed Tony. "How small are we talking here?"

"Two, maybe three, tops. Usually a male and two hens," Inle whispered, muttering profanities. "Can you handle them on your own, brother?"

Another flash of light, the shadowed figure was gone. "I don't know; it's gone."

Tremors rattled the earth and friction spiraled all around. *Shit, where did it go?* Rocks skidded and bounced down the slope past his feet. Somewhere above, Tony heard the fluttering of feathers. In reflex, he unsheathed his sword and made a wide arc in the direction of the sound. Sparks flew as claws met the blade with a loud clack and hiss, as if metal slid against nails. The weight and bulk of the creature pressed down on him, and Tony dropped to one knee.

With a flap of its wings, it landed before him. Static united and a flash of lightning shed light on the shadow to reveal a large dragon-like rooster standing eye level with Tony. It hissed and flapped its wings in frustration at him. The beak was filled with alligator teeth, and it had dinosaur legs, and the notorious spike of a normal rooster, minus the fact it was like a sharpened branch as thick as Tony's arm.

The cockatrice leaped forward, and Tony swung his blade. *Where's the venting of magic? I could really use that right now!* Another clang as he blocked the incoming claws. The spike sliced his thigh and made him stumble. *Shit, I need to stay on my feet.* A sharp metallic twang in the air made the feathers flair. Screeching, fire roared into the air and its light revealed on the boulders up ahead two more chicken-shaped shadows. *It's definitely three. Fuck.*

Focusing on the one in front of him, Tony charged forward. Swinging his sword, it flapped out of the way, clawing and snapping. Parrying with the creature, neither was gaining any ground. With every electric flash, Tony scanned for the rest of the pack but had lost them. Sweat dripped down his skin as the heat continued to sting at him. Ash painted his entire being as rocks fell, hot and sharp, cutting him on occasion. The creature retreated, and he lost sight of it.

Dammit, did the pack arrive and close in already? Tony dropped to a ready stance, unsure of which direction the creatures would come from. Spinning, he searched the cloud for some hint of movement or shadows. He was breathing harder, making the wet cloth tug inward with every inhale. Squeezing the sword's hilt, he begged it, *Please do that thing you did against the loogaroo pack.* Rocks scudding to his right made him swing in reflex. *I'm only able to do this thanks to Badbh's training.* The cockatrice rooster flapped back to dodge the strike. Blood sprayed across Tony, squirting against his bare chest like boiling water. He rushed backward, failing to slap it off before claws dug into his back. The weight of the impact shoved him forward. He lost his grip on his blade and it skidded out of view.

"Shit!" *Well, now there won't be a chance for...* "Ugh!"

Claws raked across his backside. A sickening sensation of claw scraping bone brought him alive in a roar. Horns, claws, and fangs took hold. As much as he wanted to roll and face his opponent, the claws were too deep into his flesh. He reached up and over his head, and the cockatrice clamped down on his hands. Another wave of pain shook him as a bone in his forearm snapped and mended with every gnawing motion.

Did I lose the ability to feel pleasure instead of pain? Tony dug his claws into the roof of its mouth, growing numb to the pain as it began to shift in sensation. The claws uncurled from his back. He didn't waste time and thrust it up and overhead. His hand broke free as he flung the cockatrice hen to the ground with a thud, the snapping of a bone as it rolled.

"Karma's a bitch." Panting, Tony was desperate to catch his breath from the pain. *What the hell happened? This hurts, or am I just that far out of focus since my body changed again?*

A flash of lightning arced between him and the cockatrice rooster. Alarmed, Tony took in all he could. The chest was still sliced open, and blood painted the feathers and scales below it, dripping to the ground in globs. *Unlike me, they don't heal fast. I've got that much going for me.* A shiver rolled through Tony, and he closed his eyes, fighting the instincts it stirred at his core, as the scent of the iron-rich blood cut through the ash. *It smells ... delicious. The idea of ripping it apart with my bare hands feels exciting.* His stomach churned. *It's the same as when I was in the ring or cornered in the alley. The smell is driving me into a blood rage.*

His eyes snapped open, and he caught the rooster's massive claw. The large spur split open the skin across Tony's torso like a knife grazing him slowly and agonizingly as they pushed to overpower one another. A shockwave rolled through him; pain had turned to pleasure as his horns grew to crown his head to their full length. *It's working! Just needed to relax and enjoy the fight. Shit. I feel like a minotaur with this weight on my head, but this... this is the sensation I have a tough time allowing forward. This makes me nervous, but survival comes first.* An arc lit the span behind his assaulter, exposing the other two, fast approaching from either side. *Classic pincer move.* His heart fluttered, eyes searching the obscurity of the ground. Somewhere in the darkness of the ashen cloud, he could feel the sword, as if a piece of him was longing to be back in touch with him.

"It's there!" With a grunt, Tony caught the shine of the familiar pommel. *Black on black in this place sucks, but at least putting my blood in there had another advantage, I see. Thanks, Badbh!*

Shoving the creature off, Tony ran and dove for the sword. He slid across the ground; ash plumed around him. The hilt smacked into his palm firmly, as if sliding into an optimal position. Ripping the muddied cloth from his face, Tony jumped to his feet. A flapping of feathers came from the left and the skidding of claw on rock from his right. *Then the rooster is straight ahead.* A glow filled the ashen air and his mind flashed to how many times Badbh had *killed* him in training. *But I'm healing faster and stronger now. I can do this. Will the hens retreat if I cut the rooster down? It's worth the gamble.*

Tightening his grip, he launched forward with his sword poised for the next strike. Tony could hear the confused chirps and growling from behind as the two hens knocked into one another. The fire rolling from the cockatrice rooster's mouth hit Tony in the chest as he swung through the blaze. Heat seared his flesh, but it only brought him unfathomable pleasure. The hilt pulled on the surge of incubine power his blood lust brought him and he lopped the head clean off. It fell with a thud and hiss as the flames were snuffed out. Spinning around, Tony searched the ash for the other two. Seething, he panted through clenched teeth as an arc showed two familiar figures.

His muscles tightened, unwilling to stop the fight, but he kept his body firmly planted. The chortling and flapping of wings ran past either side of him. *They ran away... good.* Tony rubbed his chest where he had felt the melting and charring of flesh, where his lungs had burned, and his heart had seemed to stop for a moment as magic drove him forward. *Nothing. Nothing but blood, sweat, and ash. I'm a fucking monster.* His chest ached with the stir of emotions; he swallowed. *But even so, I'm her monster. I can live with that idea, for some reason. That thought I feel excited for; the idea I—*

"I breathe and fight solely for my queen, Lillith," he muttered to himself.

A wave of arousal drew his eyes up and through the ash; he saw her, *Lillith.* Every nerve drew tight as he took in the wooden woman, the Nordic queen in white, and the female with the white eyes watching him with concerned expressions. The scent of fear, *her fear,* cut through the acrid air and he could hear her heart flutter. *What the fuck do I do? I don't think I was supposed to notice them.*

Inle and Irawaru walked *through* them, and Tony stiffened.

"Brother, you managed to save us from the cockatrice, but," Inle pointed to the heap behind him, "we better move before that attracts a firedrake."

"Give me a minute." Tony pushed his arousal out and Lillith's waved back like a ripple, making her visibly flinch. "I need to catch my breath." *And figure out what in the hell is happening. Who are those other goddesses?*

"Would you stop that?" hissed the white-eyed woman with dreadlocks to Lillith.

"I can't help it," Lillith blurted, eyes still on him. "I've never... I can't stop my body from replying; it's embarrassing to even tell you three."

The wooden woman met his gaze, and he dropped his own to Irawaru when she asked, "Does he sense you're close? That happened the last time we came here to observe him using Freya's astral spell."

"You and Irawaru okay?" Tony feigned, swallowing as he squatted to the dog, who looked back in the direction he had dodged, tilting his head and whimpering. *Does he sense something there, too? Am I the only one able to see them?*

"Impossible." The white-haired Nordic goddess scowled, crossing her arms. "It would take a lot of magical power or a dense enough blast for someone to sense us. Right, Alecto?"

"Freya, I don't doubt that, but..." Lillith's heart fluttered as Tony dared to peer back at her as Alecto speculated, "She's never bonded with anyone. He's technically the first and none of us know what kind of power spike that will bring them both."

"Very true," the wooden woman nodded to herself and motioned for the other goddesses to come closer. "Lillith, give us a moment to discuss this. Let's walk a little farther this way, as I want to make a suggestion for you two to consider."

"Gee, gossiping is unsightly," snarked Lillith as they left her behind.

"Are you okay?" Inle had asked it a few times, but Tony had focused on the conversation of the unknown goddesses.

"Not sure yet." Tony watched as Lillith turned her back to him. *If Inle and Irawaru walked through them, perhaps they are holographically here somehow?*

"Let's rest farther up the trail, yes?" Inle suggested as he and Irawaru looked at one another, both unnerved by Tony's unknown distraction.

An arc of lightning spiderwebbed overhead, and he caught sight of the footpath behind Lillith. *Idea!* "The footpath continues over there; I think we can shortcut and gain more distance. Looping around might provide too much time for a firedrake to sniff out the cockatrice."

"I always wondered about that." Inle marveled over it and laughed a moment. "Whether I was crossing the same beast or not, and it seems I was!"

Tony glared at Lillith, where she held her arms, her back to him as if afraid to meet his gaze again. *She wouldn't blatantly ignore me without reason. If she's in trouble, I need to know.* He motioned for Inle to lead the way and he followed hesitantly behind them in hopes of gaining just enough distance to whisper something to her without the other entities hearing him. Tony's heart pounded loud and hard. *I feel like this is a big fucking risk. She's going to hate me if...* He held his breath and halted as Inle passed through her and Lillith stiffened.

"I hate astral projection. People and things just go through me without..." She halted, turning slowly as she muttered under her breath. "You wouldn't."

Tony arched a brow, and despite the intense moment, couldn't resist the toothy smirk as their eyes met. *We both know I would.*

"He looks so dumb with dirt and ash caked on his fangs," Lillith drawled, watching how his smile faded and his lips clamped close; now, she smirked with an arched brow.

Clearing his throat, he took a few steps closer until they were nearly touching, the heat of the ashen land making it hard to read if he could feel her body close to his. His muscles twitched and stunted the next step. *Will I walk through her, or will I bump into her? Exactly how strong is this spell versus our bond?*

Whispering, Lillith warned, "Just walk through me, or they'll figure out you can see me, asshole."

"What if I bump into you?" he hissed back.

"Then you're strong enough to beat Freya's best spell," she spat, glancing back to see no sign of the others. "Fucking just do it."

"Are you in danger?" he muttered, his eyes dropping to sheath his sword, and he began to feign he needed to stretch.

"No, but you are. If they deem you a threat," she resisted the urge to smack him on the chest as she balled a hand in contempt. "Stop being so damn awkward and fucking—"

He took a step forward, and their shoulders connected. Their eyes widened and Lillith paled.

"Shit," he replied and sidled over to avoid her.

"Pretend that didn't happen." She kicked his shin, and he grunted in reply.

"See you around," he muttered bitterly.

Sighing, she covered her face. "Why have you complicated my life so much?"

He scoffed, starting up the slope after Inle.

"In just a few months, you have made so much more chaos for me than in my entire existence," she shrieked at the air.

"Scream any louder and he might actually hear you," offered Alecto as she marched through Tony.

Holy shit, that was close. We almost got caught. She went through me, but Lillith didn't. Tony paused on the path where his companions waited. *Did that juggernaut of a goddess do that on purpose? Were they watching us? Did they see me knock shoulders with Lillith? Shit, I wonder what kind of danger I'm in if she has no means of saying anything to me about what they are deciding to do with me?*

CHAPTER 34

THE MORTAL REALM

BADBH & BOTO

The cue ball clacked hard against the 8-ball, sending it sailing to the corner pocket. It bounced between the edges, teasingly avoiding its target pocket, and Badbh muttered curses in archaic languages. Glaring at Boto, she watched as he chalked the tip of his pool stick. The smirk on his face, and sparkle in his eyes, told her of the defeat that was now inevitable, and she grabbed her beer in bitter defeat.

"Corner pocket," Boto cooed.

He aimed away from the 8-ball, and she scoffed. With a hard clack, the ball bounced off the edges in a gorgeous display of geometry and slowed to gently tap the 8-ball, which eased into the corner pocket. Now he took a swig of his beer, gloating without ever saying a word.

"So, where did you go?" Badbh pulled the rack out and began filling it with balls from the pockets. "You were supposed to help me train Tony. You got your ass handed to you once, and poof, you ghosted my ass until he was shipped out."

Boto shrugged, abandoning his empty bottle into the ice bucket, and cracking open another beer. "Morrighan had empty bottles that needed to be filled." He gave a smug expression. "What man can resist helping any woman in need of filling their precious bottles?"

"But you left those bottles on my table," snarked Badbh as she stalked around the pool table and rolled a ball to the rack. "So, what bottles did you fill?" Her brow rose high, teasingly.

"Well, we both know I need bigger bottles for what she wanted from me." He chuckled, catching the rolling balls and adding them to the rack. "Bigger is better, after all," he tutted.

"Why don't you two just give up and hook back up?" Badbh pulled the 8-ball out of the corner pocket and scowled at it as if it had betrayed her.

Shrugging, Boto rearranged the balls in the rack. "It's not like there's love there. Just simply lust with no strings attached. Well, and magical materials in need of refilling." He snorted.

"Isn't that enough for your kind?" Badbh rolled the 8-ball to him and pulled the cue ball out. "Didn't think romance was a priority for sex demons."

"It can be a very big deal for anyone, especially when you can feel the difference between lust and love. So, yeah, to a sex demon, you can say it's very huge for us to eventually find someone to love and be loved by in more than the physical lust that we get from the masses." He dropped the 8-ball into its proper spot. "Finding love is like filling a void within our souls, but for Lillith, she's had to bear a curse that prevented her from fulfilling that gap, or she'd forfeit her life. Tragic."

"Speaking of gaps, I think we forgot to show him how to fly." Badbh shoved her empty bottle into the bucket and frowned when she saw there were no more beers left to replace it. "You don't think he actually walked on foot?"

"He'll figure it out." Boto pulled the rack off the balls and began chalking his pool stick. "I'm betting he breaks one wing trying to do some crazy maneuver in flight."

"Nah, I think he'll fuck one up in a fight before figuring out he can fly with them." Badbh pulled out five gold Celtic Starters and placed them on the pool table. "I'm willing to put money on it."

"Okay, I'll match that." Boto pulled out five gold coins with Spanish markings as if found in a treasure hunt at the bottom of the sea.

"Can I place a bet?" The woman's voice called their attention, her green-brown heterochromia making them stiffen. "I'll bet ten Aureii against you both that he does both. Break it during a fight in flight."

Badbh and Boto shot a glance at one another before Badbh challenged the woman. "It's a little strange for the same gypsy that caused his change to bet on his demise now. So, which of you is here to talk with us?"

"Cleo," her expression became sad, "I don't have much time, but I did all I could to push him into action."

"Who? Tony or Kronos?" Boto's horns were crawling forward, the powerful aura coming from the girl making the air buzz. "Because I don't think putting Tony in the middle of our war was wise, and as for the latter—"

"No, not them." Cleo shook her head, flustered. "I can't say his name ... for reasons that will provoke too many others into action ahead of time. A new vision, something I didn't see until now, has ... complicated the plan." Cleo's eyes glowed, still carrying the weight of the grim future she saw. "Tell Phoebe he isn't choosing to be silent as we had originally predicted and has provided the only key for when... for when... *I breathe my last breath and the world tilts back before my conception.*"

"What kind of cryptic bullshit is that?" Badbh gripped up the pool stick, not sure if she would need to use it as an impromptu weapon.

"Promise me," Cleo demanded, the aura of her power pressing down on them until they stood frozen, unable to move. "Tell her he has created *a key for when my clock stops and the worlds return to a time before...*" She gripped her chest, gritting her fanged teeth. "He's going to take this vessel from me eventually..." Sweat trickled down her temple as her aura retreated from them and they inhaled, able to breathe again. "...prepare while you ... can." With that, she teleported away in a wake of ash and smoke.

"Maybe I should have taught him to fly," muttered Boto. "I didn't know she held that power. I can't even move, and I'm a titan. Maybe I spent too much time in Atlantis and under the ocean to be of any use to anyone now."

"Me neither." Badbh broke the pool stick over her knee and tossed it on the table in frustration. "Come on, we've got a message to relay to Phoebe. Shit's gone sideways again."

Boto rubbed his forehead, murmuring, "I should have stayed in the fucking river."

The vampiress Becca trembled where she stood a few steps shy of them, a fresh bucket of ice and beers scattered at her feet where she had dropped it. To a lesser creature, the aura they had fallen under was enough to make someone wish for death. Boto and Badbh cast her tear-stricken face an apologetic glance.

"Becca, keep the gold; we've got bigger bets on the line." Badbh snapped her fingers, and she teleported her and Boto in a flurry of raven feathers.

In a flash, they stood in the grand meeting hall alongside several others. The room fell silent as they appeared in a poof of feathers. Boto brushed a few from his shoulder before winking at Morrighan, whose cheeks flushed. Phoebe straightened. She was tall and slender, her neck elegantly framed by dark locks of brown hair. Artemis stood next to her, mask laid on the table, exposing the uncanny resemblance between the mother and daughter's facial features. Badbh crossed her arms, a few steps short from them, as the other deities in the room whispered in speculation of what could be the matter now.

"Cleo said to pass a message to you, Phoebe." The old goddess and protector of oracles and prophets did not flinch at the daring reveal. "Do you want it here with ears or elsewhere with just yours?"

Phoebe cast her gaze at the room and came back to Badbh, motioning for her to speak.

"She said *he* isn't staying silent." Clearing her throat, Badbh pressed for answers. "And *he* doesn't mean Tony or Kronos, so I imagine you know of whom she speaks."

"I do." Phoebe sat down, face paling. "But has no one been in contact with *him* since they've been here? Has *he* reached out to anyone?"

Pan leaned on the table beside her, furrowing his brow at her. "As a master of riddles, curses, and blessings... I imagine we are speaking about the being who controls the true will of Avalon?"

Nodding, Phoebe sighed and thought a moment before asking, "The doors move for all of us, but have any been forced to go places against their will?"

Pan paled. "One."

"Who is it?" Artemis's eyes glowed, and she scowled. "Who has *he* chosen?"

"Whoa, wait a minute here!" Boto interjected, waving his arms. "I'm still stuck on who *he* or *it* is in this scenario?"

"R-right," Phoebe made a small triangle with her fingers. "I suppose I should start with how the realms were created..." She was stalling.

"Yeah, yeah." Badbh rolled her eyes as Phoebe told a summarized version of how the realms came to be. "Gaea hated love and humans, Aether's most precious items, so she gave her favorite son, Kronos, her eye. Turning a *blind eye* to Aether, Kronos killed him, and all the magic and emotions were divided to create all the realms as we know them to be."

"Yes, we all know, Phoebe." Pan's voice darkened as his eyes went black. He pressed his aura farther out, making several beings shuffle away from him. "But the unsolved part of that tale is that no one found his head. Aether was unkillable even if he shed his body for a more vulnerable, even humanlike version, was he not?"

"Ah, so good. We suspect Aether then." Phoebe's brow lifted high and now Romasanta pushed past everyone.

"Where is Aether?" Romasanta demanded, and everyone stiffened.

"Here." Phoebe motioned around the room. "Sort of, or so I speculated."

"What do you mean *here?*" Romasanta growled, narrowing his yellow eyes. "I have Cedric in a coma, a rookie playing with fire, and the gypsy that broke me sending my mother, of all people, messages. Whose side are you on?"

Phoebe cast her stare around the room and inhaled, steeling herself before she spoke. "His head created a realm of its own, and on that island, he built a safe haven for you all from Gaea."

Boto shot a look at Pan, guffawing, "How did we not notice we were standing on... on..."

Pan waved him off, unmoved by the information as he pressed further, "Then tell me what business he has with creating a new titan and manipulating Gaea's heart?"

"I frankly don't know," Phoebe confessed with a shrug, turning to Badbh. "Was there anything else?"

"Time's running out," Badbh announced. "Cleo says her time will stop and the worlds will restart or something like that."

"Said he wasn't silent and has made a key for when that happens," added Boto. "That creature you call a gypsy is unfathomably powerful. She gridlocked us both with only her aura. If we can't beat her, then who could even get close enough to attack her when Kronos takes over her vessel? Why wait?"

"He'll flee. She will anchor him in the only way she can so we can do him harm." Phoebe nodded to Artemis as if to hand the next part to her.

"As we were discussing before that," scanning the room, Artemis sighed, "Angeline is nursing Cedric at the moment, which gives us one chance to inform you all of what we've known since before Romasanta was fused with Fenrir." Many of the hooded deities in the room whispered in surprise at the idea. "Cleo will need to be taken down by her own parents."

"You're out of your fucking minds." Pan grimaced and started for the door. "Good fucking luck pitching that to the big guy when he wakes the hell up."

"W-wait." Phoebe stood, her hand reaching out to Pan. "But you know who Aether has spoken to, do you not?"

"I do. And as their lawyer," Pan smirked with a fanged grin, "that's none of your concern."

Boto and Badbh looked at one another as Pan left with Romasanta, slamming the door shut behind them.

"Does anyone else know?" Phoebe pleaded, looking among the familiar and unfamiliar beings in the room. "I must know!"

Mingled whispers brought no takers as silence fell again.

"So be it," hissed Artemis, scowling at the closed doors. "We will find out one way or another."

Badbh shook her head at Artemis and marched for the exit. *I want no part of a battle without honor. If I caught Pan's words right, he's talking about Tony and Lillith. No way I'm telling either of those old hags until I know which side they're aligned with. Can't bet on folks who might turncoat.* Badbh smirked to herself, pushing out the doors to catch up with Pan and Romasanta. *Oh, but the battles born of them... those are the ones I crave!*

CHAPTER 35

CLIMBING TO THE TOP

Lillith stared daggers at Tony's back as she and the goddesses followed closely behind Tony's entourage. Occasionally he'd cough and hack, sliding a glance to her before faking he was looking for trouble. Alecto, Freya, and Hamadryades were chuckling over the two battles and how cute it was seeing him struggle. Part of her wanted to defend him, but no part of her disagreed with their observations. *He's such a rookie.* She rubbed her forehead as flashes of a splashing hand and tentacles waved wildly. *It's so painful to see how quick he is to panic and how little battle experience he has, even with the smallest of matters.*

"You see any more cockatrice?" Inle's voice caught Lillith's attention.

"N-no." Tony receded his stare at her. "So hard to breathe and see in this crap." Irawaru gruffed a muted bark, and they halted. "What did he say?"

"He said we may attract a bigger predator since you're covered in blood from the cockatrice," translated Inle. "But I haven't seen anything glowing in the clouds besides the heat lightning."

"Firedrakes glow nonstop, then?" They started walking again as Tony picked up a fist of ash to attempt to rub off the blood.

"Them and ifrits," added Inle.

"Personally, I hope they run into one of them," commented Freya. "I want to see this titan when he battles an intelligent opponent."

"Agreed," nodded Alecto, patting Lillith's shoulder, and she stiffened. "No offense. He makes a terrible hunter of beasts."

"I didn't consider that as a requirement when choosing who to be with," spat Lillith, brushing the arm off. "If any of you visited the Mortal Realm, you'd know how barren of beasts it is in these times. Kronos wiped them out and sent them to the Otherworld a long time ago."

"Really?" Freya seemed intrigued. "I know many prefer to live there over the Otherworld. I assumed it was joyless, with very little to no magic to provide luxuries."

Hamadryades chuckled, aloof, as she walked far behind the group. "You assume life can't find a way without magic at all. Nature favors adaptation and survival, Freya."

"You make me feel like a child when you speak in that tone," drawled Freya, waving off the Queen of Dryads. "I will go see for myself; perhaps you can take me there, Lillith—"

Lillith groaned, muttering, "Shit, I forgot I lost Glorianda in the Mortal Realm..."

"Wait." Alecto threw an arm out and cut in to face the group. "You let the Queen of Fae loose on her own in—"

"Look, it was an accident. How I was supposed to know about the troll—"

"The troll!" Freya was beside Alecto, arms crossed and tapping a boot.

"Ladies," Hamadryades brushed past Lillith and divided the other two to keep pace, "we're falling behind the boys."

Me and my big mouth, I just give up. All my plans and centuries of scheming and preparing have been unraveled thanks to a single entity. Lillith rushed to catch up as the path began to grow steeper and cut between massive boulders. Tony and Inle worked in tandem to lift and carry Irawaru over the steeper ledges. Eventually, it hit the point at which they faced a sheer cliff rising well over fifty feet overhead.

"Damn." Tony glared over at Inle, the god looking pitiful covered in ash. "Are you sure the path continues up there?"

"I came down this way." Inle shrugged and sat La Diablesse down.

"Why are they carrying that creature?" Alecto arched a brow at the others, and they all shrugged.

"And you still went after the bounty, knowing you'd have to carry it up this way?" marveled Tony, looking at Irawaru. "Oh, and we have you as well."

"It's a bounty," announced Freya.

"I heard him," hissed Alecto.

Lillith facepalmed at the bickering goddesses, while Irawaru covered his face with a paw and groaned at Tony for other reasons.

"It's okay; you weren't designed for climbing with a body like that." Tony squatted and petted him, and his tail wagged. "How about I take the heavier one and you strap Irawaru to your back?"

Inle thought for a moment, staring up at the wall. "You sure about this, brother?"

"I don't get tired, and if we strap her to my back, we might be able to get through here faster once we get to the top." Tony stretched his arms, one, then the other, as he turned to nonchalantly stare at Lillith.

I'm surrounded by idiots. Lillith spun away and put her hands on her hips. "So, are we going back?"

"I want to scale the wall," fussed Alecto, excited to rise to the challenge, taking a few steps forward before roots glued her in place. "Hey!"

"You will do no such thing," interjected Hamadryades, who shot a glance at Tony, who turned away and scooped up Irawaru. "Freya, you can make a stairwell to the top, can you not?"

"Of course, I can." Freya smirked, fluttering her fingers as one grew beyond where they could see through the ashen clouds. "Done."

"Let's go," Hamadryades commanded as the roots withered away from Alecto's boots.

"But I want to watch them climb," protested Alecto, following Hamadryades and Freya up the icy stairs.

"Walk slower," drawled Freya.

"There, everything is strapped in place." Tony caught Lillith's furrowed glare at the start of the stairs and lipped to her, *not fair.* "Looks all clear behind us, so we dodged a bullet."

"You start first?" offered Inle.

"No, you go first. You sound more familiar with this climb, and I'll follow your lead." With that, they started their ascent.

The goddesses would pause and lean on the railing to watch as they gripped and stepped, rising past them. Freya, at one point, gave Lillith a wink and thumbs up as she stood eerily close to Tony on the stairs as he climbed past. *It's taking every fiber of restraint not to let my jealousy rage forward. If Freya reaches out and touches Tony, by the powers be ... someone is dying today.* Lillith shoved them forward, rushing them up and past where Tony and Inle were currently climbing up the cliff.

"Let's see what waits at the top for them, huh?" Lillith threw a distraction worthy of getting at least Freya and Alecto's excitement going.

"Oh, do you think there's another flock of cockatrice?" Freya's eyes lit up.

"Let's hope it's something bigger." Alecto shoved past Freya, who gave chase.

Hamadryades gripped Lillith's wrist, waiting for the others to climb ahead before whispering, "Does he just see you or all of us?"

Lillith's legs went weak, and she caught the railing with her free hand. "I..."

"So, he does see..." she pried, reading deeply into Lillith's expression.

Crafty old tree hag, Lillith hissed bitterly in her thoughts. "See me, but I honestly don't know..."

Hamadryades flicked a thorn over Lillith's shoulder as Tony came eye-level with them. A sinking sensation hit the bottom of her stomach as she twisted, her cry muffled by Hamadryades's hand. Tony blinked where he clung to the cliff, a startled expression. Lillith looked at La Diablesse on his back. The creature went limp with the thorn in her neck. Dropping her hand off Lillith's mouth, Lillith gave the old dryad a bewildered expression.

"You can see me." Hamadryades smirked at Tony, who couldn't deny he'd flinched when he thought he was being attacked.

"I ... can?" Tony offered, giving Lillith an apologetic expression.

"You were being too obvious," jeered Lillith.

"It's hard not to acknowledge a fucking ice stairwell when I have to fucking climb with a monster on my back that clearly was awake," Tony retorted. "What the fuck do you expect me to do?"

Hamadryades chuckled and motioned. "Quick, boy. The thorn, before the others notice."

Tony adjusted his grip and tried, but it proved too hard. "I can't. You two are going to make me fall at this rate."

Lillith huffed, "Come closer, then."

Tony smirked and climbed over to them. Hamadryades reached over her and retrieved her thorn, giggling some more. Lillith bit her lip, some part of her wanting to lean in and kiss him. All it warranted was heat in her face. *Am I some lovesick puppy dog? What in the hell has gotten into me?*

His eyes burned into her, and she met Tony's gaze, her heart fluttering. *Is this what makes love different from lust? Shouldn't I feel aroused instead?*

"I'll leave you two to talk for a moment, but keep it short." Hamadryades tilted her head toward Tony. "I see why you were chosen, but be warned; our world is unrelenting."

"I've noticed," Tony snorted as the wooden woman climbed the steps out of view. "So, what the hell is going on?" He reached over and sighed relief when he touched the railing and could stand on the platform's edge.

"Everything about you breaks the rules," Lillith confessed. "What you are, who you are becoming, and this power growing inside you."

Inhaling deeply, Tony nodded his head and looked away in thought. "Had a feeling it had something to do with whatever is happening to me." He blew his breath and the falling ash twirled in response. "Are you safe with them?"

"Seeing Hamadryades breaking the intent of being here in secret." Lillith glanced up, but the ashen air had hidden them from her view, and she answered, "I don't think either of us is in danger for now." He leaned in, another deep inhale and sense of arousal, *longing,* escaped him. "What do we do now?"

"We," she motioned with a finger, "don't know we can see one another. Keep pretending we're not here and stop stealing glances at me. It's painfully obvious you're looking at me."

A smirk crossed his face, and he cooed, "But I can tell you get a little excited each time. It's a little addictive."

"Lillith, dear, you're taking too long!" shouted Hamadryades.

"Shit," Lillith muttered and cupped Tony's face. "Don't do anything else dumb."

"Like what?" he seemed offended.

"Like, why aren't you flying up the cliff with your wings?" she scolded.

"I have wings?" The expression on his face seemed distraught, as if the thought slammed him; *I could have just been done with this place days ago.*

"Yes. Damn Badbh and Boto. They're probably cackling over wine and liquor over this, but..." Lillith gave him a flat expression before pressing her lips hard against his. *Let me do this much to help you through here faster.*

Tony moaned into her as their lips parted as one, tongues hot and hungry to taste one another. His arm hooked her waist, the passion behind the kiss making her heart beat like a stampede of stallions, thudding and thunderous inside her ears. Snaking a hand down his neck, then his shoulder, she reached behind him. It was tight between La Diablesse and his bareback, but it was enough to rake her claws across him. Pleasure and lust escaped him as she held his lips hard against her own. Tony moaned as the sexually intoxicating aura washed through him until, at last, wings burst into existence.

She pulled away, hot and panting. "There, I think you can figure it out from here."

"Why is it when you claw me to bits I crave more?" he panted, flapping the appendages. "I've had them out before, if I remember, but have never flown with them. I thought they were for show." With a fearful expression, he mustered a half-hearted smile. "If I fall, this is your fault."

"I'll gladly take the credit," she whispered, turning to run away up the stairs. *Don't look back; don't look down. I can't take that broken look of want on his face.*

The sound of flapping rushed past her somewhere in the ashen abyss, the wind of him making her slow a moment. Another flap of wings and a yelp as Inle squealed profanities of the Caribbean variety at his friend. She caught up to the goddesses, who stared at her with suspicion.

"I just gave him a nudge of arousal for the wings," she offered. "He's new?"

"That's funny." Alecto smacked Freya's arm. "To think, he could have flown over all this bullshit."

Freya snort-giggled. "Such a *fersking*!"

Orange and yellow light glowed overhead from the cliff's top. A column of fire burned away the ash and a roar shook the air. *Firedrake!* Lillith shoved past them all, her stomach in knots. *He's not good enough to fly away and fight a firedrake! It's too big by the looks of the fire breath!* Panic ate at her core as she cursed the steps. *What the hell is wrong with me?* Wings burst out, and she launched up and off the stairs, rising to the glowing heat.

As she crested the top of the cliff, Tony pulled his blade free, one wing half burned away, and the aura of pleasure and bloodlust flowed from him. She landed close to a charred boulder where Inle and Irawaru coughed and gasped for oxygen.

What do I do? Do I help or do I have faith he's able to do—

CHAPTER 36

FIRE AGAINST FIRE

A sizzling and popping of flesh came from his charred wing and Tony frowned as the sensation felt exhilarating. *So, this is the unnerving sensation Cedric spoke of in his story. I just figured these powers out, and I can't believe that as soon as I figured out flying, I managed to fry one wing like a burned chicken wing while the other...* Tony glared at the wing he had broken by bashing into a boulder he wasn't prepared to find just over the cliff. Tony's face flushed as embarrassment flashed over him. Granted, he managed to duck behind the boulder minus the one wing. *How does she expect me to figure extra limbs out so easily?*

Looking at the firedrake, it was everything he had imagined a dragon to be. Armored scales reminded him of the alligators he'd caught glimpses of in the swamp. Fire rolled out from the crown of horns on the firedrake's head and down the ridge of its back like hairs on a horse's mane. Long and narrow, the snout was full of teeth, much like the cockatrice's. Its wings flapped and flared in warning. *It's making it clear it can out-fly me, but shit, anything can at this point with one broken wing and a hole burned into the other.*

Tony unsheathed his sword. "Finally, something to really test this sword out on," he announced to the firedrake. "I guess I actually am on a knightly quest."

"That's cute; he thinks he's a knight," chuckled Alecto, nudging Freya. "She fell for this guy; can you believe that?"

"He's cute," reassured Freya. "But do you think he can even face a full-grown drake?"

The firedrake lowered its head and hissed, eyes glowing like dewdrops of lava in those onyx scales that made up its skin. Even the drool dripping from its jowls glowed like lava and hissed and popped as it hit the ground at its clawed feet. A growl gurgled from deep within it, heat riding its breath as it stung at Tony's skin. He winced, sweat poured from him, and his heart thudded fast and hard. *I'm excited to fight, but I'm terrified of being burned alive.*

Tony took a few steps back and nearly walked off the ledge. *Dammit, I forgot about the ledge.* The drake flapped its wings, blowing away the ash and sending a halo of heat lightning sparking out and away all around them. One step forward made the ground thump under Tony's feet. *It's tall enough; I can at least try to get on the other side if I duck under it.*

A flap of his own wings was enough to thrust Tony forward with speed. The air glowed and heated behind him where he had stood as a column of flame followed his path. Dodging between a front and hind leg, he managed to get far behind the firedrake and onto the safety of a boulder-laden plateau. *Thud-Oph!* The firedrake's tail slammed into him, knocking the wind from his lungs. His back slammed into the stonewall of a mountainous boulder, blood spilling from his mouth as his internal organs burst. No pain filled him. Instead, the harrowing sensation of erotic pleasure brought a wicked smile to his face. Blood dripped hot from his chin as he slid and fell to the ground. Shivers of gratification rolled through his entire being as Tony could hear and feel the bones snapping back to heal the injuries. The sword was still firmly grasped in his hand. *Good, didn't drop it this time.*

Rising to his feet, his own blood covered him from head to toe. "I see. This is how it's been for the others. Cedric, Romasanta, even Boto. What do you do when the only time you feel alive is when you're fighting under the worst possible odds, despite being unkillable?"

Lillith stood just in view behind the firedrake, and he lipped, *wait for me.*

Squeezing the hilt, Tony watched as the firedrake spun and came stomping toward him. He charged forward. A claw slashed out, and he swung the blade, parrying and cutting a claw off. Snapping jaws aiming for retaliation were met with a fist. Lava spit ate through Tony's flesh where it splattered, but the arousal it brought spurred his desire to fight more. The jaws snapped down once more and Tony rammed the pommel into the bottom jaw. It snapped loud, and the remaining claw reached out, slicing across his torso. Wincing from the provocative rush, Tony rammed the sword downward and pinned the claw in place. The firedrake tugged a few times until the blade cut through its toe, abandoning it to twitch at Tony's feet.

It lurched back, a glowing ball rolling up its throat. *Fire breath, again!* Glaring around, Tony's heart thudded hard in his chest. *The big boulders are too far!* Glaring down the firedrake, he waited for the inevitable. Fire rolled between its teeth for a fleeting moment, and his gut rushed him toward it. *What do I have to lose at this point?* The column of heat scorched the ground behind him, following his path. The firedrake held the attack, scudding backward to keep up with him. Swinging out, the tip of his blade sliced the scales open. Clamping its jaw shut, the drake abandoned its fire breath to flap its wings to slide faster. A dragon's equivalent of a yelp escaped it as its hind legs slid off the ledge. Its eyes glowed with rage. A few more flaps pulled it up, and it came flying at him.

"Shit!" Tony turned, running in the opposite direction as he glanced at his mostly healed wings.

It was enough to keep him just in front of the snapping jaws as he half-glided across the field, kicking off boulders. He could hear the firedrake smashing them and the scratch of claws mimicking his own technique. Another sheer wall came into view and panic filled him. He flapped harder. *There are too many holes. I'm like a shitty parachute!* Tony spun around as the firedrake slid to a stop, its tail lashing out and pinning him against the wall.

"Argh!" The pleasure it brought was intoxicating.

Peeking up at last, the roll of fire boiled on its forked tongue. It spilled forward and Tony winced, closing his eyes tight in anticipation of the inevitable. *This is gonna be bad!* The heat in the air shifted, and nothing seemed to have slammed into him. No sounds of sizzling, none of the erotic pleasure or pang of teetering on the edge, nor the overwhelming heat filling his being. *What just happened?* Tony opened his eyes; a tiny, fiery female figure floated between him and the blast, shielding him. *Now's not the time to question it!* In one fist he still had his sword, pinned between the tail and wall, but the other was a claw. Digging into the tail's flesh, Tony ripped at it until he caught a scale and ripped it from the flesh. The firedrake stumbled back, retreating as it snarled at him and his new ally.

Able to breathe easier, Tony gave the fire-girl another glance and blinked. *It's like a bigger version of the tiny ifrit from before!*

"Well, let's see if we can drop this thing together." He nodded, swallowing.

It smiled, nodding as the flames bobbed on its head.

"You shield me from the fire, and I'll do the rest, okay?" Again, it nodded, and he turned back to the firedrake as it hissed and crouched, roaring its frustrations as lava spit splattered the ground.

Again, Tony charged forward. The sword finally began to buzz and pull at his core. *Now you're awake! About fucking time!* Another blast of fire was blocked by the ifrit, and he slid under her floating form. In a pure feat of athleticism, Tony was standing again with no loss to speed. A claw rushed down from the drake, and he swung. The power left the sword with a loud *whomp!* A front leg fell to his right, and the head to the left, as the body shook the ground on impact. Tony stumbled back, wheezing as his body shook. *Fuck, it took too much power from me again. This actually hurts.* Pain burned at his chest as he dropped the sword and fell back. *Just... need... to breathe...* A roar of pain escaped him, though it did nothing for his need for air. The ifrit blinked down at him, confused by his reaction. *I'm going to die as some fiery chick looks at me like I'm being dramatic; this sucks!*

His body was burning up and he gasped in one last inhale. *I can't...* Tony tried to sit up, but his body shook with the repercussions of the magic his sword pulled from him. Looking to the sky, he could see how it had not only cut down the firedrake but cut the ashen clouds and the white ones far above that. *Way too much magic...*

"Oh, first time using magic and overshot!" Alecto chortled, leaning into his view.

Freya tsked, hovering beside her. "That one hurts." She glanced up. "I think I can safely say he does have enough power to see through my spell."

"Oh?" Alecto poked his cheek.

"Help..." Tony croaked, tears welling in his eyes as he clawed at the pain swelling in his chest.

The ifrit spat and sputtered, a sound much like a hissing campfire at Alecto and Freya.

"Great. They all can see us after that spell left his sword!" Freya threw her arms up and walked out of Tony's view.

"Look, I can't fix this." Alecto frowned at the ifrit and poked Tony's face. "This idiot wasn't properly trained for magic and spent it on one blow like a rookie! You pretended to be one of the big boys and it bit you in the ass, new titan!" She stood, laughing loudly.

Another desperate wheeze and he managed some air, anger filling him. *Come on! SOMEONE!*

"I think he's mad at us, Freya." Alecto pointed, calling out beyond his scope of vision.

"Fersking!" scoffed Freya.

A wave of arousal slammed into him. The relief it brought him was instant. He sat up with alarm as he inhaled. *I can breathe!* Lillith landed next to him, wide-eyed. She, too, was rubbing her chest. Another wave from her and the pain retreated further. Sinking to her knees, she cupped his face. Yet another wave of arousal and desire rolled through him like refreshing ocean waves. His panting, his thudding heart—it all slowed as he soaked in her magic, relished in her touch, and stared longingly into her eyes.

Lillith searched his face, her lips opening and shutting, struggling with the words until, at last, she muttered, "You're an idiot."

Enjoying the ability to breathe again, Tony smirked, "Correction. I'm your idiot."

"How is he?" Hamadryades stood a few steps back with Inle and Irawaru at her side.

"Alive," drawled Lillith, shoving him away from her and abandoning him where he sat.

"Brother, you know some very important people." Inle gave him a grim expression.

Covering his face, Tony flopped onto his back. "I had no idea, Inle. No fucking idea how important."

Irawaru rushed up, licking his arm.

"It's true," Hamadryades reassured Inle. "He's proven he is unaware of his own connections, let alone his power." A giggle escaped her as she shot a glance at her fellow goddesses. "What say you, ladies?"

"I like him. He's funny." Alecto shrugged and turned to Freya expectantly.

Freya's glare came with a chill as the heat muffled and ice spread across the ground. "He has too much magical power and not enough understanding of how to use it."

Silence fell across them all as they all stared at Tony with weary expressions.

"Then someone teach me." Tony's words made Freya stiffen as he stood, brushing off ash and dirt. "It's not that I mean to use it wrong; I just don't know the difference. No offense." He rubbed his chest and cringed. "If I can avoid that, I'm happy to learn."

Freya drummed her fingers on her arm, weighing his words.

"Would the Amazonians be willing to teach him?" offered Hamadryades.

"Oh, no." Alecto shook her head and waved her hands. "That level of power is even higher than my own. That's something... well..." She shot a look and lipped something to Freya, who raised her brow and nodded. "That's something I think is best for Hades."

"H-hades?" guffawed Lillith and Tony.

"What about Pan?" added Lillith.

"Oh, no..." Tony shook his head.

Freya cut in before anything else could be said. "It's the type of power. It's dark magic. Unlike Pan's—that's light. He needs someone who can match his level and show him when to use it."

"But the gate is locked." Lillith crossed her arms, sucking on a cheek in thought.

"Oh, with that blade and magic." Alecto picked up the sword and handed it to Tony, patting his shoulder. "You can break a teensy-weensy padlock on any gate, can't you, big guy?"

"And you are?" Tony brushed her hand off and she scoffed.

"I'm Alecto. This is Freya—"

"F-Freya?" Tony stuttered.

"—and over there is Queen of Dryads, Hamadryades."

Bewildered, he glanced at them all. Even Inle seemed uneasy to be in their presence. *These are legendary, big players in the mythology world, and here they are telling me I need to train with the one and only fucking Hades!* He looked at Lillith, who had covered her face with both hands, groaning where she stood beside the wooden woman, Hamadryades. *What fresh hell did I walk into? Or will be going to?*

"Let's move on, shall we?" Hamadryades clapped her hands as if gathering up a tour guide group. "As an apology for interfering, I'll send you to your destination post-haste."

"Wait, I have—" Roots erupted all around Tony and they cocooned him before retreating. "Where ... are we?"

"Brother, we just got sent to Salamandra's front door," marveled Inle, grasping his shoulder.

They looked at the massive doorway as two creatures started to walk apart, their steps making the earth tremble. The crystal and rock bodies were like massive boulders with four legs that reminded him of an elephant. Nowhere could he see signs of a head or tail, just a body with feet that served as a means to block the doors. A groan and creak escaped the metal doors, and they began to open. Tony spun to check what all made it in the transportation. Irawaru and Inle were walking past with La Diablesse over Inle's shoulder. Just behind him, the ifrit sputtered and shrunk until she glided to sit on his shoulder. In a giant heap beyond that lay the firedrake's corpse.

"Well, little flame, I guess I owe you for helping me." It popped and crackled in delight, and he turned, jogging to catch up. "You take the lead, Inle."

"My pleasure, brother." Inle nudged him and winked. "You're going to be okay?"

"Well, you have no idea why I came to see Salamandra, and I'm not quite sure anymore." Tony swallowed as they stepped through the threshold.

What a strange world I live in now, but where did they take Lillith? And how the hell am I to get to Hades to learn to use this magic inside me? Wait, isn't he in the Underworld? Does that mean I have to die? Wait, no... maybe it's like when I went into the Otherworld where I...

CHAPTER 37

RITES RESOLVED

L illith stood before the three powerhouses, their stares on her making her feel small in their presence. Part of her wanted to run, but gauging from their actions and words moments before, she was no longer in harm's way, nor was Tony. *So why do I still feel as if I'm being held hostage?* Alecto shifted and crossed her arms; they all seemed to be waiting for her to say something. *What could I possibly say?*

"If you are expecting an explanation or some means of excuse for him, I have nothing to offer." Lillith shrugged and took a seat on a toadstool, crossing her legs. "You clearly saw how green he is."

"Quite the cute little sapling," sniggered Hamadryades, who summoned a table with tea between the toadstools. "Ladies, we promised to give this boy a Rite of Preeminence Judgment. What is your verdict? Does he have the potential for greatness? Is he worthy of the crown Lillith not only titled him with, but for the first time since her own creation has properly bestowed on someone?"

Freya flicked her skirt back, took a seat, and after a long silence of sipping her tea, spoke. "There is no question he has the potential."

"Agreed." Alecto still stood, looming over them as she thought to herself and announced, "He's far more superior than I had expected but is untrained and lacks the experience to support the crown you thrust onto him."

"Trust me; I didn't willingly give it to him." They gave her a distraught expression and her face flushed. "Not in a creepy Zeus or Hermes way!"

"I was wondering..." cringed Alecto, making a disgusted face.

"Look, he pursued my affection, and I can't say I may ... have ... instigated a time or two." Lillith's chest ached with the confession.

"Instigated?" Freya lifted a brow, smirking. "Do tell."

"Well, um, about that." Lillith picked up her teacup and started to down the scolding hot liquid in hopes it would render her tongue useless.

Alecto sat down, grinning as she insisted, "Yes, do tell."

"Well, I'd be lying..." Glaring down at the empty teacup, *traitor,* she thought bitterly. "...about intentionally placing my mark on the back of his neck." She bit her tongue to demand it stop wagging and questioned, *did she spike this tea with truth serum of sorts?! She wouldn't... but then...*

"Oh, how thrilling, to have him bend over for you instead..." Freya's words slowed, and she smacked Alecto's cup from her hand, but it was far too late. "Hamadryades. You wicked old tree!"

Giggling, Hamadryades waved a hand, reassuring the goddesses at her table with, "Come now! We should be talking frankly; the man is worthy of the King Incubus title with those looks and that voice."

"That voice in the throes of pass—" Alecto cupped her mouth.

"Well," cooed Lillith as she could feel the rise of lust in the goddesses before her, "you should all know my thrall is only loyal to his queen."

"Th-thrall?" Alecto bit a lip, eyes darting away.

"Oh, yes." Lillith was now in a dominant situation over them as she waved arousal through them, mimicking the wave Tony would release in moments she dominated him. "That's just a sampling of when I make him bow to me, by force."

Freya made herself a fan of ice, fluttering it to calm her beating heart. "My, Ottar makes me feel hot and bothered, but this... this is far too much heat."

"But that's not a normal wave of lust, is it?" Alecto picked up the teacup and sat it on the table.

"No," confessed Lillith and sighed. "I should be dead for what I did. My curse speaks of forfeiting my life to give my love that title or even laying with someone I have *those feelings for.*"

"I knew it had something to do with you never bestowing the title," interjected Hamadryades with a saddened expression. "But that curse refers only to children of Gaea or blood relations to her and her kin."

"That's what I thought, too, until Tony took the title..." Lillith searched for the words to describe it. "I suppose I didn't bestow it on him; I simply bonded myself with the king, who found a way to obtain the title in his own way."

"I see." Alecto twisted her lips in thought before adding, "It seems you aren't quite sure what he is either."

"N-no." Lillith's chest felt heavy as she murmured, "I really have no idea if he's a titan or something entirely new and different. I do know he's the first true King Incubus."

"Is that going to upset our dear Angeline's betrothed?" Freya dumped out her teacup and frowned. "And how strong was that dose, Hamadryades?"

"Enough to break your frozen lips loose. It should be gone by now, even if you had drunk the whole cup." She winked at Lillith as if to signal she would be safe to talk further.

"I'm glad you found him worthy," Lillith concurred.

"Yes, we just need to get him to Hades and get that magic under control as soon as possible." Freya nodded, waving her fingers to summon icy cups of water. "I assure you, these are not spiked." She shot a narrowed glare at Hamadryades, who shrugged.

"Yes, his magic is the current issue more than anything. He has an unlimited well, and I agree, Hades would be the only one to teach him best how to use it." Alecto gulped down some water, refreshed. "In fact, there are a lot of similarities between them."

Lillith flinched, scowling as she rebutted, "I don't think so."

"No, there is something... familiar." Hamadryades tapped her wooden lips a moment, and the autumn leaves in her hair shifted to a vibrant green. "Yes, he fights like him."

"You're right," agreed Freya, sitting up sternly. "You don't think he is of relation?"

"No, but I'd suspect he picked up some training from one of Hades's associates in the past," Alecto reassured. She inhaled swiftly and asked, "Who trained him?"

"Boto and the Battle Goddess Badbh," answered Lillith.

"Oh." Alecto retreated into her thought and mumbled, "Well, someone taught him how to project his murderous intent."

"Look, I didn't pry in his past because I didn't want to share my own," Lillith hissed, repeating herself from before.

"We know and understand that well, Gaea's heart," snarled Hamadryades as if reprimanding a child.

"Don't call me that." Lillith's emotions were weighing down on her and her mood was souring. "I'm nothing like the body I was birthed from."

"Agreed." Alecto stood, stretching. "We should be going."

"Yes, we should." Freya gave a weak smile. "If you need us, call upon us." With that, she and Alecto were gone in a flurry of snowflakes.

Lillith could breathe again. She leaned on the table and buried her face into her arms. Nothing harmful had come from the judgment, and Hamadryades had revealed their inner attractions. *Did she do that to help me feel more confident? I wonder...* She looked up to ask but found she sat alone in the forest. *Of course, she's gone as well.* Closing her eyes, she was exhausted mentally, emotionally, and physically from all that had unfolded. She had given much of her magic to Tony, more than he needed in fear that was the last time she would have a chance to support him.

Images of the fight with the firedrake played out in her mind. The way sweat dripped across his body and patches of smudged ash. His eyes fierce, fangs and horns adding to a look that shouted *demonic* by any means. He looked worthy of any creature of the Underworld, like herself. *But he doesn't resemble Cedric at all, except for those green eyes, I suppose.* Smiling, she wondered how much longer she would be trapped in the Otherworld until someone came to get her or if she dared to leave the safety of Hamadryades's Forest.

A creaking sound of a door sent a chill up her spine, and she opened her eyes. Turning on her toadstool, an open door, much like the one that brought her here, appeared. The other side was pitch black and her heart leaped. *Do I dare see what he wants with me?* Standing, she walked slowly to the abyss as it sucked the air into itself. An arm's length away, she turned to see if a dryad or Hamadryades was anywhere to see this magic that greeted and haunted her. Looking back to the nothingness, she held her breath and stepped into the darkness. The door slammed loudly, and her heart thudded as she spun slowly, looking into the abyss. She pulled on her bond with Tony, the arousal waving back from him as he echoed it in earnest. The comfort it brought her soothed her nerves as she paused and calmed her thoughts. *I can do this. Someone needs to confront this thing, or is it him?*

"What do you want from me?" She spoke into the dark.

"...WantwantWantwantWANT..." it hissed and echoed all around her. "...what is it you want? Desire? Crave?"

Lillith swallowed, the question reflected onto her, and she answered, "To be..." She hesitated and swallowed. *Let's be honest.* "To be happy," she announced to it. "Doesn't everyone desire and crave happiness?"

Laughter rolled from all around, and a flickering of torches came to life. She stood in a circular room with no doors. Footsteps made her twist around once more and there stood a being with gleaming green eyes. *So much like Tony and Cedric.* He was unnaturally tall, easily pushing what she could only guess as close to seven feet. His long silvery hair was pulled back halfway, braids mixing with long locks of loose hair like the Vikings of old. Bejeweled hair clasps and rings interwoven between knots, adding a sense of royalty to the way it crowned his head. He had a chiseled jawline, broad shoulders, muscular forearms, and a skin tone that was a ruddy, earthy tone as if scorched by the desert sun. Unexpectedly, he wore modern clothing with a black button-up shirt with rolled-up sleeves and black slacks. The look was complete with an expensive watch whose hour and minute hands spiraled uncontrollably, as if time was of no object to this thing. He sighed, giving her a smug expression as he looked her over. *Shit, I still have ash and dirt and Tony's blood on my hands and, and...* He motioned behind her, and she turned to see a wrought-iron table and chairs. *Three, but for who?*

"Sit," he demanded in a celestial voice that touched her soul.

Her skin pimpled as she did so, her eyes still locked on this creature, the man, this powerful being.

"Did you notice yet?" he asked, taking a seat across from her, hands clasped on the table.

"Is it safe to assume you are responsible for what changed Tony?" Lillith balled her fist on the table, staring daggers at the man.

"Well, that was part of the process." He shrugged and leaned back in his chair, drumming his fingers. "Go on, ask it."

"Who are you?" she blurted.

"Who do you suspect?" He licked a dual set of fangs and her mind flashed back to Cedric.

There are only a few creatures ever known to bear those. Swallowing, she braved her suspicion, her voice trembling as she dared to say, "A-Aether?"

244

Nodding to himself, he exhaled and corrected, "I go by Avalon now."
The weight only shifted in her chest. She felt no relief or comfort
from his answer and acknowledgment. *No, this doesn't explain anything.*
It only makes this more confusing than ever before. What do I even do with
this information?

"You do nothing with it," he offered. "I only wish for three beings to
know I exist. The first is you, my most precious treasure."

Lillith flinched, deducting, "You can read thoughts and do all sorts
of magic. So why hide and be so ... cryptic? So, you want me to know. I
suspect Tony, but the third?"

"You haven't figured it out? My motive for setting so much of this
in motion?" He tilted his head and his eyes shimmered with newfound
excitement.

"No one has," she hissed, annoyed with him. "You're the worst father
possible to give birth ever so recklessly as your prize son Zeus did after
you left."

"But he will not inherit this world, so what does it matter what Zeus
or any of my sons of old have to offer?" He seemed unphased by her words
and she didn't dare to let her thoughts wander now under his presence.

"Well, clearly you wanted to speak to me?" she questioned, leaning
back in her chair to cross her arms.

"Come now. I'm playing nice for once," he mused.

"Why didn't you stop Gaea or Kronos sooner?" she demanded.

Raising his brow high, he smirked. "Forward and bold, are we?"

Lillith sat tight-lipped and firmly staring daggers at him.

"Let's circle back—"

"You're dodging," she declared.

"I am," he mused.

"Answer me," she demanded.

"No."

This man is so...

"...impossible?" he finished her thought, and she shuddered.

"Do you not consider anything sacred or private?" she spat, banging
a fist on the table.

"True love."

She flinched, giving him a baffled expression.

"Now, that burning sensation, did you sense what it was I did to you and the one trying to prove himself worthy to me?" The room darkened, though the torches were lit. "Answer me, my precious heart." Horns grew and behind him glowed magnificent wings, one of light like a fae and one dark and feathered like celestials. "I demand to hear you acknowledge me and my gift."

The aura he brought down upon her sucked the air from her lungs and rendered her soul cold. Her sole thought pulled on her bond, tugging and calling for Tony.

Help me.

CHAPTER 38

DYRNWYN

Rocks crumbled down from overhead as the cherufes shuffled behind them. Every step they made was worthy of being called an aftershock, and Tony thought back to the only time he visited Los Angeles during a minor earthquake. *Walking fault lines,* he snorted to himself. The doors shut behind them, closing off the light that had filtered in from the sky. The corridor glowed with the eerie light of the lava that dripped and hissed down the wall in places like glowing columns, moving in a way that made them seem alive. Tony followed behind Inle, who soon slowed to a stop. Paying closer attention to the metal doors beginning to appear now on either side, Tony could see the end of the hall was fast approaching. Someone had approached in his moment of admiration of the strange palace: a big man smudged with ash in leathers like in the images he'd seen of blacksmiths on television or in movies. The man leaned over to meet Tony's gaze and nodded in acknowledgment.

"Look, Inle, Salamandra's indisposed with his esteemed guests right now." The deep voice rang loud against the halls, echoing far behind them. "Besides, who's your friend?"

"Uh, Tony." He offered a hand to the burly, bearded man who shoved his smudged glasses up on his nose in reply. "Right, maybe handshakes aren't a thing here..."

A grin cracked on the man's face, and he firmly gripped Tony's hand and gave it a tight, hard shake. "Rali Gofannon, manager of the forge fires and superintendent of this operation. Expert metalworker by trade and talent."

"Uh, operation?" Tony gave a baffled look at them both. "What operation? You make it sound like we walked on to some private base somewhere. Or factory?"

"We're the last metalworkers and legendary forge in full operation still residing in the Mortal Realm." Rali scratched his beard with a look of pride in his eyes. "I bet you've never seen a magic forge before."

"But Avalon has a forge." Tony arched a brow, suspicious of the information provided to him by the man with the crushing handshake. "In fact, I've seen it and worked by it. Hot as hell."

A shine of admiration lit Rali's face and he sounded impressed. "Avalon is considered its own realm, but you've seen the forge there. Impressive. That's the one Battle Goddess Badbh is said to create legendary weapons and armor from, isn't it?"

"I helped her forge my own blade." Tony unsheathed the sword and offered for him to hold and inspect the blade. "Granted, she made it pretty; I just helped fold the metal and provided some materials for the magic in it."

"Oh, black sands of the Underworld," whispered Rali, flipping the blade one way, then the other. "I didn't think anyone had any in storage after it was locked by Gaea. Should have known Badbh keeps a little of everything on hand."

Tony swallowed, nervous he may have said too much. "I have no idea; that woman has mountains of weapons and shields. It seems she is in competition with someone."

"You're not mistaken." Rali shot a look at him and swung the blade once, whistling. "The balance and magic are something else. Here, take it before it eats away any more of my magic. Don't know how you can be standing with a blade that eats magic like a thirsty beast." Clearing his throat, Rali's expression turned sterner. "I know who Inle is and why he's here, but I don't know why you're here, Tony."

"Uh, well, Pan sent me?" Tony offered and searched his memory. "Said I was to pick up a blade... called..." Rali crossed his arms, snorting as he waited for the answer. "Da... Duh... Dooo... Durr..."

"*Dyrnwyn?*" offered Rali with an arched brow.

"That, yes, that one." Tony could see this didn't seem to invoke anything from Rali. *Was I supposed to demand the blade? Or make a big ordeal about it?*

"And again, who are you to be asking Salamandra for his most prized blade?" Lowering his brow, Rali started to drum his fingers on an arm.

Dammit, Pan! Tony cleared his throat, looking to Inle, who threw a hand up and turned away to say, *you're on your own on this one, brother.* "Can I speak with Salamandra? I'm pretty sure he knew I was coming." *Please don't let this much be a bluff; please let this much be true, or so help me when I get back, I will wring Pan's neck!*

Rali blinked and looked at a door. "Well, no offense, kid, he's in there with Prince Fire-Fade and Prince Fire-Flash waiting on a king to—"

"King Incubus," blurted Tony. "I'm a, uh, the King Incubus! He's waiting on me."

Rali looked him over and burst into laughter. "Nice try!" Wiping a tear from an eye, he struggled to catch his breath. "You barely weigh a pound, soaking wet, and look nothing like a sex demon, let alone King Sex Demon." Another wave of laughter rolled from the smith deity, loud and boastful as it echoed all around.

A blast of uncanny arousal slammed into Rali, and he went white, meeting Tony's heated glare. "I said I was the King Incubus. Was he not expecting me?"

"I, uh." Rali blinked and looked to Inle, thumbing at Tony. "No joke, huh?"

"Brother, he's a monster for sure, but a man of honor." Inle patted Tony's shoulder. "I was blessed to have him by my side on my way back, fo'sure."

"Well, damn." Rali flicked his eyebrows high, nudging his glasses up once more, and nodded for them to follow him to the door. "You boys enjoy then."

With an ear-shattering whistle, the ground shook, and the door opened. Inside, steam rose from geysers and pools of hot water; the air was filled with strong herbs and incense burning within giant clay pots. Swaths of colorful cloth draped all around and a giant gold statue of a golden dragon battling with a silver-white tiger filled the cavern wall opposite the massive doors. It was colossal, something expected in a temple or palace. *Uh, I guess this is a palace?*

Blue figures raced all around, giggling and watching as he and Inle marched farther inside the hot-springs-turned-pseudo-sauna room. Lust filled the air thick here; the waves of it from all directions felt like handfuls of stones dropped in a pool of water, with Tony at the center. There were blue-skinned women filling the room, naked other than the long hair that draped their bodies in sheets of reds, purples, or black. Every time Tony glanced at them or met their eyes, they would chuckle behind steam or cloth as their lust slammed into him and he let his sword absorb it.

"What are they?" Tony whispered to Inle.

"Ciguapa." Inle shrugged and adjusted La Diablesse on his shoulders. "Sirens of the Caribbean, really. I suppose they are a kind of succubus."

"I can feel that much," Tony muttered, watching as Irawaru yelped and ran off into a curtain of steam. "Where is he going?"

"He must have found what he was here to look for." Inle smacked Tony's arm and signaled for him to be quiet.

A chorus of singing came within earshot, and soon the largest pool in the room lay before them as two Japanese men and a large scaly salamander-looking creature ate meat from a ciguapa servant. The bulbous eyes on top of its oversized head fell to Tony and Inle as they flung La Diablesse over the edge of the raised hot spring.

"Ah! Inle!" Salamandra stood, long body built like a lizard with stubby, almost froglike fingers and short arms. "I see you caught my bounty!" He motioned to the Japanese gentlemen, who stared at the creature with deep intrigue. "Prince Fire-Fade, Prince Fire-Flash, please excuse me a moment as I do business with these gentlemen."

"No problem, Salamandra-san." One of the princes replied before they both went back to flirting and enjoying the ciguapa servants.

Water rolled up and over the edge, hot against Tony's legs and feet. *Hot springs sound so good right about now...* The giant salamander-lizard sniffed at La Diablesse and licked its hideous face. Salamandra chuckled to himself as he inspected her slender arms and sniffed her hair. Humming to himself, his bulbous eyes shifted back to Inle.

"Was she difficult to detain?" Salamandra's voice was throaty and snorty, the black scales and skin painted with splotches of yellow reminding Tony of a tiger salamander a girlfriend once kept.

"I don't know. If I'm being honest, the King Incubus detained her and aided in retrieving her." Inle kneeled before Salamandra, leaving Tony dumbfounded. "He even brought you a gift of a firedrake to your doorstep, domain master Vulcan."

Tony swallowed. *Fuck... this fucking lizard is the Vulcan from mythology.* "It was just luck, to be honest." Tony mimicked Inle's motion and bowed his respects, unsure if he should drop to a knee. *But I am a king, so ... maybe I don't?*

The bulbous eyes seemed unmoved before he started to laugh, the stubby fingers gripping the top of his head, claws digging in to bring Tony closer. "You mean to tell me this tiny thing is the first official King Incubus? Pan's going to pay for playing jokes on me again."

"No, really, I am." Tony could hear Aether's words echoing: *Prove you're worthy.* As he pried the creature's hand off him, it tilted its head. "And please, don't be rude and touch me without my permission," added Tony, sending a blast of incubine power into Salamandra, who retreated and sloshed back in surprise, nostrils flaring. "It's dangerous to touch a demon without considering the harm it may bring you." Tony ran a hand through his hair, glaring at the Salamandra with newfound authority. "I'm here for the sword. It seems Pan has made arrangements for me to get it."

A wicked grin grew on Salamandra's face as his body shook off a shudder. "Forgive me, you're right. A king indeed." He waved his stubby fingers, and some lizardmen seemed to melt into existence. "Take this thing and throw her into the dungeon. I'll see what to do with her later." They hissed and snorted, grabbing La Diablesse and were gone as fast as they had appeared. "Come join us a moment and rest, oh great King Incubus. Let us celebrate your new reign!" He spun in a grand gesture, his tail splashing water that slapped hot against Tony's chest.

Sucking a cheek, Tony looked at Inle, who shrugged. "Normally, I would be civil enough to take advantage of the springs, but where is the sword? I've got other business to tend to."

One of the princes pointed up to the huge statues. "Good luck, Gaijin. It's in the dragon's mouth."

The other one twirled a ciguapa's hair in his fingers. "And they say any who touch the white hilt is burned away to ash. It has found no one worthy for a long, long time, Gaijin."

Glaring up at the dragon, Tony could see the hilt at the center of the tongue. The golden jaws were open and large enough for anyone to stand on the platform created there. Looking all around, it was clear no one was ever meant to reach that high. No ladder or stairs led to the top of the statue where the dragon's head peaked, the tallest point of the fight scene with the swiping tiger.

"I apologize, King Incubus," cooed Salamandra, splashing back down into his seat. "There's no way to reach the sword. It's kept far out of reach for everyone's safety. Surely you understand. It's not meant to be touched at all."

Shaking his head, Tony licked a fang. "I'm really fucking tired of everyone right about now." Cracking his neck one way, then the next, Tony allowed his horns to come forth like a wicked crown. "I've had a shitty time, and I'm in a hurry." Wings stretched out from behind him, and a tail began to swish to and fro in annoyance.

Salamandra snarled, "It's my treasure. Prepare to burn before taking it. Why would it choose you as its master when I can't even tame that blade?"

"But you can't touch it because you're not worthy." Tony gave him a wicked grin, eyes glowing green with the rise of power. *Putting a King Incubus in a room full of sex demons. Who was dumb enough to give me a power high like no tomorrow and then dare challenge me?*

Salamandra lunged forward, hissing as he bared his teeth.

"Sit back down," commanded Tony, a wave of murderous intent and bloodlust sending everyone scattering away from him besides Inle and the ifrit on his shoulder.

"S-S-See you another time, S-S-Salamandra-san," muttered a prince, and they both disappeared in a flash of flames.

"You will never be worthy." Tony flapped his wings, rage filling him as he took to the air.

Tony glided across the span and slid down the tongue and into the dragon's jaws. Below, Salamandra's roar echoed off the walls. Tony's heart thudded hard inside his chest as he stepped closer to the ivory and leather hilt of the sword jammed deep into the golden tongue. He cast a glare back down at the large pool, so far away now that it could fit inside his hand. Inhaling deeply, Tony reached for the hilt. It heated in his palm and buzzed similarly to his own sword. He waited, expecting to combust into flames as Pan had implied. The tiny ifrit fluttered off his shoulder and grew to match his size. She smiled and cupped his hand where he gripped the hilt, afraid to tug it free just yet in fear that would be the moment he'd forfeit his existence. Her orange flames shifted to a brilliance of white, blue, and purple. He stared, marveling over how beautiful the sight of her before him seemed... angelic.

"You are worthy to carry my spirit, my honor," she cooed, looking at him with kindness. "You wish to protect the ones you love, and that is worthy enough cause to wield my body and soul."

Tony pulled the sword free and watched as the flames swirled around the blade, the heat comforting. "Thank you," he whispered as they died out and retreated within the hilt.

Screams cut through the air as the hot springs exploded water into the air. Scanning the chaos through the steam and streams of water, he spotted Inle running with something black and yellow tucked under an arm. Salamandra roared as the water around him clouded red and he gripped where a stubby arm had once been. Hot on Inle's heels was the familiar form of Irawaru and on his back a ghostly shape of a woman, her arms outstretched behind her as the waters rose violently in their wake.

"There's a story there, Wyn. I hope it's okay to call you that since I can't pronounce Dry, Dur, well, your full name for two-shits." Tony smirked as his companions down below vanished through the doors, and the white sword buzzed and warmed in his palm. "They don't need me, but there is someone who does." Turning around, Tony found a door waiting for him. "Let's have a word with Avalon."

I'm going to make sure he knows exactly how worthy I am.
No one will keep me from Lillith.

CHAPTER 39

A Blessing or A Curse

A door slammed shut and there stood Tony with a heated glare, a white and a black sword in either hand. "Avalon." Rage rode in his voice, ash and blood still smeared across his entire being.

He looks so monstrous. Lillith's breath caught, the horns and wings adding to the aura; he brought to the darkness something deeper than just his incubus powers.

"Come. Come sit." Avalon had a wild grin stretched across his face, the double fangs ferocious. "We were just discussing you!"

Tony looked at Lillith, who gave him a worried expression, and he asked, "Are you okay?"

Swallowing, Lillith replied in honesty, "I don't know," and shot a glare at Avalon. *Or do we call him Aether? I don't even know if this is the same, but the power is terrifying.*

"Oh, stop looking at me like I'm about to snap my fingers and wipe you both out of existence," Avalon chuckled. "Great movie. Have you seen it?"

"No," Tony and Lillith replied in unison.

"What do you want with us?" Lillith pounded a fist on the table again.

"I want nothing." Avalon motioned for Tony to sit. "But you two wanted a lot. From the world and from one another, no? I've been working hard to deliver on all fronts for you both."

"You shoved me out that last gate and told me to prove I'm worthy, and here I stand," Tony's wings stretched wide behind him as he seethed. "You don't scare me."

"Well, is he?" Avalon turned to Lillith.

"W-worthy?" she guffawed. "Of course, he's worthy." Standing, she took three steps before a force halted her movement, and fear filled her face.

"Sit down," Avalon growled and flicked his fingers, forcing her to slide back and flop into the chair.

"S-stop," she managed to stutter before he made a motion for her to zip it.

"What did you do to her?" roared Tony, and he found he couldn't move a muscle either.

"I need you two to understand that I will not give my blessing just yet." Pulling a cigar from the air, he began to puff on it, enjoying it a moment before continuing, "So let's talk about what parting gifts I've bestowed on you both, my most favored children of this world." Another long puff and Avalon blew circles into the air as he deadpanned at Tony. "You both were burning up not too long ago, but did you understand why?"

Lillith hummed and gave a heated glare at Avalon.

With a flick of his fingers, her lips opened, and she inhaled deeply. "You may speak now, but talk ill of me again, or think it, and I'll put you in an unpleasant state. Love is cruel, after all."

Lillith trembled, staring at Tony. "Our curses burned away, but I don't know how. Including the one that created me."

"But he does, don't you, big guy?" With the cigar between his lips, Avalon stared calm and unmoved by Tony's wrathful expression.

"Because I'm your son." The words tasted bitter in Tony's mouth. "Not a descendant of Kronos or Merlin, but directly my father, with no need for magic." Every muscle drew tight as memories of his mother seeming broken and muttering about how she bore the child of Gabriel, the Angel of Death, bit at him. *This asshole broke her mind to cover his tracks. Or is it possible my mother couldn't cope with the idea she had given herself to something far from human? I was in and out of foster homes until I ended up in a family that had ties to the mafia; go figure.*

Avalon scoffed. "Your mother was a looker, and the scent of Gaea's curse in her blood was enough to spark an idea, a solution, a gift for my little treasure." He winked at Lillith.

Lillith seemed calm as she closed her eyes, whispering, "So my suspicions were right. It wasn't just a descendant of Gaea. I suspected he was somehow of your lineage by some twist of fate." She opened her eyes and looked at Avalon, speaking her new deduction with confidence. "He is directly related, not because of the curse."

"Oh no, that curse just pulled out the King Incubus, though I hadn't thought of what kind of power that whole dynamic Gaea created had evolved this far from its initial conception. I don't think you can call that a curse any longer but living magic. She started it, but Cedric seemed to find a way to free himself from it all. Beautiful stuff she can create, and how it takes a life of its own, is chef's kiss." Another puff on his cigar and he snorted. "He's nothing like me, though. Sad you didn't get any of my good features. I bet you can trade up those wings in just the right mood, son. The question is whether you have wings of light," Avalon stretched out his iridescent fae wing, "or wings of darkness?" and flared out the black feathered wings.

"I don't understand: how did he get cursed if he's a direct child?" demanded Lillith, her heart racing. *We both know direct blood has immunity!*

"Because he bound me," Tony interjected; he too was piecing it together as he opened to the possibility that his life up until she entered it had all been a ruse. "The burning. It was you breaking the chains on the titan side that you had placed on me." Tony grasped at memories and thoughts as he furrowed his brow. "Pan's test would have shown me as a titan if he had tested me before the curse."

Lillith stiffened. "Yes. Considering what we know, yes, the result would have shown titan."

"Will you come sit down and talk with your old man like a big boy?" Avalon arched a brow and waved his hand.

Tony fell to the floor, the swords clattering to the ground. His body ached from the tension and being locked in place. Tony could feel his hands tremble until he balled them into fists, white-knuckled to calm his nerves. Standing, he grabbed the chair and slid it closer to Lillith, out of the reach of his *father*. Avalon rolled his eyes, waiting for him to sit. Tony reached over and clasped Lillith's hand, her entire being shaking and cold.

"Such dreadful expressions," Avalon chortled. "Keep that up, and you both will have crow's feet from hell. Speaking of which, Hades says he's ready to train you all the way now that you've come of age." He rose to his feet, arms spread out in victory. "Hamadryades has fulfilled her promise to doctrine my last son as a titan recognized by peers, and now, we simply need to have you master magic, my boy!" He pivoted on his heel and smacked the table, making both of them flinch. "But one last thing." Gripping Tony's wrist, he pulled the cigar from his hand. "I can't simply leave it to speculation. No, I want to see Kronos's and Gaea's faces when they see the sign of Aether burned into your flesh." He pressed and rubbed the burning tip of the cigar across the top of Tony's hand.

"Thanks, Dad," snarled Tony as he made no effort to pull away.

Lillith pushed her arousal into Tony where his other hand held hers, squeezing tighter. It only worked as small waves of relief as he endured it. Time knew no end; no attempts to move were made in fear Avalon would aim his ill will at them for challenging him further.

"What happened to you?" she gave Avalon a sorrowful expression, and he flinched, releasing Tony at last.

"You can say I lost my mind at sea," he sighed, turning away, marching into the darkness. "Excuse me; I have a restaurant to run while I wait for the world to end. Oh, and you should tell him sooner and not after the fact, love. That's the one little thing I can't intervene or stop. That one I didn't plan or expect, though I find it strangely ... pleasing."

"Avalon, wait—" Lillith's words were choked out by a loud thundering. The ground gave way under them, darkness swallowing them up. Tony wrapped his arms tight around her, wings wide as he floated in the nothingness. He kissed the top of her head, the smell of burned flesh still lingering in the air. Against his bare chest, she could hear his heart racing with fear as fast and hard as her own. *Monster.* A force came down hard on them. Tony rolled in a split moment, and they slammed hard against a stone floor. He wheezed as the wind was knocked from him. She lay still, cradled in his arms. After a long silence, they dared to look around and relief waved over them. *We're back in his room!* Turning back to Tony, she cupped his face, kissed him, and pulled away.

"We need to talk about—"

Tony's lips pressed firm against hers, kissing her deeper.

She followed his lead until they pulled away slowly. "I know. There's a lot about my life that I don't think is as normal as I thought." He stumbled over the words.

"And I need to be honest about what we are." Tears were streaming down her cheeks. "I have ... that night when we ... first."

Tony thumbed her tears away from her eyes as she shook on top of him. "What is it that you are so afraid to tell me?"

"I don't know if it's going to be different because of you, and ... the curse is gone, but..." She leaned down and touched foreheads with him and whispered, "I'm ... with child. Your child. It seems to be one, not the brood or vileness and..."

Tony hugged her into him, his lips whispering into her ear, "Then let's go someplace safer."

In an instant, they fell yet again, but this time landed in a bed that plumed dust all around them.

"This is... this is my castle in my domain." Lillith sat up in alarm, straddling him.

"You bonded yourself to me. It's our domain and not a damn thing will ever set foot here and threaten you or..." Tony's palm was hot on her belly, his words a murmur, "...what is ours."

"What about the others?" Lillith stared in disbelief.

"Fuck them." A fiery glare glowed in his eyes. "It can wait. The world isn't ending any time soon."

She pulled off him and shook her head, distraught as her voice cracked. "It's not that simple. You're the only one as strong as Aether. You're the last son."

"No, I'm not." Tony pumped his fist and glared at the archaic symbol burned into the top of his hand. "I will not be the one inheriting the throne, remember?"

"Cedric." She sucked on her cheek and started to search her drawers. "Come on. I keep spare phones somewhere around here. Ah-ha!" Turning it on, she frowned as it bleeped low battery, and she dove back into the drawers for another, finally getting one to stay on, the number ringing.

"Sister! Where in the fates have you fucking been? This is a shit show—"

"Pan! I need you—" A burst of rose petals popped in behind her and she spun to hug Pan.

"Well, not the welcome I am accustomed to..." Lillith trembled, and Pan caught the grim expression on Tony's face. "And what the fuck is happening between you two?"

"Correction: happening to us, not between." Tony flashed the branding and Pan paled.

"Sister, my love." Pan pulled Lillith off and cupped her distraught face. "Why does our boy toy have the mark of Aether?"

She bit her lip, and after a long silence between them, she chose to dodge the question. "He needs to see Hades."

"Fucking Hades," drawled Pan.

"W-wait! I'm not leaving you alone here!" Tony scrambled to his feet.

"If you master your magic," she poked Tony in the chest with each word, "we might be able to defend against him. On that note, Cedric is in a coma, which means I have to show Angeline how to pull on their bond. Something you clearly have an innate talent for doing, seeing as *you* managed to bring us here."

Tony stared hard into her face. "Fine. If you think I can protect us better if I do this, then ... I'll do it for you, for them." Pulling Lillith to him, he kissed her forehead and again slid a hand over her belly. "I guess I'm willing to go to hell and back for you, after all."

"Pan, I'm sorry—" The broken expression on Pan's face made them flinch as it cut Lillith's words short. "Are you okay?"

"You and them, who the hell..." Pan stopped. Cringing a moment, he, at last, started again, "You bitch. Ghosting him because..." Puffing out his cheeks, Pan motioned at her body. "Don't you control these things? What succubus doesn't control her own cycle at will? Are you fucking kidding me!" His face flushed red to maroon with the rise of his blood pressure as he marveled over everything. "I've got a passed-out Cedric, and meanwhile, Phoebe and Artemis are looking for Aether, and you two apparently are chums with the crazy old bastard, and now I have to send this one out to see Hades in hell, but the gate's fucking locked."

"Alecto said I should be able to do it with my sword," offered Tony.

"Of course, those old hags and the damn old witch of a tree most likely knew everything from the start. But who am I to challenge the greatest powers in the Otherworld alone?" Pan paced the floor, waving his hands about, and after a short silence, added, "And I still haven't found Glorianda!"

"Well," Lillith raised her eyebrows high and pitched, "how about we take a moment to rest? Since Avalon is compromised, do you have anyone willing to help us with the current state of affairs?"

Pan froze. "Yeah, I actually do." Turning, he sighed with the rise of a smirk. "Maybe all our meddling at least earned us some trustworthy companions." Looking around the dust-covered castle, Pan scoffed. "You two wash up; I'm bringing some familiar faces here and some maids."

"Wait, what about the firm?" Tony furrowed his brow.

Pan waved it off. "No worries. I found Selene and awakened her. She'll be a better opposing force for Artemis and Phoebe."

Lillith inhaled deeply before nodding. "Okay, then let's take matters into our hands once more. Time to bring my wolf home, along with anyone else who will stand with us. Let's prepare for war."

Cracking his knuckles, Pan snorted, "Finally," leaving a pile of rose petals at their feet.

To Be Continued...

BONUS STORY

WHITE RAM LAW ASSOCIATES

SHORT STORY DURING
THE ORACLE, BOOK 3

SELENE

Pulling her long black hair from her lips, Selene shivered and huddled herself tighter in her dark blue cardigan. It was freezing outside as her breath boiled up in steaming clouds in front of her face. She had taken a wrong turn somehow. The city was dark and crowded tonight; people bumping into her only made her check her pockets in paranoia; each time, she was relieved her wallet and things were still in place. Looking at the buildings' signs, her silver eyes squinted as she lipped the information. Selene found herself in a new area she had never noticed before; even the smells in this area seemed to be void of the normal intrusions of trash and sewer. Instead, there were aromatic spices, interesting colognes and perfumes, all competing for attention on the chilling breeze even though visually everything looked to be in order.

The sun had set hours ago and though she felt more comfortable at night, she was confused at exactly where it was she went wrong on her way to her favorite club. She got off at the same train station and, after, did her usual turn down the main stretch, which led to her street and the nearby club. This time she turned down her street and found herself some place new. The river of people continued to flow around her like white water rapids around a boulder, as an occasional bump would push her farther along, turning her around, adding to the confusion. It was impossible to figure out which way would head back. Sighing, she caved to the fact she would never figure it out with this crowd on the sidewalk and began to search the signs. Bright neon caught her eye, its glow warming her face as she read what the flamboyant lion head logo said next to it: The Lion's Den.

A bell rang loudly as she pushed through its doors, determined to get one drink out of this ordeal. It was a tavern-style setup, a huge bar top greeting her as she released the door behind her. She looked over the place, taking several steps inward; the tavern had booths and tables on the far-left side of the place, a single pool table interrupting the center of the rectangular room, and a line of stools at the bar, which chased the right wall. There, two bartenders furrowed their brows at her. As the door closed, the bell ceased its screaming alarm at her arrival. She came to an abrupt stop as all the men and women within the crowded establishment stared at her in sudden silence. She swallowed. Some of those eyes seemed to glow in the poorly lit tavern, and the jukebox was the only sound as it started to play "My Demons" by Starset. The aura of the place grew dark. Desperate, she turned to face the man and woman bartending, as if in a plea to help her move. Perhaps the tavern's name was a warning and not some trendy reason to have a lion logo, as she had assumed.

"You're new." The female bartender, a busty blonde, smirked at the other bartender. "What do you think, Tony?"

"Shush, Lisa. Hello, miss, what has brought you to The Lion's Den?" His green eyes cut through her, making her heart push hard against her chest as she watched him rub the side of his jaw, looking her over. "Did you take a wrong turn? Are you possibly lost, or are you meeting someone here?"

Selene's voice wouldn't come to her lips as the song echoed her thoughts: *Save me.* Her bottom lip began to quiver as her eyes jolted back to a large man in the back corner with glowing amber eyes. She could feel the heat of his glare burning through her. He shifted and smirked as if he had smelled the smoke from the fire he started. She began to back up as her panic started to pull the strings on her body. Her hand fumbled behind her, desperate to catch the door handle to aid in a swift escape. Warm fingers wrapped around her hand as gently as a lover's touch, while another hand pushed tenderly into the small of her back. The motion was soft, yet sudden, and it redirected her to move toward the bar top with ease. Her face flushed as she peered over her shoulder to see a tall man smiling at her.

Despite her slack jaw, she was too lost and confused to scream or speak as she found herself sitting on a stool next to him at the bar.

"Selene, I am so glad you made it!" The man had a strong Greek accent as he greeted her in his smooth tone. "Sorry to make you wait for me!"

She looked him over, certain she had never seen him in her whole life. He smelled like a flowery meadow on a hot summer day, bringing back fond memories of her childhood when she used to frolic with the butterflies at her grandparents' farm. Unlike most city folk, he had tan skin, and the color of his irises was a wonderful jade color, unlike the emerald of the bartender's eyes. His light brown hair was cut short; a slight fade on the sides complimented his goatee and mustache around his fleshy lips. The brown leather coat with wide folds adorned in fur looked expensive, despite being partnered with baggy khaki cargo pants and black boots. Once more, he smiled at her, winking as he spoke again.

"You didn't wait long for me, did you?" The tavern around them went back into motion, the clacking of pool balls breaking her tension. "Brenda said you quit the firm today."

"Brenda from HR?" Apparently, rumors of the fit she threw at work had gotten out, but how this man had found her while she was completely lost was still rolling in her mind. "Who are you? How did you find me?"

"Huh?" His eyes widened, shocked by her questions. "You really don't know, do you? Brenda warned me, but I didn't believe her; you know how they can be."

"The HR Department?" she questioned. "Or that I wouldn't know who you were?"

"By the fairies... Tony, make me something strong; it's going to be a long night." Rubbing his forehead, he took a moment before daring to continue the conversation. "First, let me introduce myself. My name is Nomius Panes Silvan, but most still call me Pan. As I already said, Brenda had informed me of your situation: severely underpaid, and worse, ungodly hours. If you would allow me to, I would love to make you an offer for a job at my own establishment."

"And what establishment would that be, Mr. Silvan?" It was unnerving to hear her personal business spewed so freely from a stranger's lips. "Exactly what else has Brenda been telling you?"

"You can say I run a record-keeping company that also doubles as a law firm for *special individuals*." He slid a card over to her, and once more, she lipped what she was reading on the card. "White Ram Law Associates will pay for all your living costs as well as provide you with an annual salary of fifty-thousand dollars."

"All living costs?" She snorted. "What if I live an expensive lifestyle of fine dining, luxury apartments, and shop till I drop every day?"

"All paid for, plus fifty-thousand." He gulped down the drink and looked her in the eyes as he spoke. "Is fifty thousand not enough? I can go higher."

"Is this some kind of joke?" Scowling at him, she flipped the card around, pointing at the address section, "Your address is listed as Room One on Avalon?"

"Tony, I need another drink..." He shook the glass. "It's no joke, Selene. I am desperate for someone who has goddess status but is fully capable of knowing the laws of men. On top of that, someone capable of helping me update records on locations as well as the status of clients and even potential clients."

Selene blinked a few times before bursting into laughter. "Goddess status, oh my God! Who put you up to this? I know I threw a tantrum, but you guys, you didn't have to go this far to prank me. You got me!"

Tony returned with a refilled drink, and he stopped to watch her outburst as Pan shrugged in confusion.

"No, Selene. This isn't a joke!" Pan huffed. "I don't know how else to explain this. Nature is bringing the gods and goddesses back to life to restore the proper order. But, but... Tony?"

"Oh, I don't understand it either, Pan." Tony threw up his hands, pleading to stay out of the mess. "Between Cedric, Romasanta, Lillith, and this bar, my hands are tied."

The door chimed and a petite brunette came in the door, rushing them. "Selene! You made it! You heard his call!"

"Brenda!" Selene gave her an angry growl. "Who the hell is this guy?"

Brenda canceled the hug she had aimed for, looking at the man next to her. "That's Pan."

"Are you in on this gag, too?" Selene palmed her face a moment. Sighing, she ended her laughter. "Well, it was nice being amused, but I really need to get home."

Standing, she offered her stool to Brenda. "Here, you can have my seat."

Brenda shook her head and motioned for Selene to sit back down. "No, you need to take his offer seriously, Selene. If you agree, I will quit the firm and join you as your assistant over at the White Ram in Avalon."

Flustered, she glanced at Pan, who gulped down another drink. "Tony!"

Reluctantly, she looked down at the card again: Nomius "Pan" Silvan, President. "One-hundred-fifty-thousand salary annually and no covering living costs."

"Done, but we still need to pull that magic out." He was downing another drink as if he was working up the nerve for his next obstacle. "Tony, can't you or your grandfather do this next thing? Maybe Lillith? She's always into that sort of thing; I dread doing this..."

Tony's face turned red as the muscles in his jaw twitched. "No, and don't ever call Cedric my grandfather. It's awkward and complicated. You're on your own."

"Aren't you older than Cedric, Pan?" snorted the female bartender. "You were the first King of Arcadia, weren't you?"

"Shush, you vile ampires." Pan returned his attention to Selene, who had crossed her arms in annoyance. "So, why don't you want me to cover your living costs as well?"

"I hate the paperwork involved, plus what I do is none of your business," she retorted. "I have your card, Mr. Silvan. How about we continue this discussion when you haven't downed so many drinks?"

"Oh, please call me tomorrow as well, Selene!" Brenda's honey, almond eyes glowed with excitement as she clapped her tiny hands. "I'll take you over to the office personally."

"Right, Room One, on Avalon," grunted Selene, looking at the business card with disgust. "I'll call everyone tomorrow..."

Sliding the card in her wallet, she placed it back in her sweater pocket and started for the door. She had lost her patience and the ongoing prank had lost its fun. Glancing back across the tavern, she eyed its occupants as she paused a few steps shy of the door. Once more, the yellow-eyed man glanced her way, smiling and flicking some fingers like a tiny signal of hello.

At the pool table was a loud-mouthed woman whose black hair flickered colors like on the feathers of a grand raven. She was scarred, tan-skinned, and muscular, while her pool contender was a mousy pale-looking man with a purple mohawk. Spinning about, she noticed the smells in the tavern were misplaced. Without the distraction of fear, she could make out exotic smells as if in a field of flowers from other countries. Confusion pulled at her. Lisa, the bartender, was flirting with a muscular man at the bar, but she could see a hint of a fang on her blood-red lips.

Brenda's voice pulled her all the way back around. "Pan! Do something!"

"I swear, Mother Gaea has a sick sense of humor," he mumbled, another drink meeting its death. "Fine."

Selene looked at the drunken Pan, bewildered by his complaints as she questioned, "Who are these people?"

"Who?" He lifted his eyebrows, taking a glance about the room before meeting her eyes again. "You mean *what*? You've worked in a law firm; you should know how to ask the right questions."

"Fine," she huffed. "What are they?"

"Not human." A childish grin crossed his face as he giggled. "It's your job to take names and record what exactly they are and where they really come from."

Once more, the bar's occupants paused and stared in her direction. "What they are..."

"Ask another question!" He was feeling the liquor at this point. "This is fun!"

"Why me?" she whispered. "I'm just a human..."

"Ah, that's where you are wrong!" He pointed at her, catching her full attention. "You are Selene! The Moon Goddess! Queen of the Heavens!"

Frowning, she countered, "That's who I am named after."

Without warning, his drunken lips pressed against hers. As her back smacked into the door, the bell rang loud in her ears from the impact. She could feel an intoxicating sensation flowing through her from the touch of his lips. As they began to kiss more deeply, the flavor of honey crisp apples, honey, and cinnamon exploded into her mouth as their tongues tangled. Regaining a clear moment, she pushed him away; the heat in her cheeks was a mix of anger and excitement.

"What is your problem?" Touching her lips, she blushed further. "And why did it taste and feel..."

"I am Pan, and a kiss from me is like kissing a hot summer's day, Selene." She was thrown by the grimace on his face as he continued, "Please know I did not kiss you because I like you. It was far from that, in fact. A vulnerable moment of intimacy can reveal a lot, as you see."

Pan motioned for her to turn around. Her brow knotted; her movement felt flawless as she did so. She caught her reflection in the dark glass door like a phantom from another time. Stumbling back, she gasped, her purse bouncing across the tavern's floor. There was a glowing all about her, skin pale and silvery, her lips a deep purple while her hair was so long it nearly touched the ground. Locks floated like feathers in a tiny breeze; her silver eyes held their own light while she observed the deep purple crescent and star symbols etched into her forehead. As her focus worked outward, she gasped again. Large green with silver and purple-edged moth wings stretched out from behind her, fluttering as her panic sent her heart racing. She recognized them as the wings of the lunar moth; one of her favorites when she had snuck out into the fields at night. There, under the light of the moon, she had danced with them, jealous of them as they left her on the ground, unable to join them.

Tonight, that would all change...

ABOUT THE AUTHOR

Valerie Willis is the Chief Operating Officer for 4 Horsemen Publications, Inc., an expert digital typesetter, and a fantasy romance author based out of Central Florida. When writing, she loves crafting novels with elements inspired by mythology, legends, folklore, fairy tales, and history. As COO, she oversees the design of all books including covers, typesets, and author branding where she pulls in creative print design while making versatile eBooks.

You can find her hosting workshops or attending as a guest speaker at many events (MegaCon, DragonCon, OCLS Writers Conference, Florida Writers Conference, SavvyAuthors, Women in Publishing Summit, etc.). She's been on panels with best-selling authors from Peter David to Delilah Dawson sharing her expertise in writing, research, worldbuilding, character development, book design, reader immersion, and more. You can also find her co-hosting on the Drinking with Authors Podcast speaking with Jonathan Maberry, Heather Graham, Charles Gannon, and many more on their own journeys as an author! Or talking about the spooky stuff over on Eerie Travels with topics such as big foots, mermaids, and even Bloody Mary!

Her award-winning dark fantasy paranormal romance, *The Cedric Series*, is a blend of genres that appeals to a wide range of readers who describe it as "dramatic, lustful, and fantasy fulfilling." The motto here is: "No immortal is beyond the ailments of man" that includes powerful creatures, demons, witches, and deities! Many of the monsters are derived from Medieval Bestiaries adding a fun flavor of new yet deeply-rooted assortment such as Coin Iotair, Shag Foal, Cynocephali, and more.

Like many authors, her writing journey started in grade school and carried her through high school. Many who grew up with her talk often of the traveling binders that were often kept safe in their lockers. This was the precursor to the now complete young adult dark urban fantasy of the *Tattooed Angels Trilogy* starting with *Rebirth*. This alternative historic piece about immortals and a failed reincarnation Hotan covers a wide variety of life lessons such as whether to follow your own lifepath or the one chosen for you, breaking toxic traditions, and the obligations of cleaning up our family's mistakes and destruction. Inspired by her own life tribulations, it has been the beacon to keep her moving toward the world of books and writing even now.

For readers of fantasy MM romance, check out her pen name V.C. Willis with the Traibon Family Saga starting with books *The Prince's Priest* and *The Priest's Assassin*. If you are looking for steamy paranormal erotica, chase down Urban Legends and modern retellings of fairy tales with Honey Cummings. Many have found themselves laughing out loud and fanning themselves while reading *Sleeping with Sasquatch* and *Wanton Woman in White*.

In 2021, she left her day job to join 4 Horsemen Publications, Inc. full time to bring over a decade of typesetting skills and industry knowledge to the table. Nothing is more rewarding for her than making fellow author's dreams come to life in physical format so they may share them with readers. Designing and writing books has been a longtime passion since childhood of hers and she continues to inspire and encourage authors around the world whenever possible, indulging whenever she can to chat about the books folks are reading and writing.

Keep in touch and keep reading!

WWW.WILLISAUTHOR.COM

LINKTR.EE/WILLISAUTHOR

More Books by Valerie Willis

Cedric: The Demonic Knight
Romasanta: Father of Werewolves
The Oracle: Keeper of the Gaea's Gate
Artemis: Eye of Gaea
King Incubus: A New Reign
Queen Succubus: Holder of the Crown

Val's House of Musings: A Mixed Genre Short Story Collection

Rebirth
Judgment
Death

Writer's Bane: Research 101
Writer's Bane: Formatting

ANTHOLOGIES & COLLECTIONS

A World of Their Own
Work of Hearts Magazine Release
How I Met My Other: True Stories, True Love
It Was Always You: A Thrill of the Heart Anthology

Demonic Wildlife: A Fantastically Funny Adventure
Demonic Household: See Owner's Manual
Demonic Carnival: First Ticket's Free

The Hunted—Thrill of the Hunt 3
Urban Legends Reimagined—Thrill of the Hunt 4
Buried Alive—Thrill of the Hunt 5

PUBLIC DOMAIN REMAKES

Bulfinch's Mythology with Illustrations
Book of Werewolves
The Fairy Faith of Celtic Countries

Writing MM Romance as VC Willis

The Prince's Priest
The Priest's Assassin
The Assassin's Saint

The Champion's Lord: YONDER webnovel
Champion's Love: KU short story

Writing as Honey Cummings

Sleeping with Sasquatch
Cuddling with Chupacabra
Naked with New Jersey Devil
The Erotic Cryptid Collection

Laying with the Lady in Blue
Wanton Woman in White
Beating it with Bloody Mary
The Erotic Ghosts Collection

Beau and Professor Bestialora
The Goat's Gruff
Goldie and Her Three Beards
Pied Piper's Pipe
Princess Pea's Bed
Pinocchio and the Blow Up Doll
Jack's Beanstalk
Pulling Rapunzel's Hair
The Urban Erotica Fairy Tale
Collection

Curses & Crushes: KU short story

Queen's Incubus: YONDER webnovel

BOOK CLUB DISCUSSION QUESTIONS

1. Do you believe Tony's feelings for Lillith are legitimate and caused by his change?

2. Why do you feel Lillith distanced herself? And is her reasons justified?

3. Battle Goddess Badbh plays a huge part in Tony's ability to defend himself. What did she excel at? How did she fail him?

4. How significant was the title of this book to the characters and plot?

5. Why do you think it was important to have a prior King attempt to train Tony? How did he compare in power and mindset?

6. This story has several parallels to book 4, *Artemis*. Why do you think that was significant and how did it change your understanding of book 4?

7. We get to see Pan play the big brother role in this book. What can you deduce in regard to his relationship with his sibling Lillith?

8. What do you believe Tony fears most externally? Internally?

9. What do you believe Lillith fears most externally? Internally?

10. Tony is thrown into his quest with little direction. Why do you think this was vital for his character development?

11. When do you think the two of them started to develop feelings for one another? Was it in a prior book or at some point in this one.

12. Mythology is a huge part of the series. Why do you think the author focused on Caribbean-based deities and creatures for this book?

13. What is the significance of revealing more about the concept of domains, sanctuaries, and territories in this book?

14. Share what conspiracy theories or predictions or deductions you have about the series, characters, and/or world thus far.

15. Which scene or moment was your favorite? Why?

16. Debate why pairing Lillith and Tony as a couple is a great/horrible idea.

17. Aether has a huge presence in this book as we slowly discover more about him. How involved do you think he is in Lillith and Tony's story? Cedric and Angeline? Romasanta and Daphne?

18. Hamadyrades seemed to hold Lillith hostage. Why do you think she did this? Was it to keep her from running away from Tony? As a favor to Aether? Or something else?

19. What are your thoughts on Gaea and/or Cleo's next move?

20. Artemis and Phoebe seem to be taking charge. Do you think they will be friend or foe by the end of the next book?

www.ingramcontent.com/pod-product-compliance
Lightning Source LLC
Chambersburg PA
CBHW020403110726
47899CB00006B/1843